Angel tripped on the rug b[...] before she fell, his hands spannin[...] broken her with his fingers. Instead, he crushed her against his chest and claimed her mouth with his.

His lips and hands took on a life of their own. Revenge belonged to another life. He tried to think of why she was here, why she had become his wife, but each *why* dissolved like wax beneath his lusty heat. That's what it was, he told himself as he felt the whisper of her tongue on his. Lust. He'd never felt the full force of its power until he held Angel in his arms.

His tongue raked the inside of her mouth as his fingers fumbled with her gown. It fell soft as a cloud to the floor and his hands pressed against nothing but warm satin skin.

"Is this what you want?" he asked.

"I want . . . yes, oh yes."

Her voice caressed him, touching him all over. She looked at him, her eyes dark with heat and longing, her breath coming out ragged in a single short cry. Quent forgot all else but Angel. Sweeping her into his arms, he pulled back the covers and lay her on the dark sheets.

All he could think of was touching her, kissing her, plunging into her again and again . . .

* * *

ANGEL

EVELYN ROGERS

ZEBRA BOOKS
KENSINGTON PUBLISHING CORP.

ZEBRA BOOKS are published by

Kensington Publishing Corp.
850 Third Avenue
New York, NY 10022

First Printing: December, 1995

Printed in the United States of America

To Laura and Tom,
to Larry and Sue,
and to my husband Jay—
the best people in the world.

Also, boundless thanks goes
to Beth Lieberman
for her help and support.

Prologue

Cordangan Castle, Ireland
Christmas Eve, 1867

I killed her.

Quentin Kavanagh stared through his bedroom window at the stormy night and admitted the truth. Amidst the thunderclaps came the crash of waves against the rocky shore below, too distant to be seen, but he felt their wildness in his bones. He had killed her, as surely as if he'd plunged a knife into her heart. She was gone, and so was the chance for them to make their peace.

How many years did a boy have to spend in purgatory for ending his mother's life? A man, not a boy, Quent thought. He was fifteen, old enough to accept the blame for his sins.

Somewhere in the darkness, church bells would soon ring to celebrate the season; somewhere families gathered to sing and to feast. But not at Cordangan Castle. Never there.

Quent stroked the stone sill. Stone that had been in place six hundred years longer than the beveled, rain-streaked panes. Would that he were strong enough to rip the ancient rock from its moorings and toss it through the infant glass. Helpless, he dug his fingers into the rough surface, drew blood, stared at the thin dark stain on the stone.

What had come over him tonight? Was it the storm? The season? He was no stranger to such weather, and Christmas held no special meaning for any Kavanagh. He knew never to argue with his father, but when the old man had fallen into a drunken rage at dinner, banishing one and all beneath his roof to perdition, Quent had answered the threats. Hearing the angry voices of her husband and son, Morna had taken to her bed.

For the last time, Quent was sure. Her heart was bad. His temper had killed her. He knew it as surely as he recognized his sins of insolence and disobedience. This sin was the worst. At fifteen, he wanted to die.

The door to his room creaked open.

"She's asking for you, lad."

Quent turned in disbelief to Doreen MacCabe, the housekeeper. The tall, strong woman stared back, her brown eyes cold, her hard-bitten mouth grim.

"I thought she was—" he began.

"She's holding on. Don't tarry. She's not got long."

Quent shook a lock of dark hair from his face. All his life he had longed for a summons from his mother, and now it came when she neared the end. One last time to chastise him? It mattered not. She had called and he would answer.

He hurried toward the door, the chill stillness of his room as thick as bay water. His father stood in the shadows of the long, bleak corridor that stretched the length of the castle's third story. At sixty-five he looked ancient as the surrounding walls, his white hair unkempt, his pale eyes flat and lifeless.

Father and son stared at one another. It was Dermot Kavanagh who looked away. Quent strode past him, inhaling the sour scent of stale whiskey and unwashed clothes. His pace slowed at his mother's door. He gripped the knob. Swallowing a deep breath, he entered the tomblike silence of her room.

He'd last seen it on a warm spring morning two years ago. Curiosity and longing had driven him to steal inside while his mother took a rare stroll around the castle grounds. Then and now the air held the scent of old lavender. White lace curtains hung across the mullioned windows, as out of place in the stark, high-ceilinged quarters as the son of the woman who lay dying on the poster bed.

His boots struck heavily against the thinly carpeted floor as he walked toward her. Morna O'Brien Kavanagh lay on her back beneath the covers, her silver-streaked dark hair splayed across the linen pillowslip, her papery skin colorless, as though she were drained of blood.

Quent saw no sign of breathing. Heart pounding, he stood awkwardly beside the bed and wondered what to do with his hands. He wanted to stroke his mother's hair, but touching her was forbidden. It always had been, since he was a very small child.

The only touching Quent knew was his father's cane. The beatings had ended six months ago when Quent wrested the cane from Dermot Kavanagh's hands and snapped it in two over his thigh. A passage into manhood, he'd taken it, and his father had not threatened him since.

Except for tonight, when the drunken ravings had proven too much for them both.

Morna's eyelids fluttered open. Quent knelt beside her.

"I'm here, Morna," he whispered. Never Mother, never Mama. She demanded he use her given name.

"Hungry," she whispered, "so hungry."

Quent reached for the bowl of broth on the bedside table, broke the fat congealed across its surface, but when he tried to offer her a taste, she shoved the spoon away.

"No food," she said, half sob, half gasp.

"There's food," he protested, feeling clumsy and helpless.

"All gone," she said, unheeding. "All dead." Her voice was thin and tight, a steel wire pulled to the breaking point. "It's the famine," she said. "Will it never end?"

Suddenly Quent understood. She remembered the time of starvation when she was a girl, the potato blight that had wasted so many of her countrymen. The housekeeper had told him of those days, of the suffering, and of how his mother's trials had been among the very worst.

The strain on Morna's face eased, and she smiled, an eerie, mad expression that chilled Quent to his soul. Behind the lace curtains a streak of lightning brightened the night, and a clap of thunder shook the room. Morna paid no mind.

"I was pretty then," she said, her eyes staring at images her son could not see. "Everyone said so. Even him." Drawing a long, thin hand from beneath the covers, she stroked her hair.

"You're pretty now," said Quent, and meant it. Despite the signs of age, her features still held their delicacy, and her movements their stately grace.

"He loved me."

"Of course Father did," said Quent, not knowing what else to say.

His mother showed a moment's agitation. "Not *your* father, fool. *Him.*"

Of course. Quent *was* a fool to think otherwise.

Her lips twisted cruelly, and for once she glanced at her son with eyes that were lucid and piercing. "He must pay." She grabbed Quent's hand. Her nails drew blood in his palm. "You must avenge me."

Quent nodded dumbly.

"I survived it all . . . the famine and the typhoid, the desertion, and the disgrace. But I can no longer live without love."

I love you. The words would not force themselves to Quent's lips.

For a moment he was once again two years old, climbing onto his mother's solitary bed at early morn, telling her how he felt, watching her turn from him like a flower from the sun. The scene was the earliest he could recall, the details, the hurt, the loss as much a part of him as his hands. He had never tried to speak of his feelings again.

Morna half rose from the bed, her fingers strong enough to crush his young man's hands. "Promise you will avenge my ruin."

Quent felt her strength flow into him. "I promise." He spoke from his heart.

She rested her head against the pillow. A smile of contentment graced her lips. Quent had never made his mother smile. He felt a glow of power and pride.

"Say it again," she whispered, her voice growing weak.

"I promise." When she stirred restlessly, he said, "I promise to avenge your ruin."

A long, slow breath whispered through her lips. "Only then will I rest in peace." She closed her eyes. "I'm tired. So tired." She relaxed her hold on him. Her body shivered, then grew still.

For a long while, Quent held her hand, until all the warmth was gone and the scent of lavender mingled with the scent of death.

Suddenly Doreen MacCabe was beside him. "She's gone, lad. Let her go."

Quent rested his dead mother's hand on her breast, then stood. He looked at her a moment longer, his promise lingering ghostlike in the air. Without a word he returned to his room, uncaring that his father stayed in drunken ignorance behind a closed door. He opened his window to the storm and let the spray dampen his cheeks, in place of tears that would not fall. Quent had not cried since that second year of his life when he learned rejection. He was not driven to weeping now.

From somewhere in the direction of town came the deep, steady tolling of a bell, announcing the midnight hour.

Merry Christmas. Good tidings to all.

He called himself a fool. The church lay far too distant for the bells to sound in his room. He imagined them. And they tolled not for the holiday but for the passing of a tormented soul.

The sadness that should have filled his heart was overtaken by a strange sense of exhilaration. In death his mother needed him as she had never done in life.

Avenge my ruin.

That he would do.

He knew little about the man who had robbed his mother of her innocence when she was but a lass of seventeen. He had left her to bear his babe in shame . . . the babe she had felt driven to abort.

The scandal, the shame, had driven her from the church and into seclusion. Dermot Kavanagh, approaching old age, had taken the beautiful young woman as his bride to provide him with an heir. Quent was the sole issue of their loveless union.

And now, for the first time, one of his parents truly needed him. He had a reason to curb his wild ways. He had a reason to live.

His thoughts flew to the tower at the north corner of the castle, to the dark room with its bolted door, to the proof of his mother's shame that was hidden inside. Oh yes, he thought, he had reason to live.

He knew little about the man who ruined his mother, but he knew his name. Thomas Chadwick. It had been drummed into his mind throughout his fifteen years. She talked of the man with the same hate and scorn the townspeople showed when they talked about her.

Slattern, murderess, whore. They had been hard words for a little boy to master, and harder to forget. He had learned early to stay away from the village of Cordangan, from the docks that lined the bay, from the neighboring farms. Later he had learned to fight, to roam, to ride. And to rejoice in the fear he could arouse in opponents larger and older than he.

He had not learned gentleness, nor, except for the restless feelings he felt for his mother, had he learned to love. Such sentiments were for weaklings. At fifteen, he understood his strength.

And so must his mother have understood, else she would not have turned to him in this final hour of her need. Thomas Chadwick had much for which he must answer. Staring into the storm-tossed night, rain and wind raking his face and hair, Quent vowed to bring him to destruction and to bring his mother a peace she had never known.

One

Savannah, Georgia
April, 1882

Angel Chadwick stared at the figures in front of her, at the letter from the bank, at the figures again. It couldn't be, she thought, tugging at a lock of hair, but a thorough check of her calculations brought no change.

She leaned back in the chair. No matter how many explanations she came up with, there was no denying the fact that Papa owed more than he owned. Papa was broke.

She glanced around the small office at the back of Chadwick Dry Goods and Clothing, at the cluttered desk, the worn file cabinets, the photograph of the three Chadwick sisters on the wall, all warmed by the sunlight from the window at her back. She knew this room and the store, the nearby family home, the street, the town . . . knew them as well as she knew anything, having lived in Savannah all her twenty-four years.

Still, at the moment she felt like a stranger. Familiarity with buildings was all right, but it seemed distressingly obvious she didn't know the central person in her life quite so well as she had thought.

Thomas Chadwick was flamboyantly Irish, fun-loving and affectionate, the best storyteller in Savannah, and the best papa in all the world. Mama was her guide, her teacher, her foundation. Papa was her joy. He would do anything for his beloved wife Anne, for his girls, for the grandchildren her two older sisters had brought him.

He would do so much, it seemed, that he had overextended himself, borrowing money to increase the stock, extending unsecured credit to tradesmen and farmers alike with the understanding they would pay him back with added interest. Eventually pay him back. Angel found no contracts to say as much, just scribbled notes in Papa's hand.

The bank letter was the worst of all. From the moment Michael put it into her hand a short while ago, she had felt its evil. Chadwicks were cursed with overactive imaginations, she had reminded herself, yet the paper had burned her fingers. One glance at its contents had proven her instincts right.

Harold Gash, Savannah's most eminent banker, regretted going against the oral agreement he had reached with Papa, but business considerations rendered it necessary that he call in the Chadwick loan. An exorbitant sum, she noted. And it was due by the end of the week.

Papa and Mama wouldn't be back from Texas until long after then. If only she hadn't given over her small inheritance to Jeremiah for his charity works. . . .

Angel sighed. What was done was done.

The bell on the outer door jangled. A customer, she thought without much enthusiasm. The store would need the population of southern Georgia tromping through to get out of the current troubles. Still, a single shopper was better than none. One of the Micks would take care of the purchases, Michael or Brendan or Ian. Good men they were, all three of them, helping out while Papa and Mama were gone, and her thoughts returned to the figures.

A shadow fell across the desk.

"Michael," she said, glancing up, expecting to see the smiling Irishman. Instead, she saw the solemn, handsome face of her fiancé.

"Jeremiah," she said in surprise.

"Good day, Angel," he returned with a slight bow of his tall, angular body. "Sorry if I'm disturbing you."

Angel stifled a moment of longing. Jeremiah Godwin was the kindest, dearest man in all the world, a doctor who ministered to the care of rich and poor alike, a tireless worker, a true gentleman, and if he didn't rush forward to sweep her into his arms, it was because he had so much on his mind.

The fact that he had never done so, even on the day he proposed, was nothing to be concerned about. She had listened too much to her sisters talk about how exciting the physical part of marriage could be. Excitement would come soon enough after she and Jeremiah were wed.

"Angel," he said, "are you all right?" As always, his brow was furrowed, and behind his wire-frame glasses his pale eyes bore a kindly cast.

Angel chastised herself. How foolish to be thinking of silly things like excitement when she was faced with real disaster. Carefully folding Harold Gash's letter, she set it aside. No need to trouble Jeremiah with her problems. With a fever spreading among the plantation workers and an outbreak of measles in town, he had enough worries on his hands.

"I didn't think I'd see you until dinner this evening," she said.

"That's why I'm here now. I fear I'll have to beg off. Mrs. Reynolds is expecting her baby any moment, and the Danville twins have started a rash, and Sam Shoop's appendix is acting up again. Could be it'll have to come out tonight."

"Don't worry about me, Jeremiah. I'm not so selfish as to ask you to leave your patients." Or, she silently added, burden you with Chadwick woes.

She came around the desk to take him by the hand. Long-fingered and supple, it was the hand of a healer. Angel used to brag to her sister Raven how she would some day marry a saint. Skeptical, Raven had scoffed against the existence of such a creature. Jeremiah's goodness proved Raven wrong.

And he *was* handsome, tall and strong for all his leanness, his even features unmarred by the wire-frame glasses, his dignity and concern both constants in his life. She loved him. She really did. The fact that he was fourteen years her senior and devoted to his work served only to deepen her affection.

"You're a good woman," he said with a smile, and his pale complexion took on a hint of color. "You'll make a fine doctor's wife."

She looked up expectantly, wondering if he might kiss her, in a physical way providing the strength she needed right now. Maybe she ought to tell him about the letter. . . .

She couldn't do it, not until she had tried all other avenues of help. To seek help right away would be burdening him with her problems, and she wouldn't be his wife until the fall.

Together, they moved into the store, where the three Micks were straightening stock. Her middle sister Flame had met them years before when she'd moved to a Texas fort. After mustering out of the Army, the men had migrated to Savannah; when needed, they helped Papa at the store.

They hailed from County Cork, a part of Ireland Papa knew well. He never talked much about his days there, or his family—all dead from the terrible famine that swept the country in the forties—but he was easily roused to tales and song about the country in general, especially when the Micks were about.

Michael, the leader of the three, abandoned the bolts of cloth he'd been stacking. "Be gone with you," he said to Angel, a twinkle in his eye. " 'Tis late in the day. We can care for the business we're liable to be getting."

"Aye," said Brendan from the cracker barrel, and Ian, standing behind the counter, echoed his sentiment.

If only she could leave, thought Angel. But that would be running from her problems. Anyway, Jeremiah needed to return to his work.

The Micks knew it. She could tell from the mock innocence in their eyes. It was no secret they found her fiancé far too serious and inattentive. Ian sometimes called him Doctor God, but she pretended not to hear.

She walked beside Jeremiah toward the front door. "Don't apologize about tonight one more time," she said. "If I can be of any help, please send word."

"Ah, my Angel, you are truly well named," he said, leaning down. For Jeremiah, the declaration was quite romantic, and she lifted her lips. He kissed her on the cheek, then was gone, setting off a draft as he opened and closed the door, ruffling her skirt and her hair.

Something drew her attention to the front window. A man stood watching. She saw only his dark eyes, gazing at her from beneath the brim of his hat, and the smirk on his lips, but they were enough to startle her and cause her to gasp.

She shook off her momentary distress. After all, she hadn't done anything wrong, just accept a chaste peck on the cheek from her intended. Whirling away from the window, she looked at each of the Micks. They stood transfixed, their stares on the stranger outside.

" 'Tis an apparition," said Michael, and Brendan agreed. Angel glanced back at the window, but the stranger was gone.

"Nay," said Ian, "that was no apparition. As sure as I'm standing here, that was the devil himself."

Late evening, long after the store was closed to business, Angel labored over the books in the office. No solutions to imminent bankruptcy came to mind. She would simply have to talk to the banker in person, to ask for patience and generosity, to beg if necessary.

As the youngest of the Chadwick girls, the golden one with the wide blue eyes, Angel had always been considered sweet and slightly simple-minded. Raven was the strongest and smartest, the dark-haired accomplished actress and now wife of an English earl. Flame, married to a Texas rancher, was as quick to temper and action as her red hair suggested.

Angel was neither as tall as her sisters, nor as outgoing. But she had surprised everyone by showing a talent for running the business, for keeping the books, for judging human nature better than either of her sisters. They laughingly said she always looked at the good side of everyone, but that wasn't true. She emphasized virtue, that was all, instead of faults.

Surely Banker Gash had a good side to his nature. The fact that she had not found it yet meant she hadn't tried hard enough.

The outside doorbell jangled. Angel sighed impatiently at herself, irritated that she hadn't remembered to pull the bolt. She wasn't worried, however. The Micks knew she was working late. At least one of them would be hovering nearby.

She felt the presence of someone out in the store. "Michael?" she called. "Jeremiah?"

All was silent, and then a shadow fell across her desk. She looked up into the midnight-blue eyes of the stranger from the afternoon, the man who had watched Jeremiah bid her goodbye, the man whose lips twisted so naturally into a smirk. He wasn't smirking now, just staring with his incredibly piercing eyes. Again, the look of him caused her to gasp.

His hat was gone, and she could see his sharply hewn face, the strong nose and chin, the tight lips that looked as though they never smiled. His shoulder-length hair was black as pitch, matching his suit and shirt. He wasn't a hulking man—nowhere near it—yet he filled the doorway with his presence, blocking her escape. The devil, Ian had called him, although a steady stream of customers until closing time had kept him from explaining why he thought so. Right now, with alarm flowing like warm liquid to the marrow of her bones, she saw his point.

Her thoughts flew to the gun Papa kept in the bottom drawer. Not much comfort there. She had never learned to use it.

Angel straightened. "Wh-what do you want?"

His lips twitched, his only movement, and the lines of his face deepened.

"The store is closed for the night," she said, wishing her voice were not so soft, regretting she lacked the command of her sisters.

Why did he keep looking at her like that, as though he could peer into her soul? She had never seen a man like him before, so darkly quiet and on the edge of menacing. Too harsh in appearance to be handsome, exactly, he was definitely arresting. As different from Jeremiah as night from day, he pinned her in the chair with his eyes.

"Ah, Miss Chadwick," a man behind him piped. "Didn't mean to frighten you, coming in so late and all."

She recognized the voice of Harold Gash. Remembering his threatening letter, she shivered. The devil and the banker had her trapped.

"Please, sir," Gash said to the stranger, "allow me to enter so that I might introduce you."

The stranger almost smiled. He had caught her shiver. Somehow it amused him. Angel felt all the more ill at ease.

Gash sidled past him into the small office. His cloying cologne caught in Angel's throat. A short, squat man, his complexion pocked and pale eyes narrowly set, he dressed nattily as befitted his position. From his velvet lapels and stiff collar to the ivory-handled cane at his side, he was every inch the prominent citizen.

And as ever the avaricious financier, Angel could see by the light in his eyes. He seemed especially pleased with himself this evening. Her apprehension grew.

"Miss Chadwick, may I present Mister Quentin

Kavanagh, a visitor to our shores. He's been generous enough to—"

One glance from the stranger stopped him. Angel had never seen anyone hush the banker so effectively, except for his bombastic wife.

She got the impression she was supposed to be intimidated by the two men. In truth, she was, but it would do her little good to let them know it. She stood, smoothing her skirt, wishing she were tall.

Kavanagh looked her over, and the liquid alarm inside her turned hot. He made her far too aware of all her parts. If only she were a little less—voluptuous was the way her sister Flame put it, which seemed silly. Her bosom had outgrown her small waist, that was all. Men noticed. Most men. Not Jeremiah, but she figured he would take notice in the fall.

The stranger showed no such reluctance. He was, she saw right away, no gentleman.

"Miss Chadwick," he said. Something in the way he pronounced her name made it seem like a curse.

"Mister Kavanagh—" Gash began. Again, a dark look silenced him.

"I'd like to conduct my business with Miss Chadwick in private," Kavanagh said.

Gash stared dumbly at him.

"In private," Kavanagh repeated.

The banker summoned his dignity. "Am I not your representative?"

"I represent myself." The stranger's tone forestalled argument.

Gash nodded once and tapped his cane against the floor. "Very well. I'll be in my office in the morning should we have further business to complete."

Angel watched in dismay as the banker departed. The stranger glanced around the room, then returned his attention to her. No one in all her life had looked at her so thoroughly. And he studied with such authority, as if no one would dare criticize or complain.

"You're Irish, aren't you?" she said, attempting to sound casual. "I'm familiar with the brogue. My father—"

His eyes glittered with a flash of feeling so hot it should have seared the papers on the desk. Angel was stunned to silence.

"Your father is out of town, I understand."

Somehow she found her courage. She was, after all, a Chadwick, and Chadwicks held their ground.

"He and Mama are visiting their grandchildren in Texas."

"How pleasant for him."

Her courage grew. "You don't sound sincere, Mister Kavanagh."

His dark brows lifted slightly. "Isn't it pleasant for him?"

"Of course. I meant that you don't really care—" She broke off, realizing that whatever she said seemed only to feed his dark reactions.

He leaned across the desk. She fell back in her chair.

"You are in deep trouble, Miss Chadwick," he said, telling her nothing she didn't already know.

She took a deep breath. Quentin Kavanagh must have recently arrived from abroad, for she caught the scent of the sea on his skin. His cheeks were shadowed with bristles, and his thick brows gave him a dark, hooded look. The devil, she thought. Yes indeed.

"Trouble? Whatever do you mean, Mister Kavanagh?" she said.

His eyes roamed over her face and bosom. She brushed her hair from her cheek, wishing she had pinned it into a bun instead of wearing it loose.

"You're in no danger from assault, if that's your worry. I prefer my women riper."

Indignation burned her cheeks. "That's a terrible thing to say."

"Are you ripe, then? Would you welcome my assault?"

"Why, no, I only meant . . . that is . . . Oh, never mind. If you're trying to upset me, you are succeeding. As if I didn't have enough troubles already."

"That you do, Miss Chadwick." He seemed to take pleasure in grinding out her name. He backed away, easing toward the door, taking the air with him as he moved. "You can't imagine just how much."

He paused in the doorway. "I've bought your father's mortgage papers at the bank. Within the week I intend to foreclose."

Before she could so much as yelp in dismay, he was gone.

Two

"That man outside the store yesterday. You called him the devil. What did you mean?"

Angel tried to make the question sound casual, but, fearful and anxious as she was, she couldn't keep from staring at Ian across the cracker barrel.

Ian settled the lid firmly on the newly stocked barrel. " 'Cause that's how he's known throughout County Cork. If he's the same man, that is. Appeared to be, but there's no explaining why he's here in Georgia."

He gave further thought to her question. "And why might you be asking about such a dark one on this fine bright morn?"

Because he'll own the floor under our feet by week's end.

Angel couldn't bring herself to say the words. Too harsh, too dreadful. Besides, they might not be true. Quentin Kavanagh hadn't bothered to elaborate on his terrible announcement. He had simply gone, leaving her to a hundred questions, a thousand worries, and a long, sleepless night.

She didn't want to distress Ian with her problems, but she couldn't lie to him, either.

"Mister Kavanagh stopped by the store after you left."

"What?" Ian's explosion brought Michael out of the stock room and Brendan away from a customer who was placing an order at the counter.

"The devil was here last night," said Ian to his companions. "Kavanagh himself."

Brendan made the sign of the cross.

"Are you sure it was our devil?" asked Michael.

"The lass knows his name right well enough, isn't that so?"

Angel nodded. "Quentin Kavanagh. That's how Mister Gash introduced him. I was working in the office when they stopped by."

"The two of 'em were here?" asked Ian. "The banker and the devil? There's a double dose of trouble for sure."

"While it's none of our business, Miss Angel," Michael said, "could you be telling us the nature of their visit?"

Angel tried to smile. Michael was the leader of the Micks, the dependable one who would feel most responsible for her well being while Mama and Papa were gone. He was also likely to see through her evasions.

"The topic of investing in the store came up."

Brendan rolled his eyes. "Saints preserve us, we'll be dealing in brimstone afore the first of May."

Sorry she'd mentioned the man, Angel edged toward the counter and the waiting customer. When the woman was gone and the store once more empty of customers, the Micks came at Angel in force, throwing questions one on top of the other.

"Mister Kavanagh only hinted at his intentions," she said in answer to their barrage. It wasn't exactly the truth, but it wasn't a lie, either, considering the details he had failed to deliver. "I'm certain we'll see him today."

"Bar the door," said Brendan, "and put out the gone fishing sign."

"Sure and he'd find us," Ian said. "There's black magic in the fiend."

"There's no such thing as black magic, and you know it," said Angel with more volume than conviction. Remembering the dark look about the man and the aura of power he wore, she wasn't certain she was right.

"Don't be too sure," Michael warned. "There's forces in

the old land you'll not be finding here in your new country."
Angel was surprised to find the normally sensible Irishman
as serious as his mates.

"All right, let's say there is such a thing as black magic.
So what is Mister Kavanagh, devil or witch?"

"He's something in between, or so the stories go."

"They say he's sprung fruit from barren trees," said Brendan, "then turned it to poison afore the eyes of Cordangan folk."

"Cordangan?" asked Angel.

"Aye, in our blessed County Cork on the southern coast
of Ireland. That's where you'll find his lair."

"Come now, Brendan, you'll be calling him a beast of
the wild next."

"Depends upon who you're asking as to what he's called.
Devil seems to be preferred."

Ian spoke up. "They say he roams the seaside at night,
his horse taking wings and soaring over the waves as they
crash against the rocks. There's none to follow and none to
see when he returns."

Angel pictured yesterday's visitor on such a mount—
black of course, like everything else about him. A stallion
with powerful, shiny flanks and nostrils breathing fire. The
image sent a shiver down her spine.

"He dwells in a castle high on the highest rock overlooking Bantry Bay, so dark and grim no light is ever seen there,
and no people come or go," said Michael.

" 'Tis taking your life into your own hands to venture
up the rock," said Brendan. "There's them that's never returned to Cordangan, nor have ever been seen again."

Angel looked from Michael to Brendan to Ian. Young
men all, not yet in their thirties, red-haired and freckled,
their fair faces lined with concern.

Unpeopled castles . . . poisoned fruit . . . horses that
fly . . . mad stories all, but told with solemnity. The Micks
truly did seem worried for her, as though the evil from

Cordangan, County Cork, Ireland, would drift across the ocean and creep into Chadwick Dry Goods and Clothing on a busy Savannah street.

The idea struck her as preposterous, and she laughed. It wasn't a very loud laugh and she was immediately sorry, but she couldn't call up a serious face to save her soul.

"You're having me on," she said. "No one could be so bad."

The three spoke at once, each defending his story.

"Have any of you met the man?" she asked. "I thought not. Have you seen this castle, or the flying horse?"

"We've heard from those who have," said Ian.

Angel's eyes twinkled. "And maybe you've each kissed the Blarney stone. It's in County Cork, is it not?"

"I'm admitting we're not from Cordangan or anywhere close," said Michael. "Our village lies nearer Cork. But we saw him in the city once. There were Kavanagh stories aplenty in the taverns and on the streets, in Cork and as far away as Dublin. Too many to ignore. The Irish are a fanciful lot, as you know, but there's truth behind our tales, sure as you're born."

"Then tell me a truth. Has he a family?"

"They say he lives alone," said Brendan.

"In a castle? All by himself high on a rock?"

Brendan nodded solemnly. "Cordangan means fortified hill, lass. 'Tis true the crossbows are gone from the castle, but the devil's darkness keeps the good folk away."

Michael joined in. "You ask for truth, lass, but it's facts you want. 'Tis a fact he lives alone in a high old castle. 'Tis a truth there's terrible bad in the man. Where there's smoke, there's fire, you've no doubt heard. Considering the stories about him, I'd say there's a fire burning in his soul that bodes no one well."

Angel was not to be daunted. "And where does this evil recluse get his money? I'm not so sure about devils, but don't witches have to eat?"

"Quentin Kavanagh lives on the flesh of fair-haired virgins," said Brendan with a shudder.

Ian slapped him on the arm. "Why do you want to be talking such vulgarity? Virgins, indeed. You'll have our Miss Angel frightened he's after her."

Angel fell silent. The way Quentin Kavanagh was looking at her last night, he might very well have wanted to take a bite. Except that she wasn't ripe enough. Or so he had said.

She wasn't exactly sure what he meant, but it hadn't sounded like a compliment. Looking past the Micks, she was relieved to see several customers had wandered into the store. "Oh, my. We'd best get to work."

Reluctantly they left her and the topic. She stared absently into space. No matter how she rejected the Micks' description of Quentin Kavanagh . . . no matter how hard she tried to look for evidence things were not so bad as they appeared, she couldn't forget her visitor's final words.

I've bought your father's mortgage papers at the bank. Within the week I intend to foreclose.

Foreclose was such an ugly word, like *maim* or *kill* or *hurt*. Surely he couldn't have been serious. He wanted to frighten her, for some reason she couldn't imagine. Well, he had certainly done that. And it was serving her little good to stand around moping or even asking questions of the Micks. They had said themselves they didn't personally know him. But Harold Gash did.

Excusing herself, leaving the store in their hands, she hurried next door to the Chadwick family home, tugged on a bonnet and fetched a parasol as protection against the warm spring sun, then made the short trek to the bank. She had to wait a half hour before seeing Gash. He welcomed her into his private office with a smile. Remembering his part in her predicament, Angel was not impressed with his cordiality.

It took only a few questions to learn the worst: Quentin Kavanagh had indeed bought up Papa's notes. "With cash," said the banker admiringly, as though that were the greatest accomplishment the Irishman could have achieved.

"And he can do with them what he wishes?" she asked.

"Payment for the debt is due upon notice. It's in the papers I turned over to him. Papers Thomas willingly signed."

"But what would someone from Ireland want with a Savannah dry goods store?"

Gash cleared his throat. "It's not the bank's business to interfere in a private individual's transactions."

"But you didn't have to sell him Papa's notes."

"I owed it to our depositors. Mister Kavanagh came in here yesterday asking about possible investments. It seems he had noticed your store, wondered if it might be for sale. I had no choice but to tell him the way things stood with your father and the bank."

"He must have been here about the time I got your letter. The one threatening foreclosure. The one you sent knowing Papa was out of town."

For Angel, it was a harsh comment, but the banker took it without so much as a raise of his thin gray brows.

"His arrival was quite fortuitous, I must admit. For the bank's customers, you understand. It was their money which your father borrowed."

He went on to explain the way financial institutions worked, as though Angel lacked a firm perception of such complicated and manly matters. But she understood far too well.

"Thomas borrowed to finance improvements in the store," he concluded, "and to pay for these rather extravagant trips he and your mother have been taking."

"To see their grandchildren in Texas and England."

"Just so. Forgive my saying so, Miss Chadwick, but there was no telling when your father might come up with so much money. With the current economic conditions, it has become necessary for me to call in bad debts."

The banker's words stung, and Angel had to bite her tongue to keep from responding sharply.

"Papa has extended credit to several men in the county. When he returns, he will call in the money he's owed."

"Ah, his ability to do so is only speculation, my dear. The fact is your father is not a very wise businessman."

Angel's temper was not easily aroused, but such constant criticism of another Chadwick was enough to raise her ire.

"There's nothing wrong with Papa. He has many friends, as a matter of fact. Don't you think they will be upset at you over all this?"

"As businessmen they will understand," he said, brushing at his lapels. "As depositors, they will applaud."

Angel wanted to stamp her foot in frustration. Mister Gash really was not a very nice man. In fact, he seemed almost to be taking pleasure in her predicament. Raven had once hinted she had been forced to rebuff his advances. Imagine, a married man twice her sister's age approaching a single woman. Was he now seeking revenge for that rebuff?

She would like to think the residents of the town would rise to Papa's defense, but she knew all too well that most of Gash's customers were of the gentry and considered themselves above a shopkeeper and his kin.

A few of their sons made no such class distinctions, however. She had received several offers of marriage over the years. Could she approach one of these swains now for a loan? For Papa, she would have swallowed her pride and done so, but she knew in her heart she would receive nothing more than a return of the rejections she had handed them.

As Gash showed her to the door, he made one last observation. "I truly regret the situation, but the truth is, matters are out of my hands. Even if I chose to be charitable, I no longer hold the papers on the store. Those belong to Quentin Kavanagh. Any further discussion about the matter should be directed to him. He is, I believe, abiding at the Georgia Hotel."

Out on the street Angel whirled the ruffled parasol over her head and considered what next to do. As much as she hated to take the banker's advice, she knew she had to face the Micks's devil sooner or later, and his hotel was in the next block. Would he be there this close to noon? There was only one way to find out.

To Angel's way of thinking, the hotel's dim interior was overfurnished and terribly oppressive, as befitted the occasion of her calling. The desk clerk eyed her carefully as she scribbled a note on a piece of hotel stationery, then asked that it be delivered to Mister Kavanagh's room.

He smirked, too. Angel ignored him, as well as the stares from a half dozen men lingering in the lobby. There was not, unfortunately, another woman in sight. She tapped the tip of her parasol against the carpet, remembered the way Harold Gash habitually tapped his cane, and forced herself to stillness.

The clerk returned within minutes, his smirk broadened to a leer. "Mister Kavanagh asked that you come right up."

"I meant we should talk in the lobby," she said, keeping her voice low, knowing every man around was listening to what transpired at the desk.

"Be that as it may," the clerk said ever louder, "Mister Kavanagh is waiting. His suite occupies the top floor."

Further argument would bring only further attention, and with a nod she lifted her skirt and hurried up the stairs. The suite was three flights up. Out of breath, she knocked on the door.

He answered right away, giving her no time to formulate her appeal. He was dressed as he was the previous evening, all in black. One arm propped high on the doorjamb, he leaned forward. But he did not smile. Oh no, he just looked at her with those dark blue eyes, his strong mouth set in a line, everything about him seeming to reach out and wrap her in its power.

Or more precisely in its heat. As Michael said, he did indeed burn with an inner fire.

The devil.

She stopped herself. She was sounding like the Micks.

"Miss Chadwick," he said, and her name did not sound quite so harsh on his lips as it had last night.

"Mister Kavanagh, I was wondering—"

"I'm certain you were wondering many things. As was I."

He had a deep voice enriched by the hint of a brogue. Enriched and darkened. Everything about him seemed shadowed, even the look in his eyes.

"I was especially wondering how long it would take you to offer me something to win back your father's effects."

"Offer you something?" Angel asked, distressed by the squeak in her voice.

"You do that innocence very well. Please come in. We'll see how long it lasts."

Three

Quent stepped aside to admit his visitor. Her skirt swished as she entered the sitting room, hips swaying in the natural way of a woman. He watched the movement. Despite her look of wide-eyed innocence, Thomas Chadwick's youngest daughter knew how to entice a man.

She turned to face him. Her bonnet was blue to match her dress, and within its enclosing brim yellow curls framed her face and the curve of her neck. Her thick-lashed eyes were wide and deep, the color of a springtime sky, and her features delicate. Her small nose wrinkled and her chin tilted against his perusal. She was a small one—except for her breasts. These were swollen to full womanhood, natural and taunting like the sway of her hips.

She was, in truth, the picture of angelic innocence and a luring Jezebel. Would she prove to be a formidable opponent? He hoped so. He had been a scrapper for so long, he preferred fights where no holds were barred.

"Mister Kavanagh," she said, her hands tight around the handle of her parasol, "we need to talk about your visit yesterday."

She spoke in a soft voice, rolling out the words with gentle sibilance, definitely American but not so southern as others he had heard in Savannah. Her Irish father and her English mother had passed on an accent that was pleasing to the ear, as well as features that were pleasing to the eye.

Not that anything about her mattered. He would do what he had come to do.

"Didn't I make myself clear?" he asked. "I hold the mortgage on your father's property. It is time he paid his debts."

She blinked once, but she held her ground. "I had hoped we could discuss the matter."

"The matter being the method of payment. You've come up with cash." It was, he knew full well, a task she would find impossible.

She winced. "The matter being the best way to approach our shared concern."

As if he were concerned about Thomas Chadwick. Pretty Angel had a great deal to learn.

He took her parasol and set it aside. "Sit down," he said. She hesitated, studied the small sitting room, then chose a straight-backed chair beside the small sofa. He caught her glance into the adjoining room, where the unmade bed was clearly visible.

Studying the terrain, he thought, noting her options, planning her approach. Miss Angel Chadwick looked as innocent as her name, but there was nothing foolish or stupid in her wide blue eyes.

Sitting primly, hands folded in her lap over a small purse, she said, "I've been to see Harold Gash."

"The man's a fool."

Her gaze lifted to him. "You're blunt spoken, Mister Kavanagh."

"Does that bother you?"

"No, not really. I'd rather we were both honest and straightforward. So that we can trust one another."

Just wait, he thought. *You'll soon wish I had the silver tongue of most Irishmen.*

She took a deep breath, an act that did interesting things to the bosom of her gown. "Mister Gash mistakenly assumed Papa couldn't pay his debts. Once he's back from

Texas, he will make things right. You have my promise he will do so within the month."

Quent answered her with silence, letting the moment drag out until the tick of the clock on the table seemed like a bell tolling the doom of some unfortunate soul.

Good tidings to all. The phrase came to him out of the distant past.

Impatience ate at him. "Take off your bonnet, Miss Chadwick. I find it distracting."

"I beg your pardon?"

"How wide-eyed you are. I asked that you remove your bonnet. It reminds me of blinders on a horse."

"I don't see why—" She stopped, then sighed. "Very well."

The hat joined the purse in her lap. She smoothed the golden curls around her face. Her back upright, her chin at a tilt, she looked him straight in the eye.

"I'm afraid you're mistaken about something, Mister Kavanagh."

"And what's that?"

"Chadwick Dry Goods and Clothing is not as profitable as it appears."

Quent stifled a laugh. He knew exactly what income the shop was capable of producing, having studied it as well as the town yesterday before approaching the bank. He had found the establishment small and plain, with far more goods than customers. Old Thomas must have worked hard to do as well as he'd done. Give the devil his due.

"Are you saying it's not worth owning?"

"Not for you. You're obviously a man of means. Why on earth bother with our little place?"

"Call it a whim."

"A whim!"

She almost came out of her chair, then took a deep breath as she settled back. There was spirit in the lass, he would give her that.

"I'm sure you don't mean to cause my family injury," she said. "We're reasonable adults. We can work something out."

Ah, was she at last getting to an offer, one she assumed he couldn't refuse? Her only asset was her person, and while Quent was not immune to physical pleasure, Angel Chadwick's admitted charms were inadequate to sway him from his course.

His impatience grew. Let her present an offer and be done with it. She clearly needed a little goading. He leaned forward on the sofa. "Who was the man who kissed you in the store yesterday?"

She shook her head. "You have the most disconcerting way of changing the subject. If you must know, he was Jeremiah Godwin, my fiancé."

"Your fiancé? How curious."

"What? That I'm betrothed?"

"Not in the least. I'm surprised you are not wed with a trio of brats tugging at your hem. How old are you, approaching thirty?"

"I'm scarcely twenty-four," she said with an indignation that revealed a sensitivity to age. A feminine weakness, to Quent's way of thinking, otherwise he would not have provoked her. What other weaknesses did she possess? A lascivious nature would not be unwelcome. She did have the most extraordinary breasts.

"You're still beyond the first blush of maidenhood," he said.

"I postponed marriage until I found a truly good man."

She spoke sincerely, as though she believed there really were such a thing. Quent suddenly thought of home, and of a cottage nestled on an island of Bantry Bay. In certain circumstances good men did exist.

"Does Jeremiah ever give you more than a brotherly kiss?" he asked.

She blinked. Extraordinary breasts, extraordinary eyes. He felt a moment's disquiet.

"Mister Kavanagh, please get back on the subject."

"Then the answer is no. Poor Angel. You've cold nights awaiting with him in your marriage bed."

"What happens in my marriage bed is between me and my husband. We've never even discussed—" She stopped suddenly, her fingers pressed to her lips.

"Does he know you're in a man's hotel room?"

She looked away. "No."

"You didn't tell him, I assume because he might have insisted on accompanying you. And he might get in the way should we reach an agreement we find mutually satisfying."

She gave no sign she understood him. "Jeremiah is a doctor. He has other worries to deal with. I chose not to tell him, but he would understand my being here."

"Then he's a fool. If you were mine, you would play hell visiting another man in secrecy."

"Mister Kavanagh!"

"At last a little passion. Could there be more such feelings seething beneath those fine full breasts?"

She jumped to her feet, purse and bonnet falling to the floor. "I have to leave."

"Have you turned coward, Angel?"

"Not in the least," she said, but a blush gave lie to her words. "You've made it obvious this is the wrong place for a serious discussion."

"I was very serious about your breasts."

Sighing in exasperation, she knelt to pick up her belongings. He was in front of her in an instant, hands on her shoulders, forcing her to stand and look into his eyes.

She felt soft and warm within his grasp, and his hold on her tightened.

"If you were mine, I would know how to tell you goodbye."

"Let me go."

"But aren't we supposed to be working something out? I can be good. Very good."

"You really are the devil."

"Has my reputation preceded me? Then I must live up to it. You want to leave, and I wish to show you a genuine goodbye."

In that moment Quent felt no passion, no hunger for a woman. He felt only anger, and a turmoil that burned in his gut. He wanted to punish this Chadwick trapped within his power, to let her share the anguish of his years.

His mouth took hers quickly. She stiffened under his embrace. He held her slender body against him, felt her breasts brush against his chest, her lips flatten against his assault. He broke the kiss, she started to speak, and he took her mouth again, this time with lips and tongue.

She tasted sweet and wet and womanly. Despite his anger and his anguish, he sensed the flare of desire. He deepened the kiss. She softened against him, and he forgot who she was. Heat rose in him more quickly than it had since he was a randy lad, and blood pounded in his veins. He held her tight, raking his tongue against hers, ravaging her mouth, wanting to take her on the floor.

Her small cry brought him to his senses. He broke the kiss. She stared up at him with searching eyes that did not seem to understand what had almost passed between them. Her lips were red and swollen from just a moment's passion, and her hair, fighting the bun into which she had tried to force it, formed an unruly golden halo around her head.

Were all Chadwicks so enticing? Was it the curse of his family to fall under their spell?

Goddamn it, no. He let her go. She swayed, then got her bearings, grabbed her purse and bonnet, and without another word or glance, fled from the room.

The slam of the door echoed in the room. Quent closed his eyes until the pounding of his blood slowed. Unmoving, he stared at the parasol she had left behind, propped against the wall. A frilly thing with more ruffles than substance, it would not hold off an Irish mist, much less a storm blowing off the sea. Like Angel Chadwick. He doubted there was much substance to her, beyond a few pallid feminine charms. The arousal that had been so quick to heat just as quickly cooled

The tick of the clock unnerved him. He strode to the window and stared down at one of Savannah's tree-lined squares. And he thought of Angel Chadwick with the wide blue eyes and the full soft lips and the parentage that damned her to hell.

If he found her attractive, it was because she was available, and he had been celibate the few weeks since learning for sure about Thomas Chadwick's whereabouts. Deprivation fed desire, as did a sense that, after fifteen long years of burning for revenge, the end of his journey was at hand.

Early in his search he had come to the home of a wealthy Englishwoman, Anne Pickering, who became Chadwick's bride. Anne and Thomas had long ago disappeared, and the trail had ended in bitter frustration, yet always in his travels he kept eyes and ears alert for news of the couple. Last March he read in the *London Times* about an American actress married to an English earl. Raven Chadwick Bannerman, wife of Marcus Bannerman, Earl of Stafford, and daughter to Thomas and Anne Chadwick of Savannah, Georgia, in the United States, had begun a regional theater near her Sussex estate.

The *Times* reporter had been greatly impressed with Lady Stafford's successful efforts, given the position she held as helpmeet on her husband's prosperous estate and as mother of a young son. She was compared with a sister in Texas, a mother of two small children who helped her rancher husband while establishing several flourishing businesses in a nearby town.

A quick investigation showed Lady Stafford's mother had been a Pickering and Quent had experienced a satisfaction hitherto unknown to him, and an anger as well. Damn these Chadwick offspring for their happiness. Damn them for their success. The smoldering resolution struck at his mother's deathbed had burst into flame.

Too well did he remember Morna O'Brien's suffering, her mental lapses, her estrangement from the world, from her husband and son. The memories fed his obsession for revenge. It burned within him more powerfully than physical desire. Since his early years, his mother's enemy had been his enemy as well. He would see the man destroyed in whatever manner it took.

Angel Chadwick had said her Papa could repay his debts. That he could. Her problem was she didn't know everything that her Papa owed.

Angel paused on the sidewalk outside the Georgia Hotel, catching her breath, straightening her hastily donned bonnet, trying to understand what had taken place in Quentin Kavanagh's hotel suite.

Her visit had been a mistake. Mister Kavanagh had misunderstood her purpose and her offer to negotiate. She had meant a redrawing of the papers, adding to Papa's debt in return for an extension of the loan. Apparently the man believed she meant otherwise. She wasn't so naive she didn't understand *that*.

A woman in red walked past her and strode boldly into the hotel. The scent of patchouli hung in the air long after she'd gone. Angel wasn't so naive, either, to mistake the woman's profession. She knew women sold themselves for financial considerations, even in Savannah. Quentin Kavanagh had hinted that was what Angel was about.

Angel's cheeks burned. She could never do such a thing. Never. Not even to—

She caught herself. Not even to save her Mama and Papa

from being thrown out on the street? The answer did not come quickly.

Never, she at last whispered to herself, but the word had a hollow ring. She was left with the unsettled feeling that in trying to help her family, she was traveling down a dark and dangerous road.

If only she hadn't given the whole of her Pickering inheritance to Jeremiah to aid in his charitable works. Jeremiah had few funds, refusing to charge much for his services, saying he ministered the sick the way the Reverend Altwhistle ministered their souls. If only Jeremiah weren't quite so noble, but then that was why she loved him, why she had finally agreed to become his wife. Mama and Papa were worried their spinster daughter would never find a good man to love, but she had.

A truly good man, just as she'd told Quentin Kavanagh. She thought of the way the Irishman had kissed her, showing her, he claimed, how her fiancé should have bade her goodbye.

But Jeremiah was a gentleman and a saint. The Irishman sprang from the underworld.

You've got cold nights awaiting with him in your marriage bed. What nonsense. Whatever happened in her marriage bed was no business of Mister Kavanagh's.

And yet, when she turned to hurry back to the store, her thoughts weren't on her Papa's troubles or her saintly husband-to-be or her foolishness in going to the hotel. She remembered nothing but how the devil had taken her in his arms and kissed her. To her everlasting shame, she hadn't twisted or fought to get away. Oh no, she had felt a small hot spark deep inside her, an impulse to do more than they were doing, the kind of impulse her sisters said they felt in their husbands' arms.

She had never felt that spark with Jeremiah. She was, in truth, no better than the tart who had entered the hotel. What would she do to save the Chadwicks from ruin?

She did not know for sure.

* * *

Quent took his meal in his room. For all its graceful beauty, Savannah offered nothing to entice him outdoors. He had almost accomplished what he had come to do. He would have liked to see Thomas Chadwick's face when he learned about his losses, but now that seemed impossible. Texas was another world away, and while he didn't mind the journey, he could easily pass the returning Chadwicks en route without knowing it.

He must be content with sailing to Ireland, and with taking the mortgage papers to his mother's grave as proof of his promise fulfilled. He hadn't visited that particular hilltop in years, for to do so was to admit the failure of his cause. Surely with the evidence of success laid at her headstone he could find the peace that always evaded him. Surely Morna O'Brien Kavanagh might find the same.

A knock at the door startled him from his reverie. Could it be Angel returning to renew her efforts at a settlement? If so, she was more foolish, or more brazen, than he had thought.

He opened the door to find three red-headed men staring at him in earnest anger. Irish, every one. He would recognize the breed anywhere.

"Quentin Kavanagh," said the man in front, "we've business to discuss."

Quent looked at each. They had the look of determination about them, of men on a mission who would not be denied. He stepped aside to let them enter, thinking that if it was solitude he was after, he'd not find it in the Georgia Hotel.

"I'm Michael Mallon," the speaker said, "and these be Brendan Faulkner and Ian Craig. We work for Thomas Chadwick and for his daughter while he's away."

"And you're wondering, I suppose, whether you will be working for me."

"No such thing," said Michael with indignation, and his companions echoed his feeling in strong terms.

"Mister Thomas's daughter Flame befriended us when we were in the army," Michael continued, "and he gave us jobs when we mustered out. We owe him a great deal."

"Ah, and you're here to pay your debt."

"We're here to see that Miss Angel comes to no harm," said Ian Craig.

"Shouldn't her fiancé be doing this?"

"Jeremiah Godwin?" said Ian with a hard laugh. "Doctor God has more important things to consider than his betrothed."

Quent was not surprised. "She's gone, I'm glad to report. And little the worse for wear."

"I knew she came here," said Brendan Faulkner. "Right into the devil's lair."

Quent raised a brow.

"Our village lies in the hills of County Cork," said Ian. "We know of your reputation."

"Then you ought to be trembling in your shoes. When my name comes up, so I'm told, fear leaps in the hearts of men."

"And of women?" asked Michael. "Do they fear you as well?"

"Not so much," Quent said with a shrug. "If Angel looked afraid when she returned to the shop, it was because she feared herself."

"You're making little sense, man," said Michael. "The lass is innocent as a newborn babe and sees only the good in us all. She tried to keep her troubles a secret, but she confided in us today about the mortgage you hold. She's fair crazy with worry, she is. I've never seen her in such a state."

"Then you ought to be offering her consolation, instead of bothering me."

Michael's hands fisted at his side. "From her own sweet lips I heard her call you the devil. You must have harmed her in some way to rouse her to name-calling. 'Tis not in her nature."

"Rest assured, men, I am not a despoiler of virgins. I did nothing that fair Angel's nature didn't expect or want. I suspect I did far less."

"What are you getting at, you bastard?"

"Ask her yourself. She did not back away from me. On the contrary—"

Brendan came at Quent. His companions dragged him back, easing their hold only when he was subdued.

Michael stepped close. "See here, Mister Quentin Kavanagh, almighty owner of Cordangan Castle and practitioner of deeds that cannot bear the light of day. You can take Thomas Chadwick's belongings, his store, and the roof over his head, and he'll somehow find a way to survive. He's friends and family to help him as much as he needs. But harm a golden hair on that maiden's gentle head and you'll have to answer for it."

"Even the devil has his reckoning day," said Ian.

"Aye," said Brendan, "Miss Angel is the most precious creature in the world to everyone who knows her. Mister Thomas will seek you out no matter where you hide, even on that high black rock you call home. He'll carve out your entrails and hang them on the castle walls for the birds to dine."

Hard words they were, but Quent was not distressed. "If I harm her in any way."

"Aye," the three Irishmen said.

Quent nodded solemnly. "Thank you for the warning. You've certainly given me much to think about. In private, that is."

They started to protest, then found they had little more to say. He showed them the door, ignoring the belligerent, triumphant light in the eyes of Brendan and Ian and the skeptical look of Michael. He had spoken no more than the truth. They had given him much to think about.

Financial ruin had seemed the perfect revenge, since most men cared about their pride and personal well being above all else. Thomas Chadwick, it seemed, had other priorities. With two of his daughters married to prosperous men, his concern centered on his youngest and virginal child.

This most precious creature in the world must not be harmed.

The same precious creature who had hinted at liaisons less than respectable, who had responded in a most unangelic way to his kiss.

To harm her was to tear at his enemy's heart. It was a prospect much to be desired.

He had meant to remain in seclusion until the mortgage papers were in his name, then close down the shop and leave. Now it seemed he would have to venture out and corner Miss Angel Chadwick once again.

Four

"Rest your heart and your head, Miss Angel," Brendan announced as the Micks strode into the store.

Angel looked up from where she was working behind the counter. "What do you mean?"

"I mean we've settled your woes."

Michael shot Brendan a dark look. "Don't be getting the lass's hopes up. Our mission scarcely reached such lofty goals."

"We've come from the Georgia Hotel," said Ian.

"You went to see him?" she asked, dropping a package of pins and sending them skittering across the counter. There was little need to identify whom she meant. Since yesterday evening the universe had settled into one dreadful *him*.

"Aye," Ian said with a nod, "that we did. For sure Devil Kavanagh knows the lay of the land now. He'll be thinking twice about the dastardly deeds he's been considering. Talk fearsome before a helpless maid, will he? We let him know you're not alone."

"He agreed to hold off on the foreclosure?"

"Not in so many words," said Brendan. "But we got him to thinking, that's for sure, and pondering his course. When we left, he wasn't the cocky bastard that greeted us at the door."

Gratitude and doubt stirred Angel's heart as she looked at the Micks. How proud they looked, even cautious Michael, but the devil's threats were surely not so quickly dispatched.

They were her stalwart champions, however, and she could do no less than come around the counter to give them each a hug. When she turned to gather the pins, she felt a stinging in her eyes, the tears as much in affection for the men as for the foreboding sense that they may have done more harm than good.

She kept herself busy the rest of the afternoon, and when closing time arrived she assured the Micks she would lock the door against late visitors, then exit the back way for the short walk home.

In truth she craved solitude, a moment to gather her thoughts and calm the pounding heart that had never quite slowed since she left Quentin Kavanagh's suite.

Drawing the front blinds against the glow of twilight and throwing the front bolt, she began to turn down the lamps, strolling past the shelves and counters, breathing in the scents of spice and sugar and sawdust, the familiar comforting mustiness that had perfumed the air of Chadwick Dry Goods and Clothing for as long as she could remember.

She loved it all. And so did every Chadwick, Papa most of all. An only child, he had never said much about his parents back in Ireland, only that they were the poor Irish relations of a famous English labor reformer named Edwin Chadwick. They had been Dublin shopkeepers who lost everything in the potato famine almost forty years before.

After their death, Papa had sought work in England, had met his beloved Annie, had traveled with her across the Atlantic when her father objected to their love. The Savannah store was his creation, a testament to his ability to care for his high-born wife and their three girls. It was Papa who had named them at birth for their coloring. Raven, Flame, and Angel, each as different in habits as in the shade of her hair.

People laughed, Angel knew, but Chadwicks paid no

mind. They weren't the most revered people in town, not among the gentry at least, but they were honorable and hard-working and certainly respectable. They were good citizens with friends and a comfortable home.

The loss of that home would hurt as much as the loss of an income. Papa and Mama had worked hard through the years. It would be difficult to begin anew.

Too restless to return home, she settled in the office to study the store's finances again. Concentration came hard, and she did little more than shuffle papers. She sought the impossible. If Quentin Kavanagh pursued in his stated purpose, there was no way to save Papa from ruin.

She thought of the Irishman's kiss. Strange it was that she could feel his lips on hers, even now hours later, could feel the invasion of his tongue, could still taste him when she couldn't remember dinner from a short while ago.

Shameful, she told herself, and tried to think of Jeremiah. Surely when they were married they would bring each other pleasure in many ways. It was a shallow consideration, given her current circumstances, but it brought her a moment's comfort even though it did not remove her doubt.

A chill came over her, and she rubbed her sleeves. What could she do to help Papa? Would she really give herself to a man out of wedlock in order to save her family? Quentin Kavanagh obviously thought so, but what about her? How far would she go to gain time on Papa's debt?

Tiny nerves tightened along her spine and settled in the pit of her stomach. She would go as far as necessary. Flame had faced savage Apaches when she first went to Texas, and Raven had conquered both the peerage of England and the critical world of the stage. The least Angel could do was give herself to one lone Irishman for an hour or two.

Jeremiah's gentle face came to mind. She sighed in impatience. A moment ago she hadn't been able to summon his image no matter how hard she tried. Jeremiah would have to understand. Or maybe he didn't have to know.

She pushed the thought aside as unworthy. The good doctor did not deserve being deceived.

At the heart of her problem lay the character of Quentin Kavanagh. She couldn't imagine anyone drawing pleasure from ruining the lives of strangers, yet that seemed to be what he was doing. He was a type of man totally beyond her experience.

A *type* of man? No, she corrected. There could be no one else like him on the face of the earth.

A hard knock sounded at the front door. She jumped in her chair.

Ignore it, a small voice said. When the knock sounded again, Angel pretended not to hear the whisper of advice, instead hurrying through the dark store and peering through the blinds. Quentin Kavanagh peered right back.

With his hat pulled low on his forehead, he looked as sure of himself as he had at the hotel. He looked, she had to admit, as though he had come to collect what he assumed she was offering. And she had been wondering how far she would go.

Her heart pounded against her ribs. It was one thing to decide on surrender while alone in her office; it was quite another to face the devil with such a conviction in mind.

Chadwicks weren't cowards, she reminded herself, and she threw open the bolt. "Come in," she said, relocked the door, then taking a wide berth around him hurried toward the lighted back room as though it offered sanctuary. Taking refuge behind the desk, she looked at him standing in the open doorway, just as he had done the night before.

Just as dark, just as arrogantly certain of himself, just as menacing. He was like a furnace, heating her whenever he got near.

Had it been only twenty-four hours since they met? Surely it had been a year.

"Do you venture out only at night, Mister Kavanagh?" she asked, trying to stand as straight as he.

"Like a vampire? No, I'm a devil, remember. It's best you keep in mind the particular monster you face."

She couldn't look at him for long. He was just too . . . formidable.

Rustling the papers before her, she said, "Please tell me you've decided to give Papa additional time."

He didn't respond. She looked up to see him studying her with a regard that sent the blood pulsing through her veins. Heat stole from her stomach to her breasts, right up to her hairline. She even felt a tingling along her scalp.

She cleared her throat. "I know why you've come. I'm not so innocent as everyone believes. I understand the ways of the world."

His brows lifted a fraction. "Do you now?"

"I've two married sisters who have talked a bit. And Mama, of course. She never believed in keeping her daughters in ignorance about what goes on with a man and a woman."

But they had spoken of coupling in the marriage bed between two people in love. With the Irishman it wouldn't be the same thing at all.

If only he wouldn't keep staring at her. She could hardly think.

"Have you a family, Mister Kavanagh?"

The twitch of his lips was unmistakable. It was like a curse from a less stoical man.

"They're all dead."

"I'm sorry."

"Don't be. My parents died a long time ago."

"And have you no brothers or sisters?"

He didn't respond. She looked up to see a hardness in his eyes that struck her as harshly as a physical blow.

She took a deep breath, and then another. "Would your parents approve of what you're doing now?"

The hardness settled into what was close to amusement. "I think they would. Morna, most certainly, although little in life pleased her. Old Dermot Kavanagh cared little for anything outside a bottle."

"You call them by their given names. They were not loving, were they? I'm sorry." She meant what she said.

"I'm not here for sympathy, Angel," he said, tossing his hat onto the stack of papers in front of her. "Save your selfless sentiments for those who want them. I'm after something else."

Here was the moment that he claimed his victory. Why he wanted her she couldn't imagine, when he could have far more worldly and beautiful women than she. Her task was to take each moment as it came.

He came around the desk, standing close enough for their clothing to touch and for her to feel the heat and determination burning within him. He was a furnace, all right, blazing out of control. It took all her courage to stand her ground, to close her eyes, to lift her lips.

But he did not kiss her. She looked up to see him regarding her again with what appeared to be amusement.

Her cheeks burned with embarrassment.

"Don't tease me, sir."

"But you're eminently teasable. Do you really think all I want is another kiss? Maybe a little groping under your skirts and a fondling of your breasts? Is that what you believe?"

She fell backwards into the chair. "Oh, my," she managed. This wasn't at all how she imagined things would go. She hadn't imagined any kind of talk.

He leaned forward, his hands on the arms of the chair, his breath stirring her hair. "When I ravage women, I want far more. Shall I tell you exactly how much? First I'd like you naked—"

"Mister Kavanagh!"

"Maybe not naked right away. Before we begin, I'd like to hear my name on your lips. Say it. Quentin. It's not difficult to pronounce."

She concentrated on his mouth. What heat he aroused in her. Maybe if she didn't look into his eyes she could keep from melting.

"Quentin," she said, thinking how crazy was this entire scene. Her head whirled. She must be caught in a dream.

"Good," he said in a voice that was all too real. "Next comes the naked part. Don't look so startled. I don't mean here and now. My room offers far more comfortable accommodations than a hardwood floor."

She remembered the unmade bed in his suite and imagined him pulling her down onto the tousled covers. *I'm doing this for Papa,* she told herself, but the words seemed to come from someone else. Certainly the tingle of anticipation in her breasts and in her belly held no hint of sacrifice.

"I'll undress you and you'll undress me," he said. "And we'll touch each other all over, and look at each other, and kiss wherever we want to kiss. Is the skin of your thighs as soft as your cheek? I would imagine so."

She felt as though he were already undressing her, and looking, and Lord help her, even kissing. She truly was in league with the devil.

"A man's never lain between your legs, has he, Angel? We're not so heavy as we look. Leastwise few women object. Do you know what I'll be doing? Do you suspect how it will feel?"

Perspiration beaded on her upper lips, and her heart pounded in her ears. She shrank back in the chair, unable to take a breath to save her soul.

"A lamb to the slaughter, aren't you?" he said, backing away. "You'd lie stiffly beneath me, thinking of your wonderful Papa and your noble Jeremiah, of your own noble sacrifice. One time, one quick thrust, and all would be well."

He made her feel like the wrongful one. Perhaps she was,

but not for any reason he could imagine. When he moved close, no other man had been on her mind.

She found her breath and her voice, and found, too, the strength to stand. Her legs were shaky, but she felt far less vulnerable than when she cowered in the chair.

"Once ought to be enough," she said, her chin tilted in defiance.

"Don't you know by now what ought to be seldom is?"

His voice was sharp, and he stared past her. She watched him carefully. He seemed to be somewhere else, caught in a nightmare of his own. An expression of such despair flashed in his eyes that for a moment she forgot her own distress.

"Is something wrong?" she asked, wondering why she cared, instinct driving her to reach out to him. She stopped herself just in time.

The despair vanished as quickly as it had appeared, and she saw that his thoughts had returned to her in all their scorching intensity. "Nothing permanent. Nothing I can't settle after so many years. A thought occurs. What if your belly held a child after our one joining? Would your family rally around you? Would Jeremiah understand? Would he give you his name and take our bastard as his own?"

She hadn't considered a child born of their union, but she did so now. The thought emptied all her insides.

"That's not—"

"Answer!"

His voice came at her like a shot. "He would," she said in haste, then added more softly, "At least I believe he would."

"I thought as much. Then one night will not do. I want your father to imagine my hands on your pure white body every night. I want you far from his reach and his protection, far from your Doctor God's forgiveness, far from your loving home."

He ground out each word. Angel heard them with a growing sense of horror.

"What is this all about?" she cried, wondering if the darkness in which he clothed himself went all the way to his soul. "I don't understand. I've never known a man filled with such hate."

"Return with me to Ireland and I'll tear up the mortgage. That's the only offer you'll get from me."

"Ireland!" Angel stared up at him in disbelief. The man was mad. "I . . . I can't," she stuttered, suffering the inadequacy of her words. "My home is here."

"You're a saintly sort, are you not? Your home is where you can do the most good."

A relentless fist clutched her heart. Leaving with him was beyond all possibility, yet if she didn't—

He continued to stand there, watching her as she tried to sort things through, but she couldn't think, not with any clarity.

"What demons drive you to do this?" she asked, letting all her anguish cry out in her words.

His eyes were hooded and his voice flat as he spoke. "Listen well, woman. I want you far from Thomas Chadwick. I want him to think about what I do to you every night. I won't hurt you, but he might well imagine that I do."

A breeze from the open window cooled the room. She hugged herself against its chill.

"This is all about Papa," she said, feeling stupid because she had not seen it right away. "You want to ruin him however you can."

"Ah, the innocent Angel is not so stupid after all."

"How can you hate him so much? And why?"

"You'll find out soon enough. But you'll find out on Irish soil."

Angel felt as though she were slipping into the madness that had overtaken him. "Papa couldn't harm anyone. How could he have harmed you? He must have been gone from Ireland before you were born."

"I've said all I intend. Will you go with me or nay?"

But she could not stop. "Your family . . . your home, your fortune. What do you think he's done?"

"Yes or no. I want an answer."

She searched his face for signs of his secrets, but he kept them hidden behind a rock-hard visage. Time, she thought. She must stall for time until she could be alone and work out a plan.

She brushed loose hair from her cheek, unmindful that her fingers trembled. "I'll need a trousseau and there's the marriage to arrange."

He threw back his head and laughed. Angel shivered at the sound and thought it strange how a man could laugh and yet not smile.

The fist twisted harder on her heart. "Have I amused you?"

"Surprised me. I said nothing of marriage."

"But surely you didn't think I'd go with you otherwise."

"You were ready to sleep with me without the appropriate vows."

"But that was for one time."

"And repeated couplings would be far worse?"

"Leaving home is what is wrong." She could barely say the words without a flood of tears.

He looked her over as he might study a sheep or a cow. To him she was no more than chattel, a stock in trade. "Then marriage it is," he said curtly. "I accept your proposal, for it makes little difference to me."

"*My* proposal!"

"Aye, you were the first to mention marriage. But not before a priest. I have no use for them."

"We're Presbyterians," she said. "The Reverend Altwhistle will perform—"

She caught herself. How could she sound so reasonable when she now dwelled in a crazy world?

"You don't love me," she said, as if that made a difference.

"And never will. Make no mistake on that part. Loving is not a part of my nature. But neither will I beat you. There should be consolation in that. And you'll have a roof over your head without fear of devils like me foreclosing on the mortgage. I'm a wealthy man, Angel. There's many a woman who would gladly take your place."

"Then find one, please," she said with all her heart, "and go in peace."

"Ah, you speak bravely. Remember Papa out on the street. It will happen, I promise. Is his heart strong enough to take the loss of his home and all he's built? He's not a young man. If anything happens to him, you'll have only yourself to blame."

Something was wrong with his reasoning, but her thoughts were so in a jumble she couldn't figure out what it was. She turned from him to stare out the window into the night.

"How will Chadwick react when he returns to find his precious Angel gone with a stranger?" he said. His voice was colder than the breeze. "Will your leaving be any worse than financial ruin?"

She pictured Papa with his smiling face and the happiness shining from his eyes. And she pictured his puzzlement when he found out the news.

She shifted back to meet his cynical gaze. "You think so, don't you? That's why you want me to leave."

"I misjudged you, Angel. You're far more clever than I thought."

"He'll come after me, you know."

"Good. He can see for himself the damage he's done."

Angel twisted her hands at her waist. "What damage? What is this all about?" She spoke leadenly, knowing as she asked that she would get no more satisfactory reply than she had already received.

"You'll find out soon enough. Since marriage was your idea, make the arrangements. The next ship leaves day after tomorrow. I want the newlywed Kavanaghs to be aboard."

"I haven't said I'll go."

"You'll go, all right. Loving daughter that you are, you have no choice."

He headed for the door, then returned to take her by the shoulders.

"We need to seal our betrothal, do we not? And I'd like another sampling of what I'm getting for my money."

He kissed her as thoroughly as before, until she was dizzy from loss of breath, until she was incapable of a single coherent thought.

He pulled away. "Not bad. I've had better, but you'll improve with practice." Once again he started to leave, pausing in the doorway, and she saw from the bleakness deep in his eyes that his own private demons had returned.

If only he would share his troubles with her, she could help to lessen their weight, and in the doing they might reach a compromise. Instead, he chose to mock her and to suffer alone.

"Marriage to a Chadwick." He stared past her into the night outside the window. "What improbable things we do because we have no choice."

And then he was gone, leaving Angel to wonder why his scorn seemed directed toward himself as well as toward her.

She wondered, too, in the midst of her own turmoil, why his troubled soul moved her in ways that Jeremiah's goodness had never done.

Five

They were married two days later by a justice of the peace in the Chatham County courthouse. Only the Micks served as witnesses, the Reverend Altwhistle having refused to preside over what he called a Godless union. He made the judgment after a brief, private conference with the groom.

Angel wondered if Jeremiah might burst through the judge's door demanding—requesting—she return to his side. Or maybe wishing her well, which was more in keeping with his character. But he did not appear, and she was not really surprised. He probably didn't even know about her desertion of him, a consideration that caused her no little distress.

After dawn yesterday she had hired a carriage and ridden out to the Reynolds farm. He had sent word from inside the house thanking her for coming to help, assuring her she was not needed. He would see her later, he said, and she had gone away.

Later. As far as she and Jeremiah were concerned, later would never come. For the first time since her betrothal to him began, she was grateful their relationship was not a passionate one. In truth, she saw her love for him as what it was: admiration and gratitude for his kindness, and for the unselfish way he used his extraordinary skills.

Jeremiah would lose himself in work, and there were other women around, in particular a widow she could name, who would move in to offer consolation. Within a month or two, the good doctor would forget whatever heartbreak she brought him now.

It was both a lowering and encouraging thought.

Unable to reach Jeremiah, she had returned to the store to face the Micks, knowing she must announce to the skeptical Irishmen her change in fiancés in such a way that they wouldn't rebel against the news. Quentin Kavanagh offered a chance for travel, she said, for adventure and for riches beyond her expectations. Under their astonished stares, she also hinted at other, more physical reasons for the marriage, but she'd had so little experience with passion, she doubted they got her point.

"I cared little for Doctor God as your mate, Miss Angel," Ian responded, his voice stricken with distress, "but you've gone too far the other way."

"Too far? Hell, yes, she has," said Michael in a rare moment of profanity. "We can't let you do this, lass."

Angel fought a momentary panic. "You have to," she said, then forced herself to a composure she did not feel. "You have no choice."

"But he threatened to bring your family to ruin. And now you're marrying the bastard."

"He's not so evil as you think," she said, wishing she could sound more convincing. She thought of the moments in which his thoughts turned inward and decided that in a curious way she might be speaking the truth.

But the Micks were not of a mind to believe her, and she had to draw on their sympathy in different ways.

"He's not threatening me in any way. Just the opposite." She lowered her lashes and took on the unfamiliar role of coquette. "Do you think I'm not pretty enough to attract him? Maybe he wants me as his wife because . . . he wants me."

"We've no intention of insulting you, Miss Angel," said Michael. "He'd be demented if he didn't see your worth."

Brendan and Ian hurriedly agreed.

"Please accept the fact that I'm marrying him. It's a decision I made of my own free will. All I ask is that you stand beside me in the place of Mama and Papa." Here she almost came to tears. "They'll want to know all was proper."

"Is that what we're to say?" asked Brendan. "That all was proper? The wedding's too rushed. They'll want to know why."

"The ship leaves for Ireland this week and he must return." One by one, she looked them full in the face. "This is a far more complicated world than I ever imagined, yet I know in my heart I'm doing the right thing." She managed a smile. "You were friends to Flame in Texas. Be a friend to her sister now."

She could see the reluctance in their eyes, even as they gave their assent. Perhaps she should claim to have fallen in love, but they wouldn't believe her. At least, she thought with a slight lift of spirit, they weren't threatening to shoot Quentin in the knees.

He was Quentin to her now, both when she thought of him and when she mentioned him aloud. She had to call him so if she were to convince anyone they held regard for one another. But deep inside her, he was Mister Kavanagh, a stranger in some ways, an enemy in others, and an enigma she might never solve.

Had any woman before her ever entered into such a union? She believed not, and so she declined to inform the few young women who were her friends.

Until the ceremony she busied herself with choosing what to take with her. She made it to the courthouse and through the exchange of vows with a calmness that would have made Raven the actress proud. In no way could she have the Micks describing to her parents what a gruesome thing the sharing of vows had been, with the groom growling through the whole thing and the bride weeping miserable tears.

And they would do so, despite all their promises.

As it was, Quentin almost growled and she almost cried, but she knew that no one else took note. The judge, mindful of the groom's terse instructions, kept the proceedings short and to the point. Throughout, Angel managed to forget her determination to marry a truly good man. When she promised to love, honor, and obey, she told herself that somehow she would manage to do just that. The saddest part of the occasion was the knowledge that at the same time her husband followed tradition and slipped a wide gold band onto her finger, he lied in every vow.

He hadn't bothered to wear other than his usual black suit and shirt. For his lapel she'd brought him a rose from the bush at her back door. He wore it without protest or thanks, as though it were another part of the ceremony to be endured.

Angel had chosen one of her white summer gowns for the service, and a matching lace-trimmed bonnet she had bought on a whim but never worn. Brendan, the most sentimental of the Micks, gave her a nosegay to carry, a brightly colored array of spring flowers. They were almost her undoing.

Quentin treated her politely enough, settling for a Jeremiah-type kiss at the end of the ceremony instead of the usual Kavanagh attack. After the proper documents had been signed, he did the one thing that brought happiness to her day. He burnt the mortgage papers, lighting them from the wedding candle that was another of Brendan's offerings, then tossing the conflagration onto the cold chamber hearth.

Angel stared at the ashes.

"It's my wedding gift to you, Mrs. Kavanagh," Quentin said. "That and what I'll give you on board ship."

He shot her such a look with his midnight-blue eyes that she couldn't mistake what he meant. Their marriage bed would not be cold tonight. The certainty of it weakened her knees.

He stepped close. "My brave little bride," he said in a low voice where no one else could hear. The lines fanning from his eyes deepened. "Trying to put on a good show. Apparently Lady Stafford is not the only actress in the family."

He echoed her thoughts closely, as if he could read her mind, and Angel felt a moment's panic.

"May I say goodbye to my friends?" she asked, daring to touch him, avoiding his gaze. "Alone, if you don't mind."

He stared at her hand on his sleeve, and at the wide gold band around her finger. He gave no sign of the inner turmoil that she had witnessed that strange night in the store, but she sensed that somewhere deep inside him it lurked like a storm hiding over the hills.

"Why not?" he said. "The deed is done."

Pulling a wallet from an inside pocket, he nodded to the judge. They left the room, and Angel turned to the Micks. Now was the time to give in to sadness, to a sense of loss, to despair. But she didn't, and for that strength she was proud.

"Here," she said, thrusting two letters into Michael's hand. "One's for Jeremiah. He's been tending Mrs. Reynolds in a difficult childbirth, and I haven't had a chance to tell him about—"

Her voice broke. Tell him about what? She had betrayed him; there was no putting a good light on what she had done.

The second letter was for Papa and Mama. It had been difficult to write because it was filled with lies . . . about how an Irishman from Papa's native land had swept into town and in a few short days fallen in love with her. He was so wonderful (she wasn't skilled enough at deception to come up with specifics) that she returned his feelings with all her heart.

"I love him the way he loves me," she declared, "and isn't that what you've always wanted for your daughters?" The words were the closest she came to the truth.

As a wedding present, she wrote, he had paid Papa's debts. "Wasn't that a wonderful thing to do?" She used the word *wonderful* a half dozen times. *Devil* appeared not once.

She lied to everyone but herself. Her husband had taken her as a bride to get at her father, to hurt him, to bring him to ruin or to Ireland. He looked at both as the same. In Ireland Papa was supposed to learn a terrible secret. The situation made no sense. Quentin had never met Papa, had said his family was dead and gone—

She stopped herself. Had Papa killed someone? She pictured his round, ruddy face, his laughing brown eyes. No, she thought, Papa was incapable of inflicting harm on another human being, certainly nothing that would warrant a thirst for revenge. Quentin was wrong. She needed time to prove it. To that end, Papa must remain at home.

And so she claimed in her letter that she and Quentin were deliriously happy, madly in love, passionately embarking on an extended honeymoon The Chadwicks just might believe it since their other daughters had found such a relationship.

She added that they could visit when the honeymoon was done, and the bride settled into her magnificent new home. She would let them know when that would be. After she learned Quentin's secret, she could have written, after she knew the truth of why they had wed. And, she hoped in her heart, after she and her husband had reached some kind of truce.

Right now that seemed impossible. She glanced at the ashes in the fireplace to remind herself that sometimes miracles did happen, even with the Kavanaghs.

Leaving the judge's chamber, she and the Micks found

the bridegroom waiting on the courthouse steps. Angel watched as he thrust a letter into Michael's hand.

"See that Chadwick gets this as soon as he returns."

Michael glanced at Angel. She smiled an encouragement she did not feel. He looked back at Quentin.

"Aye," he said without enthusiasm. "I'll do as you ask."

"Give Angel your word, not me. You'll not be so quick to lie to her."

Michael's eyes narrowed, but he did as he was told.

Quentin snapped a finger and as if by magic a hired carriage appeared on the street. Secured to the rear were the two suitcases holding Angel's possessions. She had never been much for material things. Mostly she was taking with her the myriad memories stored in her heart.

Halfway down the front walk, she stopped, muttered a hasty "just a minute" to her husband, and ran back to the Micks. She wanted to tell them to destroy Papa's letter from her husband, but she was afraid Quentin would again read her mind and figure out what she was doing.

Instead, she gave them each a big hug and promised to write about how things were at Cordangan Castle.

"I really am happy," she said with a smile and a lift of her chin. "An angel can manage a devil any day of the week."

The Micks watched as the carriage disappeared down the street.

" 'Tis a dark day in Savannah to see such as this take place," said Brendan.

"And the three of us just standing here and letting it happen," Ian said.

"What would you have us do?" asked Michael. "I fear we've already done too much."

"What do you mean?" the others asked, but he was not of a mind to tell them. The suspicion that they had set the devil onto their innocent Angel twisted like a double-edged knife in his heart. Curse their visit to his hotel room, and curse their foolish words about what a precious thing Miss Angel was to her Papa. It was after their bold, thoughtless words that the wedding had been set.

Could she really manage him? Angel Chadwick was pure of heart, and that gave her strength, but was her goodness powerful enough to overcome the evil of Quentin Kavanagh? Angel claimed so, but she always looked on the bright side of things.

Good against evil, a struggle as old as man. He would visit the priest today for reassurance that good really could win.

In the meantime . . .

He ripped open Kavanagh's letter to Mister Thomas.

"Should we be doing that?" asked Brendan. "We promised Miss Angel—"

"It wasn't a promise she asked for."

"Aye," said Ian. "If Michael hadn't done it, I'd 'a opened it meself."

Michael read it, then passed it around.

May you never know a moment's peace, Thomas Chadwick. I have your precious Angel. Morna O'Brien is avenged.

"Who's Morna O'Brien?" asked Brendan.

No one had heard the name.

"There's evil here, mates," said Michael. "Worse than we thought. I can feel it like a black cloud blocking the sun."

"Are we giving the letter to Mister Thomas?" asked Ian. "It seems our devil wishes to torture the man."

"I'm inclined to do little Quentin Kavanagh asks. We'll not deliver it right away. We'll wait until we hear from Miss Angel. It could be he'll find satisfaction with taking her as his bride and leaving the father to miss her. She's a wonder, she is. We'd best be telling ourselves she's happy with what she's done."

He spoke for the others, little believing his words himself. But Miss Angel had wanted them not to worry or fight the wedding. He would have to trust she knew what she was about.

Quent arranged for separate cabins aboard the ship that would take them to Ireland. A private man by nature, he would share his bride's bed for a while but he wouldn't share her room.

The consummation was a matter of necessity. No annulments for the Kavanaghs. Divorce maybe, later, after her cursed father came to call. If a child should come from their union, Angel could take the brat back with her when she returned to the Chadwick fold. Families weren't for him, other than the responsibilities he already faced.

And she would return. Of that he was sure. She was nothing to him but a means to an end. To her, he was the money that kept her Papa from ruin. She had saved the Chadwick store, all right, but no power on earth could save its owner from his ultimate moment of truth.

He gave her ample time to prepare for his conjugal visit. The meal he ordered for her was returned from her cabin untouched. Was the lass so beside herself with desire that she couldn't eat? It seemed unlikely.

She had looked fine enough in her white gown, her wide blue eyes, her quivering lips, the dress equally proclaiming her virginity. Damned fine, as a matter of fact, with her woman's breasts and hips and her small waist. Her lips had a right to quiver. He wasn't a gentleman, nor a gentle man. Not that he would hurt her; that was not his way. But he liked his women lusty and practiced. His wife would be neither, and he was impatient to be done.

Quent waited on deck for night to fall. He had booked

them aboard a cargo ship that carried few other passengers. Just as well. He hadn't the patience for the card games and social gatherings that were a part of most ocean travel.

Alone, he watched as the ship sailed down the Savannah River, and later he watched the land slip away and the dark, rolling waves of the Atlantic beckon him back to Ireland. To home. He had spent much of his adult life traveling the world, especially since his father's death nine years ago, but he had never taken much pleasure in it. He'd been setting up his business, the Pride of Ireland Imports/Exports out of Dublin, but always the name *Thomas Chadwick* burned at the back of his mind.

His efforts had brought him a prosperity the Kavanaghs hadn't known since the days when there had been an earl at the helm. The title was taken from the family several generations past when the last earl seduced a nun in church. He had suffered a fatal heart attack in the process, and the title was revoked by the Crown. Just as well. Quent would have made a poor peer.

Few people outside his immediate staff knew who was behind the Pride of Ireland. Quent liked it that way. He was a very private man.

Pacing the deck, watching the fall of night, he came upon a cage lashed to the base of a mast. Feral yellow eyes peered at him from behind the bars. He knelt to stare back and was greeted with a low, menacing growl.

"Be careful there, sir," one of the mates said behind him. " 'At's a nasty beast we're carrying on board."

"Some kind of leopard, isn't it?"

"Man who brought it on board called it a puma. Caught in the States. We're taking it to a private collector in the north of Ireland. The bastard. Ought to be caned." He hesitated a moment. "Beggin' yer pardon, sir, but ye ain't a collector of such yerself, are ye?"

Quent shook his head, and the puma's growl deepened.

"Cats is all right," said the sailor. "The domesticated

kind, although gi' me a dog any day. This 'un belongs in the wild."

For a moment Quent was one with the cat, suffering the tyranny of the bars, the hatred of oppression, the longing for a night run through the forest, alone and unfettered. Months had passed since his last ride across Kavanagh lands. He thirsted for one now.

Quent wasn't a drinking man. He took his pleasure from his rides, often at midnight when the clouds swirled across a starlit sky and the world lay quiet and pulsing, as if hiding from the day. Other times he ventured from the castle just as dawn was breaking and the purple light over the bay turned golden through the branches of the trees.

The rides were wine in his veins. They offered respite from the worries of his world, from the memories of a deathbed promise, from his thwarted search for revenge. A promise such as he had made could form a cage just as surely as iron bars, though the promise had been gladly given and would be gladly kept.

And yet it was a cage. He felt a sudden fury to destroy those imaginary bars and be done with the past. His fury became a frenzy to be free. He fought the turmoil. Too often it threatened to overtake him, but the necessity for self control always won out, as it must now on this, his wedding night.

His thoughts caught on the last few days, the words spoken before a judge, and the cramped cabin where Angel Chadwick Kavanagh awaited. He watched the cat a while longer, and the cat watched him, each breath of the animal a low growl that crept under Quent's skin.

He stood and turned, but the wildness stayed with him. His body pulsed and heated. He was ready for his bride.

Six

Angel pulled the bedcovers high under her chin. He would be here any minute. He had said he would visit tonight and while she understood little else about Quentin, she knew he would keep his word.

She was dressed in a white nightgown that covered all but her extremities. Beneath the soft muslin, she was naked as the day she was born, and she felt vulnerable and wanton, stretched out like this in the bed with the ocean swelling and falling under her. She was waiting for a man . . . her husband, she reminded herself, but she had a difficult time thinking of him that way.

He was a stranger who had walked into her life and changed everything. Still, he was not done with change. Tonight, a time that should be filled with loving tenderness, promised a different kind of experience she could scarcely imagine. Her first time was to have been with gentle Jeremiah. Instead—

A shiver ran down her spine. Whatever words could be used to describe Quentin Kavanagh, gentle and loving and tender were not among them.

Where was the bravery she had shown to the Micks? She needed it now more than she had ever done.

She had brushed her hair until she thought it would come out by the roots, donned layers of underclothing, then feeling foolishly childish, removed all but her gown. Close to an hour had passed since she had readied herself. Maybe

he had lied about the visit, to taunt her, or maybe something
had happened to him. People did fall overboard.

She chastised herself. Some people, maybe, but not
Quentin. Neither the idea of his death nor of his resurrection
provided her with relief.

The handle on the cabin door turned and he entered. Her
entire body tightened. Get this over with, she told herself,
then try to get some sleep. She glanced at the narrowness
of the bed. But how? There wasn't sufficient room for one
person, much less two.

One glance at her husband and she forgot the technicali-
ties of her wedding night. Quentin would work things out.

He stood inside the closed door, no more than a half
dozen feet away. Sitting up and bending her knees, hugging
them against her breasts, she studied him in silence. A brass
lantern on the wall cast flickering light on his face. He
hadn't shaved since before the wedding, and his bristled
cheeks had a sunken look to them. His chin seemed stronger
than ever and his lips flat and unsmiling.

As always, it was the look in his eyes that got her . . .
the stare that peered into her soul. Or at the very least,
peered through bedcovers and gown to the naked body of
his bride. Nerves along the surface of her skin prickled, and
her heart rose to her throat. She would have thought her
breasts actually swelled if she didn't know such a thing
were impossible.

His hair, cropped just short of shoulder length, fell back
from his face, as though he had raked his fingers through
it a hundred times. She noticed what a high, wide forehead
he had, from his thick black brows to his thick black hairline. In the dim light his skin color reminded her of Irish
whiskey, and his eyes seemed darker than the night sky.

He'd taken off his coat and unfastened the top buttons
of his shirt. Black hairs curled at his throat. He looked more
muscular than he ever had before, his shoulders wide, his
arms strong, his stomach flat and tight.

She looked lower. His trousers fit him snugly, so snugly she could see—

Her eyes flew to his. His mouth moved a fraction. It was the closest to a smile she had ever seen on his face.

Visions of her family, of her home and friends refused to come to her. She saw only Quentin. Quent. The name had a curt, hard sound to it, like the man himself.

"Still awake, Angel?" he asked as he took the few steps to the side of the bed.

She cleared her throat. "I've been waiting for you."

"How dutiful you are."

"Of course it's my duty—" Something in his expression stopped her.

Feeling awkward and ignorant, she straightened her legs and lay her head back down on the pillow. She held still, held silent, her arms at her side. Whatever she said or did would be wrong or ignorant or irritating. Probably all three. She tried to work up some irritation of her own. After all, he *had* kept her waiting, and now he was trying to scare her to death.

He wasn't doing a bad job of it, either.

He pulled back the cover. "My sacrificial virgin."

What could she say? He spoke the truth. But for all her innocence, she was not a child. The curling heat in her belly served as proof.

In defense, she shifted to her side and curled into a fetal position, facing in his direction, wondering how he would feel if, like an infant, she suckled her thumb. One thing was certain: he would not be amused.

He tugged his shirt loose from the waist of his trousers and unfastened the buttons. The shirt fell open, and she saw a narrow band of his chest, from throat to trousers, the skin dusted with black hairs thick in the center and sparse at his waist. It was an interesting sampling of everything under his clothes.

Her gaze naturally slipped lower to the unmistakable

bulge at the base of his abdomen. A strange thing happened. Angel's fear left her. What could only be called interest took over her thoughts. He was her husband and she was his wife. She had said he was not evil, and with little evidence, she truly believed her words. He had promised not to hurt her, and she trusted he spoke the truth.

He might not take their vows seriously, but she did. Obey had been part of the ceremony. Love and honor, too, her inner voice said. She would work on those later.

She sat up and shook her hair about her shoulders, staring into space, waiting for the inevitable. She felt him watching her. His gaze fell like hands on her body. A tingle shivered from the nape of her neck down to her toes. And she waited.

At last she looked at him. "I don't know what to do next. You'll have to show me."

"Such a good girl," he said. He made it sound like a sin. She started to offer a protest, some kind of defense, but he spoke again. "Kneel in front of me," he said.

Angel obeyed. The bed was attached high to the cabin wall. Positioning herself as he had asked put her on a level with him. His thighs were pressed against the bedframe, and his hands were at his side. He didn't say anything, just kept staring and standing there only a few inches away.

It seemed clear he expected something of her. Follow his lead, she told herself. If he could unbutton his shirt, she could do the same with her gown. The buttons went halfway down the front. The gown didn't fall open the way his shirt did, and she gave each side a little tug until the inner swells of her breasts were revealed.

His sharp intake of breath hollowed her insides. Tossing his shirt aside, he gripped her waist and pulled her close, his thumbs shifting her gown open wider, until the bared tips of her breasts touched his skin. Her nipples hardened with a strange kind of longing she didn't understand.

But she liked it. God help her, she liked it very much.

"Touch me," he said, his voice husky.

Where? She didn't know. He was so contoured, and there was so much of him that was naked. Tentative hands rested on his shoulders. He was hot to the touch, and so hard she could imagine the muscle and sinew and bone beneath the stretch of taut, pale-whiskey skin.

She stroked him in exploration. His muscles tightened beneath the pads of her fingers.

His tongue touched her lips. "Open your mouth," he said, and she did. He teased her lips, her teeth, her tongue. His kiss was deep and long and thorough and left her so weak she rested her body against him . . . rested her full, eager breasts against his warm skin.

Instinct drove her. She rubbed her nipples against him. He broke the kiss and leaned his forehead against hers, muttering something in what sounded like Irish. She didn't understand the words, but she knew that whatever else he felt, he was scorning her no longer.

Angel's head reeled, and every muscle tensed. Surely, she thought, he could hear the pounding of her heart. This was all going so fast, and it was all so much more . . . involving than she had ever imagined. She tried to pull away, but her husband was having none of it. He pulled her gown down her shoulders, letting it pool at her knees on the bed. And his eyes raked her. He saw everything—the high, full breasts with their embarrassingly erect tips, her trembling stomach, the triangle of pale hair between her legs, her milk-white thighs. Mostly he looked at the hair.

Too much, her mind protested. She scarcely ever looked at her body, even when she bathed, and now she was exposed to a man. Shoving her gown aside and still kneeling, she pulled the bedcovers over her nakedness while Quent stripped off the rest of his clothing. Never once did he move his eyes from her face.

When he was as naked as she, he jerked the cover from her hands. With movements as sure and swift as a sorcerer, he laid her back on the bed and eased beside her, fitting tightly in the narrow space, one hand cupping a breast, the thumb applying a gentle torture to its tip. He suckled at the tip, then turned his attention to the other nipple, at last running his tongue across the valley between the swells, up to the pulse pounding wildly in her throat.

Cradling her close to him, he ran a hand down her side, across her buttocks, lingering in the narrow crease until she thought she would go mad. At last he eased around to rub his palm against her abdomen in an insistent, taunting massage. Angel's body burned, but she could draw no breath to ease the heat.

Lost to instinctive urges, she lifted her hips to him, stroking his body wherever she could reach, impatient for things she could not imagine. When she pressed her lips against a pebbled nipple, she tasted salty sweat and wanted more. Remembering what he had done to her, she touched him with her tongue and felt him tremor beneath her gentle assault.

Her name was a whisper on his lips, so soft she thought she must be imagining it. Still, she felt a soaring of spirit that was nothing less than joy.

He parted her thighs and lay on top of her, his mouth covering hers once again. Her private part was wet, so wet. His private part rubbed against her, and she began to pulse in a steady rhythm that quickened, grew so intense she thought she might die from its power.

Everything was so new, so strange—the thundering heart and hot blood, the ragged breath, the throbbings that drove her insane.

He thrust inside her, quickly. She cried out in pain. He swallowed the cry, held still, then began to pump his body steadily into hers, and she forgot that he had hurt her. She knew nothing more than where their bodies touched and rubbed. He pounded into her so fiercely that she was almost afraid of the violence. Almost, except that he brought to her sensations she could never have dreamed existed.

Her world exploded, and small cries escaped her lips. She clasped herself to him as wild tremors took possession of them both. His seed spilled into her. He held her tight. Dizzy with a thousand feelings that tore at her, she welcomed the strength of his embrace. The cabin had been cool, but their bodies were slick with sweat and her hair clung to her face. She had never felt such abandon; it shattered everything she'd ever thought about herself.

She had imagined sweet thrills; she discovered rapture. It was a word that at last she understood.

And she was married to a man who made her feel this way, a man who claimed her in a loveless union, a man who had touched not only her passion but something deep inside her, something she did not fully understand.

She liked what he had done. More than liked. She felt wild and joyous, without restraint. He had turned her into a woman she did not know.

Tears burned her eyes, not in grief, but in astonishment. No longer afraid of her husband, she felt lost not knowing herself. She seemed young as spring and old as Eve, severed from her orderly past, sucked into a world of primal pleasure where reason had no place. If he touched her again, and kissed her, she would brazenly welcome everything he wanted to do.

His breathing grew regular and he raised himself to one elbow. She didn't want him to see the tears, thinking them foolish, but she knew he did.

"Goddamn," he said, and in an instant he was out of the bed. With his back to her, he stared out the closed porthole into the pitch-black night.

"Quent," she said, wiping her cheeks, but he did not turn around, and whatever else she thought to say caught in her throat.

He stood so straight, so rigid, so far away. A sense of loss overcame her, and wherever she had felt hot, she felt cold. She wanted to cry out for him to return. Fool that she was, she wanted to hold him, to explain the emotions tearing through her, but how could she when she didn't understand them herself?

And he could only curse her, and scoff.

Nothing in their mating had been a disappointment, yet in her inexperience she had disappointed him. A small voice reminded her she had wanted the incident quickly done with, but that had been a different woman who felt that way. A sacrificial virgin, he had called her. She was a virgin no more.

She couldn't look at him . . . at his bare back and tight, white buttocks, at his strong thighs and calves. At least she couldn't look at him for long. To stare and to study was a kind of intimacy she could not accept. She couldn't handle what she had already done.

With the ship falling and rising in the deep ocean swells, she covered her nakedness and used the edge of the cover to dry her eyes.

"It wasn't supposed to be this way," he said in a voice no longer husky. Instead, he sounded angry.

He glanced over at her. "Are you through whimpering?"

He might as well have slapped her.

"I'm done," she said. In truth, she thought she might never cry again.

He returned his gaze to the night. "I meant to be quick. And not so thorough." His voice was low, and she wondered if he spoke to himself or to her.

She wanted to say something, but her words seemed inadequate, and they caught in the lump in her throat.

"A lamb to the slaughter," he said, and her heart twisted at the cruelty of his words. "Do you know that's what you sounded like, moaning beneath me the way you did? A lamb bleating over the sight of a knife. I cut you all right. Look close and you'll see the blood."

Angel, protected all her life, and loved and cosseted, felt a humiliation that blistered all the brief wild joy of becoming a wife. Whatever her husband had stirred inside her shriveled and died under the bitterness of his words. Let him solve his own cursed turmoil. She had her own to deal with, and it would take all her strength.

He returned to the bed and leaned close, his hands spread for support on the covers beside her. She drew a quick breath. He shook his head as if in disgust. "Don't worry. I'll not bother you again. I'll not have a Chadwick with power over me, lass. My soul should burn in hell before I let that happen."

He dressed quickly and was gone, leaving her to suffer the raw wounds of his lacerating tongue. She forced herself from the bed to clean herself, using the tepid water from a small basin, scrubbing at the blood and the semen that stained her thighs. Never had she felt so cold and alone. In trying to save her Papa, she had given herself to a stranger. But Quentin Kavanagh was no ordinary man. She had been told it from the beginning.

She'd also been told what a bad person he was. She had chosen not to believe it, but now she was not sure.

What had she done? she asked herself the rest of the night. What had she done?

True to his word, Quent did not bother her again. He seemed to know when she strolled the deck, for she seldom saw him and he had her meals sent to her room. She was glad of their separation. It helped her forget their wedding night.

It took the full store of her optimistic nature to ease the misery of loneliness. Life had changed so much the past few years, she reminded herself, first Flame's leaving, and then Raven, and now Papa and Mama traveling so much. Her time for leaving had arrived, that was all. Sometimes she even managed to forget the strange, dark circumstance that had set her to sea. Sometimes.

In the moments that despair threatened, she reminded herself of why she was where she was. She was saving Papa. She refused to consider the fact that her husband believed the reverse.

And so the weeks passed. She soon gained her sea legs, as one of the mates put it, and never was she sick. She liked the ocean with its constant rise and fall, liked the feel of the salt spray against her cheeks, liked the taste of it on her lips. If the crew and the few passengers occasionally studied her in puzzlement, she told herself they were surprised at the ease with which she took to sailing. In her heart she knew they wondered what kind of bride it was who could not entice her new husband into her bed.

One of the sailors who fancied himself a geographer described for her the land to which she journeyed, from north to south, concentrating on County Cork.

"We'll dock on the River Lee at Cork City," he explained, "as fine a harbor as ye'll find anywhere. The village of Cordangan lies some fifty miles to the west, on the far side of Bantry Bay, close to the town of Glengarriff and the Caha Mountains. I've not heard of this castle ye speak of, but I'm betting it's near the water. We've a thousand castles throughout Ireland, ye ken, and I can't be knowing every one."

Angel assured him she understood.

"There's hills and forests surrounding Cordangan," he added in a return of enthusiasm, "and wooded inlets all 'round the bay. Ye'll have as splendid a view of the water, stretching out to the ocean, as ye'll find anywhere. If I weren't a traveling man, I'd envy yer new home."

When he was gone to his chores, she tried hard to concentrate on the beauty awaiting her. If only she had someone close to guide her, to help her know that Ireland would make a wonderful place to spend the rest of her life. But she didn't, and she was left to raise her spirits as best she could.

To ease her worst moments of loneliness, she began talking to the wild cat caged on the deck.

"Ireland's the home of my father's people," she said, as she settled on the deck, unmindful of the damp, salty wood beneath her cloak. "It's true he's never mentioned them, except to say they're all dead, but their blood flows in my veins."

Ceasing his tight pacing, the cat stretched and bared his teeth, but he did not utter a sound She swallowed and went on. "Mama said little more about her English family, but when I visited Raven and Marcus in London two years ago, I felt at home," she reasoned. "Why should Ireland not be the same?"

The animal stared at her with unblinking eyes that held a lost and feral look bleak enough to break anyone's heart. He reminded her of something or someone. It took her a few days to understand who.

In some strange way the beast was like her husband. She couldn't imagine why. While there was more than a hint of savagery about Quentin, there was nothing to suggest he was caged. Yet when she looked at the cat—really looked at him—she saw not yellow eyes but deep, dark orbs the color of a midnight sky. And she felt a primitive quality about him that brought back memories of when Quent had stepped into her room.

She felt so strongly the resemblance between animal and man that the shattering shame of her wedding night returned to her. She could not escape. Memories and confusion stole her serenity, replacing it with worry about what lay ahead. Too well she remembered the judge's pronouncement that in the sight of God and for all eternity, she and Quentin Kavanagh were man and wife.

For all eternity. Somehow she must deal with this strange marriage, she told herself, whether or not her husband returned to her bed.

She vowed, too, to learn the truth of his hatred for her

family, and to dissolve that hatred, if she could. Never would she forget the way he had burned the papers that could have ruined her Papa. A man who could do such a thing—even one as unloving and troubled as Quent—deserved patience and whatever tolerance she could summon.

She knew he also needed help, though he would have denied it with his dying breath.

I'll not have a Chadwick with power over me.

He had spoken from his soul. She didn't want power; she wanted understanding and, for them both, a kind of peace that would help them get through the years.

How strange that she was losing the hurt of the wedding night. Stranger still that she sensed her husband needed her, not for revenge, but for something far different, something she could not name. In this need, as in so many other ways, he was as different from her first fiancé as he could be.

As the voyage neared its end, she wrote her parents a reassuring letter about the calm ocean crossing and the beginnings of her married life. Both, she said, were wonderful. Knowing her husband would not approve or agree, she gave the letter in secret to the geographer sailor, who promised to post it as soon as the ship reached port.

When at last the vague outline of Ireland appeared on the horizon, she felt ready to take on the challenges that awaited her. How bravely she had sworn that an angel could control a devil. It was time to find out if her brash words held any truth.

Seven

Quent brought his bride to Cordangan Castle on a stormy Monday afternoon in early May, five days after disembarking the ship in Cork City. Instead of rail, he chose a hired carriage, refusing to endure the stares and speculation sure to accompany them on the more public ride.

He soon had cause to regret the decision. A broken axle and steady spring rains doubled the usual time needed for the journey. By the time they were rumbling up the final steep road leading to home, the tension between husband and wife was as thick as the outside air.

The first view of the old stone walls came in a flash of jagged lightning. All seemed dark inside the castle, which rose from a rocky headland high above them. In the brief flash of light the lone turreted tower that remained of the original structure looked like a stub-fingered hand clutching the sky.

A harsh, forbidding sight to most, Quent thought as the carriage jounced upward, but it was one of the few that gave respite to his restlessness.

"I've never seen a castle before," said Angel. She hadn't spoken since noon, and her voice, subdued though it was, took him by surprise. Indeed, since he left her bridal cabin a month ago, neither had said a word that was not essential.

She sat straight-backed beside him on the hard narrow seat, a damnably prim bonnet hiding her face, but he could imagine her eyes wide with fear as she stared out the window. For all he knew, she was crying, too, the way she had—

He stopped himself. Her tears still ate at him, on those rare moments he allowed himself to remember his wedding night. Damned if he knew why he thought of it now, except that she was close and her voice was soft, and they had been confined in tight quarters for what seemed an eternity.

He could think about her now, staunchly hiding her fear of the beast she had married, so close he could prove with a few kisses she judged him rightly . . . or he could think about her then. It seemed easier to remember the past.

She'd been soft in his arms, responsive in ways that belied her obvious innocence, an enigma who drove him wild. He had been ready to take her again and again, thinking in his aroused state that she felt the same mindless urge. But she had been crying. Like a baby. He hadn't meant to hurt her until those tears . . . and until the shattering realization of her power over him.

For a while he had been beside himself with want, but it was a temporary condition, he told himself, the result of taking his first virgin. She wasn't a virgin anymore, and besides, whatever power she held was only in bed. She wouldn't get a chance to taste control again.

Quent did not care. There were willing women around should he feel the need for them. As far as her Papa knew, the devil that called himself husband possessed the precious Angel every night. Listening to the tales of his Irish lackeys, Thomas Chadwick would understand his adversary was capable of every debasement, and he would suffer.

Quent took special satisfaction in knowing the pain was over nothing, since he could find satisfaction in little else. To make certain the wedding night would not be repeated, he had provided separate rooms in the inns where they stayed on the overland journey from Cork. But he had not slept.

"Is your home very large?" Angel asked. "From here it seems to cover the top of the hill."

A persistent woman, he decided, despite her silent stoicism on the difficult journey. His hands tightened on the reins.

"It's not much of a castle as such buildings go." He cracked the whip over the tired team of horses. "But then the Kavanaghs have never been much of a family."

Thunder volleyed across the countryside that rolled in humps around them and the rain pelted onto the carriage roof, so loud they had to raise their voices to be heard. Quent took the weather as proof the marriage would go badly. He intended that during its brief existence it should never go otherwise.

The uneven road wound toward the bay side of the promontory, at last leveling as it passed through a high arched gate. Lightning heralded their approach. A pair of massive stone dogs, rising on haunches at either side of the gate, snarled in silent greeting as they rumbled past.

"Oh!" said Angel with a start.

Welcoming the sight of the dogs, Quent met his wife's timidity with harshness. "You're safe enough. They're not alive. 'Tis said, however, a third ghost dog haunts the castle. Three heads, each with teeth sharper than the others, and each with a taste for blood."

The carriage jostled over the rutted driveway and she fell against him. Righting herself, she laughed softly. "The statues surprised me, that's all. And I don't believe in ghosts. Not for a minute."

He cursed her good cheer as equally as he had her fear, giving scant notice to his inconsistency. "You've not been in Ireland before," he growled.

She started to reply, then fell into the silence that he preferred. He stopped the carriage at the front steps. Settling his wide-brimmed hat lower on his forehead, he helped Angel to the ground. Her gloved hand was small in his, and bore no more weight than a butterfly. Quent wasn't a tall man, but his wife still seemed small beside him. Small and insignificant, he told himself as she hurried past him up the stairs to the high carved door.

A gust of wind rounded the corner and buffeted them both. She swayed but held her ground. Her billowing black cloak seemed to give her substance, but he knew full well the slenderness of the body beneath its folds.

With a glance at the shuttered windows, he stepped around her. Before he could grip the knocker, the door creaked open. A gnarled hand lifted a lantern against the night and a wrinkled round face peered into the dark.

"You're home," an old voice cracked.

"Aye, Mrs. MacCabe, that we are."

Quent stepped into the entryway, followed at a short distance by Angel. They stood in silence for a moment, rain from their cloaks dripping onto the cold stone floor.

"We got your message from Cork," the woman said. She pulled herself to her full, formidable height as she looked down at the stranger behind her master. Like him, Mrs. MacCabe was dressed in black, and like him, she did not offer a smile.

"A wife, it said," she continued, her voice stronger. "This be she."

Angel stepped forward to extend a hand. "I'm Angel Kavanagh, Mrs. MacCabe."

As Quent expected, the housekeeper ignored the proffered hand. "Found her in Georgia, did you?" she asked.

"Aye," he said. "Angel Chadwick Kavanagh is the full name."

The woman's dark eyes narrowed a fraction. "I should'a known."

Quent looked at his wife, who was studying the vaulted ceiling, the damp walls, the water puddled at her feet. Within the confines of her bonnet, with her fair hair darkened by the rain, she looked like a lost, lonely wren.

A twist of conscience surprised him. It lasted only until her darting glance reached him and he caught a spark of life behind the loneliness. It wasn't so much a challenge as a reminder that she had agreed to this union and was ready to face all that it offered, even the torment of sharing a bed.

Deluded fool. She had much to learn.

He left to gather the belongings from the carriage, reappearing shortly with the scant pieces of luggage. He set them on the floor.

"Show her to her room," he said to Mrs. MacCabe before returning to the carriage. "The last one by the tower."

"But—"

One glance stilled the housekeeper's protest.

"I'll see to the horses," he said. "You see to her."

Angel reached for her suitcases, but Mrs. MacCabe's large hands grabbed them first. He watched as the two women walked up the staircase, the older stooped but strong and as familiar a fixture at Cordangan as the steps over which she trod. And the younger, slight but straight-backed, a temporary resident, as out of place in the castle as would be a laugh or a sigh or a song.

Had he done the right thing in bringing her here? He thought of the island lying off the foot of the promontory and knew the question to be useless. Right or wrong figured into little he did. The course of his life had been set long ago.

Standing by the open door, he watched until they were out of sight, then went out once again to the storm.

By the time Angel hurried up two flights of stairs and down an endless corridor, she was out of breath. The housekeeper showed no sign of such distress. Pride kept her from gasping for air . . . pride and the cold, damp mustiness that surrounded her. Forestalling speech, she looked around her room while Mrs. MacCabe lit the bedside lamp.

A low peat fire glowed in the hearth, barely strong

enough to ease the spring chill. The furniture was spare but heavy and intricately carved: a wardrobe, poster bed and table, a basin stand in the corner closest to the door. The room could have held twice as much furniture and still been spare.

Not a single decoration offered relief from the starkness, except for the dark marble framing the fireplace and the lace curtains at a pair of matching shuttered windows, each recessed in its own small alcove complete with a cushionless windowseat. It was a shame the marble had not been polished in decades, and the curtains were gray with age. Despite the coolness of the air, she felt as though she were suffocating, and she hurried across the room to open one of the windows. The latch refused to budge.

"They've not been opened since last summer," said Mrs. MacCabe. It was her first utterance directed to her new mistress. Angel turned and ventured a smile.

"Can we open them now?"

"You'll take ill. I'll not have Master Quent blame me for his bride's demise."

Angel doubted he would much care, but she refused to let the thought get her down.

"Master Quent?" she said. "That makes him sound like a little boy." And her hard-hearted husband, she could have added, was as far from boyhood as a man could get.

For just a moment the harsh lines of the housekeeper's face softened. "I've known him since the day he came into this world."

Hope flickered in Angel's heart. Here was someone who might reveal something of the mystery surrounding Quentin Kavanagh.

"And when was that?" she asked. "I know so little about him. I don't even know his age."

A mask slipped over the woman's expression, as efficiently concealing as the shutters that blocked out the night.

"You'll have to ask him yourself, Mrs. Kavanagh." She uttered the name as though it tasted bitter on her tongue.

Undaunted, Angel persisted. "Was this ever his room?"

"Nay." The woman hesitated. "It belonged to his mother. Fifteen years ago this Christmas past she died in that bed."

With those final words, Mrs. MacCabe departed, closing the door so quickly behind her she almost caught the hem of her black gown, leaving Angel in the damp closeness to stare at the fragile lace coverlet that matched the grayness of the curtains.

She took a deep breath. She had been strong for more than a month, keeping quiet when her husband was near, accepting whatever he arranged, and she was growing weary of the part. But it was useless to break down now, when her courage was needed most. Once she got some rest, and once the rains stopped, she would be able to think more clearly, to summon a braver heart.

Quent's mother had died in her bed, her inner voice whispered. And it was where he expected her to sleep. He said the Kavanaghs had never been much of a family, but she wondered if he lied. Early on she had decided he was ignored and unloved in his early years, but such an assessment was only part of his tale.

She thought of his dark eyes peering at her from beneath the brim of his hat . . . in the carriage, in the castle, everywhere their glance chanced to meet. Rather than getting used to him, she felt a hollowness inside that seemed to grow with time. It was one thing to think brave thoughts when she was out at sea, and quite another to keep up her optimism in the gloom of an ancient castle. It was no exaggeration to say her new home seemed right out of one of Raven's Shakespearean tragedies. She knew both of her sisters would agree.

Thunder rattled the windows. Angel jumped. It must have been close, she thought, to shake the panes behind the protective shutters. She lectured herself against being so skittish. Wild storms raked Savannah in the springtime with regularity; she ought to be used to the wind and the rain.

Irish wind and Irish rain were different, the small voice said; they brought with them little good. Nonsense, she answered as she tossed her bonnet and cloak on top of her baggage, trying to think of how the sailor had described the beauty of her new home.

But she had seen nothing on the overland journey but rain and black, roiling clouds and muddy roads, and her feeling of doom would not go away. No flickering lights behind cottage windows had welcomed them as they bounced along. As far as she could tell, there wasn't another home for miles.

Using the heel of her shoe, she hammered open the window latch and unfastened the shutters. A strong draught whipped them from her grasp and set them to banging against the high castle wall. It took her a long, wet while to lash them open. By the time she was done her hair fell in damp ringlets around her face, and her sodden dress clung to her body, but she did not move away from the rain blowing into the room.

Let the heavens divide, she thought in a moment of poetic exaggeration that would have made her sisters proud. And let the angels weep their wildest; she must be strong enough for any event. As though drifting in out of the storm, unexpected thoughts of Papa and Mama struck her. Had they returned from Texas? Had they read the mysterious letter Quentin Kavanagh left for them?

And what, oh what, had the letter said?

She would be more afraid of her husband, would think of him truly as the devil, except for that ridiculous story about the three-headed ghost hound haunting the castle. He had been trying to frighten her; she wasn't so foolish and ignorant that she hadn't seen that right away.

He was the foolish one not to know what truly frightened her . . . the unknown future and the memories of their wedding night. She could be strong for Papa, determined enough to carry through on the arrangement that kept him from ruin. But she hadn't been at all strong in her husband's arms. In truth, she had lost herself. On the ship she had usually managed to keep the details of that night from her mind, but here in his home the remembrance returned full blown.

Would he come to her bed? She couldn't want him to; their first encounter had been far too shattering for her to wish for a second time.

Or a third . . . or more. A woman had to love a man to hunger for his touch. No matter how strong her optimism and her hope for a contented life, she could not imagine holding a tender feeling for Quent.

Still, she could imagine his stroking her, stripping her clothes from her body, kissing her wherever he chose.

Stop remembering, she warned herself. All her energies must be directed toward beginning her new life. She was still a Chadwick, and Chadwicks did not grow faint of heart. Especially when what they did was for the family.

Forget his body and his hands. Remember his wedding gift, the ashes of the loan papers lying impotent on the courthouse hearth. And try to remember the times he had shown a vulnerable side. True, it had been weeks since he had done so, but that didn't mean his troubles had gone away.

Reluctantly she closed the window, drying her hair and upper body with the hem of her skirt.

Mrs. MacCabe returned with a heavy blanket and a tray of food, a hearty lamb stew and chunk of rye bread, studiously ignoring the wet condition of her new mistress. Under questioning, the housekeeper admitted she also served as the cook.

"A fine one, too," Angel said in all sincerity after sampling the stew, but Mrs. MacCabe, departing the room, showed little pleasure at the compliment.

She would have thought she could not swallow a bite, but she ate everything, sopping up the liquid with the last crust of bread. Whatever the housekeeper lacked in warmth, Angel decided, she truly made up for in her cooking skills.

Weary, she prepared for an early bed, using the adjoining dressing room for her necessary ablutions. Thank goodness, she thought, the castle had the latest in personal amenities. It was her brightest thought on a very gloomy night.

As she pulled the covers gently back from the down pillows, she wondered if the linens were those upon which Quent's mother had lain.

She died in that bed.

Huddled beneath the blanket, Angel could hear the housekeeper's words and knew for certain that regardless of why or for how long her husband slept apart from her, he would not renew his conjugal visits here.

The thought did not give her the comfort it should have. Where was he now, feasting with a crowd of friends below? Drinking himself into a stupor in the solitude of a lonely room? Was he thinking about his bride the way she was thinking about him? Knowing so little about him, she could not guess at the answers. She suspected he was doing nothing she could begin to envision.

In the restless hour that preceded sleep, she imagined the howling of hounds echoing down the hall outside her door.

Eight

"The time's long past to quit your wandering, Quentin Kavanagh. Sure and it's grand to have you home."

Quent glanced up from his desk to see his assistant Neill Connolly standing in the library doorway. The sight of the lanky young man with the red hair and quick Irish smile brought the same pleasure he had felt on seeing the castle yesterday eve.

"I'll be the first to welcome you," Neill added, "since it's doubtful Mrs. MacCabe put forth the effort."

Quent set down his pen. "It's good to be back." He meant it, despite the poor night's sleep and a general feeling of grumpiness that had come to him with the dawn.

He looked out the window at the morning, cool and bright after the passing of the storm. "I wanted to take a ride, but you left me too many reports, too many contracts to be gone over. You know what a lazy bastard I am."

Neill laughed. "You can work us all to an early grave, as you full well know. But choosing to toil on such a fine morn is something else again."

He wore his usual attire—work shirt and trousers and a brown cap pushed to the back of his head. To the casual eye he appeared a simple worker, but there was intelligence behind the green eyes darting around the room and Quent trusted him as he did no other man.

Neill had earned that trust a long time ago in an unpleasant incident in town, speaking out to a crowd of malcontents bent on causing trouble for whatever could be linked to a Kavanagh. Quent had no use for the villagers of Cordangan, no more than they had use for him, but he appreciated courage and loyalty, both traits of Neill's. He had taken the young man into his employ and into as much confidence as he was able to share.

"Are you alone?" Neill asked. "I would have thought you'd still be a-bed."

"Ah," said Quent with a knowing nod, "you, too, have heard about the bride."

"The whole of Cordangan can speak of little else. Already there be stories from Cork to here and back again to Dublin."

"Are there now?"

"Aye. Most concern the nature of the woman who gave herself to the devil. They began the moment you walked the dock at the River Lee. You're a man who's noticed, you know, whether you wish it or no."

"I don't wish it," said Quent, feeling increasingly crotchety. He had expected to return home with a sense of accomplishment, if not outright triumph, the pleasure privately enjoyed, but his expectations had yet to be fulfilled.

Neill settled his long body into the chair opposite the desk. " 'Tis said she has the powers of the little people, for it would take such to get you to the altar."

"Are these the same tale-bearers who swear I rot fruit on the trees?" he asked, remembering the blight that had ruined the apples on his lone apple tree.

"More'n likely. They also say she towers over you like the tallest oak in the forest, commanding you do her will."

Quent pictured his wife in her sheltering bonnet and cloak, hurrying beside him down the gangway, her attention more on her new homeland than the man who brought her here.

"None who observed us on the dock would make such a claim."

"A tiny one, is she?"

He answered with a shrug.

Neill grinned. "There's also those who claim you bind her to the bed every night and have your wicked way with her until the dawn."

"Good God," said Quent, running a hand through his hair. "It's hard to believe I've only been in the country a few days."

"Time enough for an Irishman to tell his tales. They flew faster and farther than your carriage through the muck and mire."

A momentary silence fell between them. "Is there truth to these marriage stories a'tall?" Neill asked. "Not that I'm asking about the nights, you understand."

"There's truth enough. I am a married man."

Quent knew his friend awaited details . . . a description, a purpose, an explanation for the unexpected turn of his affairs. He had nothing to tell him. Only Doreen MacCabe knew the full details of the past, and that was the way it would remain.

Until it was time for the Chadwicks to know. How long would it take Thomas to come to these shores? Tomorrow would not be too soon, although common sense put the likely time as weeks away.

He riffled the papers on his desk. "These contracts with the linen mills have been handled well. There's markets for such products in the States."

Neill straightened, and the teasing in his eyes sharpened into businesslike concern. "So you said in your letter. Did you not notice the proposal I worked up for trading with the people close to home?"

"I noticed."

"Have you nothing to say?"

"Nothing you'd care to hear."

"But there's products here as fine as any in Ireland. Our sheep produce a wool that would make the millers of Scotland weep with envy. And there's pottery and lace and embroidery that would suit the Queen herself."

"To make Victoria's palace grander, is that your purpose?"

"I'd rather increase the Pride of Ireland's coffers."

"And the coffers of County Cork as well."

"Have you never noticed how the creatures of nature depend on one another, the worms enriching the soil, the birds eating the worms and scattering seed—"

"And I'm to enrich the good folk of Cordangan and its environs, is that your point? Tell you what, you find some good folk and I'll see what I can do."

Neill was not so easily deterred. "Now that you've a family, why not expand the Pride of Ireland and at the same time let the people hereabout know the identity of their benefactor?"

It was an old argument between them, this privacy concerning his business, and its potential in the country around Bantry Bay. Now it seemed that Quent's marriage was adding a new element.

"No," he said flatly.

"But they might take a mind to understand you better, especially if you brought them a more prosperous life. They'd fare well with the Pride shipping their products around the world."

"I don't care how they fare. And have you never wondered whether they might refuse to deal with the devil?"

"They're a practical lot who want to better themselves. Like you, who brought the name Kavanagh from the ranks of the poor. They can't help wondering how you get your money, you being the richest man around."

"Let them believe I get it from black magic, or thievery, or some practice so evil that the pure minds of Cordangan cannot conceive of the details."

He spoke from his heart. He had no wish to satisfy the curiosity or aid in the well being of anyone, least of all the townspeople and farmers who had helped Morna O'Brien to ruin.

The young man's brow furrowed. Suspecting he was considering his employer's new bride, Quent veered to a different subject.

"In going over the accounts this morning," he said, "I found more profit than expected. You've earned an extra bonus."

"Little good it will do."

Quent looked in surprise at his friend. Here was a bitterness he had not heard before, a bitterness that almost matched his own.

"If it's more money you need, you have only to ask."

Neill looked past him to the open window, to the trees and the hills and the sky open to view.

"There are things in this world that money cannot buy."

How well Quent knew. It was the reason he was wed.

"Nevertheless," he said, "you'll get the bonus." Neill answered with a shrug.

The song of a lark drifted into the somber library, and for a brief time the men were left to their separate thoughts.

"Padraic Scully's been showing up lately in the taverns here about," said Neill at last.

Isolated though he kept himself from his neighbors, Quent could not like the news. A Dubliner who occasionally traveled throughout the county, Scully stirred up troubles wherever he went, from arguments over Irish Home Rule to tavern brawls to night riders who scourged the countryside. Never did he participate in any of the troubles, but when they came he always seemed to be nearby.

Quent had no proof Scully was behind the raids, but he had his suspicions. The man had yet to bring harm to Kavanagh property, but when he did—

"What's the son of a whoremonger up to?" he asked.

"I've no idea, but he brings up your name from time to time."

"Not in connection with the Pride of Ireland."

"Nay, not so far as I've heard. I would've told you straight off if that were the case."

Quent was about to return to business when a soft knock came at the door. Both men watched as Angel Kavanagh came into the room.

She wore an emerald-green dress that accented her womanly features, and her sun-colored hair was piled in loose curls atop her head, lengthening the sweep of her neck and giving her an appearance of height she did not possess. Where he felt edgy and tired, she looked beautiful and rested . . . except for the half circles under her wide blue eyes, but they were so faint he doubted anyone but him would detect them.

She looked at him in unspoken question, then offered a tentative smile to Neill, who stood and introduced himself.

"Mister Connolly," she said, shaking his hand, "it's a pleasure to meet an acquaintance of my husband."

"I'll have no *mister*," Neill said.

"Then I'll be Angel to you."

"Aye, that you will." He glanced over his shoulder at Quent, who remained stubbornly seated behind his desk. "And what, pray tell, did you do to capture such a prize?"

"I bought her."

Angel gasped, and Neill shook his head in surprise. "You're a wealthy man, Quentin Kavanagh, but not so wealthy as that."

"My husband likes to tease," said Angel with a soft, shaky laugh.

Neill looked from man to wife and back again. "Does he now? It's a trait we've not noticed here before."

Quent ignored the sarcasm. In his imaginings about bringing a Chadwick to Cordangan, he hadn't considered what anyone would think of her. He didn't give a damn whether anyone approved, not even Neill, but he wouldn't have her getting in the way.

He stood and came around the desk. "I've business to attend this morning," he said to her. "You'll have to keep yourself occupied elsewhere."

"Of course," she said with a brisk nod of her head, but the wounded look in her eyes was unmistakable.

"I'm the one in the way," said Neill hurriedly as he moved to block her exit. "We'll meet later in the week, Quent. There's no business that can't wait 'til then."

He was gone before Quent could protest, closing the library door behind him, leaving the newlywed Kavanaghs alone. They faced one another, only a half dozen feet apart. Outside the lark continued to sing.

Angel lifted her chin a fraction. "Please accept my apology for the interruption. I know how demanding business can be."

"I had forgotten you're an expert at paperwork. But then you didn't handle your father's affairs very well."

"Papa didn't tell me—" She stopped herself and looked away. "I never called myself an expert at anything."

How meek she was being this morning, so apologetic and reasonable. And fragile. Too well he remembered her wild thrashings in bed. And then the weeping. Which signified the real Angel Chadwick, the abandon or the tears?

He stepped closer to her, irritated that despite all she had been through, she could still manage to entice. "Not an expert at anything? What about fornication?"

"Oh," she said, covering her mouth with her fingers. And then she surprised him with a shake of her head. "I didn't think I was any good."

"You what?" said Quent, not bothering to hide his astonishment. He could have imagined a thousand replies and not included the one he heard.

She blushed. "I'm not asking for a compliment."

Quent ran a hand through his hair. "I hadn't planned to extend one."

"Could we please change the subject? I'm simply wondering what I'm supposed to do. I'm not used to idleness."

Quent groaned inwardly. The last thing he needed was a busy wife.

"Mrs. MacCabe is in charge of the household."

A shadow darkened Angel's face. "So she told me this morning."

"Then take a walk."

"I've walked for more than an hour, but the grounds are muddy and I couldn't go far."

"It would seem you've already had an active morning."

"I . . . couldn't sleep, and I wanted to get a better look at the stone dogs. They don't seem nearly so fierce in the daylight. Do you have any pets that are alive?"

"I've no time for such foolishness."

"Oh. With all this land, it seems a shame. My sisters and I always wanted a dog, the biggest one in Savannah, but it seemed cruel when we had no place to let him run."

"Don't be thinking you can bring a worthless animal onto the grounds." He spoke sharply, wanting to get her out of the room and as far from his mind as he could.

But his wife was proving to be stubborn on this first morning in her new home. She stepped toward him. "Worthless like me, you mean?"

Good God, the woman had deep blue eyes, and a pair of full, soft lips that could break the heart of a man . . . if the man had a heart to break, that is.

"You serve a purpose."

She reached out, not quite touching his sleeve. "And what purpose is that, Quent? To worry Papa? Is that all I'm supposed to do?" She had long fingers, and a graceful curve to her wrist. And she smelled of sweet flowers he couldn't identify, scents that seemed to waft all the way from Savannah.

Quent cursed the desire that tightened his loins. "Why,

you're to dance naked on the tabletops of the castle, didn't you know?"

"But—"

"You did swear to obey. Take your clothes off. I want to see you naked now."

Her fingers clasped the fastening at her throat. "You're teasing me."

"You told Neill I like to do so. Perhaps you were right. Besides, we're alone. No one but your husband will see."

He eased closer to her, and she edged away, stepping backwards toward the door. He kept up his slow, steady pursuit until her back was against the stuccoed wall beside the massive oak doorjamb, her hands at her sides.

"It's all legal and natural, Angel. We ought to be wrapped in each other's arms and still abed."

"It can't be natural to ask your wife to bare herself on top of your desk."

"It's an old Irish custom that's seldom mentioned outside the home."

"I'm sure it is not." Her deep breath filled her lungs and sent her breasts dangerously close to his chest. "But if that's what you want—"

Quent shook his head in amazement. "You'd do it, wouldn't you? Precious Angel, giving her all for her Da'."

She answered him with silence, her eyes locked with his. A picture of her standing above him naked seared his mind . . . Angel with her milk-white skin and yellow hair curling against her shoulders and down to her breasts . . . her graceful thighs and thick pubic hair . . . Angel willing to do all that he asked.

Hunger possessed him. He wanted to take her here against the wall, hard and fast. It would be legal and natural, this claiming his wife when the mood was upon him. It would be damning, too.

He backed away. "Amuse yourself elsewhere. I've work to do." He turned so that she wouldn't see the evidence of

his arousal. And she would look at him, this innocent, con-
fusing woman he had taken as his wife. Before their marriage he had thought she would be tremulous and cowardly
and weak, yet he was the one with the shaky knees.

He strode to the window and looked at the spring grass
that grew outside the library, at the broken stone wall some
twenty yards away, and on to the trees and the distant hills.
He couldn't see the bay from this vantage point, but he
could imagine the waves driving against the rocks.

He should have taken his ride this morning, he should
have stayed out of doors. But with the way things were
going for him, he would have run into her on the castle
grounds.

He waited until he heard the door open and close, then
returned to his desk. Five minutes of looking through contracts and pages of figures and proposals by Neill were
enough to convince him he had no more head for business
today.

Calluragh Island beckoned far more. It lay a short distance off the base of the Kavanagh headland. He thought
of its heather and gorse and rocks and in the center of its
wildness a small, neat cottage that he had helped to build.

In that cottage he would find contentment, and a rare
moment's peace, two conditions he would never find with
his wife.

Angel heard her husband leave through the front door.
She started to follow him, then held herself back, deciding
she had endured all the insults she could for the day. And
it was not yet noon.

Instead, she went on a tour of her new home, self-
conducted since Mrs. MacCabe seemed little inclined
to give her a moment of time. She did learn from the
woman that the original parts of the castle had been
built late in the thirteenth century, when the Normans

ruled the land. One whole wing had been destroyed, a few remaining sections restored, and there had been rooms added, too, most of which featured stuccoed walls instead of rough medieval stone.

"Used to be an earl lived here," Mrs. MacCabe said as she was kneading bread in the kitchen, a trace of pride in her voice. "But he raped a novice from the convent, and the title died."

"I see," said Angel, not seeing at all. Her knowledge of the peerage came through her sister Raven's marriage to the Earl of Stafford. She thought titles went on forever, from generation to generation, passed down to honorable men. From what the housekeeper said, apparently such was not so.

Ireland was not England, she reminded herself. It was a fact she must keep in mind.

Alone she walked the three floors of the castle proper, leaving the outbuildings for another day. A long, single-story hall extended the full length from the entryway, its vaulted wooden ceiling offering a spaciousness that left her dizzy the longer she stared at it. Opening off the Great Hall, as the housekeeper called it, were several smaller rooms, one of them her husband's library. She remembered the walls of bookshelves, the standing globe, the cluttered desk . . . and Quent. She did not investigate the library again.

Another of the rooms was an abandoned chapel, which had long ago been stripped of everything that might have a religious nature.

At the rear was the kitchen and storerooms; a back stairs led to the dining room on the floor directly above, and beyond it a drawing room as large as the main hall. The bedrooms were at the top, the highest part of the castle save for the locked corner tower. She made herself a promise to ask Mrs. MacCabe for the key.

When she was done, she hastened out of doors for a

breath of fresh air and for an escape from the gloom that lurked everywhere in her new home. No one had bothered to open the shutters to the beautiful day; no one had bothered to light the fires or the lamps, or to do anything that might bring signs of life to the castle.

Little wonder. As far as she could determine, the entire domestic staff consisted of Mrs. MacCabe.

She sat on a low section of wall near the front gate, contemplated the two dogs growling down at her, and decided they needed names. After much thought, she settled on Saint Patrick, the patron saint of Ireland, and Finn MacCool, the great hero of Irish legend. Pat and Finn, for short. They frequently figured in Papa's tales of home.

"Finn," she said to the nearest statue, "there's hope for the place. Not much, I'll admit, but at least there's some."

She thought especially of the marble fireplaces, a few with magnificent lines, others of more simple design, and all of them ignored for years. The stucco work also stayed in her mind, the broken scrolls over the high window niches in the Great Hall and the decorated ceilings in many of the rooms.

Throughout, the furniture was as dark and massive as the pieces she'd found in her bedroom. A little polish, a little light to break the darkness, and there might be real beauty lurking behind the dust.

Worthless, was she? If Quent really thought so, he didn't know her in the least.

Angel sighed as she thought of her husband. Somehow she must concentrate on her tasks, furniture and walls being far safer topics than the memory of Quent's lips and Quent's eyes.

When she approached him in the library, it was to ask what was expected of her in the way of domestic duties. She knew he'd been goading her about the naked dancing, otherwise he wouldn't have stopped her when she offered to do what he asked. Somehow she had known he wouldn't let her proceed. And if he had? She grew warm inside thinking about what might have taken place.

She rested a hand over her pounding heart. "Pat," she whispered, speaking to one of the dogs, "what is happening to me?"

To keep her sanity, she spent the next hour making lists of all she had to do, in the general order in which her tasks should be completed. First she would send a letter to Mama and Papa, letting them know how happy she was, how wonderful her new home, and most of all—she barely flinched at the lie—how loving was the man who had taken her for his bride.

Nine

By late afternoon, Angel was dressed in her fourth-best gown—other than her wedding attire, she had brought only four—and with sleeves rolled above her elbows she sat on the dining room floor scrubbing at a patch of mildew on the wall.

One rule governed the enormous project she had set for herself: think big, work small. If she concentrated on only one corner of the castle at a time, eventually all the corners could be reached.

By the time she was eighty, her inner voice said. So be it, she answered back, but not so firmly as she would have liked.

The work proved hard, the soap solution she had borrowed from the kitchen acrid, and her palms susceptible to blisters. Still, she hadn't been so contented since the first night Quentin Kavanagh strode into the store.

To augment the natural light from the windows, she had rounded up a half dozen lamps from around the castle and scattered them about the floor and tables of the room. She had expected the wall to be a dull, pale brown; instead, under the scrapings of a hard-bristled brush, the stucco emerged a lighter shade that was nearer to white. As she stared at the surprising surface, she was reminded of the clotted cream Mama served over strawberries in early spring.

Grinning, she set her imagination free. Things were not

so hopeless after all, at least as far as her new home was concerned. What this dark old room needed in addition to a thorough cleaning was a splash or two of red. The red of ripe berries to go with the cream-colored walls, a painting or two, perhaps, some flowers, and a nice thick rug to cover the wooden floor. The heavy dining table with its massive carved legs, the dozen high-backed matching chairs, the sideboard, the cabinets—none of these would seem nearly so oppressive if what she envisioned in her mind proved feasible.

Setting bucket and brush aside for a moment, she leaned back on her hands, stretched her legs in front of her, and, ignoring a few complaining body parts, allowed her thoughts to roam. First the dining room, and then the ad-joining drawing room, perhaps the Great Hall and a bed-room or two, and these would be only a beginning. The outside of the castle needed just as much work, but she would grow dizzy if she took on too much at once.

As if she hadn't already done so in just this one big room. Despite her governing rule, she felt like an ant con-templating a freshly baked pound cake he planned to steal. How did the ant manage? He moved the cake crumb by crumb.

Think big, work small. Brave words, and wise . . . but did she really want to wait until her dotage to be done?

What she needed was the little people Papa talked about to scurry from behind the furniture and join in the work. Each equipped with bucket and brush, she added quickly. If she were going to conjure up helpers, she must likewise conjure up their supplies. Not always was she the naive, optimistic baby sister of the family. She could, if necessary, be as practical as Raven and as impetuous as Flame.

Like them, she was also a worker. She returned to the wall, and within the hour had scoured a three-foot high band stretching the width of the room.

Mrs. MacCabe found her just as she was tossing the

brush into a bucket of very dirty water, the third such bucket she had used since she began. She stood, dried her hands on the towel she was using as an apron, and rolled down her sleeves.

"It's a start," she said.

The housekeeper studied her accomplishment. "Does Master Quentin know what you're about?"

"I haven't seen him since this morning."

The woman said not another word, just kept on looking at the patch of scrubbed wall. Angel did the same. To her dismay, instead of looking beautiful, it made the rest of the stucco look drearier than ever. And even in the clean parts there were streaks that would need more work.

"Your food's ready," Mrs. MacCabe said at last.

"I didn't realize it was so late."

"We eat early in the castle."

"Oh," she said, "I see." Tucking a strand of hair behind her ear, she looked in dismay at her damp and dirty gown. A gray muslin, it wasn't very festive to begin with, but it was a disaster now. "I'll have to bathe and change. Is my husband here?"

"You'll be dining alone."

She should have known; she had to fight a surge of disappointment.

"Where?" she asked, feeling foolish and far too inadequate to serve as mistress of the house.

"Wherever you'd like."

She met the woman's stare. Despite a slight stoop of her shoulders, Mrs. MacCabe was of a formidable height, a big woman without being stout. Her gray hair was knotted away from her face, her strong features marked with deep lines, her brown eyes narrow and cold and hard. She must be close to sixty, but she gave no impression she had tired with the years.

Used to friendliness, Angel couldn't accept the judgment in those eyes. She took enough of it from her husband.

Somehow she must make the woman her friend. But first she must earn her respect.

"I'd like to eat in here," she said, then couldn't stop herself from adding, "if you have no objections."

"It's not up to me to object. I didn't bring you t' Ireland."

Angel's heart sank. Winning the housekeeper's regard would be a great deal harder than scrubbing a stucco wall . . . and far more important, she was sure. Something told her the woman would not approve of weakness, however, and she grabbed up the bucket and brush.

"Take care of this for me, would you? I'll change and be here in half an hour. If my husband returns, please let him know. Otherwise, I will eat alone."

"Your food'll be cold."

"I've eaten cold food before."

But she had never eaten it seasoned with loneliness, not even on the ship, where she believed her isolation temporary. When she finally made it back to the dining room, she could do little more than toy with her dinner. Mutton stew, again, and dark rye bread. It lacked some of the flavor of the night before. She probably ought to speak to Mrs. MacCabe about the menu, about what was available, about what she could prepare.

Too soon, her inner voice warned, and she agreed.

Sitting in the hard, high-backed chair at a table the size of her bedroom back in Savannah—a table badly in need of a dusting—she felt small and insignificant. Night embraced the unshuttered windows, and the lamps burned around her as though she feared the dark. If Quent were to stroll past on the castle grounds and spy her at her solitary meal surrounded by all that sparkle, he would think she had lost her mind.

He would, of course, be wrong. Spine stiffened, she picked up her fork and ate what she had been served.

Early the next morning she stretched a hundred crying muscles and arose from bed to look out her window. Along with the dawn, the sight of her husband on a magnificent black stallion greeted her, and she felt a tingle of excitement.

He rode outside the castle walls. She caught only a glimpse before he disappeared into the trees. How easy it would be to imagine him sitting astride a winged mount and flying off the edge of the land. But the horse had no wings, and he rode on solid ground. He was a man, not a creature from the underworld. Whatever darkness he possessed lay in his heart, not his soul.

She stared for a long while at the place where he had last been visible. She longed to soar out the window and join him on his ride, whether he welcomed her or not. Or join him in a more conventional way. But she must be patient. After all, he didn't beat her or imprison her or starve her behind locked doors.

What he did was tempt her with insinuating words, and then leave her alone. After almost seven weeks of marriage, she knew little more about him than she had before they were wed.

She knew how he was in bed, though, and she knew how he made her feel. She also knew he was content with taunting; he didn't show signs of wanting her again.

With a sigh she donned her third-best gown and went downstairs. Breakfast was warm bread and cold cheese served in the kitchen. Mrs. MacCabe excused herself, and once again Angel ate alone. The dining room wall, she thought with less than complete enthusiasm. The wall awaited.

Her eye strayed to a ring of keys suspended from a nail by the back door. Should she ask permission to take them? Probably. But the housekeeper was gone, she had no idea where, and she had no idea when she might return. Gobbling down the last bite of bread, she grabbed the ring before prudence could force her to wait.

The larders off the kitchen proved clean and practically

empty, and the wine cellar cobwebbed and overstocked. Staring at the rows of dusty bottles, she realized she had never seen her husband take a drink of any sort of alcohol . . . but then neither had she seen him take a meal.

Before she grew maudlin over that ridiculous situation, she turned her thoughts to other places she could investigate. The nether regions of the castle having proven uninteresting, she decided to go to the top.

And that meant the tower near her bedroom. Keys in hand, she hurried up the stairs. It took several tries at the lock before the heavy wooden door finally creaked open. Lamp held high, she stepped into a tiny space that led to more stairs, these winding and steep and dark. Surrounded by cold stone, she did not slow down until she reached the landing. Another locked door greeted her, but eventually she found the right key on the ring.

Behind the door was a wide bed and a chest of drawers and a rag rug on the floor. Narrow openings let in bands of light. Knowing little of castles, she suspected these had once been lookouts, or slots through which medieval weapons had been aimed.

The room had once been lived in, although many years had passed since that time. She couldn't shake off the feeling she was invading someone's privacy, and she moved on to the door in the far wall. It opened easily. She entered slowly. Here were windows, real, unshuttered windows that let in the sun. It was an observatory of some sort, she decided. Setting down the lamp, she forced the sashes open to let in the cool morning air.

From here she could see Bantry Bay, and a little of the rocky shoreline with its many wooded inlets. Morning sunlight sparkled jewel-like off the surface of the water, broken by the sails of a dozen boats, as well as a small island just off the Kavanagh headland.

Beautiful, she thought, from the water to the hills to a distant band of mountains. And then she turned to see what the room held. Her eyes widened, and her heart began to pound. What she saw took her so by surprise she could only slip to the floor and stare.

"She's where?" Quent's bellow echoed from the kitchen through the Great Hall and all the way to the front door.

Mrs. MacCabe was not perturbed. "In the tower," she repeated. "She took the keys when my back was turned."

Slapping a riding crop against his thigh, he forgot the breakfast he'd been anticipating after the morning ride. He took the backstairs two at a time, then it was through the open door of the tower and up more stairs, past the bedroom, and into the observatory.

He found her sitting on the floor, in profile, her head bent, her hair pinned loosely away from her face and falling against her shoulders. Her dress was chocolate brown, and spread bell-like around her, its sleeves rolled above her elbows.

The sight of her stopped him, and his anger evaporated like morning mist. He saw her so seldom that her presence struck him with a totally unexpected force. Somehow the reality of her so close . . . so alive . . . differed from the image that never quite left his mind.

Her arms had a gentle curve to them; he'd never noticed before, and for a moment they were all he could see. He felt a sharp, unexpected twist in the pit of his stomach . . . and then he looked around her.

She sat in the midst of family belongings he had hoped never to see again—stacks of frames, rolled rugs and tapestries, and against the far wall an upright suit of armor, visor closed and lance held high, as though it were standing guard. Balanced on the floor in front of her was a gilt-edged oil painting of an elderly man in ruffled shirt and red cloak.

She looked up at him with eyes bright with pleasure. "He has your chin, I think. Is he your father?"

Quent pulled his gaze from her and looked at the similar paintings close to her skirt and a pair of unrolled tapestries stretching across the floor.

Then he looked at his wife, whose eyes were no longer quite so bright. He forgot her arms and the graceful tilt of her head. No matter what she looked like, she was intruding where she didn't belong.

"What are you doing here?" he asked.

"I'm—" She stopped, her fair cheeks blushing pink. "I guess I'm doing something wrong."

"Right you are. This is a private storeroom. It's been locked for the past decade, and that's how it was to remain."

"I see," she said, but he could tell she didn't see at all.

Setting the painting aside, she stood and brushed the dust from the folds of her skirt. She looked small and delicate and out of place in this high stone-walled room, yet when her eyes met his, he saw a determination that was not in the least delicate.

"Are you going to beat me with that?" she asked, gesturing toward the crop.

"You deserve it."

She sneezed. "I *have* stirred up a great deal of dust." She rubbed at her nose. "But then there's so much around."

Light from the window at her back circled like a halo around her head. He could not look away.

"Dammit," he snapped, running a hand through his hair, "most people would be shaking in their boots if I spoke to them like that."

She smiled. How brave of her, he thought with scorn, yet the warmth of that hesitant little smile cut the chill of the room.

"Papa taught—"

She stopped, seeming not to breathe. The air between them crackled. Even the light faded, as though a cloud had passed over the sun.

Quent felt a burning emptiness inside. "Thank you, Angel. For a moment I forgot who you were."

"I'm your wife," she said softly.

"Only because you insisted. To me, you're Thomas Chadwick's daughter."

"Of course I'm Papa's daughter. That's the reason you brought me here. It's the reason I agreed to come. But reasons have a way of changing with circumstance, Quent. Will I never be anything more?"

Quent cursed the sincerity in her voice, the unspoken plea. She wasn't supposed to confront him, she wasn't supposed to question what he did. He wanted her quiet and submissive and out of the way. He wanted her meek and mild. Hadn't that been part of their bargain? Wasn't that the idea behind the burning of the mortgage papers? The marriage itself?

So why did he feel a grudging admiration for her as she faced him and dared to stand her ground?

If he were an enigma to her, so was she to him. Never had she complained of hardship, not on the ship, not on the carriage ride, not here in the stark, isolated castle where she had been brought. He'd thought her docile, but in this forbidden room he saw a new Angel, a woman tougher than he had supposed.

Could toughness be gentle? It seemed so from the velvet blue of her eyes as she looked up at him. He glanced away, fearful his own eyes would betray the turmoil she aroused. He saw the paintings, the tapestries, the suit of armor badly in need of a shine. The doors of an ancient mahogany cabinet hung partially open. She must have studied their contents in haste—the fine linens, the embroidery work, the hand-painted porcelain vases—then gone on in her furtive search.

All were Kavanagh treasures, although his father had shown little appreciation for them. Nothing was here that had belonged to his mother. She had brought nothing of material value to Cordangan Castle. She had brought only her ability to bear a child. He couldn't count the times she'd told him fertility was a woman's curse.

He looked again at his wife, at the narrowness of her waist and the slender sweep of her hips beneath her loosely falling gown.

"You're not pregnant, are you?"

Her head jerked back as if he had slapped her, and she wrapped her arms around her middle. "Do you want me to be?"

"God, no."

"Then it's a good thing I am not." But she didn't sound happy about her condition, as if she would have preferred bearing his child.

"Accommodating little thing, aren't you?" he said, wanting to hurt her, letting the cruelty that lived within him take hold of his heart.

"I try, but you make it very difficult."

A hypocrite. She had to be. "My little saint. Come here," he said. She hesitated. Tapping the crop against his leg, he repeated, "Come here."

She stepped gingerly past the paintings and made her way close enough for him to see the rich thickness of her hair framing her face, the darker honeyed strands mixed with the gold. He thought of touching those strands. Instead, he clutched tighter at the crop.

"Aren't you afraid I'll beat you?"

"I know you could. But you won't."

"Don't be too sure."

He tried to think of her milk-white body marked with red welts, but all he could picture were the smoothness of her skin, the shape of her high, full breasts, and the way she had lain beneath him on their wedding night. He cursed himself for his weakness, even while he took pleasure from the images in his mind.

"Tell me, wife, would you have danced naked on a tabletop for me yesterday?"

She swallowed. He watched the movement of muscles in her throat. "I don't know. I think so."

"What if I had asked you to dance for Neill?"

"Oh, no," she said quickly. "I couldn't have done that."

"Why just me?"

"You're my husband. You've the right to see me."

"And you're a strange little creature, Angel. Is the sometime spirit within you an illusion? Do you harbor no hate?"

"If you think it takes no spirit to face you like this, with that ridiculous whip in your hand, then you're not as clever as I thought you were."

"Ah, a criticism. It's taken you long enough."

"There's more I could say."

"Such as?"

"Such as how"—she hesitated and drew a deep breath—"how cowardly it seems of you to avoid me."

She came so close to what he had been thinking himself that he could not answer her right away.

"I've never seen you take a meal," she continued, "or do anything in the normal way of living."

"You've seen me undress." A limp response. He'd meant it to sound crude, but it came out more like a weak defense.

"Once. The only time you bothered to visit my bed."

"And set you to whimpering."

"I wasn't whimpering!" Her fervor took him by surprise.

"What would you call it?"

She looked away, her hands twisting at her waist. "I wasn't hurt or afraid or . . . sorry. I liked it." She spoke so softly, he could barely hear her. "I didn't know it would be like that, and then the tears came, and you saw them. . . ."

Her voice trailed into silence.

Hunger for her surged through him. He cursed her, but he desired her, too. "You want it again."

Her eyes met his. "Not on a tabletop." She touched him,

her fingers scarcely weightier than the air, but he felt their heat as though they were a brand.

He grabbed her hand, and she winced. He looked down at her blistered palm. "Goddamn, what have you been doing?"

She tried to tug free, but he wouldn't let her go.

"Cleaning, that's all. My hands will grow stronger with time."

"I didn't bring you here as my slave."

"Then why did you bring me? Why is vengeance necessary? Oh Quent, please tell me everything."

Whatever he said she managed to turn on him, and his desire died. "So you can sympathize, is that it? So you can talk me out of whatever I have planned for Papa?" He spat the name out, and he felt a raw disgust for himself and for his wife.

He dropped her hand and backed away. "You're the clever one, shifting all our confrontations onto me."

"I want no confrontations. I want to know you."

"In every way? Do you really want to know me in the physical sense?"

"I want to be a wife to you. Right now, I am and I'm not. I don't know why I'm here in Ireland, not really, but I do know we were pronounced wed for all time. I can't run away from that fact. I have to live with it, not in a man's way, but in a woman's. That's why I took the keys. I wanted to open doors."

Again the hypocrite, he tried to tell himself, but all his anger, all his prejudices couldn't erase the sincerity in her voice. Something stirred within him . . . something sweet and sad and insistent . . . something he had never felt before. The stirring hurt. He stilled it right away.

"You're a means to an end, nothing more," he said, as harshly as he had ever spoken to her. She had to understand.

"I'm also a human being. Not a painting you can lock in a tower."

He knew too well how human she was . . . how close and warm and ready to be a wife. She had no idea how impossible that was.

"What a brave little thing you are." He put all his scorn into the words. "It's not a quality I admire."

"I'm not brave, Quent. I'm trying to survive."

She swayed toward him, as though she would touch him again, but something held her back. "There's one simple fact about me you ought to understand. I'm used to work. It's a Chad—it's a personal trait. That's also why I came up here. I'm not trying to change your home, just make it livable. I saw no sign you cared for it, no more than for me. I didn't think you would mind what I did, as long as I stayed out of your way."

He tried to mock her declaration, but the words wouldn't come. She understood one thing about him—he wanted her apart from him.

As he looked at the disarray of the room, as he considered the memories all of it aroused, the will to fight went out of him. He didn't want to think about the portraits, the artwork, the Kavanagh past. He hardly thought of himself as a Kavanagh; all his ancestry came from his mother's side.

But he thought about the Kavanaghs now. Angel, it seemed, had stirred more than she could ever know.

"So many things," he said. "So many objects I've forgotten. My mother started putting them in here, then lost interest. And then my father took up the work. The vases mostly, to protect them when he was drunk. I added the rest after his death. It was a family project. The one thing in which the three of us shared responsibility."

He looked at his wife. Were those really tears in her eyes? They shook him as much as anything she had said or done. Maybe he preferred her tough after all.

"Do what you wish to this old place. You couldn't harm it more than the years have already managed. Besides," he said, turning from her, "you could be right. Perhaps it will keep you out of trouble."

He made it almost to the door before she spoke.

"I have no funds."

Her words brought him up short. "Be careful, Angel, or you'll be sounding brave again."

"You said you were wealthy. I don't want much for myself, but there are some things needed for the house."

The house. Quent almost laughed. Never in its seven-hundred-year history could Cordangan Castle have been called a house. He doubted, too, that it had ever been called a home. Not even his intrepid, busybody wife could do so.

"I'll speak to Mrs. MacCabe. She will get you whatever money you require."

This time he made it to the doorway.

"The painting," she said. "You never told me who was in the painting. Could it be the last earl?"

"Ah, you heard about him," he said in resignation. Whatever else she was, his wife was a stubborn woman.

"It's not the earl. If there ever was a portrait of him, it was long ago destroyed. That is my grandfather," he said, picturing in his mind the dark, hooded eyes, the strong face, the proud bearing that the artist had captured on the canvas.

"My grandfather," he repeated, more softly, then closed the door between him and his wife, between him and his hated past.

Ten

Angel stared at the door, blood pounding in her ears, her heart going out to Quent in the knowledge of his pain. The demons she had sensed in him back in Savannah caused him a suffering she had never known.

Did he know how much he had revealed to her? He was such a private man she couldn't believe he had done so on purpose. Whatever the source of his anguish, he preferred to bear it alone.

And how could she comfort him really? He came from a family as unlike her own as possible. But she could listen, and she could sympathize. And maybe she could give him love. In her heart she had a bountiful store of that emotion ready to give to the man of her life. And the man of her life had turned out to be Quentin Kavanagh. Enemy of the Chadwicks, he claimed. Enemy to himself.

How she had dared speak to him in such a way, she did not know. She had practically begged him to be a real husband to her, to confess all, to come to her bed. He hadn't been interested . . . except to wonder if she carried his child.

Most men wanted—

She stopped herself. Quentin Kavanagh was not most men.

He wasn't unaware of her, or even disinterested. She had seen raw hunger flare in his eyes. If he had been watching carefully enough, he would have seen her shamelessly feel the same. But the flare had been temporary, for him more than for her. He had been eager to leave.

She went to an open window and stared out at the bay. The sky had turned cloudy, and the air had a bite of cold that hadn't been there earlier. A curl of smoke drew her attention to the small, wooded island that lay just off the shore below the castle. It seemed to come from a chimney, although she couldn't see a house. Someone lived down there, she thought with surprise. It looked so isolated.

No one could be more isolated than she, her inner voice said. She had left all behind her, and after weeks she was no closer to knowing exactly why than she had ever been. The castle was quiet . . . too quiet . . . and she was used to noise, to music, to laughter. At times she would welcome the howling of Quent's ghostly three-headed dog.

She sighed. She shouldn't have mentioned Papa. But she couldn't deny his being, nor his influence on her life. Thinking of the details of this new existence, she came close to despair.

And where would that get her? She might as well throw herself out the window and save decades of misery. Through the burn of unshed tears, she managed a smile. Papa's daughter she was, but she was Mama's daughter as well, and she could not leave a dirty house. The thought was an attempt at humor—small, certainly, but it brought a lift to her spirits. Quent cared little for the castle, but right now she saw it as her salvation.

And he said she could spend whatever she chose. Silly man. To say such a thing, he either didn't know much about women or he was richer than she had supposed.

Shoving her unhappiness beneath the surface of her resolve, she composed another list in her mind, this one for immediate purchases, including a few items her husband would find surprising. She might not be learning much about him, but she could certainly let him know a few things about her. After all, he had told her he hadn't wanted her for a slave.

Changing into her second-best gown, she grabbed up her cloak and bonnet and went down to confront Mrs. Mac-Cabe. The housekeeper confirmed that Quent had kept his word about providing money.

"I'll have to go into town," she said.

Mrs. MacCabe's brows furrowed. "I'm not so sure—"

"I could hardly buy anything up here, could I?"

"Old Tully will get what you want."

"Who is he?"

"He runs the stable."

"Ah," said Angel with a smile, thinking that with the introduction of the stablehand, the staff of Cordangan Castle had just doubled.

"Are there any other people around I don't know about?"

The housekeeper took a moment to answer. "Master Quent hires help from time to time. He's not one for strangers about the place."

I'm a stranger, she wanted to say, but could see little purpose in doing so.

With a nod and *thank you,* she hurried out the back door and across a dirt-packed clearing, stopping at the open stable doors. The half-timbered building was two stories, and looked practically as old as the castle itself. Outside was the carriage Quent had hired for the ride from Cork City two days ago.

Two days. Angel sighed. Time passed slowly on this limestone hill.

She stepped into the dimness, momentarily blinded. A horse whinnied. "Mister Tully?" she called. She heard a rustling, and the sound of footsteps moving slowly, heavily against the straw-strewn floor.

A shaft of light from the door fell on the small, wiry figure of an old man. His hair was white and his leathery face carved with wrinkles, but there was an alertness to the eyes peering at her that was unnerving. Everyone in Ireland, it seemed, had excellent eyes.

"Mister Tully?" she said

"Tully Fitzgerald. Old Tully, I'm called. For reasons that must be obvious. Ye must be the wife."

"Angel Kavanagh," she said, stepping forward and extending her hand.

He took it in a grasp that was firm and warm. She liked him right away.

"Mrs. MacCabe said you ran the stables. You must have been here for a long time."

"Fifty year next September." He said it with pride. He would know much about the Kavanaghs. Remembering how she had antagonized the housekeeper with questions about the past, Angel decided not to interrogate him. Not just yet, that is.

"I need a ride into town," she said.

Old Tully's bushy white brows lifted. "Do ye now?"

Angel swallowed guiltily, embarrassed because she felt compelled to defend herself. "I've spoken to my husband about making some purchases in town."

"And he said aye?"

"He didn't say nay."

The old man's pale eyes twinkled. Taking her by the hand, he pulled her into the sunlight at the stable door, then studied her with the same care her husband had frequently shown. Unlike Quent, however, he concentrated on her face.

"Master Quent did right well fer himself. I'm surprised."

She curtsied. "Thank you, sir." She could have kissed him for being kind. When she got to know him better, she would.

He thought a minute. "I'll be going into the village shortly to take the hired carriage and team."

"I'll go with you, if that's all right."

"Only one horse to ride back . . . Old Brenda. In horse

years the nag's near old as I and won't ride double. 'Course, I could walk."

"You most certainly will not. Is my husband riding the stallion?"

Old Tully clutched at his chest. "Ye weaken me heart, lass, to ask such a thing. He'd have both our hides if ye was to ride Vengeance."

"Vengeance?"

"That's what he's named him. Says the beast carries him through wind and rain, up hills and down. I've not felt called upon to criticize."

Angel understood.

"Do ye ride well?"

"Papa—" She caught herself, but saw no harshness in the man's eyes. "Papa saw that my sisters and I learned."

"Then ye need a mount o' yer own."

She smiled. "I do."

"Gi' me more t' care for, too."

"I suspect, Old Tully, that like me, you don't like idle hands."

He watched her for a moment, then slowly shook his head. "Two days here, and yer still smiling. Yer a rare one, lass." He glanced toward the castle, then back to her. "And who have ye met?"

"Just you and Mrs. MacCabe. And Neill Connolly, of course. Is there anyone else?"

"Mebbe. Mebbe not." He turned from her. "We'll be leaving within the hour. I'd be obliged to have ye ready to ride."

The village of Cordangan was a half hour away. Angel found herself entranced by the countryside, the rolling hills, the mountains in the background. The land around Savannah was mostly flat, but here everything was rise after rise, all the way to the horizon. And covered with trees, at least the part she could see from the road, the forest such a rich, deep green she understood why Ireland was called the Emerald Isle.

Cottages lined the road as it neared the village. Cordangan itself was charming with its half-timbered houses, as well as brick and frame, and thatched roofs and narrow, winding streets. Every other building seemed to be a tavern, all of them doing a brisk business on this weekday afternoon.

Away from the heart of the hamlet she could see the masts of sailboats.

"That's the harbor," Old Tully explained. "Fishing's big in these parts."

He let her down outside a row of shops, promising to return within two hours. He glanced at her long skirt and heavy cloak. "Be prepared t' ride, lass."

"I will," she promised. Purse in hand, its contents a goodly sum of money provided by Mrs. MacCabe, she went into the nearest shop, a small establishment reminiscent of Chadwick Clothing and Dry Goods of Savannah, Georgia, U.S.A. The smell inside was the same, too, goods and sawdust and commerce, which as any business person could attest had an odor all its own.

Taking off her gloves, she smoothed her skirt. And she looked at a half-dozen middle-age, sharp-eyed women staring at her with open curiosity, if not outright hostility.

"Good afternoon," she ventured, her heart sinking to her toes. "I'm Angel Kavanagh."

No one spoke. She got the feeling they knew full well who she was, and more, that they didn't approve.

"I need to buy some things."

No one moved.

Papa always claimed Ireland was the friendliest land on earth. "They have a way of making you feel that if you hadn't come along, the day would not have been so pleasant."

It was a reaction Angel had yet to experience.

Well, she thought, she had to start somewhere, and she headed toward a rack of dresses hanging at the rear. She was after workclothes; she found a few gowns that would need little alteration. She took them down and went to the counter at the side of the store.

No one made a move to wait on her. As far as she could tell, no one made any move at all.

"I don't know how things are done here," she said to the general populace. "At the family store back in Savannah, we let the customers help themselves if they can, take orders for the rest, then total up what they've bought and present the bill." She dropped her purse heavily on the counter. It would have taken someone deaf and blind not to realize she was carrying cash.

At last one of the women started toward her.

"Yer family has a shop like this?" she asked as she went behind the counter.

"Yes," said Angel with a smile of relief. "For many years. I've worked there since I was a child."

"Humph!" said a woman behind her. "Tell me, Mrs. O'Flaherty, do ye plan t' do business with a Kavanagh?"

"I plan t' do business with any customer who can pay, Mrs. Dunne," the store proprietor responded, a challenging light in her eye.

"Then ye'll not be doing business with me."

The door opened and closed. Angel turned around to see that two of the women had exited with Mrs. Dunne, leaving Angel, Mrs. O'Flaherty, and two others in the store.

"Oh, dear," said Angel, "I hope I'm not causing trouble."

"She'll get over it," said the proprietor with a shrug. "Mrs. Dunne always likes to take a stance. Besides, there's no place else in all of Cordangan where the gossip's half so choice."

"Ah, and we've got the devil's bride. She'll be back to hear what we've learned," said one of the other customers, who stepped up beside Angel. "Mrs. Plunkett here, and pleased t' meet ye. This be me sister-in-law, Mrs. O'Dowd."

"I'm pleased to meet you," said Angel with a nod. Quiet descended. She felt compelled to speak. "You have lovely weather here in Ireland."

"If ye don't mind occasional storms," said the proprietor.

"Oh, I don't mind."

"Imagine it's stormy much of the time up at the castle," Mrs. Plunkett said, a glint of interest in her crafty, close-set eyes. Mrs. O'Dowd moved in closer to hear Angel's reply.

A bug caught on a pin, that's what she was. And she didn't much care for these strangers calling her husband the devil. She was surprised at the strength of her loyalty.

"We must have the same weather there that you have down here."

"You're a young one t' be wed," said Mrs. Plunkett, not in the least daunted.

This was new sentiment for Angel, who at twenty-four had been considered a spinster by Georgia standards.

"We marry late in Ireland," Mrs. O'Flaherty explained. "Since the famine, ye understand. Keeps down the number of children and the mouths we have t' feed."

"Not that Kavanagh is worried about such," said Mrs. Plunkett with a sniff. "He's got the money to feed a dozen brats, though where he gets it the Lord only knows."

Angel's ears burned, and she was grateful that her bonnet covered what must be a tell-tale red. With all the calm she could muster, she gave all her attention to Mrs. O'Flaherty. "I'll need sewing supplies to alter these dresses. And would there be some place I could buy a riding habit?"

"Around here, we generally hike up our skirts."

Mrs. O'Dowd giggled, and her sister-in-law shot her a quelling look.

"There's the dressmaker two doors down," volunteered Mrs. Plunkett. "She keeps a few such frills for those who care for 'em."

"Thank you," said Angel, deciding then and there to buy the fanciest habit she could find. She gave full attention to her order, noting the strange brands on the shelves, guessing at their quality, picking out a few tins whose purpose she couldn't imagine. But she was determined to fill the castle larder, whether Mrs. MacCabe wanted it done or not.

If she picked out the wrong things, she would give the housekeeper the satisfaction of pointing out her mistakes.

The counter was soon piled high with goods; she also ordered a few additional staples, as well as fresh fruit and vegetables whenever they became available. As an after-thought, she purchased the ingredients for a sugar cake. She was used to taking her turn in the kitchen, and it didn't make much difference to her whether the oven was in a castle or a cottage. Mama always said the smell of fresh-baked cake could get a man's attention when all other charms failed. Somehow she didn't think sweet cooking scents would work with Quent, but she planned to give it a try.

Her business was taken care of under the watchful eyes of the sisters-in-law. Mrs. O'Flaherty just kept helping, a small, tight smile on her face.

"This will have to be delivered," she said when she was done. "Except for the cake ingredients. I'd like to take them with me now."

"We've a lad who can take care o' it," Mrs. O'Flaherty said.

Angel paid the bill, taking the woman's word as to what was what with the shillings and pounds and pence. It was clear she was being cordial out of curiosity and profit. The other women were just plain inquisitive, without a sign of real friendliness in their eyes.

And so she chose not to linger, though she had a million questions to ask about the village and life as it was lived in the area, and what people did for pleasure and what they did for work. These women wanted to learn about her and

Quent and she wasn't going to tell them . . . not that she knew all that much herself.

Still and all, as she left the store, she didn't feel bad about how the morning had gone. She'd let them know the devil had married a woman without horns or two heads or whatever they had probably been imagining. They knew now he'd married a woman who could bake a cake.

As soon as she stepped into the dressmaker's shop, she knew things would be different from the store. For one thing, she was greeted with a smile and a handshake.

"Come right in, lass," said the dressmaker, who introduced herself as Nellie Ahearne. "Nellie, please," she said, a genuine smile crinkling her hazel eyes. She was about the same age as the other women, somewhere around forty, but she had an air about her that was as soothing as Mama's broomrape balm.

"You'd be Mrs. Kavanagh. Don't look surprised. There's not a woman from here to the bay wouldn't recognize you on sight."

"But I came at night, and this is the first chance I've had to get into town."

"Mrs. Kavanagh, you were spotted coming off the ship with your husband in Cork City. Word spreads fast, especially about someone as pretty as you walking alongside the most interesting man in these parts."

"Thank you," said Angel with a sigh of relief.

"Whatever for?"

"You didn't call my husband the devil."

"Didn't call him a saint, either."

Angel laughed at the thought. Saint Quent somehow didn't have the same ring as Saint Patrick; it was not a name to catch on. "You can call me Angel, if you'd like." At the woman's look of surprise, she went on to explain how Papa had named his girls for the color of their hair.

She didn't mention Papa's name, though, or anything else about herself except to say she and Quent had met in Sa-

vannah and decided to be wed. It was clear from the way
Nellie was listening that she knew there was more to tell,
but the only thing she asked was how she could be of help.

"I need a riding habit. I guess it's a frill—"

"You've been listening to Mrs. Plunkett."

Angel grinned. "I plan to do some riding and I'd feel
more comfortable in the right clothes."

"That woman calls lace on her underdrawers a frill, and
maybe she's right. But that doesn't mean we women can't
feel a tad more feminine with a ruffle or two beneath our
skirts. Besides," she added, hands on her rounded hips,
"there are women around Cordangan who make some of
the finest lace in all of Ireland. Tell them they're wasting
their time and you're liable to get a poke in the eye."

"A contentious group, are they?"

"This little island has been invaded so many times we've
learned to defend what's ours. Now about that habit—"

As luck would have it, she had a green wool outfit that
needed only a little alteration to serve just fine. "You'll
need something warmer in the winter and cooler in the summer, but for spring, this is just right."

The next half hour she concentrated on fitting the outfit
to Angel. "You've got a fine figure for a small woman,"
she said with obvious appreciation. "No wonder Mister
Kavanagh took you as his bride."

For a moment, the pleasure of the afternoon fled. Quent
didn't care about her figure, no more than he did what she
wore or what she ate or how she spent her time . . . except
where it infringed on his privacy.

Nellie must have sensed her change in mood, for she
started talking about the village and its people, her late husband, the good fishing in the bay, the dances, the stores and
what was available in them. Angel was so relieved by the
woman's tact, she went on to order two dresses and some
undergarments—"with as much lace as you can get on
them."

Within the time allotted by Old Tully, she was dressed in the riding habit and carrying two bundles—the clothes she'd worn from the castle and the ingredients for the cake, the latter including a dozen carefully wrapped eggs. She was about to go outside to look for him when the door opened and a woman burst inside.

"Oh," she said, looking at Angel with wild green eyes. Her red hair was half tumbled to her shoulders, and she clutched a small bundle to her worn cloak as though someone might take it from her.

She smoothed her hair. "I thought you were alone," she said to Nellie, her eyes still on Angel. She looked no older than twenty-five, a sturdy woman who somehow reminded Angel of the Micks. She was pretty, too, in a wholesome way, healthy and hardworking. She also looked afraid.

She thrust the bundle into the dressmaker's hands.

"Thanks for the delivery, Mary," said Nellie. "I'll be needing this lace for Mrs. Kavanagh." She introduced the newcomer as Mary O'Callaghan. "Mary goes around to the women out in the country and picks up the lace and embroidery work and brings it to me. I pay for what I can use."

"You live at the castle," Mary said. "You know—" She looked down, clutching her hands at her waist.

Nellie pulled a few coins from her pocket. "Here, Mary. This is for your trousseau."

"Oh," she said, a catch in her voice. She glanced at the two women, opened her mouth to say more, then with a small cry darted outside.

Nellie stared after her. "Poor woman," she said, but she gave no sign she wanted to say more. Remembering too well the gossipy women at the previous shop, Angel appreciated her discretion. With a heart-felt *thank you,* she followed Mary's path.

Outside she saw no sign of Old Tully. She was looking

down the street when an anguished voice spoke from behind her.

"I'm glad to make your acquaintance, Mrs. Kavanagh, for I'm needing your help as sure as sweet air to breathe."

Angel whirled. "Miss O'Callaghan—"

Mary clutched her arms, almost spilling the bundle with the eggs. "You've got t' help me. If you don't, I might as well throw meself into Bantry Bay."

Eleven

Angel's heart went out to the woman. "What do you need?" she asked. "If it's money, I'll do what I can."

"Nay," Mary said with an impatient shake of her head. "I need—"

Her voice broke, and she turned away in anguish. "I need more than anyone can give. Any woman, for sure."

"You thought I could, or you wouldn't have waited for me."

"I hoped—" Mary broke off as a pair of women strolled by. They took their time, their eyes cast sideways toward the objects of their interest. When they were out of earshot, Mary pulled Angel into a narrow alley that ran beside the dressmaker's shop.

They stood behind an old wooden cart. Angel was startled to see a shaggy-haired donkey in the traces. The donkey brayed in answering surprise.

"Hush, Josephine," said Mary. Thrusting her arm from beneath her cloak, she rolled up her sleeve. "Look," she commanded. "And there's more I could show you."

Angel stared at the ugly purple bruise on her forearm. "How did you get this?"

"Fergus Malone," she said. "My intended." She spat out the words.

"He beat you."

"He wanted a sampling, was the way he put it, since it's three years 'til the wedding. He caught me out on the road

as I was riding into town." Her chin tilted. "The only sampling he got was of me fist. He tripped and fell. Lying there
on the ground, like a great hairy log, making me wish he
were dead, but his big body drawing too many breaths to
give me comfort."

Angel had no adequate response. She hugged her packages to her bosom, for a moment forgetting the eggs.

"Do you have to marry him?"

"In the new country maybe daughters do as they wish,
but here in Ireland we do as our father says. And me Da'
says I must wed Fergus Malone, so that our two farms will
be joined. 'Tis been a dream of his. I'm an only child, you
see, me mother having died when I was a babe. Da' has
long been bitter I was not a boy."

"Have you not tried to talk with him?"

"You don't know Seamus O'Callaghan. He wouldn't listen, so close is he to Owney Malone. Me father-in-law,
eager to get his hands on me dowry. He says he's settling
cheap for a milk cow and some sheep, but he knows there's
the deed to O'Callaghan land after me Da' dies." She
sighed. "Ah, I'm in trouble t' be sure with the pair of them
deciding me fate."

A more pitiful tale, Angel had never heard. Worse than
her own. At least Quent didn't bruise her. And he didn't
demand a sampling.

"You had something in mind when you spoke to me."

Mary lowered her eyes. "I was thinking . . . ah, it was
a foolish thought. I was thinking that if I could get up to
the devil's castle, no one would bother me there."

"Oh," said Angel, taken by surprise.

The woman touched her arm. "I'm not asking for charity,
understand. I'm a hard worker. I'll earn me keep. And Neill
says the devil isn't as bad as folks claim."

"You know Neill?"

The blush that stole onto Mary's cheeks looked out of
place. "I know him."

She knows him very well, thought Angel in dismay. What was she getting into? She thought of the bruised arm and she thought of Mary's fear. Whatever the woman was or wasn't telling her, the bruise and the fear were real.

"I do need help," she said. "It's charwoman's work, nothing easy, but neither is it anything I won't be doing myself."

"I'll work for free."

"That won't be necessary."

"I'll sleep in the woods. You won't know I'm about."

"We can find a room for you somewhere," Angel responded with more confidence than she felt. Her inner voice protested she was making a terrible mistake, but her conscience would let her do nothing less.

"What about your father? Will he worry?"

Mary laughed sharply. "He has a woman on the place to care for his needs. He'll scarcely know I'm not about. I'll send word I'm earning money for me wedding. He won't like it, but he hasn't the fire in him to come after me and see I'm all right."

Angel smiled at her, and received a tentative smile in return. She liked Mary O'Callaghan. She liked her fighting spirit; she understood her fear. To marry a man she didn't love could be a frightening thing.

And she was someone to work with, someone to talk with. . . .

Stop, the voice said. You're not buying a friend, you're buying trouble. Again, Angel refused to listen, although the fact that Mary knew Neill presented a nagging worry. There was more to the acquaintance than she was being told. She thrust the worry aside.

A sideways glance showed Old Tully was waiting in the street astride the ancient mare Brenda. He had a white mare in tow.

"Can you come with us now?" she asked.

Mary's smile was broad. It did wonders for her face. "I'll follow in the cart with Josephine."

And so it was that within minutes the strange procession headed down the main street of Cordangan, Old Tully and Brenda moving slowly in the front, the new Mrs. Kavanagh in her fashionable green habit riding sidesaddle on the high-stepping mare Solas (Irish for light, Old Tully explained), and Mary O'Callaghan following triumphantly in the trailing donkey cart.

The villagers, pedestrians and riders alike, stopped to stare. In a rare moment of devilment, Angel removed her bonnet and thrust it beneath the parcels behind the saddle, letting the afternoon breeze loosen tendrils of her golden hair. Let them see what Mrs. Kavanagh looked like. She might be a bundle of nerves inside, but she refused to let it show. Such was the Chadwick way.

Without incident they made it past the shops and cottages and halfway to the winding road leading to the castle. Old Tully was the first to sense something was wrong.

He reined Brenda to a halt. "We've trouble, Mistress Angel," he said, his rheumy eyes casting to the woods alongside the road. Brenda whinnied in agreement.

Angel listened, but she could hear nothing that caused alarm. In truth, she could hear nothing at all except her heart, the wind having died in the warming afternoon. Even the birds had fallen silent. The mare stomped impatiently against the ground, and behind her the donkey cart creaked to a halt.

"Why are we stopping?" asked Mary.

The answer came right away as a monster-sized man in dirty workclothes emerged from the woods, his muddied boots stomping through the high grass all the way to the road, not halting until he stood directly in their path.

"Fergus!" cried Mary, and crossed herself.

Even high on her horse, Angel felt small and vulnerable as she stared down at the farmer's son. Everything about him was big, including his coarse features . . . except for the beady eyes he pinned on his betrothed. Another man loomed behind him. An older version of the brute, only somehow meaner and smarter and tougher. Angel wished for her husband's crop.

Old Tully tried to ride on, but Fergus grabbed the reins.

"Owney Malone," he said, looking past the son to the father, "you'll regret this. Be sensible, man. Let us be."

"We've no argument with you, Old Tully, or"—Owney's crafty gaze shifted to Angel—"any Kavanagh. Leave my son's woman and be gone."

"Better do as he says," Mary said. "I'll not be the cause of injury to you good folk."

"We'll have no such nonsense coming from you," said Old Tully. Angel felt a rush of pride at his courage and a clutch of fear for his safety, both emotions overtaking her at the same time. All of this was her responsibility. She had to be in charge.

"Mister Malone," she said, speaking to the father, "Mary is in my care now. And in my employ. Anything you do to her you do to me."

Fergus cackled. "Now, ain't that just what Da' and me would like. The two o' ye out in the woods, one fer each."

Old Tully raised his riding whip. "Get away. Leave the women alone."

"No," cried Angel, more fearful for him than for herself.

Fergus grabbed the whip and pulled the old man to the ground. He fell hard against the rock-strewn dirt, the air rushing from his lungs as he grabbed his arm.

Without thinking, Angel sprang from the saddle and kneeled beside him.

"I'm all right, lass," Old Tully managed as he struggled for breath, but Angel didn't believe him. Staring at the dirty boots of the farmer, at the broad, blunt hand holding Old Tully's whip, she felt a rise of panic that would not go away.

And then she felt the vibration in the ground. Someone was coming. She looked down the road and saw a rider and horse moving fast in their direction. Everyone watched. Muttering a curse, Fergus backed away.

The horse thundered on. The black horse with its black-clad rider. Quent, she thought with a swell of relief. Her elation lasted until he reined to a halt, the stallion Vengeance snorting and stamping, her husband's eyes boring into her.

She held onto Old Tully, as much to receive comfort as to give it.

"Quent—" she began, but her words of gratitude died in her throat. With his hair blown wild by the ride and his stare hot with fury, he looked ready to fight, but whether he wanted to hit her or the Malones, she didn't know for sure.

He chose Fergus. The farmer outweighed him by fifty pounds and had a half foot in height advantage, but Quent came off Vengeance like an unswerving streak of black fury, landing full against his bigger foe, knocking him to the ground and sending him sprawling. Fergus attempted to scurry crablike toward the tall grass at the side of the road, but Quent was having none of it and the two men rolled in the dirt.

The mare's frightened whinny rose high above the grunts of the men, and Angel's alarm became a panic for the safety of her husband.

"Quent!" she cried, wanting to go to him, but Old Tully held her back.

Fists flew, mostly Quent's, and it was over as quickly as it began, with Fergus stretched out on his back, eyes closed, his body shaking as he gasped for air, and Quent beside him on one knee, his dark eyes trained at the edge of the woods where the Malones had first appeared. The father Owney was nowhere in sight.

Quent stood and turned from Fergus as if he offered no more threat than a slug. His clothes were streaked with dust and the dark hairs at the throat of his open shirt curled tight with sweat, but otherwise he looked none the worse for the fight. He shook his head to fling the wild black hair from his forehead as his eyes picked out his wife.

Relief flooded through Angel, blunting the edge of the fear she knew he meant to arouse. "You're all right," she said in a whispery rush as she stared up at him.

"I'm always all right." It was a statement of fact, not a boast. "You'd best fear for yourself. What the hell were you about?"

The power of his stare pinned her to the ground. Old Tully's roughened hand took one of hers " 'Twas the Malones. They're a bad lot, fer sure," he said, then added in Angel's defense, "The lass meant no harm."

"She never does," said Quent, his accusing eyes still on her. Guilt stung her. Quent was right. This was all her fault. Behind her husband, the fallen farmer groaned, then pulled himself to his feet and staggered toward the woods. His hulking figure disappeared through the grass and trees without a glance from anyone but Angel.

She looked at her husband, wanting to touch him, to say she was sorry, to . . . oh, foolish thought, to take him in her arms and offer comfort, to make sure he was truly unharmed. But that would be like embracing the puma from the sailing ship deck.

She started to speak, but Quent shifted his anger to Old Tully. "And what about you, old man?"

Releasing Angel's hand, Old Tully stood without help. He gave slight favor to his left shoulder, but the light in his eye shone militant. " 'Twill take a better man than a Malone to harm this tough old body."

Angel rose to give him the hug she could not give her husband. "I'm sorry," she said, gingerly inspecting his shoulder with her fingers, deciding he had received no more injury than a bad bruise. "I shouldn't have asked you to take me to town."

"Ye shouldn't have brought me," said the forgotten Mary

O'Callaghan, who sat low in the donkey cart a dozen yards behind the battle scene. She glanced once, quickly and nervously, at Quent, then turned her full attention to Angel. " 'Twas good of you, Mrs. Kavanagh, t' offer help, but there's little anyone can do—"

She broke off as she stared past Angel up the road leading from the castle. "Oh." For all its softness, the cry held a world of wonder and joy.

Angel followed the direction of her stare. Neill Connolly rode toward them, his bay horse kicking up a cloud of dust. He reined to a halt beside the stallion. "I got worried when you didn't return—"

He saw Mary and his words to Quent faded to silence. Angel knew the look that passed between them. She had seen it shared by Mama and Papa, by Raven and Marcus, by Flame and Matt. Neill and the betrothed woman were in love. In that instant she felt a flare of jealousy because she never would share such a look with Quent.

The feeling stunned her. There were so many other considerations to worry about now. What a ninny she could be.

She looked to her husband. "How did you know we were in trouble?"

"When you're out of sight for long, there's cause for concern."

" 'Twas a strange thing," said Neill, drawing his eyes from Mary, but moving the bay nearer the donkey cart. The squat, hairy Josephine blinked her deep brown eyes once but did not shift from the center of the road.

"We were working in the library when suddenly he stopped his writing and threw down his pen. A mistake, I thought, or a blot of ink on the paper, but no. He said . . . ah, never mind. His words were not for the delicate ears of a lass. He ran from the room, and the next thing I knew he and Vengeance were thundering beyond the wall near the library window. I waited, but when he didn't return—"

He shifted his long, lank figure to the ground beside the

cart, his eyes only for Mary. "I hardly knew what to expect. In a million years I would never expect to see you."

"Mrs. Kavanagh offered t' take me on," said Mary. "Fergus was not of a mind to let me be."

Angel looked at the bleak expression on the woman's face, looked at the horses cropping grass at the side of the road, at the proud black stallion and the smaller white mare standing close together away from the other animals. At last she forced her eyes to her husband. "I was going to tell you as soon as I could."

Quent's hard-hewn expression was impossible to read. "You're a good woman, aren't you, Angel? Well named and all that. 'Tis what I heard in Savannah, and now you've brought your goodness here."

He sounded far from pleased, as if goodness were a crime, and her heart turned heavy in her breast. He mocked her as he had in the tower, as he would ever do any time she crossed his will.

"Do not believe that I am of the same good temperament," he added before she could defend herself. "Or ever will be. Take care. I'll not ride to your rescue again."

"I'll remember," she said. For a moment no one uttered a word, and she could hear nothing but the pounding of her pulse.

In the awkward silence, Old Tully pulled himself as straight as his aged body allowed. "Don't be hard on the lass, Master Quent. 'Tis my fault she went t' town. And 'twas my idea to get the mare. I'd heard Solas could be bought cheap."

Quent gave no sign he heard the old man's defense. "Can you ride Brenda back to the castle?"

Old Tully sniffed and pulled at his nose. "I'm stiff and old, and I'll be stiffer and older t'morrow, but I can still take care o' meself."

Accepting no argument, Quent helped him into the saddle. He made no such gesture of help toward Angel as she walked toward the mare. He whistled for Vengeance, easing himself astride the horse and taking the reins in his hands.

His dark, strong figure loomed above them all, stark against the cloud-streaked afternoon sky. "Bring the woman with you," he said to Neill. It was clear he meant Mary O'Callaghan. He made no reference to his wife.

He started at a trot down the road, a straight-backed, solitary figure in black. Neill helped Angel into the sidesaddle, and they all followed in Quent's wake, moving slowly, the cart creaking in a belabored rhythm, Angel's heart beating heavily in time.

I'll not ride to your rescue again. But he hadn't this time, she wanted to tell him. He had saved Old Tully and Mary, but not his wife, who was never really in danger. Surely he knew.

He wasn't after accuracy, her inner voice said. He wanted everyone, especially her, to understand she was beyond his care.

She understood, yet she could feel nothing but sorrow for him. Right now he could be riding with them, sharing the talk between Mary and Neill about what had happened in town, and with Old Tully about the quick fight in the road. But he chose to ride alone. An infinite sadness settled like a cloud over her. Everything she did where her husband was concerned proved wrong.

He had forced her into this marriage for reasons as mysterious as they were ugly, he had threatened her loved ones, he had scorned her at every turn. She had no reason to look for anything from him but hurt and rejection. She had no reason to look for love.

But Angel's heart was a curious thing. When Quent had flown off that horse and attacked Fergus Malone, her foolish spirit had soared, and all her being had warmed for him, both in anxiety and in pride. She couldn't imagine feeling any other way.

She ought to avoid him, yet she missed him when he

wasn't around. She ought to hate him, yet she yearned to share his pain. Somehow in that sharing she knew that the trouble between him and Papa could be settled.

The fact that Quent held no such conviction could not deter her. Maybe she was trying too hard to make herself his wife. Or maybe she was trying in all the wrong ways.

As they passed the main gate, she glanced up at the snarling dogs. "Pat," she whispered to herself, "and Finn, you've growled down at him all his life. Is growling all he's ever known?"

She glanced back at the bundles tied behind the saddle. As best she could tell, the eggs remained unbroken. She had wanted to bake him a cake, to demonstrate for him her domestic skills. The idea seemed silly now. She'd have to find another way to Quentin Kavanagh's heart.

Twelve

Padraic Scully sat by himself at Bantry Bay Tavern's rearmost table, nursing a pint of ale. He stared through the smoky shadows at the coarse, ruddy faces of the men around him, trying to ignore their loud laughs and quick, ribald songs.

Sometimes their talk shifted to declarations of independence. With Gladstone as prime minister, they declared Home Rule as sure as done.

Never, thought Scully. Not while there was a breath of air in his body. Irishman though he was, he had much to lose should Ireland separate from England. Patriotism be damned. A man had to take care of himself.

"Let's have a round fer independence," someone in the haze cried out. Every voice in the tavern shouted agreement, including that of Padraic Scully, there being no purpose served in showing the truth of how he felt. Several men turned to grin at him. Nodding, he returned a humorless smile.

These men of Cordangan are fools, he thought as he sipped the ale. Puppets. Worse than the drunkards in Dublin, the city he called home.

Dublin, he thought in disgust. Not much of a home . . . not with his wife and daughter there. His muling, scrawny wife and his cretinous daughter. They were reasons to stay away.

Scully took another swallow of the bitter brew. He wasn't

much of a drinking man, but, considering the way life had turned on him, he had reason to be. In his youth, he had married for money. He was set for life. But the money hadn't lasted, not with that bastard Quentin Kavanagh running him out of business without a fare-thee-well.

Kavanagh, with his obsession for privacy and his damned instinct for success. Kavanagh, who stupidly thought no one knew he owned the Pride of Ireland. But Scully knew. He hated the man with all the force that was within him. Someday he would bring him to ruin. He was not without plans. He was not without means.

For the present he would let the stupid folk of the county believe the devil's money came from sources too dark to bear the light of day. He would add stories to strengthen that belief, the old tales of poison fruit and magic midnight rides. Fearing Kavanagh, they would never call him friend.

Two figures loomed out of the smoke. The biggest fools of all, he thought as he gestured for them to join him. But useful fools, and so he waved at the wench behind the bar to bring a round of drinks.

"I'll kill 'im, I will," growled Fergus Malone as he dropped heavily into a chair at Scully's right.

"Ye had yer chance," his father Owney shot back from across the table.

"He took me by surprise, jumping off the horse that way. He's the devil fer sure."

His snarling words piqued Scully's interest, enough for him to study the man's broad, flat face, to note the purple bruises swelling one cheek and eye.

"You fought Kavanagh," he said.

"He served as a bloody punching bag," Owney snapped.

" 'Twern't a fair fight, Da'," Fergus whined in response.

Scully looked from father to son. A well-matched pair, he decided, each more stupid than the other, though they had their uses, especially Owney Malone. Too bad, thought Scully with a sniff, that he smelled so rank.

"You attacked him in the light of day," Scully said to Fergus. "Some deeds are best done by night."

"He owns the night," said Owney. "Leastwise he thinks he does."

"But we know different, don't we?" Scully said and Owney nodded that he agreed.

"He was taking Mary," Fergus said.

Ah yes, thought Scully, the round-rumped woman who was betrothed to the younger Malone. He would have felt a bit of sympathy for her if sympathy was within his ken.

"What do you mean he was taking her?"

"The bitch he married was taking her to the castle," Owney explained. "We saw them ride out of town and followed."

Scully's interest lifted by several degrees. "This Mrs. Kavanagh. Did you get a good look at her?"

"Aye, and felt the lash of her tongue," said Owney. "A runty thing she is, and fair. Not at all the sort I woulda picked for the black-hearted devil."

Scully would have picked no bride at all for his nemesis. Kavanagh seemed to need no man or woman. The fact that he'd brought a wife back from the States was the cause of much conjecture in these parts, most deciding she must be evil indeed to serve as the devil's mate.

Scully finished his ale just as the serving woman arrived with the full tankards. She set them on the table, and he studied the width of her rear. He felt an urge to thrust his hand under her skirts and pinch her buttocks. He and half the men in the tavern knew she wore no undergarments to prevent him. Later, he promised himself. Business first.

Fergus took a long draw on the ale. "With only that old fool from the castle stables along, we woulda had the two of 'em."

His father barked a laugh. "Ye fool, ye couldn't handle Mary when ye had her alone."

"She took me by surprise," said Fergus, drawing again on the ale.

Scully withdrew into himself, letting the farmer and his son bicker. 'Twas a fact that Quentin Kavanagh lived a solitary life, running his business in secret, depending upon no one else except that naive fool Neill Connolly. 'Twas also a fact that he had traveled to the States supposedly to take care of business and had brought back with him a woman who, unlike her husband, ventured into town.

Kavanagh never dealt with the people of Cordangan or any of the neighboring farms. He hated them for reasons that dipped into the past. And the villagers hated him.

Yet Kavanagh's bride dared to visit amongst them. Clearly there were things he did not know. Things he had to learn.

But Scully was not his own boss. Not entirely. Not yet. He had other matters to attend to besides the newlywed Kavanaghs.

He waved for another round of drinks. "It's time again," he said to Owney.

"I thought it might be," the farmer said.

"Can you manage it tomorrow night?"

"Aye, but there are costs involved."

"Have I ever stinted you on the money?"

"Nay," said Owney while his son concentrated on his ale.

"If not tomorrow night, the next," said Scully, and the two set to working on the details.

After the Malones were gone, he turned his thoughts to more immediate needs. He thought of Kavanagh and his bride. She must be a lusty wench, he decided, for the devil would settle for nothing less. A woman unlike Mrs. Scully, who never cared for sex. Scully liked it, with women plump and ripe.

A tall, thin man with a penis to match his angular frame, he rubbed it to fullness while he watched the serving woman move around the room. He liked his sex mixed with pain. His stupid wife objected. But not this one. Not if he paid her enough.

He rubbed himself so hard he almost spilled his seed. She caught his eye. She caught his meaning. Later in the room he rented above the tavern, she would satisfy his needs.

And then he could concentrate on Quentin Kavanagh. The more he thought about the unexpected marriage, the more he liked it. Perhaps he could get at the devil through his wife.

Quent spent the waning hours of day riding hard through the woods, up hill and down, urging Vengeance to stretch his legs and soar across the land.

Mostly he avoided the castle and the people it sheltered. Mostly he avoided his wife. Damn her. She had no business going into the village. And she had no business bringing a stranger to the hill, even a working woman to help her scrub the walls.

Most of all, Chadwick that she was, sacrificing everything for Papa, she had no business transforming his life.

He didn't care a farthing about the walls. He wanted peace. He had thought it was within his grasp, but it seemed further away than ever. Where the hell was Thomas Chadwick? Knowing he suffered afar was not enough. He wanted to see the pain in his eyes.

And so he rode, hard and long and fast, at last bringing Vengeance to a slow, careful descent to the edge of the bay beneath the Cordangan Castle headland. The shoreline was rocky and uneven, ragged with inlets and thick brush and trees. He chose a small, familiar clearing where he kept the rowboat that carried him to Calluragh Island. He considered rowing to the island, then decided he was in a mood to be alone.

Unsaddling Vengeance, he stood in silence as the stallion lapped at the cold bay water. The sunset was behind him, casting pink and golden light across the water, while the sky turned a purplish gray. He breathed deeply of air rich with the scents of spring. At such a time as this the world should be at peace. But he felt no peace in his heart.

He had always been a gambler, taking chances, knowing he had little to lose. In the process of throwing out challenges, he'd made a great deal of money, although the besting of others had been his primary aim. He had gambled, too, in taking Angel Chadwick as his wife. She hadn't seemed like much of an adversary. She was proving him wrong.

Maybe he should tell her everything, let her know the real agony of her Papa's betrayal. Maybe he should drag her down to the rowboat and take her—

Nay, he thought with a sigh of disgust. He could darken the brightness in her eyes soon enough, but something held him back.

He thought about his mother's grave . . . and his father's as well, although he rarely gave Dermot Kavanagh's burial site consideration. After returning with his bride, he had pondered whether or not to pay a rare visit to the family cemetery, but there had been little he could report to his mother . . . little that would rest her soul.

And so he stood at the edge of the water and stared at Calluragh Island looming out of the twilight. While he stood, he wondered whether his marriage had been a good thing. Two scenes conflicted in his mind . . . Angel's gentle persistence in the tower and her wild responses on their wedding night.

Mostly he thought about her in the ship's bed.

I liked it, she'd said in the tower.

So why had she cried when he held her in his arms?

I didn't know it would be like that.

She knew now. And she wanted him to believe she

wanted it again. Damn her, and damn the way she stayed in his mind.

He was not a man given to sentiment or overt gratitude. Seldom did he give Doreen MacCabe a moment's thought, although she had served him from his birth, first as nanny, later as teacher when the jeers at school drove him away, lastly as housekeeper when he turned to the Kavanagh books for his learning.

Old Tully had likewise served faithfully through the years, yet he couldn't describe the man's eyes to save his soul.

But he could describe his wife in great detail, from the contrast of pale brows above black curling lashes to the puckered, beckoning tip of each full breast, down to the pin-sized dot of brown skin an inch above her pubic hair. With such aspects to remember, it was no wonder she wouldn't leave his mind.

Everything about her disrupted his life, even when she was not near. Like today in the library. He had been writing one of the contracts Neill talked him into when a flash of panic struck him. Something was wrong with Angel. He didn't know what and he didn't know why the realization hit with such force, but he could no more have ignored it than he could ignore the castle bursting into flame.

He'd saddled the startled stallion in less time than he usually took to smooth the saddle blanket, and he'd ridden out as if the hounds of hell barked at his heel.

Never would he forget the look on her face as she crouched in the roadway giving succor to Old Tully . . . the spread of her green skirt around her, the wild play of her sunlit hair, the joyous light in her eyes when she saw he was there. He had wanted to embrace her and then he'd wanted to shake her until she collapsed into his arms begging forgiveness.

She had no business riding into the village, no business bringing a Cordangan woman back with her, no business interfering in his life. He had married a woman with more courage than good sense. The sooner she returned to Savannah, the better for them both.

He whirled at the sound of rustling behind him. Something inside him twisted sharply as he recognized the figure of his wife astride the mare Solas riding cautiously down the twisting path that led to the bay. She handled the horse with an expertise that gave credit to her equestrienne skills.

It was another Angel surprise.

Watching, waiting, at last he called out, "Stop."

She did as he bade. Dropping to the ground, she made no move to approach him. "You're nothing but a shadow, Quent," she said. Her voice was soft as a caress in the dusk.

"How did you know I was down here?"

"Old Tully pointed out the path. We couldn't see you, but I took a chance you were here."

"Ride on back to the castle," he said. "I prefer the solitude."

"I will," she said, a catch in her voice. "But first, there's something I want to say."

He remembered that persistent tone from the tower. Let her speak and then be gone.

She looked small and vulnerable, standing there on the trail a dozen yards uphill from him, tall trees rising around her, making her look all the more in need of protection. He had to remind himself her safety was her own concern. He had made that clear enough today.

A shaft of late-day sunlight filtered onto her face for a moment, and he saw the tilt of her chin and the unswerving way she gazed at him. The light passed and, like him, she stood in the lengthening twilight as no more than a silhouette.

"Say what you will and leave."

But she did not speak, and he was aware of the insects buzzing and chirping in the dark around them, and the rustle of wind in the leaves, and the lap of bay water against the rocks. The air was cool, but he felt only heat as he stared at the shadowed figure of his wife.

He wanted her gone, and yet. . . . Goddamn it, he wanted her gone.

"I'm sorry for today," she said, and then more quickly, "Please let me finish. And then I won't bother you again."

He nodded once, curtly.

"If I go slowly, forgive me, Quent. And I'd rather you not interrupt."

"Giving orders, are you?"

"I guess I am." He could imagine the small smile on her lips. "But this is difficult for me and I want to get it right."

Vengeance raised his dark head from the water as he caught scent of the mare. Quent saw he must keep the two apart, else they would mate.

"I knew well enough when we married that you had secrets I couldn't imagine. I was fool enough to think you would eventually tell me what they were. But you haven't. Nor should you, since I'm not in any sense of the word your wife. Except legally, of course, but I see now that that's the weakest sense of all."

She paused. Behind her Solas sniffed the fecund air, and Vengeance stirred restlessly at the water's edge.

"I keep telling myself I ought to feel great resentment against you, but I can't. Back in Savannah—please don't laugh—I decided that while Jeremiah had his ailing patients, I had you. I thought of the pain you carried with you, which seemed as bad as any fever Jeremiah treated. Anyone who wishes to inflict suffering the way you do must be suffering terribly himself. And suffering can be relieved."

She laughed softly, but there was sadness in the sound. "I've always been such an optimist, but I guess there are some things that good will and wanting just can't bring about."

Good will and wanting. The words tore at Quent. How

aptly she described the way he had felt as a child, loving his mother, wanting her to love him in return. At times he had even wanted his father's respect, which showed just how stupid he could be.

He wondered how Angel could so easily remind him of times he did not want to remember. He wondered how she could get beneath his skin.

She fell silent for so long, he thought that she was done.

"The next part is the hardest to say." She took a deep breath. Quent found it hard to breathe at all.

"You can't be unaware of the way I've thrown myself at you. It seems every time we're alone and you start to touch me, I'm ready to do whatever you want. But of course, you're only teasing. You've made it adequately clear that once in my bed was quite enough."

She took him by surprise. He closed his eyes and tried to ignore the heat and hunger that suddenly raced through him. He'd never met anyone like Angel, whose softest words could inflict such passion and pain. He stood still, very still, and wondered at the thundering of his heart.

"It's hard to understand everything, Quent, when I know nothing. I see now how foolish it was of me to want to be a real wife when that's not what you're after. And so I make this promise to you. You don't have to bother with teasing or insults to turn me away. I will not pester you again."

With that she turned and, maneuvering uphill from the mare, lifted herself with graceful ease into the saddle. As she sat high above him, he felt the intensity of her gaze, but he knew that in the dusk she could not make out his expression, nor could she see the physical effects of her words.

He listened to the thud of the horse's hooves against the hard ground as she rode away. He listened until she was truly gone. And he kept himself rigid, forgetting who she was and why she was here, wanting her as he had never wanted a woman before. She spoke of fever, but how little she knew of her husband's body heat. His skin would sizzle under her touch.

When at last he did move, it was to pull off his boots and shed his clothes. The evening air did nothing to chill him nor lessen the hardness that his wife had aroused.

Under the baleful eye of Vengeance, he strode down the damp bank to the water's edge, then kept on walking, letting the waves lap against his legs, his thighs, the swelling evidence of desire. With a sharp intake of breath, he dove beneath the surface of the water, welcoming the cold and painful comfort that was offered by the bay.

Thirteen

Angel arose early the next morning to learn that Quent and Neill had gone to Dublin. Mrs. MacCabe offered no details about the journey except to say she had no idea when they would return.

It's best, she told herself. After all her boldness of the night before, she dreaded facing him in the light of day. So why did she feel such a sharp disappointment when she heard the news?

The housekeeper was even less communicative to Mary O'Callaghan when she came into the kitchen from the small room next to one of the larders.

"Did you sleep well?" asked Angel, concerned by the circles under the woman's eyes.

"I will," Mary said. "You've given me quarters better than home, Mrs. Kavanagh. Never you fear. I'm willing and ready to work." She bit at her lower lip. "Beggin' your pardon, ma'am, but you look none too fresh yourself on this fine day."

"Call me Angel, please. And don't worry. Like you, I'm willing and ready to work."

She offered Mary a helping of the warm bread and tea that were her daily breakfast, and they ate in silence under Mrs. MacCabe's watchful eye. Angel wore one of the work dresses she'd bought in town the day before, the necessary alterations having been completed during the night when she could not sleep. Within the quarter hour the two women were scrubbing away at the dining room walls. Without being asked, Mrs. MacCabe brought in buckets of clean water and offered the rags of old sheets to protect the wooden floor.

Angel hid a secret smile. The housekeeper must be warming to her. As further proof of her softening, she did little more than scowl when her new mistress asked about a ladder to reach the higher portions of the wall. She brought not only the ladder but a long-handled brush as well.

The women worked long and hard, not stopping until well past noon, when Mrs. MacCabe served a meal of potatoes and eggs—the eggs, Angel supposed, that had been destined for her cake.

The cake made her think of Quent. And of course, as she should have expected, Quent made her think of exactly what she had told him yesterday eve. How she had found the courage to go to him in such a brazen way, she would never know. She had certainly put his mind to rest, hadn't she? She had done it so well he departed as soon as he could.

With a wry smile directed to herself, she admitted she missed him. She seldom saw him, and when she did they always clashed. Yet she missed him. He wouldn't leave her mind. Ordering Mary to rest following the meal, she sought out Old Tully in the stable. He was brushing Brenda in one of the middle stalls. Lined up in the stalls in front of him were Solas and Josephine. Finding a curry comb in the tack room at the rear, she got to work on the mare.

"If you stay much longer, Mistress Angel, we'll be needing t' add another stable," Old Tully said, winking at her over Brenda's swayed back.

"Draw up the plans, then, for I'm staying the rest of my life."

He started to say something, then fell silent. Angel did not like the look on his face.

"Do you know something you're not telling?"

He looked at her with such innocence that she hastily added, "I meant about my husband and me."

"I'm a hired hand, lass. What would I know?"

Feigned innocence, she amended.

"Pshaw. My sister Raven said the upstairs maid knew she was expecting her son before even she was sure."

"Are you asking me if you're increasing?" He slapped a weathered cheek. "Saints above, listen t' me. Me mother would turn in her grave to think I would ask such a thing."

Angel smiled. "You know I meant nothing like that."

Besides, she could have added, a wife had to share the greatest of intimacies with her husband before she could bear his child.

She concentrated on the mare's white mane, letting the animal learn her scent and her touch.

"Did you hear about the night riders?" Old Tully asked. "The lad who delivered the groceries from town was full o' the news."

"I didn't hear. After the War between the States, we used to have night riders around Savannah." She shuddered. "It was an ugly time. I was a little girl, but I knew."

"They're no better over here, I can tell you. Burned down a small barn at one of the farms, and tore up some fields as they went galloping through."

"Why? Were they trying to ruin someone?"

"There seems no pattern t' the destruction. Nor a reason, except to stir up trouble. Ireland's ripe for such as that, what with demands for independence from England and hard times on the farms. Most of us are Catholic, you ken, and there's few outside of the fishermen who're more than tenant farmers."

"Cordangan seemed so peaceful yesterday. A few gossips, of course, but theirs was a minor harm."

"Peaceful aye, until the ride home. You're not forgetting that."

"No," she said softly, but the threat of harm wasn't what

she remembered. Instead, she thought of how Quent had thundered to her rescue. Old Tully's rescue, her inner voice corrected, and she admitted such was the truth.

"We've good folk here and good land," the stableman continued, "and there's no place on God's green earth more beautiful. But there's evil, too. Saint Patrick drove the snakes from the island, sure enough, but no one can drive the darkness from men's souls."

"All men?" she asked, thinking of only one.

"Arrah, not all. Some are good and some are bad, and most are a bit o' both. Same as with women. 'Tis a curse that the bad seems more powerful at times."

Angel stroked the mare's forehead. When Solas dipped her head for more, she saw her reflection in the animal's soft brown eyes. "And where does Quent fit in?" she asked.

Solas blocked her view of Old Tully, but she could sense his hesitation.

"Do ye truly care, lass?"

"I care." She spoke the truth, but it brought no lightness to her heart. How much she cared was not for speculation, not now. She simply wanted to understand.

"He had a kitten once, when he was a wee lad. The pitiful creature fell under the wheel of a tradesman's cart and Master Quent would not eat for days. He was a stubborn rascal, even then. I took it upon meself to get another animal, but he would have nothing t' do with it."

"He told me he didn't want a pet."

"Sometimes 'tis best to look at what a man does and not at what he says. He treats the stallion with great kindness. A better fed horse you're not likely to find from here to Galway."

"Why are you telling me this?"

"I'm a foolish old sod, that's why, and I ramble on more'n I should. Now be gone with you. I've got that flea-bitten Josephine to deal with. And I thought I wanted work to fill my days."

He spoke gruffly, but Angel caught the spirit in his deep, rough voice. As she made her way to the back door of the castle, she thought about what he had said. People were good and people were bad, with mixtures of both. And Quent had a feeling for animals, no matter how gruffly he denied it. To her mind, that put him on the side of the good.

She found Mrs. MacCabe in the kitchen scouring a cast-iron pot. The tea kettle had been kept warm; she helped herself to a cup and settled uninvited into a ladder-back chair by the big wooden table in the center of the room.

"We've scarcely spoken since I got here," she said.

She got no response.

She looked at the grate over the hearth and the bank of ovens to her right, then the copper pans hanging on the opposite wall. Last, she looked straight ahead to the tall, strong back of the housekeeper bent to her work.

"This is such a quiet house compared to my home. Three girls. You can imagine the giggles and the singing and the chatter. Has Cordangan Castle always been like this? I scarcely hear a human sound."

Again, no response.

Angel sighed. "Please help me, Mrs. MacCabe. You've known my husband longer than just about anyone. If you won't tell me about him, who will? He doesn't seem inclined to reveal anything personal."

Mrs. MacCabe made no reply for a while, and Angel thought she was going to have to leave, that or throw herself bodily on the woman to get her attention.

But at last she did speak.

"These halls have always known silence," she said, dropping the scouring brush and staring into space, as if she could see the past. "Except for the fights, of course. The arguments between Master Dermot and his wife, and later between him and the boy. He drank, you ken."

As if that explained everything. Why did he drink? Why

fight his wife and child? Angel feared the questions would bring this fragile moment to an end.

"He was much older than Morna, married her when he was near fifty and she still a young woman. I'd known her since we were tykes. We'd been through the famine together, when we knew such hunger our skin hung on our bones and we could barely stand. But we survived, that and more."

"Papa said more than a million people died, and a million more fled to other countries," Angel said, wondering if she erred by mentioning her father.

The housekeeper gave no sign her thoughts were anywhere but on the sad, distant past. "With all the suffering going on, there were those believing the dead were the lucky ones. Considering some of the ugliness that followed, I'm not so sure they weren't right."

There was such pain in her voice, Angel teared in sympathy.

"I married," Mrs. MacCabe went on, stronger, "but my husband succumbed to a fever, and Morna brought me here to . . . well, to tend to matters. I came willingly. And then Master Quent was born, a lusty lad from the start, quick to laugh and to question and to get into scrapes. Neither mother nor father knew what t' do with him, and his care fell to me."

Her voice turned inward at the end, and Angel had to strain to hear.

"He changed as he grew to boyhood, and more when he became a man. There was little I could do."

Her pain flattened to helplessness. She turned, her rough red hands rubbing against her apron, her brown eyes not quite so stern as they had been the times before when she looked at Angel. Even the deep lines of her face softened.

"He grew up lonely and he grew up hard, letting few get close to him. He believes with all his heart that he needs no one, and perhaps he's right."

"Do you really believe that?"

"A better question would be, do you?"

Angel considered her answer with great care. She wanted to be honest, but there were so many things about her husband she could only guess.

"I was brought up to believe in the necessity of love, and its power, too, for all humans. I know that Quentin Kavanagh is no devil as the people believe, and so that makes him very human. But he's also like no one else I've ever met. Does he need love? I want to believe the answer is yes."

"He loves this land. He could have left it long ago, but he chose to stay. That's why when he's restless at night he roams about on that wild stallion of his, with only the stars as witness to the ride."

"Does he always go in solitude?"

"Always. Neill Connolly has been as close a friend to him as . . . almost anyone, but he's never ventured out with the master at night." An expression of tenderness further softened the housekeeper's face. "And he loves this drafty old castle, make no mistake about that. I'm not certain he realizes how much."

"Then why has he let it go? Why are all those lovely possessions locked away?"

"Did he not tell you?"

"He said something about his mother putting them there, and then his father. He finished up the storage himself, although he did not seem proud of the fact. Why? Why did any of them engage in such a pursuit?"

"That's something you'll have to work out for yourself."

"He indicated I could do with them what I wished."

"Did he now?" said the woman in obvious surprise. "I thought your coming here was wrong, but now—" She broke off, but she stared long and hard at Angel, as if she would see into her soul. "You've a great responsibility on your young shoulders. See that you do not make a mistake."

She returned to the scouring, leaving her warning hang-

We've got your authors!

KENSINGTON CHOICE is the only club where you can find authors like Janelle Taylor, Shannon Drake, Rosanne Bittner, Penelope Neri and Phoebe Conn all in one place…

…and the only service that will deliver their romances direct to your home as soon as they are published—even before they reach the bookstores.

KENSINGTON CHOICE is also the only service that will give you a substantial guaranteed discount off the publisher's prices on every one of those romances.

That's right: Every month, the Editors at Zebra and Pinnacle select four of the newest novels by our bestselling authors and rush them straight to you, usually *before they reach the bookstores*. The publisher's prices for these romances range from $4.99 to $5.99—but they are always yours for the guaranteed low price of just $4.20, up to 30% off the publisher's price!

All books are sent on a 10-day free examination basis, and there is no minimum number of books to buy. (A postage and handling charge of $1.50 is added to each shipment.)

As your introduction to the convenience and value of KENSINGTON CHOICE, we invite you to accept

4 BOOKS FREE

The 4 books, worth up to $23.96, are our welcoming gift. You pay only $1 to help cover postage and handling.

Plus as a regular subscriber….you'll receive our free monthly newsletter, Zebra/Pinnacle Romance News which features author interviews, contests, and more!

To start your subscription to KENSINGTON CHOICE and receive your introductory package of 4 FREE romances, detach and mail the card at right *today*.

We have 4 FREE BOOKS for you
as your introduction to
KENSINGTON CHOICE
To get your FREE BOOKS, worth
up to $23.96, mail the card below.

FREE BOOK CERTIFICATE

As my introduction to your new KENSINGTON CHOICE reader's service, please send me 4 FREE historical romances (worth up to $23.96), billing me just $1 to help cover postage and handling. As a KENSINGTON CHOICE subscriber, I will then receive 4 brand-new romances to preview each month for 10 days FREE. I can return any books I decide not to keep and owe nothing. The publisher's prices for the KENSINGTON CHOICE romances range from $4.99 to $5.99, but as a subscriber I will be entitled to get them for just $4.20 per book or $16.80 for all four titles. There is no minimum number of books to buy, and I can cancel my subscription at any time. A $1.50 postage and handling charge is added to each shipment.

Name _____

Address _____ Apt._____

City_____ State_____ Zip_____

Telephone (____) _____

Signature _____

(If under 18, parent or guardian must sign)

Subscription subject to acceptance. Terms and prices subject to change.

KP1195

We have
4
FREE
Historical
Romances
for you!

(worth up
to $23.96!)

Details inside!

ing in the air and Angel gripping a cup of tea gone cold. It was clear their talk was at an end.

Pushing away from the table, Angel went to find Mary and renew their assault on the dining room. She moved slowly, and she worked slowly, much on her mind. *Do not make a mistake.* The words echoed in her thoughts. Her worst fear was that they came too late. She had already made so many. She had even driven her husband away from his home, the one place in all the world that he loved.

Over the next few days she and Mary, aided by Mrs. MacCabe, finished the cleaning of the dining room.

"What it needs is a coat of paint," said Mary as she eyed the result of their work.

Angel agreed. "A lighter shade, to balance the dark furniture and the red."

"The red?" Mrs. MacCabe asked.

"It's something I've been thinking of."

She glanced up at the fancy plasterwork in the ceiling, some of which had been damaged through the years. It fanned out in potential splendor from the points where a pair of chandeliers had once been attached.

"That's so beautiful," she said. "It's a shame it can't be repaired. Is it original with the castle?"

The housekeeper shook her head. "That and the other work like it were done at the beginning of the seventeenth century. 'Tis likely the stuccodores are long gone."

It took Angel a moment to realize the usually dour woman was making a joke.

"And in all that time no one else has taken up the craft?"

"Not that I've heard," piped up Mary, "not in these parts." Mrs. MacCabe agreed.

"Well," said Angel, giving in with great reluctance, "I guess we'll have to settle for a coat of paint. Still and all, it seems a shame."

Mrs. MacCabe left, only to return shortly with the news that Mistress Angel had a caller.

"Who?" asked Angel dumbfounded. A look of wariness settled on Mary's face.

"A villager," the housekeeper replied. "She's got some packages for you."

Angel smiled. "It's the dressmaker Nellie Ahearne, I'll bet. With the clothing I ordered."

She hurried through the adjoining drawing room, then down the front stairs to meet her visitor, regretting that she had no place to welcome the woman, nothing clean and open and bright. After a few words of greeting, they ended up in Angel's bedroom, where Nellie could fit the dresses to her and make a last-minute alteration or two.

When all was put away, including the petticoat ruffled in Cordangan lace, they settled on the bed to sip the tea Mrs. MacCabe served. Angel complimented Nellie's work and that of the women who had tatted the lace, and Nellie responded that the castle didn't seem nearly so frightening from the inside.

"It needs so much attention," said Angel with a sigh. "Attention and care."

"Like a man."

Like Quentin Kavanagh, she might have said, thought Angel, knowing the dressmaker wished to discuss the mysterious owner of this equally mysterious castle on the hill.

"Consider this room for instance," she said, ignoring Nellie's watchful eye. "It needs a new coverlet for the bed, and curtains, and cushions for the window seats. All that just to begin with."

Nellie eyed the room with professional care. "There are those who could do the work for you, and you not having to go all the way to Cork or Dublin for the finest to be had."

"You make it sound so possible."

"We're no different from the folk where you were born.

We're willing enough to work, where there's money to be made."

Angel thought of the delicate craftsmanship on her new petticoat. She pictured the same fine touch put to her new home. And she felt a tingle of excitement inside. Mama always said that like birds, women wanted to fancy their nests. As in other matters, Mama was right.

Forgetting the tea, the women fell to discussing the possibilities for the room. Before Angel knew it—and before she could consider the wisdom of the plan—Nellie announced that early the next morning she would bring a couple of seamstresses to the castle, along with swatches of cloth that might serve as coverlets and curtains.

She even asked if Angel would like to consider refurbishing the master bedroom as well as her own quarters.

"No," Angel said so quickly, so forcefully Nellie's eyebrows raised to her hairline. Angel blushed. Refurbish Quent's room? Impossible, since she had not once seen where he slept.

True to her word, Nellie showed up with the seamstresses shortly after breakfast. The newcomers said nary a word—frightened into silence, Angel decided, as much by the condition of the castle as by the scowl in Mrs. MacCabe's eye. But they looked and they nodded to one another, and she knew they were coming up with ideas.

The following day Nellie put the ideas to her, wonderful suggestions that made Angel see the potential of her home. During the next two weeks she threw herself into her chosen tasks, marking off items on her list of projects, adding more, feeling like a naughty child at first, then later with a trace of confidence telling herself she was nothing less than the considerate mistress of a long-neglected house.

And Quent had told her she could do what she wanted. With much effort she managed to ignore what he might say if he knew all that she did. She managed to forget, that is, until each evening when the workers she had hired went back down the winding road to their homes. Falling exhausted into bed, she stared into the dark and thought about Quent. Would he never return? Was he sleeping each night in the arms of someone else? Someone *not* a Chadwick?

And why, oh why, oh why, she asked herself on each of these nights, did she care so much about what he did, or if he would ever return?

Three weeks and four days after leaving, Quent returned in the new trap he had bought in Cork City. Stepping smartly in the traces was a blood bay gelding, Lorcan by name. Vengeance trailed, his proud head bobbing in obvious impatience at being tied to the rear.

"For your bride?" Neill had asked concerning the purchase.

Quent had denied it, in a voice that was perhaps more forceful than needed. He had been thinking a long while about such a conveyance. He'd found a good buy, that was all.

He had departed the castle with one strict order for Mrs. MacCabe—to let him know if he had a visitor from the States—but she had not written. The impatience he felt as he rode up the final hill came from Thomas Chadwick's absence, he told himself. There was no one else he wanted to see.

He ought to go to the island—and he would, soon after he saw his wife. Not that he'd missed her. But he had invested time and effort into getting her here; for that reason alone, he wanted to make sure she was still around.

Neill rode on ahead, claiming he wanted to check some figures they had left in the library, but Quent wasn't fooled. Mary O'Callaghan's figure was the one on his assistant's mind.

By heaven, Quent thought, he would burn in hell before he yearned for a woman like that.

As soon as he rode past the snarling stone dogs, he knew something was different. It took him a moment to decide just what. The weeds were gone from the front grounds, and the grass trimmed, and a pair of saplings flanked the steps leading to the castle door. Hedges, too, lined the castle front from right to left. The place looked almost respectable. Quent did not care for the change.

He found Old Tully outside the stable hitching a pair of mules to an old wooden cart.

"Saints above," the old man said with a start of guilt as Quent stepped out of the trap.

"What the devil——" he began, and then he looked past Old Tully, past the stable, to the flat, bare ground that had held a water trough three weeks ago when he left. The trough was gone, in its place a wire pen enclosing a dozen chickens clucking and pecking at the ground.

He strode to the pen and stared on beyond to the once open grazing field that was now plowed into neat furrows. He walked around the pen, stopping at the edge of the field. It was clear the mounds were freshly sown, with crops he could probably name. His wife had planted a vegetable garden. She had probably brought in a milch cow or two, as well. He had been gone less than a month, and she had turned his castle into a goddamned farm.

Behind him, a door opened and closed, and he heard the sound of women's laughter. He turned to see three of the creatures, in the simple clothes of workers, helping one another into the mule-driven cart. He couldn't make out their words, nor did he recognize any of them, but he knew them for women from the town. Pious women not too old to have been the tormentors of his youth.

Cold fury sliced through him. The first one in the cart spied him. She fell silent, and the others did the same. Reins in hand, she cracked the whip over the flanks of the mules, and the cart creaked around the side of the castle and was gone.

Yanking at his tether, Vengeance neighed in distress. For the first time since buying the stallion, Quent did not see to his care, nor did he glance at the equally fretful Lorcan. Instead, he strode past the guilt-faced stableman, stomping through the back door and into the kitchen.

Mrs. MacCabe stood by the stove. "Master Quent—"

"Where is she?"

"In her room." She spoke flatly, with none of Old Tully's guilt on her face.

Throwing his hat and gloves onto the kitchen table, Quent took the back stairs two at a time. He found his wife on the far side of the room sitting at a high, wide desk he had never seen before. As the door crashed open, she dropped her pen and shifted to face him. Her smile came and went so quickly he scarcely took note.

He held himself still, legs apart, hands fisted at his side, wanting to hit her, furious that he could not bring himself to do so. Instead, he glanced around the room at the freshly painted walls, the flowered curtains and bed covering, the embroidered pillows and wall hangings, the fresh flowers on the desk. She'd brought spring into this room. His mother's room. Morna, who had never noticed the passing seasons, nor the passing years.

He had put Angel here so that she might feel the oppression that had been his mother's legacy, might sense the darkness, the realization that all hope had fled. Instead of cowering, she had erased the darkness. She had replaced it with light.

"What in hell do you think you're doing?" he asked.

Her lips parted, but she did not speak and all color fled from her cheeks. She looked small and helpless, her hair falling in soft curls against her shoulders. Too, she looked as lovely as he remembered her, and he hated her for it.

She attempted a smile. "I wanted to look better for you when you returned," she said, her hands fluttering around her plain gray dress.

He strode around the bed and pulled her to her feet. She felt even smaller and more defenseless than she had appeared, yet firm and warm beneath his grip. He shook her. A lock of hair fell across her cheek.

She looked good enough, he thought. Too good by far.

He pulled her close, liking the sense of her helplessness beneath his hands, liking the pinpoints of fear in the depths of her eyes. He wanted . . . heaven help him, he wanted her, and all his rage could not obliterate that fact.

He let her go. "It's beyond you to stay out of trouble, isn't it, wife? You force me to do something to you. Something you will never forget."

Fourteen

Angel swayed in front of Quent, trying to say something in her own defense, but she could make no sound other than a ragged sigh. Her head still reeled from the way he'd burst into her room, looking like nothing so much as a brigand, his hair wild, his cheeks flushed, an untamed light in his eyes . . . ready to take everything she had.

Her husband had most definitely come home.

Other men might knock, might enter with gifts, a *hello, how are you?*, a peck on the cheek. Not Quent. He'd arrived with challenges and accusations and the same hard stare that set her heart pounding so fast, so furiously that she forgot the letter she was writing, forgot the tasks still on her list, forgot all the world except him.

Twisted soul that she was, she preferred the man she had to all those tamer men.

"I asked what you're up to," he said, standing close, but not quite close enough. "Have you no answer for me? No gentle admonition that might unman me?"

She watched the words form on his lips. His mouth was strong, as was his chin, and she studied the beginnings of a moustache he would probably shave before long. Such inconsequential thoughts, she told herself, but they would not quite leave her mind.

"You told me I could do what I wanted," she managed at last.

"You were scrubbing dining walls at the time."

He backed away long enough to remove his coat and toss it on the bed. "I meant other walls in other rooms, some of them hung, if you must, with a picture or two."

His partially unbuttoned shirt revealed a neck as muscled as all the other parts of him she so well remembered, and a patch of black hairs curled beckoningly at his throat. Everything about Quent was so different from everything about her, yet he did not make her feel small and insignificant. He made her proud of all the differences.

He held her once again, stroking her hair, massaging her shoulders, circling his palms against her tense body. When he eased beneath her fall of hair and traced the flesh above her neckline, she shivered under his touch.

"Afraid, Angel? You ought to be."

Afraid? Oh yes, of him and of her and his anger and the ripples of excitement shooting through her when she ought to be terrified. She closed her eyes lest he read too much in their depths.

His hands encircled her neck and his thumbs rested at her throat. "Your pulse is pounding. I could make it stop."

Her gaze flew to his. "Can't you just lo—"

She started to say *love me,* although the words took her as much by surprise as they would have him.

"—let me alone?" she asked instead. "I'll stop whatever it is I'm doing wrong."

His lips twisted into a smile. She could not look away from his lips.

"You ask what I cannot do. Besides, you never seem to know what wrong is. I married a woman in need of constant instruction."

He made the word sound ripe with meaning. Pushing her against the desk, he held his hips hard against hers. "Before I left, what was it that you promised?"

"Not to . . . pester you."

"Ah yes, pester." His hips shifted and she could feel his

arousal pressed against her belly. "I did not, in turn, promise not to pester you."

Gripping her waist, he seated her on the edge of the desk, then wedged himself between her thighs. She had no will to fight him, not with his eyes burning into hers and his breath warm on her cheek and his lips the most enticing lips she had ever seen in her life.

She wanted him tender, she wanted him gentle, but she could not, she knew, have everything. He meant to punish her with his touch, but he set up such a pounding inside her and a heat and a tightness that she told herself she must take whatever he gave.

For he would not hurt her. She knew it as well as she knew anything.

He cupped one of her breasts. In an instant her nipples hardened and thrust against the layers of soft fabric that covered her. Surely he could feel the firm tips, especially when his thumb kept doing such wonderful things.

Deft fingers unbuttoned the front of her gown and her chemise, freeing her breasts to his hands, to his thumbs, and when he bent his head, to his lips. He licked where he had stroked. Without shame, she arched her back and lifted herself to him, her greatest fear that he might see her pleasure and cease his assault. He wanted to punish her. Let him think that he was.

He kissed each breast, then slipped gradually, teasingly to her throat and to the corners of her mouth. His lips moved slowly against hers, back and forth, their delicate friction sparking flames of desire in places far away from her lips. His tongue touched her and her mouth opened to him. She lost herself in his kiss.

So lost was she that only belatedly did she realize he was pulling her skirt above her knees. Working throughout the day, she'd worn no hampering petticoat, and he found only the slippery softness of her underdrawers.

Her damp underdrawers, she suddenly realized. She was truly without shame.

She held tight to his shirt sleeves for support, pressing her bared breasts against the rough fabric, letting a thousand sensations race through her as he traced the contours of her eager inner thighs. As deftly as he had bared her breasts, he found the slit in her underclothing, found her most intimate place, and with a low moan she took to be a sign of his pleasure, he continued his attack.

Opening her legs wider, Angel wrapped her arms around his neck and held on for dear life. She didn't care that she wasn't supposed to like this. He must like it, too, else why would he persist with such electric thoroughness?

In truth, she wanted it as she had never wanted anything before. The tremors she remembered from her wedding night came at her again, only this time they were all the more thrilling because she knew where they led. She felt hot and hungry and wanting and impatient and excited and a thousand other racing emotions all at once.

Mostly she felt good. The goodness built. She thrust herself against his slick fingers, gasping when he slipped one finger inside her. She licked the firm, sinewed side of his neck, sucking at the salty warmth of his skin. The peak of pleasure struck her with tremendous force. She embraced him until the tremors passed. It took a long, long time.

He moved his hand from between her legs and rested it on her thigh beneath her gown. Neither spoke. As glorious as this moment had been, she knew it was not enough. Quent needed release as much as she had needed it. She wanted to give it to him. No, she had to feel him inside her where a husband ought to be. She wanted to lie beneath him in bed, to curl against his naked heat. She wanted so many things she couldn't, in her ignorance, put a name to. But Quent would know.

"Quent," she whispered against the curve of his shoulder, holding him tight, letting him understand she knew they were not done. He shifted her closer, his body wedged more firmly between her parted legs, his arousal solid against her thigh.

He was hot and yielding in her arms, his body melting into hers as much as she melted into him, his hands curved in gentle supplication to all her contours, and she knew that any minute he would carry her to the bed to finish what he had begun.

And then he changed, gradually, his body and his hands no longer quite so yielding, everything about him slowly stiffening until it seemed she did not embrace the same man. A single shudder went through him, not of release, but of something far different, something that chilled her heart. He continued to hold her, but it wasn't the same. It wasn't . . . good.

It was as though he willed himself not to want her. She swallowed a protest, knowing she was losing him, although how or why she had no notion. She fought against clinging to him, for that would be a mistake. Not for long could she hold him if he wanted to get away.

He gave no argument when she pulled back and looked into his eyes, hard, storm-blue and scornful. She recoiled, stunned and hurt, but he did not soften his stare.

"I keep forgetting who you are," he said, and then he looked past her to the papers strewn across her desk . . . the open letters she had received from home, the letter she was writing in return.

She slipped sideways to stand beside him, smoothing her skirt and buttoning the front of her gown, embarrassed at her nakedness. And she followed his gaze to the envelope she had already addressed . . . to the name on the envelope: THOMAS CHADWICK. It must have leapt at him from the paper while he held her in his arms.

He grabbed up the letter she had been writing, scanned it quickly, and then he looked at her.

"Do you truly believe that all is well in our little love nest?"

She reached out for the paper, trying too late for some semblance of pride. "That's meant for my father's eyes."

"But I am your husband, Angel. You have no secrets from me."

Her hand fell, and she hugged herself, too well aware that he was right. She might think sometimes that she could keep her actions private, but always he found her out.

He glanced across the desk, saw other letters, hurriedly inspected them. They came from Texas, from England, from Georgia. All rejoiced in Angel's good fortune.

"You've been busy," he said. "Do they know their precious Angel lies?"

"Papa was sick for a while," she said, holding her ground, feeling her own sickness inside. "I could not write the truth. Besides, I keep hoping—" She looked away and her eyes filled with tears. "I keep being wrong."

Quent did not respond right away, but when he did, his voice was sharp and hard, like the edge of a knife.

"I lost my rage, Angel Chadwick. I lost sight of what I had to do. It will not happen again."

"Kavanagh," she said, baring all her anguish in her voice. "I'm Angel Kavanagh now." He gave no sign he heard.

"My mistake was keeping you in ignorance. It's time you learned the truth." He took her by the wrist and started for the door. She felt weightless behind him, and she made no attempt to fight.

"Prepare for the worst, wife," he said as he strode down the corridor toward the back stairs. "We're going for a ride."

They rode double on Vengeance, Angel seated in front of Quent, her bottom bouncing against his hard thighs as he whipped the stallion into a frantic gallop. They rode from the castle, through the trees, Quent reining with unerring accuracy through the denseness to the twisted path that led to the edge of Bantry Bay.

He barely slowed for the descent, and she knew he had made this journey a thousand times. But not, she thought, with so much urgency, or so much rage.

Bounding from the horse, he took her with him, dragging her across the damp bank to a small boat chained to one of the trees. When the chain was loosened, he gestured for her to climb in. She did so awkwardly, paying scarce attention to the puddle of water in the bottom of the boat. He shoved the boat from shore, then hopped in, using one of the oars to propel them from land into the choppy waters of the bay.

She gripped the sides to keep her balance, her eyes on Quent as she skimmed backwards through the waves. He stared past her in unrelenting concentration, his muscled arms working the oars, his powerful legs spread wide.

The late afternoon sun rested at the horizon high behind him, dropping a golden light upon the turrets of the castle. For the first time she saw its role as fortress for its Norman builders. One of the Micks had told her Cordangan meant fortified hill, but until now she had forgotten.

After three hundred years Cordangan Castle still served as a fortress, protecting its owner from all who would invade his privacy.

Until he had married. It must have been a great surrender for him. This evening she would find out why he had made the sacrifice. Her heart raced in anticipation, and this time she knew a real fear. Nothing that she was to learn could come to any good.

The landing was bumpy. Quent jumped into the shallow water and pulled the boat onto the rocky shore. He made no offer to help her, and she managed under her own shaky power to disembark.

He struck out on a path only he could see. More than

once from her bedroom window she had noticed a ribbon of smoke curling from the thickness of the island forest; she had taken the smoke as sign of a lodging of some sort. Nothing had prepared her for the quaint, thatch-roofed cottage in the clearing where he took her.

It seemed out of a fairy tale, with its freshly painted white walls and green shutters, and flower bed across the front.

Quent whirled to face her, and she brought herself up short, out of breath, her gray dress torn from the branches that choked the path leading from the water. Her hair tangled and her face doubtlessly flushed, she must look like the emotional wreck she was.

Not so her husband. He stood like one of the Bantry Bay rocks, cold and unmoving, his expression unreadable as he stared at her across the clearing. With the afternoon light falling against the hard planes of his face, he was no longer the man who had embraced her in her bedroom, who had brought her such sweet joy. He was a stranger. He was someone she did not like.

"I want to tell you a story before we enter. So that you will understand exactly what you see."

Angel held herself motionless, barely able to breathe.

"Long before I was born, in the days of her youth and her innocence and her poverty, my mother was courted by a traveling man. Promising much, he gave her only sweet words. By force he took her virtue one night in a cave, while the storms raged around them, and in the morning she found he was gone. She returned home, keeping her defilement a secret. Until her belly grew and she could keep her secret no more."

Angel could hear the pain in his voice; he could not keep it from his words. But she knew he would accept no solace from her, no word of sympathy. Looking past him, she saw a face at one of the front windows, but the face disappeared before she could make out any details, and she returned her attention to her husband, unable to consider exactly what he had meant by *traveling man* or what he had yet to reveal.

"It was during the famine," Quent went on. "Everyone suffered, and in their suffering they turned on others. Morna O'Brien was abandoned by her family, and the good Catholic people of Cordangan called her a slattern and a whore."

The last words hung in the air. Feeling her husband's hurt, Angel brushed a tear from her eye.

"One childhood friend, a recent widow, stood by her side, but she was poor as well and could do little good except provide shelter and an occasional cup of broth."

Angel knew he spoke of Doreen MacCabe. Her heart went out to the woman, as much as it did to Quent.

But she kept herself very still, knowing he meant for her to suffer his same pain, her entire being denying the implications of what he said. This tale was tragic, but it had no special meaning for her. It couldn't . . . it couldn't.

"She sought refuge in the church. A priest as ancient as the Cordangan hills labeled her evil, and she believed he spoke the truth. After all, she had been taught from birth that priests did not lie. An evil woman must by nature bear an evil child, or so he proclaimed to all who listened. She sought to kill the infant before his time."

He fell silent for a moment. In the thickening shadows that surrounded them she heard nothing but the rustle of the leaves. And she heard her own frightened, ragged breath.

"She used a stick to mutilate herself." Quent's words were hard and brusque, but otherwise without emotion.

Angel cried out, then pressed a hand to her mouth to still another cry, but she could not stop the tears that stained her cheeks. Nor could she picture what her husband described. The despair that had led Morna O'Brien to such a violent act was beyond all her imagination.

Quent's mother. Angel thought of her own precious, gentle Mama, who had known trouble but nothing like this.

How could anyone suffer so, either parent or child, and not become filled with hate?

The silence between her and her husband lengthened, and for the first time she saw he had difficulty in telling his tale.

"Her attempts to abort the baby failed. He came early. He came out wrong."

"Wrong?"

"Aye. Different. And the good people of Cordangan fell on the innocent babe as they had the mother. Called him evil, and proof that the mother was tainted. The old priest died and another took his place, a more compassionate man, but the damage had been done. The child knew nothing but taunts and condemnation from his earliest years. It was both his blessing and his curse that he did not always understand.

"When the recluse Dermot Kavanagh offered marriage if she would bear him an heir, she had no choice but to agree. She was still beautiful, despite all that had gone before, and as separate from the world as he. But high in her castle prison, she never forgot what had happened to her. Nor was anyone around her allowed to forget."

Having said so much, he fell silent. She needed to hear more, but when he turned to open the cottage door, she knew his discourse was at an end.

He motioned for her to enter. She knew that once she did so, her life would never be the same. Calling herself coward, she led the way inside. The interior had a warm and cozy feel to it, but nothing could remove the chill that had settled around her heart.

A woman stood to the side, short and round and gray, old as Old Tully with the same kindly look to her eyes. Quent made no introductions. Instead, he directed Angel through the small parlor, past the kitchen with its table already laid for supper, and into a grassy garden at the rear.

She didn't see anyone at first. It was the sound of metal against stone that drew her attention to the figure of a man at the forest's edge a dozen yards away. He sat cross-legged, his attention directed to his work. Like a beam from heaven, a glow of late sunlight flooded him. On the ground nearby were a half dozen small stone carvings, none more than a foot in height, most smaller by far.

They were birds, she saw, intricately formed from stone, much like the unfinished sculpture he was laboring over. She had never seen anyone work with such concentration, unaware that anyone was close.

Quent knelt beside him. "Good work," he said, and at last the man looked up at him and smiled.

"Yes," he answered. "It's good."

The man was slight of build, and dark, his straight hair falling to his shoulders. This was all she could make out, turned as he was.

"I brought a visitor," Quent said.

"A visitor?"

"Aye. Someone you need to meet."

"A friend."

Quent did not answer yea or nay. Both stood. They were close to the same height, but in his slightness the stone carver seemed more tentative, Angel thought. Suspicions flew at her, and fears, but she could scarcely give credence to them, so wildly was her heart beating.

"He goes by the unchristened name of Chadwick O'Brien," Quent said to her. "We call him Chad."

Angel could not swallow, could not breathe. All the forest fell silent, in fear of the moment.

"He's your brother, Angel, as surely as he is mine."

She stepped forward, barely aware she was reaching out, looking at the smiling face that turned to her.

"Will you be my friend?" asked the man named Chadwick O'Brien.

She nodded, taking in the round features, the brown eyes, the crooked grin. Looking at Chad was like staring at her Papa as he might have been twenty years ago.

Fifteen

Quent watched in silence as his wife met her brother for the first time. The tears in her eyes seemed genuine enough, so too the wonder and the surprise. She gave no sign she questioned anything he had said. Of course she wouldn't. He had known from early on that Angel was smart. Misguided and weak, for sure, but smart.

She stepped forward to take Chad's hand. "Hello," she said softly. "My name is Angel."

Chad grinned. "Like in heaven?"

She nodded, and Quent saw something else in her eyes, something that made his skin crawl. She saw the way her brother was wrong. Chad was a grown man, slight but otherwise physically fit—a man with the mind of a child. And she pitied him for it.

Chad didn't need her pity. He didn't need her any more than did Quent.

Disgust and disappointment vied for control of him. "Get in the house, Angel," he ordered.

Both Angel and Chad looked at him in surprise.

"I like her, Quentin," said Chad. "She's pretty."

"Of course she is. But it's cool out here and she has no wrap. You wouldn't want her to catch a chill, would you?"

"I could give her my shirt."

"Oh," said Angel, the word almost a cry. Some more of her pity, Quent thought. His sideways glance told her how he felt.

She lifted her chin as if she would defy him. But he kept on staring, informing her with his eyes that now was not the time for argument, and at last she looked away.

"I'll be back again," she said, then kissed her brother quickly on the cheek before doing as Quent had bade. The silence was deep around the two men after she was gone.

Chad touched his face where Angel had kissed him. "She's nice, too."

"Oh, yes. She's certainly that."

"You've never brought a friend with you before."

"I . . . wanted you two to meet."

Quent's conscience bit him. He had used his brother to upset his wife. But Angel had to know. She had to understand. Now that she knew, he would keep her away.

And what about his plans for confronting Thomas Chadwick with his bastard son? What if he showed revulsion stronger than his daughter's pity? The plans would have to be amended. He would not hurt his brother for all the world. He would kill anyone who did.

Still, he wanted the son of a bitch on Irish soil. And he would get him here, too . . . through his wife.

"Are you mad at me?"

Quent started, then smiled at Chad, and for a moment anger melted from him. "Of course not. I was thinking of something else."

"You've been gone a long time."

"I went to Dublin. Remember the map we put in your room?"

"I know where Dublin is," said Chad with an edge of impatience.

"Sorry. Of course you do. And you remember I have a store in Dublin where I do business. Sometimes I have to go there, even when I don't want to. But I always return."

"Can I go with you sometime? It gets awfully lonely out here with only Agnes."

"Maybe," said Quent, stalling his brother as he always

did. Chad lived on Calluragh Island because here was the
one place he could be safe. It was both his blessing and
his curse that he didn't remember the way of things the few
times he had ventured into town.

But that had been a long, long time ago. Chad was safer
by far where he was.

"Did someone hit you in Dublin?"

"No," said Quent, surprised. "Why do you ask?"

"You have a hurt." It was Chad's word for cuts and sores
and everything that seemed wrong to him.

Quent touched the side of his neck where his brother was
staring, and his gaze drifted to the window and to the shad-
owy figure of his wife as she stood inside the cottage. She
must have bruised him with all her licking and sucking.
Sweet little Angel marking him that way, like a woman from
the Dublin docks. Surprising Angel, spreading her legs for
him, clinging the way she had.

Memories tightened his loins. In her room, with his hands
on her, and her softness curling against him, he had slipped
into an insanity of desire, hungering to lose himself in her
sweet depths, forgetting how dangerous she could be. The
next time he taunted her, he would remember.

"The hurt is nothing," he said, turning to his brother,
willing his thoughts away from his wife. "What are you
working on?"

Chad picked up the half-finished bird, holding it out with
pride.

"Another gull. I wanted to get the wings just right, spread
out the way I see them over the water."

Quent's heart swelled with an equal pride. "It's perfect."
And it was, just as all the other carvings were as perfect
as his brother's tools and the hard stone allowed. It always
seemed to him a particular cruelty that Chad had such talent
in his hands and in his powers of observation, yet understood little in the world that was complicated, and could
read only the simplest words.

He took people as they came, never looking for hidden motives, never picking up on lies. He believed everything his brother told him; in turn, Quent told him the truth as often as he could. In the same trusting manner, he accepted Angel's friendliness without questioning its cause.

Always, thought Quent with a sense of self-disgust, in any situation of late his thoughts focused on his wife.

"Work on that gull for me, will you? I've got to leave now, but I'll be back." He shook Chad's hand. "That's a promise. And then I'll tell you about Dublin, and you can tell me about what you've been doing."

He turned to see Angel still watching him from the window . . . watching and listening and pitying.

Hurrying inside, he spoke briefly with Agnes O'Toole. A gentle, caring soul, she had taken care of Chad since the building of the cottage. He trusted her the way he trusted Neill and Mrs. MacCabe.

"Are you getting supplies all right?" he asked her.

"The lad rows out twice a week, regular as clockwork. We want for naught."

"Good. I'll be back in a few days." He glanced at Angel, who had not moved from the window. "Alone."

At that, her wife shifted her gaze to him. "I want to come with you."

Her eyes were wide and deep, darkened by concern to the color of sapphires. Quent held to his resolve. "Alone," he repeated.

"You can't bring me here like this and then shut me out."

"Oh but I can. And I will." Nodding goodbye to the obviously curious Agnes, he guided Angel from the cottage, down the overgrown path to the water, and into the boat. The sun had fallen, but Quent knew every step of the way. Among the stories about him were the ones that called him a creature of the night. The stories were not far wrong.

The return journey was much like the first, Quent rowing in silence, his wife balancing herself on the narrow facing seat. But she had lost her agitation, and she didn't look at him with her damnably expressive eyes. This time she stared out at the dark water, silvered by a rising moon, and he knew her thoughts were not on him.

Silent, too, was the ride on Vengeance back to the castle stable. She sat stiffly in front of him, the night wind stirring her hair. Good, he thought, let her hold herself straight-backed as best she could. He didn't need her softly cuddling against him, he didn't need her pliant, he didn't need her needing him in any way at all.

She was necessary for one thing only. And that one thing was revenge.

Sometimes the strands of her hair blew across his cheek. At those times he held tighter to the reins.

And once she stared at the bruise on his neck, the mark of her passionate kiss. She didn't stare for long.

Old Tully met them at the stable door. He looked from husband to wife and back again as the two dismounted.

"Master Quent, is the carriage ours?"

Quent nodded.

"And the gelding? Does he have a name?"

"Lorcan," Quent answered brusquely, wishing he had never purchased the trap.

"Little fierce one," said Old Tully, translating the Irish name. "He's that, all right. You made a good buy."

Quent followed Angel into the kitchen, stopping long enough to tell Mrs. MacCabe he would not be wanting supper.

"Will you be taking a tray in your room?" she asked Angel.

Angel stared at her vacantly, as if the question were too complicated for her to answer just now.

Quent left her to her thoughts, stopping in the library long enough to gather some papers he wanted to go over, then hurrying upstairs to his room. His bedroom was down the corridor from his wife's, but it might as well be a star-length away for all he intended to share it with her.

He built a fire against the night chill and settled into his chair, but the papers remained unread as he stared into the flames. With the lamp at his elbow remaining unlit, he thought about Chad and Angel and about Thomas Chadwick and he thought about what he had to do.

His thoughts lingered on Angel most of all, the stillness of her in the boat as they returned to shore . . . the stiffness as she sat on Vengeance . . . her hot, eager pliancy of the afternoon. A woman of contrasts, a constant surprise. After two months he did not understand her. He wondered how much she understood herself.

He must have dozed, for the opening of his door jerked him awake. The hour was late, after midnight, probably. Who the hell. . . .

He should have known. Settling back in his chair, eyes half closed, he watched his wife ease through the door and close it softly behind her. She was dressed for bed, in something filmy and white. The dying fire cast strange shadows across her slender figure as she came deeper into the room. Halting, watching, barely breathing, she kept her silence. With her long fair hair and ivory skin and her flowing white gown, she looked like an apparition hovering in the dim light.

But she wasn't. She was flesh and blood, and she was trouble. Trouble he didn't need.

"What are you doing here?"

She started. "I thought you were asleep." A tentative step brought her closer. "We have to talk . . . about Chad."

"You know all you need to know."

"But not all I want to know."

"Do you doubt who he is?"

"No. He looks just like Papa. When Papa had hair."

Her smile was half-hearted, almost sad. Quent hardened himself against its appeal.

"Your saintly Papa is not so much a saint after all, is he?"

She looked past him to the dying fire. "Don't ask me to judge. I can't."

"You've heard the facts."

"As you believe them."

"As they were told to me by the woman who bore us both. Who better to know the truth?"

Her dark-lashed eyes returned to him. "Would she approve of what you're doing now?"

"Oh, yes. She would approve."

"You sound very certain."

Quent hesitated, and then he told her something he had not intended to tell.

"She asked me on her deathbed to avenge the wrong done to her. I swore that I would, and so I shall."

"To put her soul to rest."

Quent did not respond. His wife understood too much.

"And yours as well," she said more softly.

Inwardly, he cursed. "Get out. I do not want you in here."

Instead of cowering, instead of fleeing, she looked around the shadowed room, at the dark canopied bed, the heavy wardrobe, the draperies drawn against the night. He asked himself what it would take to terrify her.

"You burst in on me," she said, "and I cannot visit you?"

"I make the rules. You are my wife."

"And we share a brother. Does that not seem strange to you?"

"It's not incestuous, if that is what you mean."

"I know, but still it's strange. Please, Quent, I'd like to talk about Chad."

"As in so many other things about our marriage, you're to be disappointed. I will not discuss him with you. He does not need your interest or your pity or any belated concern you might conjure up for him."

"I don't—" She broke off, then sighed, blinking twice as if she would hold back tears. She had a fine, subtle way of lifting her chin to show her bravery. Quent clutched the arms of his chair.

"It doesn't matter what I say, does it?" she went on. "You will believe what you want. At least tell me how old he is."

"Why? So you can compare his age with the way he acts?"

"It's a simple question. I just want to know how old he is."

Simple? Quent doubted it and with reluctance said, "Thirty-five."

"And you?"

"I forget sometimes how persistent you can be, usually to my regret. Our brother was five when I was born. Does that satisfy your curiosity? Are you drawing up a family tree?"

She held her ground against his sarcasm, as she so often did, taking a step forward instead of back. Her eyes moistened, their opalescence reflecting the fading light of the fire.

"I have a brother." She made it sound like the most wondrous thing in the world. "Raven and Flame have a brother. We had only sisters and never wanted for more. But all our lives we've—"

She seemed to search for words, ending simply with, "—we've had a brother."

Quent hated her tears and hated, too, the twist of strong emotion they set up around his heart. Rage and something far more primal surged through him. She had no right to be touched by Chad. She had not seen to his care, had not made sure he survived in a world determined to destroy him because of who and what he was.

She's done no wrong. He crushed the thought as ruthlessly as he crushed the feelings she aroused.

Rubbing at her arms, she came closer, all the way to the hearth. Poker in hand, she stirred the embers to flame, then tossed a pair of peat logs onto the fire. He felt the rising warmth.

She stood and turned to face him, the light at her back outlining her womanly figure beneath the filmy gown. He locked his gaze onto hers so that he would not look at what he should not want to see.

She was a woman and he was a man, but they were also enemies.

"He's not a freak, not a child that you can play with, Angel."

"I know that." She sounded angry. "You really don't think much of Chadwicks, do you?"

He let his silence serve as answer.

"Did your mother always feel the same way? She named her newborn baby after his father."

"His first name, since it could not be his last. Oh, she felt the same, all right." Even going so far as to reject that son . . . but Angel need not know everything.

He thought of his mother lying on her deathbed, her loveliness faded, her reason lost to bitterness. He was a long way from fifteen, but the anguish of the moment lingered still.

"How could she feel otherwise?" he said. "She had been raped. My mother raped by your father, raped and abandoned. Not a pretty picture, is it? But I didn't bring you over here to describe pretty pictures."

"I know you didn't," she said, her voice so low, so hesitant, he could barely hear her. "But I didn't realize—"

She stood looking at him for a moment, no more substantial than the smoke from the fire, and as real as the heat.

"I'm sorry, Quent," she said, but she made no attempt to explain what she was sorry for.

Was she pitying him as she had pitied Chad? Quent would not have it.

Suddenly it was all too much—Angel in his room in the darkest hour of night, wearing her vulnerability like a shield—or was it an enticement? Did she understand the effect she had on him?

He rose from the chair. "Why did you come in here half naked? What exactly did you want? A little tête-à-tête? A family conference? Or did you have something more personal in mind?"

"No," she said, wide-eyed. "I couldn't sleep—"

He walked toward her and she backed away. He liked having her on the run.

"Still trying to use sex to soften me? Tsk, tsk, Angel. You ought to know by now sex makes a man hard."

She was backed halfway to the bed. "We can talk in the morning."

"Right. Give me your hand. I'll show you what I mean about the hardness." He could have, too, she had such an immediate effect on him.

She thrust both hands behind her. He almost laughed. "I thought you liked it," he said. "Remember the things I did to you this afternoon? Wouldn't you like me to do them again? Perhaps we ought to finish what we began."

She closed her eyes, and he knew she was remembering, her breath coming in short little gasps between her parted lips. Angel, it seemed clear, had a very good memory.

She tripped on the rug beside his bed. He caught her before she fell, his hands spanning her upper arms. He could have broken her with his fingers. Instead, he crushed her against his chest and claimed her mouth with his.

His lips and hands took on a life of their own. Revenge belonged to another life. He tried to think of why she was here, why she had become his wife, but each *why* dissolved like wax beneath his lusty heat. That's what it was, he told himself as he felt the whisper of her tongue on his. Lust. He'd never felt the full force of its power until he held Angel in his arms.

He was tight and full and stiff from wanting her. His tongue raked the inside of her mouth as his fingers fumbled with her gown. It fell soft as a cloud to the floor, and his hands pressed against nothing but warm satin skin. His heart thundered as he broke the kiss. He would have welcomed her fighting him, but when she arched her breasts to his lips, he welcomed her willingness all the more.

He kissed her nipples, his teeth gently jagged against the evidence of her own arousal. He could climax just kissing her this way. He pulled free. The light from the fire played provocatively across her skin, highlighting the contours of her body, the high, full breasts, the narrow waist and curving hips, the thighs, the patch of hair protecting her treasure.

His trousers almost split from his response.

He cupped her breasts, playing his palms over their fullness. Her head lolled back in languid submission, and her hair flowed over her shoulders like liquid gold.

"Is this what you want?"

"I want . . . yes, oh yes."

Her voice caressed him, touching him all over, though their only point of contact was her breasts.

She looked at him, her eyes dark with heat and longing, her breath coming out ragged in a single short cry.

Quent forgot all else but Angel. Sweeping her into his arms, he pulled back the covers and lay her on the dark sheets. Her body appeared porcelain; he did not take his eyes off her as he undressed and lay beside her. Everything was happening fast, though he moved jerkily, awkward as a schoolboy in his impatience. All he could think of was touching her, kissing her, plunging into her again and again, feeling her wet tightness hold him until he was done.

She was slick and smooth and warm beneath his hands

and his tongue, and she writhed in taunting abandon as he kissed and stroked the length of her.

She did not keep idle, not this passionate creature he had taken to wife. She fondled and kissed everywhere she could reach while he was doing the same to her, her fingers thrust in his hair, then stroking his neck, his chest, his thighs. When her lips found the side of his neck, he knew he would have another bruise.

Let her mark him. He would do his marking inside her. She parted her legs, and their bodies joined, his entrance smooth and tight and good. She came almost right away . . . he'd never had a woman reach satisfaction before him, but Angel did.

She clung tightly to him, her tremors burning their way into his blood. When he began to move inside her again, she joined him in the rhythmic thrusts, her passion returned in all its full, amazing force. He forgot everything but pleasure as their bodies pounded together. This time they climaxed together, his satisfaction hard and fast, reaching more of him than just that part buried inside his wife. He felt the rapture touch his soul, or he would have considered it so if he were a religious man.

He held her tight, not letting her move, willing her to a silence she seemed to welcome. No crying out this time, the way she had done on the ship, just a trembling in his embrace, a delicate tremor that had nothing to do with fear or cold.

They were good together. He cursed the notion even as he admitted it was true. More than good. He had never had sex so moving . . . so thorough . . . so complete.

Lust, he told himself, fed by denial and unremitting temptation. He would admit to nothing else.

And yet, as they lay in a tangle, the shadows of the firelit room dancing over the bed, he knew that he was not the only creature of the night. Angel—fair Angel, golden Angel—had come alive this midnight, and in the doing had brought him with her to a pleasure that was beyond his ken. Tonight the pleasure of Angel and the pleasures of the flesh were one and the same. He wondered if they would always be so.

Her skin moved slickly, damply against him as she nestled close, her hair spread wildly across the pillow, staking claim. He could have held her forever, yet to hold her a second longer was madness for them both.

Fighting for sanity, he shifted away and sat on the side of the bed. Sanity? He'd settle for one coherent thought. The nerves along the surface of his skin still tingled from their joining. If she had touched him . . . if he felt her fingers against his spine . . . he would have taken her again.

But she didn't, and he pulled on his trousers, covering his rapidly hardening shaft before he changed his mind. Standing, he forced himself to look at her. She was sitting, the covering sheet pulled to her chin. And she was looking at him with questioning velvet-blue eyes. As though she wanted answers from him concerning what had just taken place.

He had . . . taken her. Even in his mind, he couldn't bring himself to use a cruder word. It didn't fit what he and Angel had just done, even though he knew the act had come from lust.

But such primal hunger would not lead to anything stronger, anything more permanent. Surely she understood.

"You didn't cry this time." He used the words as a wall.

She did not respond, just kept gazing at him as though her simple stare could force him into saying—

What did she want him to say? That he had some feeling for her? Such a declaration would be a lie.

And so would allowing her possession of his bed. She did not belong in this room, no matter how much warmth and pleasure and beauty she brought to it.

He ran a hand through his hair. "You're not sleeping here."

Her eyes widened. "Oh. I hadn't thought that far." Surprise mixed with disappointment. He ought to like the reaction. So why did he feel like taking her into his arms and telling her that he had changed his mind?

Because he was a fool, that was why, a man temporarily deranged. She was trying to change his world. By God, he couldn't allow it. He eased into his shirt, leaving it loose and unbuttoned. Her eyes followed each movement, lingering at his chest, gazing at him the way men usually gazed at women.

Her simple act of looking at him was almost his undoing.

"When you get to your room," he said, purposefully harsh, "write your father. Tell him the truth this time, as much as you can bear to put on paper. Tell him to get over here as soon as he can."

Slowly her eyes raised to his. "Is that all you have to tell me?" She held the sheet tighter against her throat. "I thought after what we just did—"

Her voice trailed off, but she did not look away.

"You'll have to pardon my manners. I don't usually talk after sex. But don't worry. It was good. I assume that is what you want to hear."

She blinked, and he saw the glisten of tears in her eyes. "I didn't know it could be bad."

Quent caught his breath. For all her weakness, his wife had a way of speaking that hit him like a fist in the gut.

She was, as ever, a difficult woman to suppress.

But he had to try. "Oh, it can be very, very bad. It can also be meaningless."

She looked past him into the fire. "More for a man, I should think, than for a woman."

"Don't try to tell me what we just did had any special significance. You don't even like me."

Since Quent didn't particularly like himself, he knew whereof he spoke.

He turned away from her. "Put your gown back on." He

listened to the rustle of the sheets and the creak of the mattress, imagining the scene at his back. Imagining the details far too well, the white gown flowing slowly over her golden hair, her rose-tipped breasts, her womanhood damp with his seed.

For a long moment only the crackle of the fire sounded in the room.

"I'll write Papa tonight," she said at last.

He turned to face her. She stood closer than he'd thought. Too close. In the fireglow he could see the redness where his whiskers had burned her cheeks.

"Nothing to appease him. Nothing to make him feel good. Give me your word."

Her chin tilted. "That's not—" and then, "You have it."

Brave Angel . . . cooperative Angel. He ought to—

Hell, he felt like doing what he'd already done.

"Get him here fast, and then you two can be gone." He spoke quickly, as much to himself as to her.

She paled, for porcelain-skinned Angel quite a feat. "What did you say?"

For the first time since introducing her to Chad, he had truly stopped her.

"You didn't think you were going to stay in Ireland, did you? I can't imagine that you would want to."

"Of . . . course not."

She didn't lie very well, no better than his recent attempts to think things through. He should have known that to a woman like Angel marriage of any kind would be for life. But then she hadn't met many men like him.

Angel here forever . . . in his bed every night. He could not contemplate the possibilities.

"I won't send you back without compensation," he said, with all the cruelty at his command. "You are a means to an end, and for that you should be paid."

Her head snapped up. "I don't want your money." Anger laced each word.

"Nevertheless, you will have it. You might be pregnant, in which case you'll take what I give."

"You'd send your baby away?"

"Listen carefully, Angel. What I say is exactly what I mean. I don't want any more family than I've already got. I've never seen much good in them, but if you should bear a child I will not have him raised in want."

She closed her eyes, tears like crystal beads on her lashes, but when she looked at him again, he saw no sign she continued to cry. A single teardrop fell on her cheek. She did not brush it away. Instead, she held still, as if wanting to say more, then with a sigh hurried from the room. The door closed behind her softly, yet solidly, and he was left to his solitude.

One thought loomed paramount in his mind. He must not question what he did, or what he had done.

Why, then, did he feel as though he were committing the worst mistake of his life?

He stared into the fire his wife had built. For all her gentleness . . . for all her weakness, he corrected . . . she had a way of stirring embers into flame, then escaping the conflagration.

Except she hadn't quite escaped tonight. For whatever reason she had visited him, she left with far more than she expected. A roll on the bed, and then a talk that was long overdue.

He should have explained earlier and more clearly the way things were between them. He should have realized when she started washing walls that she was settling into a permanent home.

And all as sacrifice for her beloved Papa. The burning knowledge ate at him like a cancer. He must never lose sight of why she did what she did. Even her sympathy for Chad came from the same motivation. He was, after all, Papa's only son.

Anger flared within him. Or was it jealousy? Impossible.

He meant everything he had told his wife. She was a means to an end. Chad was the only thing that mattered, Chad and the settling of the past. Nothing more. He had no business feeling like the worst cad on earth.

Tugging off his clothes, he climbed into the bed. It smelled of sex and of Angel. The two scents intermingled in his senses until he could scarcely tell one from the other. They seemed to mean the same thing.

He didn't want a wife, he reminded himself, no matter how enticing she was. He wanted revenge.

There was no question in that to keep him agitated. Still, he knew sleep would not come easily despite the late-night exertions. Staring into the dark, remembering the past hour, he regretted he was not a drinking man.

Sixteen

Angel loved Quent.

Completely, soaringly, gloriously, the way a wife ought to love her husband, wanting to share his joys and sorrows, craving his touch, feeling his lips and his hands on her body long after she had left his bed.

She loved him painfully, too, achingly, desperately, the way a woman loved a man who did not love her in return.

Curled on the cushioned window seat near her bed, she dwelled on the whole pitiful picture. In the hour since leaving his room she had picked out the most salient points. Married little more than two months, separated from him most of that time, they hardly knew one another. To him, she was his enemy's daughter; to her, he was a powerful and enigmatic figure who struck fear in most of the world.

Sensibility told her to hate him, but the passions of her heart had nothing to do with good sense. After a long absence, he had been home only one day, but it was enough for her to see the way things were. She loved him and he didn't love her. Worse, he never would.

One minute her spirit soared, the next she felt leaden inside, her throat so thick with unshed tears she could not swallow. Hearts really could break. She hadn't realized it until tonight.

Wrapping herself deeper in her blanket, she gazed up at the stars. When had this dark, forbidding Irishman first stirred her feelings? The instant she saw him staring into the store and felt shivers down her spine. Each time they met, the shivers became something more solid, more meaningful. Otherwise she never could have offered herself in sacrifice for Papa.

Sacrifice? For Papa? She saw now she had been acting more than a little for herself, fascinated by the arrogant stranger who demanded everything she had to give, unwilling to let him get away without understanding him more. Papa had been a reason, a motivation, a cause . . . but he had also been an excuse. She had given everything to Quentin Kavanagh as soon as she could, and she would give it again and again whenever he wanted.

Oh, she was a shameless wretch.

The depth of her feeling had loomed clear when she walked into his room tonight and saw him by the fire, legs stretched toward the fire, hands lax in his lap, dark lashes shadowing lean cheeks. For once he hadn't looked steely hard and defensive, but . . . gentle, almost vulnerable.

Staring at him, wanting to run to him, she had remembered the way he made her feel in the afternoon, and she'd grown warm despite the chill in the room. She had thought, too, of how he was with Chad, kind and understanding without being patronizing, and about his attachment to the land and to the past. She had at last understood his demons, and she had felt love swell in her heart.

He hadn't remained gentle for long.

Before and after the lovemaking, she had peered into the darkness of his soul, heard cruel words, watched him turn from her in bed. And still she loved him. She must be the most foolish Chadwick of them all. As far as he was concerned, once her usefulness was done she could go to hell. Harsh words for her, but they described a harsher truth.

In this room, with the same stars shining down, Morna O'Brien had wreaked a terrible wrong on her second son, forcing him into a life of revenge for the sake of her firstborn. The result was the hard-hearted man Angel called husband. He offered her money. Never had she felt so ashamed. He thought little of the Chadwick clan. He thought cash would keep her satisfied.

A spark of anger flared within her, the raveled edge of her pride. She ought to do as he ordered . . . write Papa, wait for his arrival, then go home with him after the suffering had been played out to Quent's satisfaction . . . leaving her husband to the unhappy world he was determined to keep for himself. That's what she ought to do, all right.

But sometimes, she reminded herself as she propped her chin on her hand, Chadwick women didn't follow the expected course. Against her own father's will, Mama had run off to America with the man she loved. Flame had gone to Texas, Raven to England, neither revealing the complete truth about her respective journey until much later. And everything had worked out right for them.

Could the same apply to Angel? Impossible. Not even her stalwart optimism came to her rescue now. Everything Quent had said before and after taking her to bed had been calculated to hurt. He couldn't behave in such a manner, not under those intimate circumstances, if he felt a fraction of the love she felt for him.

Her situation was hopeless, so much so that even her guiding inner voice had nothing to add. She would write the letter to Papa, just as she had promised, telling him that matters in Ireland were not as she expected, that she needed him here before anything could be made right. And to come alone. That part was important. Mama should not be present when Papa met Chad.

She would write the letter and ride into town later to post it. Get the cursed thing on the way. No talk of love nests— hadn't that little phrase drawn all of her husband's scorn?— no postponing the inevitable. She couldn't tell Papa outright about his son. That sort of thing should not be left to the written word.

And then she would learn about Chad, the one person

her husband seemed to care about. Quent had said he wasn't a freak, nor a child she could play with. As though she didn't understand, as though she considered her brother a curiosity. The times she worked alongside Jeremiah, she had been exposed to patients suffering more than just fever and difficult pregnancies . . . patients who were *different,* she thought, using her husband's word.

Her heart had gone out to them all, regardless of their problems. She could feel no less sympathy, no less love for her own kin.

Through all her pain and confusion, she was certain of two things. First and foremost, Quent was wrong about Papa. The kind and loving man who had raised her was not the rapist her husband described. Clues concerning the truth must lie in the castle, or on the island, or in the town. It was both her duty and her destiny to find them. With the truth might come understanding, and a laying to rest of bitterness.

Second, she knew that she would see Chad again, with or without anyone's permission, not because it was her duty but because it was her heart's desire.

Late the next morning, when she should have sprung from the bed full of determination to see her course through, she dragged herself to her feet in a full-blown bout of depression. Weary from lack of sleep, too long without food, beset with a thousand worries, she was ready to admit defeat.

Whatever the cause, in the gray light of day she felt all her energy sapped from her. How could she help a man who didn't want to be helped? The same way she could love him when he didn't want to be loved. The reasoning sounded good enough, but it did little to lift her spirits. Knowing only a trifle about seduction, she doubted she could do so much as get her husband back in bed, short of parading around him naked. Which was not entirely out of the range of possibility.

Hadn't he told her that sex between the two of them was meaningless?

Maybe for him. Not for her.

And how could she hope to prove her Papa hadn't raped his Mama? The incident hadn't taken place before an audience. Besides, no matter who said what, Quent would never deny the evidence that came to him from the grave.

Still and all, she had to try. Writing the cursed letter, tucking it into her pocket, she went down the back stairs to begin her investigation.

"Master Quent rode out an hour ago," Mrs. MacCabe reported.

For the first time since arriving at the castle, Angel was grateful he was gone. Husbands, she was discovering, could get in the way.

"Where is Mary?" she asked.

"Feeding the chickens."

For a moment Angel gave consideration to problems other than her own. Too well did she remember the looks that had passed between the farmer's betrothed daughter and her husband's assistant Neill Connolly on the day the Malones tried to take her back. Like Quent, Neill had departed the next day. Unlike Quent, the younger man loved the woman who loved him. Angel was certain of it, even though Mary had avoided any personal conversations after that day they talked in the alley.

"Did Neill return with my husband yesterday?"

"Aye, that he did. Later, by train." Mrs. MacCabe hesitated before continuing. "He was talking to the lass not an hour ago, then rode off shortly after Master Quent."

Angel sipped her tea. "Did Neill and Mary . . . did they seem to be getting on all right?"

"I'm not one for gossip, but 'twas a row, to be sure."

Angel sighed, gloomier than ever. Cordangan Castle, it would seem, was not the setting for happy endings.

Mrs. MacCabe surprised her by joining her at the table. "He took you to Calluragh Island yesterday," she said without prelude.

Startled into silence, Angel could only nod.

"And what did you think of the lad? Oh, I know he's a man full grown, but he's a lad to me, and I mean no disrespect."

It was a measure of Angel's depression that she did not question the housekeeper's initiating a confidence.

"You know of our relationship?"

"That he's your brother, too? Aye. I've known since the night you arrived, Master Quent taking such care to tell your maiden name."

Angel didn't know whether to feel resentful or glad. She settled on the latter. It felt good not to bear all her burdens alone.

Her thoughts turned to Chad. "He's a dear person," she said after a moment's thought. "Gentle and friendly and open. And he's got the hands of a genius. But he seems lonely." She met Mrs. MacCabe's solemn gaze. "Like Quent."

"You should have seen Master Quent leave here this morning. A more woeful sort I've seldom seen. You're no beacon of sunshine yourself."

The woman's frankness put her on the defensive. "I had a bad night."

"From the looks of the master's bed when I made it this morning, I would have thought otherwise."

Here was a housekeeper Angel did not know. Her cheeks burned with embarrassment as she stared into her cup. "It wasn't all bad."

"Saints preserve us, I should hope not. Quent Kavanagh would be a poor excuse for a man if he couldn't satisfy his wife once in awhile."

Every two months. Angel kept the detail to herself, but as the housekeeper had pointed out, she made the beds. She would already know. And somehow, she might understand. The light in her eye was certainly sympathetic, if somewhat more probing than Angel would like.

"I don't think I'll be staying long," she said.

"Giving up, are you?"

"No," she answered, stung. "I may not have come here by choice, but I very much want to stay."

"Even though you've done little but work and pass the time alone?"

Angel managed a weak smile. "So I'm not very smart."

The two women looked at each other for a long time.

"You're smart as they come, Mistress Angel, seeing the needs of Chad and Master Quent as you do."

Angel's spirits lifted at the compliment.

"The question is," Mrs. MacCabe added, "are you tough?"

"Nobody in my family ever called me that. My sisters yes, but not me."

"And are you accepting their judgment?"

Under the woman's steely stare, Angel straightened her spine. "All right, then, I'm as tough as they come." If her response was more a wish than a declaration, that was something she would keep to herself.

"You'll have to be," Mrs. MacCabe said, looking not in the least convinced. "Tell me, how did things go yesterday?"

Angel wilted right away. "He said such harsh things to me. When he wasn't being wonderful." Her voice broke. Some toughness, she thought. She couldn't even speak.

Mrs. MacCabe cleared her throat. "I didn't mean last night, Mistress Angel. I'd not be asking such private particulars."

"Oh." If only she could swallow her words.

"Now that you bring the subject up, did you not think

his harshness strange given the circumstances? The master is a man lusty as any, if talk in the village is anything to go by. And you're a comely lass. Did his manner not seem calculated to keep you away?"

"Calculated?" Angel looked at the housekeeper in astonishment. "I hadn't thought about that."

She thought about it now. Why, indeed, should Quent bother to keep the chasm between them? If he had no feelings for her, he ought to take what she offered, not just once or twice, but every night, and then put her on a ship with Papa. If the sex were meaningless, that's what any ordinary villain would do.

But there was nothing ordinary about Quent. He wanted her out of his sight, out of his life. Could it not be in part because he was afraid of her? Afraid of the effect she had on him?

It couldn't be . . . and yet Angel felt a ray of optimism in the darkness of her despair. No blinding ray, of course, but she would take what she could get.

"And how were things on the island?" asked Mrs. Mac-Cabe, drawing her away from her speculations. Just as well. If she kept thinking about her husband's motivations, she might allow herself to hope.

"We weren't there long. Quent didn't explain many things . . . except how my brother came to be born. He was very explicit about that."

"He would be."

"He's very protective toward Chad. He seems to care for him greatly."

"Aye, that he does."

Angel leaned toward her companion, weight on her elbows, hands pressed together as if in prayer. "When we talked before, you told me Quent's parents argued all the time, and then later it was father and son. Were the arguments over Chad? Did Dermot Kavanagh know about him? I mean, *all* about him?"

"The late master knew about Chad from the beginning. She brought him here that first time when he could barely walk, dragging him behind her up the hill, begging for work."

"That's how they met?"

Mrs. MacCabe nodded. "What a sight they must have been, the slight woman from the village with curses fairly echoing at her back, and the small boy with the friendly smile and the far-away look in his eye. Laundry was what Morna was good at. That and making a fair appearance, with her dark hair and dark eyes and skin white as the clouds. Frail and uncertain she was, like she didn't know all the ugliness the world had in store for her, nor whether she could take another blow."

"Not at all like Quent."

"Nay. He took after his father, although he'd swear 'tis a lie. Poor Morna. She came to the castle at the wrong time, or maybe it was the right. Who's to say? No matter. Dermot Kavanagh was close to fifty, feeling the passing of the years, deciding he wanted an heir. He saw her and within the week offered his name. It mattered little what they said about her in the village. They said bad things about him, too, about the way he lived here away from everyone, too lordly to speak to common folk. O' course, the talk had it wrong. He'd been raised the way of his people, keeping apart. Not lordly a'tall, but lonely, if you know what I mean."

"The way he raised Quent."

"I've always suspected he wanted his son to be different, but they didn't get along. Not after he put Chad in the tower."

"The bedroom," said Angel said, remembering the neatly kept quarters next to the treasure room. "I thought someone had lived there."

"Morna was little help, so filled with self pity she was, caught in a loveless marriage, feeling like a prisoner instead of a wife. She'd entered the contract believing that food and shelter were all that mattered in those terrible times, but she found out different. 'I've been with only two men in my life, a night with each,' she told me once. 'And both times I conceived a son.' A loveless marriage, as I said. Her husband knew no words to woo her. She felt rejected all over again, and she took to her room."

Angel's heart ached for the woman who was her Papa's accuser. Married to stern, reclusive Dermot Kavanagh, unwanted, unloved. She could feel a kinship with her, but it was a feeling she couldn't dwell upon.

"You came with her to help with Chad."

"To keep him out of the master's way, although I'm thinking now if we had started out sharing our days and our worries, we might have known better times. After Morna died, Master Quent used to sneak his brother from the castle, as much in defiance of his father as in a desire to show Chad the world. But they ran into townspeople who . . . were not kind. When his father passed on, he spread talk that his brother had died as well and put him on the island. Calluragh is an Irish word for an old burial ground. An appropriate site for the cottage, would you not say?"

"Who takes supplies to them?"

"A lad from town. I do not know his name. And Master Quentin would not favor your asking around."

It was the first sour note the housekeeper had sounded. "Is that a warning not to do it?"

" 'Tis a warning to be careful, lass. I've had hopes for you, and I've not changed my mind But I've also warned you not to make a mistake. Now that you've met your husband's lone blood kin, 'tis more important than ever you heed what I say."

She stood. "You'll need a hot breakfast in you, whatever you decide to do." In quick order she placed a bowl of porridge and a thick slice of warm bread in front of her.

Angel ate it all. Just as she was finishing, the back door slammed and Mary O'Callaghan ran into the room, pulling up short when she saw the two women.

"Oh," she said, looking away, but not before Angel caught the redness of her eyes.

Mary had been crying, but she doubted if she would tell her why . . . certainly not with Mrs. MacCabe as witness. Could it be over the words she'd had with Neill, or had something else happened? Around the castle, anything seemed likely.

"Sorry t' get such a late start," Mary mumbled, hurrying past them. "The village women have not shown up, but never you fear, Mrs. Kavanagh. I'll get t' the dusting right away."

Angel caught Mrs. MacCabe's eye. "Did my husband frighten them off yesterday?"

" 'Tis a possibility."

Angel saw it as a certainty. With the housekeeper turned to the ovens, Angel debated whether to follow Mary. She chose instead to go outside. She arrived at the stable door in time to see the hunched figure of a man hurrying across the vegetable garden, kicking up the neat furrows before disappearing over the brow of the hill.

Old Tully emerged from the stable to stand beside her. "Who was that?" she asked.

"Seamus O'Callaghan. Miss Mary's da'."

"He made her cry."

"None too fond o' the Kavanaghs for taking his daughter away."

"None too fond of me, you mean. He wants her back?"

"More like he wants the money she's paid." Old Tully shrugged. "Me hearing's not what it was. That's all I could make out afore they moved away."

Angel tried to smile. "I've got my husband avoiding me, Mrs. MacCabe warning me, and now Mary fighting with the two men in her life. How about you, Old Tully? What have I done to you?"

"Given me work, lass." He scratched at his gray-grizzled face. "You've made me feel important again, and that's no small task for a man old as the hills."

Impulsively, Angel hugged him and kissed him on the cheek. "Thank you. And now, if you'd like to feel more important, please saddle Solas for me. My husband rides this land by night, and would no doubt take a dim view of my company. There's nothing been said against my riding it by day."

For the next hour, the skirt of her workdress tucked awkwardly around the sidesaddle, Angel rode over Kavanagh land, up hills and down, never moving very fast, unsure of the rocky ground, coming at last to a grassy cliff overlooking Bantry Bay. Here she found the Kavanagh family cemetery—a dozen headstones, crudely carved, Quent's ancestors having scant regard for ostentation either during or after life.

Tethering Solas in a patch of sweet greenery, she studied the headstones, making out some of the carvings, attempting to read others with her fingers, matching the names to the portraits she planned to hang throughout the castle. She wondered if anyone could help her with the identification, even Quent.

Perhaps. For all their isolation, the graves were well tended, especially the two newest additions, set apart closest to the cliff's edge where Calluragh Island could easily be seen.

MORNA O'BRIEN KAVANAGH
1828-1867
GONE TO A BETTER WORLD

Fifteen years ago, thought Angel. Half of her husband's life. Papa had been born in 1826, making him two years older than Morna. She did some fast calculating. Their thirty-five-year-old son had been born when they were twenty-one and eighteen. Younger than Angel, yet they were hardly children, not in a famine-stricken land where people grew up fast.

The second tombstone bore a simpler inscription:

DERMOT BRYAN KAVANAGH
1801-1873

Well-tended graves, although they bore no sign that flowers had ever been placed upon them. She would have been surprised otherwise.

She stood for a while looking across the bay, mostly at the island and at the smoke curling from the chimney, wishing she had a telescope. Like the one she had found high in the tower among the porcelain vases. Mounting Solas, she made a hasty trip to the castle, greeting the stone dogs with a wave and entering the seldom-used front door. She made it up to the tower without being seen, and into the rooms now kept unlocked, then with the telescope clutched to her bosom, back down to the mare.

Heart pounding, she found the path to the shore and to the boat. She rode down cautiously, only to find the boat gone, in its place a restless Vengeance, who sniffed the air and pulled at his tether as the mare grew near.

The brothers were visiting. And she was not wanted, at least by Quent. Chad did not share the feeling. She knew from their brief meeting and from the way he had talked about her when she'd gone into the cottage.

Leaving the path, she found a place far downwind of the stallion, dismounted, and settled in for a long wait, the telescope trained on a pair of boats on the island's rocky shore. Yesterday there had not been a second boat. Delivery day, she thought, a small thrill shivering through her. She couldn't have asked for anything better short of a gilt-edged invitation to sail across the bay.

When the supply boat left, she concentrated on its stern as it made its way through the waters toward the unseen harbor at the village of Cordangan. LEPRECHAUN II, she made out after much concentration. An apt name. Weren't leprechauns supposed to reveal the way to treasure? Treasure of sorts—in the form of an unknown brother—was exactly what Angel Chadwick Kavanagh sought. Whether Quent approved or not, she would see Chad, and she would try to discover the truth of his conception.

Thrusting her hands into her pocket, she found the letter she'd written to her Papa. She really ought to go into town and post it. It was what her husband would want. And while she was there, she would see to other matters. Matters he did not have to know about.

The wind caught her hair. Suddenly chilled, she hugged herself. It would take Papa at least two months to get the letter and sail across the Atlantic to find out what was going on with his youngest daughter. Two months to do what she could . . . two months to accomplish the impossible. In all her life she had never been more aware of the importance of time.

Dutiful wife and Pinkerton detective . . . she would have to be both. She made note of the date: Wednesday, June 21, 1882 . . . the day she began her double life.

Seventeen

"Quentin Kavanagh's black soul should burn in hell!"

Owney Malone's voice roared over the noise in Bantry Bay Tavern, thick and crude as the man himself.

Padraic Scully stood in the shadows, unnoticed, watching and listening. He had coached the farmer in what to say, and thus far the fool was following his script.

The two men seated with Owney nodded agreement . . . his spineless son who couldn't whip a defenseless woman even when he took her by surprise and Seamus O'Callaghan, who couldn't keep his daughter under his roof.

That they were one and the same woman spoke not of Mary O'Callaghan's strength, but of the weakness of her foes.

Scully had aligned himself with fools. It was a mark of his cleverness that no one knew how deep the alliance with the elder Malone went. In this harsh world, he had to be clever to survive.

"He's got me daughter up there, doin' the Lord knows what t' her," Seamus said where one and all could hear. The noise around them abated.

"Leaving me poor son to grieve for his lost love." Owney glanced at Fergus, who belched in response. Owney turned to the crowd. "And there's others who've joined her, spirited by the promise of good wages."

"Aye, he's spirited 'em, all right," said one of the men sitting in the smoky dimness. "Me wife is one of 'em.

When I heard the devil had returned, I made sure she stayed home today, though she put up a fight, saying the mistress of the castle would be needing her. But I say no wage is worth a trip down into hell."

That the castle was up from town instead of down seemed not to bother him. Fools, thought Scully, the lot of 'em. Fools easily led.

"More ale," bellowed Fergus.

Owney raised his tankard. The only one to hesitate was Seamus, but then, Scully recalled, he was the one paying for the drinks. From money his daughter had earned at Cordangan Castle. Seamus had been proud enough to wave it about and brag how he'd invaded the devil's land, but spending it was another matter. An additional tankard or two would ease his miserly ways.

The tavern door opened, letting in a shaft of light and another pair of customers. Scully squinted past them into the brightness of day just as a well-turned trap clipped smartly along the street. He got only a glimpse of the carriage, but it was enough to see the woman at the reins. He knew her from the descriptions he had heard. Angel Kavanagh had come to town.

Scully's interest sparked. Here was an opportunity he could not let pass. Through representatives in Dublin, Pride of Ireland had recently begun to deal with several merchants in Cordangan, and there was talk of exporting the handwork of the women, as well as opening a linen mill. During the weeks he had been gone, Kavanagh must have been making the arrangements.

Too easily could the fools around here learn he owned the company and was thus their benefactor. He would be making friends right and left, probably be elected mayor of the village. And the more popular a man became, the more difficult he was to bring down.

Right now Kavanagh had nary a friend in the world, outside the people who worked for him. Scully planned to keep it that way. Let the bastard build up his company, then bring him to ruin and step in to reap the rewards of all the hard work that had gone before.

Scully knew the business. Hadn't he been close to success as an importer and exporter? Aye, that he had, though the firm had been inherited from his father-in-law. He could be successful again. Even his sour-faced wife and daughter would find little to complain about if he made them the wealthiest family in all of Dublin.

All he needed to do was shoot down the high-flying devil of County Cork.

He stepped from the tavern's shadows to stand between the Malones. "Save your money, men," he said with a grand gesture. Then to the crowd at large, "And the rest of you as well. This round's on me. In recognition of the Home Rule that's bound to come our way."

A cheer went up.

"And why, you say, is Home Rule so certain? Because it is right, no matter who in the county objects."

"There's none who'd be such a fool," yelled out one of the men.

"And so you would think," Scully threw back. "We remember too well the days of tenancy, when good Catholic men like yourselves could not own land . . . when you tithed to the bastard landlords who lived far away."

"Who would let those days return?" the man said.

Scully held up his hands in protest. "I've heard only rumors, though they're strong in Dublin and Cork. I'm not one to be spreading what could be lies."

"You're a good man, Padraic Scully," another said. "Tell us what you've heard."

He looked slowly around the room, making sure all eyes were on him. "Who is it that comes and goes without turning his hand to an honest day's work? Who is it who lives better than the lot of you put together? Who might be under the pay of foreign forces who would keep you and your kin their slaves?"

"Quentin Kavanagh!" More than one man yelled out the name.

Taking pleasure in attributing his own sins to his enemy, Scully forced back a smile. Foster a man's fear and he was yours. He knew he had the support of every man in the tavern, only some of whom participated in the night rides.

"Rumors only," he said, gesturing for attention. "Although 'tis said he's in the pay of a Member of Parliament."

He let that particular seed germinate for a few minutes, listening to the talk of hate and threats as another man might listen to music. The fools would sober up soon enough, but not all the hate would go away.

The trouble was the devil frightened them. They were not quite ready to be led against him in open revolt. But soon. Very soon.

"Men," he shouted, and gradually they fell silent. "Let's turn our thoughts to more cheerful fare. I've ordered the next round. Drink hearty and think of Home Rule."

Another cheer, this one loud and long. In the melee of celebration and the serving of ale, he motioned for Owney to join him outside.

"Can't talk in there," he said, leading the farmer to the alley that ran beside the tavern. "Don't worry. You'll return soon enough to your ale."

The red-eyed Owney blinked and scratched at his grizzled face. "What's so important we have t' talk? I don't get into town but once a week."

The rebellious bastard. He needed a reminder of where his money came from.

"I thought you would be interested in what I just saw. But if drinking's more to your liking—" He let his voice trail off.

"I'll give ye a minute," Owney growled, hunching his massive shoulders toward Scully.

The farmer was a big one, all right. It was said he could throw a ram over a stile without breaking a sweat. Or snap a man in two, if need arose. Half Owney's weight for all he matched him in height, Scully preferred using his brains.

"She's in town," he said.

Owney squinted. "Who?"

"The mistress of Cordangan Castle. The woman who stole your son's betrothed. I just saw her ride by alone."

Owney spat through a gap in his yellowed teeth. "She's here, is she? Somebody ought t' do something about the bitch."

"Someone who understands just how much trouble the Kavanaghs can be."

"Just tell me which way she was heading. There's a score o' men inside who'll help me put the fear o' God into her."

"Talk, you mean. Call her ugly names. Frighten her. Is that what you consider doing something?"

"I can hardly beat her senseless, now can I? She's nothing but a woman—"

"Whose husband wishes to keep Ireland the slave of England. Do you think she's ignorant of his politics? Of course not. American women are a pushy lot who don't know their place. Here she is, a foreigner, telling the good people of Ireland they have no rights."

Scully talked slowly, drawing out the picture, confident Owney was too stupid to see the gaps in his logic.

"And she's got your son's woman, remember. Who knows what lies she's telling her, getting her all stirred up." Scully shook his head in disgust. "One thing's for sure. The longer Mary O'Callaghan remains in that castle, getting a taste of the fancy life, the more unlikely she'll wed the likes of Fergus Malone. And with the wedding goes the deed to O'Callaghan land."

"Never ye worry," Owney growled, "we'll do more'n talk."

"And cause a ruckus? The whole crowd of you? Think

again. Kavanagh has evil on his side, you've said it yourself. He would find you one by one, even you, Owney, strong as you are, and he would take his revenge. Those men you want to join you understand the way things are. They're cowards. Not like you and me."

"First ye say don't do this, and then don't do that. Why tell me the bitch is in town?"

Scully's thin lips twisted into a smile. "If Kavanagh didn't know who harmed his wife, he would be helpless to avenge her, wouldn't he? Everyone in the county would know he's not so powerful after all."

Owney's pig eyes squinted. "Yer thinking of something."

"Let's say I'm investigating the possibilities. Go back to your ale, and I'll see where she's gone. But I'm warning you, don't drink too much. There will be more for you later. Another round of celebration."

Grunting his agreement, Owney returned to the tavern. Scully took to the street, looking for a trap with a handsome blood bay in the traces and a beautiful woman at the reins. To his surprise he found her down at the harbor, a quarter mile off the main street, on a pier where women did not often go alone. At least the so-called decent women.

The water was too shallow at this point to allow for big ships, but enough smaller trade came in to bring the sailors. And they brought the whores.

Scully had been known to hire a few himself, the meaty ones who liked it rough.

His thoughts were on only one today. Before he was done with the Kavanaghs, he would find out what she had under her skirts that had brought her husband to bay. And she'd get it rough, whether she liked it or not.

But that was an issue for another day.

She stood beside the carriage talking to a young sailor he did not recognize, the damp summer wind off the water whipping her gown against her body, threatening to tear her bonnet from her head. From this angle, she did not look so puny after all, but then he'd never thought Kavanagh a fool. The charms of his wife made him hate the devil all the more.

The lad waved a hand about, as if in argument, then gestured toward a boat tied at the next slip. A few words more, and they parted. Scully would have sacrificed his daughter to know what they said.

Keeping well away from her on the dock, he contented himself with watching and waiting while the hate festered in his soul.

Angel rode from the dock telling herself she had done the right thing. The youth who delivered supplies to Calluragh Island had refused to admit that he did so. Leprechaun II was not for hire. He did finally, after much beseeching, direct her to another sailor, Hogan, by name, who admitted he'd heard rumors of an old recluse on the Godforsaken piece of rock.

"If ye wish t' go there, I'll take yer money soon enough."

"This is to be done in secret," she had said.

With a hitch of his baggy trousers, Hogan had agreed. "Yer money'll spend the same, whether or no 'tis known from whence it came."

He had almost balked when she told him she wouldn't know in advance when she needed to hire him, or where they should meet. After much wrangling, they came up with a point on the shore a mile from where Quent kept his boat, a place accessible to Angel by horseback. She would rig up a bright red flag. If he saw it, he would come get her. If not, she would leave and try again another day.

Angel flicked the reins over Lorcan's flanks, thinking a double life was not an easy thing. On the main street she spied the store where she had met her first residents of Cordangan. On impulse she reined the bay toward the front rail. A large carriage occupied most of the space, and she ended up leaving the trap in the alley that ran beside the store. The same alley where she had listened to Mary O'Callaghan's sad tale.

Inside, she seemed to be reliving the first visit. The proprietor Mrs. O'Flaherty talked to Angel's severest critic, Mrs. Dunne, the customer who had refused to remain in the store with the devil's bride, while to one side were the sisters-in-law, Mrs. Plunkett, the talker who thought riding habits were frills, and the mouselike Mrs. O'Dowd.

To a woman, they watched her enter, curiosity more than friendliness in their eyes. Buoyed by her success at the dock, she smiled and called them each by name, asking how they were on this fine summer's day. Only Mrs. O'Dowd answered with more than a nod, saying she was well and how was Mrs. Kavanagh. An elbow jab in the ribs from Mrs. Plunkett silenced her soon enough.

From such as these Angel had to learn about the past. Her spirit flagged. *Two months,* she reminded herself. *Two months until Papa arrived.*

She took her letter from the pocket of her cloak. "I need to post this, but I'm not familiar with the system here. Since I arrived, our stablehand has brought letters down for me, but I decided it's time I learned to fend for myself."

"They'll take care o' you two doors down," said Mrs. O'Flaherty, giving no sign she was impressed by Angel's belated independence.

Every woman in the store eyed the letter, clear as day wanting to know who the mistress of Cordangan Castle was writing.

"It's to my father," she said to one and all, as though she had no secrets. "In Savannah, Georgia. Thomas Chadwick is his name. He used to live in County Cork when he was a young man. Does anyone recall him?"

"Chadwick," said Mrs. O'Dowd. "That sounds familiar. It's an English name—"

Another elbow ended whatever she had to say.

"Oh, we're not English," Angel assured them, aware of the enmity her audience would feel toward such rabble. "Papa's distant relatives come from England, it's true, but he's mostly Irish. At least, that's what he always claimed, telling us tales of County Cork and of Dublin that made my sisters and me long to travel across the sea."

Much of what she said was a lie. Except for fairy tales and songs, Papa rarely mentioned the country of his birth, but women leading a double life couldn't always tell the truth.

Mrs. Dunne, the most formidable of the women, both in size and demeanor, made her way closer. "Did you meet the dev—Mister Kavanagh in your homeland?"

"Yes. He was there on business."

The woman's eyes narrowed. "And what kind of business would that be?"

Warning bells rang in Angel's head. She was not about to reveal anything personal about the very private man she had wed. Besides, what could she tell them? Other than knowing he owned some kind of business in Dublin, she had no idea where his money came from.

"Oh, I'm a ninny about such things," she said with a wave of her hand. "I couldn't say for sure."

"You did mention your father owned a shop like this one, did you not?" asked Mrs. Plunkett.

"Yes," she said with a little laugh, "but Chadwick Dry Goods and Clothing is much too small an establishment to interest someone like Quentin Kavanagh."

Mrs. Plunkett was not satisfied. "So what kind of business might draw such a man to your town?"

"Yes," said Mrs. Dunne, "tell us, do. We know so little about the States."

All the women moved in on her, like dogs scenting a bone.

"I really have to get this letter posted," she said in a rush.

"Thank you for the information on the post. You ladies have business of your own to attend to. I'll be on my way."

Mrs. Dunne maneuvered herself between Angel and the door.

"They say your husband's returned to the castle."

"Yesterday," said Angel, wondering what else *they* said. The woman did not leave her wondering long.

"For a man new to the marriage bed, he travels a great deal, does he not? I remember well when Mister Dunne and I were wed, I couldn't get him out of the house." She glanced over her shoulder at Mrs. Plunkett. "Do you not recall the way it was?"

"Aye, that I do. You used to complain—"

"Enough of us," said Mrs. Dunne, cutting her off. Her attention shifted back to Angel. "The master of the castle is such a stranger to us. The thought occurred he might be a stranger to you as well."

Angel's temper snapped. "The thought occurs that you should not be talking about such things." She headed straight for the woman, who barely managed to step aside in time for her to pass.

She fairly ran from the store, proud of her courage, yet thinking she hadn't handled the encounter very well. She had confronted the women to gather information, but all she found out was that they wanted information, too.

Could they tell her anything except rumors about Chad? None of them would have been past childhood when he was born. She had hoped the Chadwick name might stir some talk. And so it had, but not the kind to do her any good.

Posting the letter, she stopped by the dressmaker's shop for a cup of tea with Nellie Ahearne, as much in hiding from her interrogators as she was in need of a friendly face. Keeping her troubles to herself, she talked of clothes and decorations. It was an hour before she returned to the trap. Lorcan appeared none too pleased at the wait.

She fed him a handful of the oats Old Tully had stored at the rear of the carriage, and they were soon under way out of the village and up the narrow, winding road that led to home.

Her temporary home. All of the optimism that planning and talking and doing had brought her during the day evaporated when she thought of her destination and of the man who awaited her at the top of the hill.

Maybe he awaited. Maybe he had returned from visiting Chad and decided to leave again, in case she invaded his room during the night. Maybe he'd put her so completely out of his mind, he forgot to do so much as think about her, going about his business and his own private activities as though she did not exist.

Angel sighed. If only he would ride down the hill, sweep her into his arms, and take her to some hidden glade where he could make love to her until the dawn.

She thought of his holding her, undressing her, kissing her, telling her she was the most beautiful woman in all the world, that marrying her was the single greatest accomplishment of his life, that she made him know goodness once again, she made him know love.

Warmth filled her, and her heart began to pound. Holding lightly to the reins, allowing Lorcan to lead the way, she remembered what it was like to lie in her husband's embrace. So absorbed was she in her fantasy, she did not notice the lurch of the trap as it rounded a bend, the right wheels coming dangerously close to a rocky embankment that dropped into thick foliage all the way to the bay.

She noticed soon enough when the horse neighed in alarm and she was pitched sharply against the side of the carriage seat. Dropping the rein, she grabbed for something solid to regain her balance, but the trap took another lurch and she grabbed only air as she fell headlong into space.

She seemed to fall forever, and then she struck branches that scratched and pulled, her body twisting and tumbling, terror striking her heart as she dropped to what surely must be her death.

Her last coherent thought before she hit the ground was of Quent, and then blackness descended.

Angel came to consciousness staring into the eyes of a stranger. She screamed, then lay back holding her head, otherwise it would surely split in half.

"Mrs. Kavanagh," the man said. "I mean you no harm."

She peered at him through parted fingers. The light where she lay—wherever that could be—seemed dim enough, but even the hint of a pale glow started agonizing throbs behind her eyes.

The face leaning close was so thin, the features so sharply formed, she was reminded of a cadaver. Another scream rose in her throat, but she remembered the pain and she held herself still.

"Where am I?" she managed.

"You've taken a nasty spill. I happened to be passing and saw you."

Holding herself as motionless as possible, she tried to remember what had happened. She remembered town, the harbor and the sailor Hogan, the store, the ride back home. . . .

The trap. Something had been wrong with the trap. She must have brought it too close to the road's edge. She remembered being very, very afraid. And then all was dark.

She must have fallen out of the blasted thing. Shame rushed through her. Oh, how Quent would laugh. No, he never laughed. He would ridicule, he would scorn.

She couldn't stifle a sigh, no matter how each little motion pained her. He thought her foolish enough as things were. What would he think now?

Strange hands stroked her arm. She jerked away and paid the price, a searing pain in the back of her head.

"Forgive me, Mrs. Kavanagh, but I must find out if you're hurt."

"Who are you?"

"Padraic Scully is the name."

Scully. It sounded to Angel like *skulk*. She gave him a more careful look. Cadaverous face, spare brown hair slicked straight back, eyes so pale they were almost colorless, pink lips as thin as a pencil line. Padraic Scully. Somehow the name suited him.

"Shall we see if you can stand?" he asked. His voice had a thin, slippery sound to it, not in the least reassuring.

But he was right. She had to find out how hurt she was. Testing several muscles, she felt no extraordinary pain anywhere from her neck down, just a stiffness that promised she would be sore in the days to come.

She gave him her hand, and with some maneuvering and no little discomfort she was soon on her feet. Her bonnet was lying against her back, the ties pressed against her throat, and her hair was half undone. Leaves and twigs clung to her gown. Dense shrubbery and trees blocked out the world.

A wave of dizziness joined the pressure in her head, and she found herself leaning against Scully.

"There, there," he said, "you'll be all right."

He held her too tight. She was not comforted.

"I can walk on my own. Which way is the road?"

He gestured straight up. "You fell down a rather steep hill, I'm afraid. You'll have to let me carry you."

Angel took a step unassisted, but her knees buckled and she came close to falling onto the rocky ground. Scully picked her up. She didn't like being held this way, but she had no choice, not if she were to get home before midnight.

Midnight reminded her of Quent. Of his eyes and his solitary rides. Quent. Somehow if she could reach him, she would be all right. Where the idea came from, she did not know. But she believed it.

Instead of pushing away from her rescuer, as instinct demanded, she forced herself to rest against him, to pull in close and make the journey as easy as possible. It seemed the best thing of all to ignore the scratch of his tweed coat, to rest her head on his shoulder, eyes closed, and think of her husband.

They had walked only a few yards—struggled, more accurately—when suddenly Scully halted. His intake of breath was sharp. She felt his alarm.

"A charming picture, to be sure." The voice came from somewhere above them, deep and hard and familiar.

She opened her eyes to see her husband, clad as always in black, standing straight and strong and forbidding directly in their path.

Eighteen

A fury raced through Quent such as he had not known since the day Chad was stoned in town, obliterating the relief of knowing Angel was alive. She was alive and apparently well, and she was in Padraic Scully's arms.

He strode down the sharp incline, heedless of the rocks and branches on the uneven path, stopping in front of the pair.

"I'll take her," he said. His gaze flitted to Angel, who stared back at him with a watchful, wondrous expression on her face. He knew her too little to interpret exactly how she felt, but the strength of her emotions twisted something in his gut.

Maybe she felt guilt at being caught.

"I'll take you," he said to her, "unless you prefer Scully as your rescuer."

She came out of Scully's arms so fast Quent barely caught her before she fell. How she managed the feat without touching the ground, he had no idea, but one moment Scully was holding her and the next she had her arms around his neck and he was cradling her next to his chest.

Scully looked as surprised as he.

"It would seem she prefers her husband," Quent said. She felt light in his arms, but warm and solid and he imagined he could hear the beating of her heart.

"Oh, Quent," she said against the crook of his shoulder, her hair tickling his cheek, her voice trembling as though she might burst into tears. "I did a very stupid thing. I rode into town to mail Papa's letter, and on the way back I had an accident. Lorcan could have been killed."

She hesitated, then lifted her head to stare at him with eyes as wide and deep as the sky. "He is all right, isn't he?"

Quent tightened his hold on her, not trusting himself to speak right away. "The horse is fine." He looked from her to Scully. "The trap is damaged, however."

Scully cleared his throat. "It's a good thing I was riding by—"

"Get off my land."

"See here—"

"Off. Now."

Angel tensed. "Mister Scully found me, Quent. No telling how long I would have lain out here if he hadn't."

Her defense quickened his anger once again, and he forgot the softness of her eyes. Goddamn them both. He settled his fury on the man; he would deal with his wife when they were alone.

It took only one glance for Scully to hurry past him up the hill, thrashing through the brush, slipping and righting himself as he hurried toward the road.

A moment of silence descended, then came the sounds of a horse galloping into the distance, down the winding pathway that would take his rider to town. In the renewed quiet, husband and wife stared at one another, their lips so close their breath intermingled. Around them the woods lay hushed as if waiting for whatever would pass between them.

Angel's bonnet had fallen to her back, its ties limp but still holding at her throat. Wisps of golden hair framed her face, and a smudge of dirt marred the silken smoothness of her face.

"I'm sorry to be so much trouble," she said with a swallow, lowering her lashes onto her pale cheeks.

"Aye, you're trouble, all right."

He spoke gruffly, or at least he tried to. No need to let her know how shaken he'd been when Lorcan returned to the castle pulling the damaged, empty trap. Shaken, hell, he had been out of his mind. And there was no need to let her know he still felt the same, no matter how angry he became. She might want an explanation of his feelings when he couldn't explain them to himself.

He held her close and in the dying light of day began the journey up the hill, more sure-footed than Scully, not stopping until he stood on the road beside Vengeance.

Resting her sideways in the saddle, he settled himself behind her. On his own, Vengeance began the short journey home. Angel held herself stiffly at first, the way she had when he brought her back from visiting Chad. Gradually she rested against him, softening her body to the shape of his, her head against his shoulder, her lips close to his neck.

For just a moment he thought she kissed him. Impossible. She did that only when he motivated her to do so. Must be the combination of her breath and the twilight breeze. Either that or she remained dizzy from her fall.

A delegation of Mrs. MacCabe, Old Tully, and Mary O'Callaghan met them at the stable door.

"She's all right," he said, as he eased her from the saddle, once more cradling her in his arms. He made no move to set her on her feet, and she made no move to suggest that he do so.

"I'm sorry," she said to the small gathering. "The accident was all my fault."

Quent glanced at Old Tully, warning him with a shake of his head to keep silent. With orders to Mrs. MacCabe for a light supper upstairs, he carried Angel to his room.

"In here?" she asked. "I thought I'd go to my own bed."

"Later," he said. Much later. Like maybe the next day.

"Can you stand?" he asked.

"Of course. I'm really fine. It's funny. My head hurt terribly when I first came to, but I can barely feel it now."

She avoided his eye. "I told myself I would be all right if I could just be with . . . if I could just get back here. It seems I was right."

He set her on her feet. She swayed, but he caught her and led her to the bed. She sat at the side, untying the sashes of her bonnet and tossing it aside, then pulling at the pins in her tangled hair.

Quent watched her as long as he could, then took over, freeing the remains of her once-neat bun, letting her hair fall in golden ripples that caught the light from the fire. All the while he studied the graceful line of her neck and throat, the ivory skin above the rounded neckline of her grass-green gown, the slope of her shoulders, the rise of her breasts.

Unable to stop himself, he stroked her hair, and in the doing found a small lump close to her spine.

She winced and he cursed himself for hurting her. "Are you sure your head's okay?"

Her smile, though small, seemed natural enough. "I'm sure."

A knock sounded at the door, and he stood to answer. Mrs. MacCabe entered, looking not in the least surprised to find the mistress of the castle in the master's room. She carried a tray containing two bowls of potato soup and a loaf of bread.

"I thought you would want to take your supper with Mistress Angel. She ought to eat light and not exert herself overly much."

Was the woman smiling? Quent found it hard to believe. Dismissing her for the night, he set the tray on the table by the fire, poked at the peat logs, then turned once again to Angel. She sat quietly, hands folded in her lap, her deep blue eyes following his movements, her full lips parted and imminently desirable.

With the smudge on her cheek, she looked younger than her twenty-four years, yet every inch a woman. Familiar hungers stirred inside him. He shouldn't want her the way he did, certainly not under these circumstances. But he did.

"Do you want to eat now?" he asked.

"Not just yet."

"The fire will keep the food warm." As if he cared. "I'd like to know that you're really all right."

"Won't you take my word for it?" Her voice was breathy, where his was thick.

"Nay, that would not suit my purpose."

"Which is?"

"To make sure you're not hurting anywhere."

That's all he would do, he told himself. She'd taken a nasty fall.

And ended up in the arms of a bastard.

"I didn't know you knew Scully"

He didn't know where the question came from. Suddenly it was on his lips.

"I don't," she said with an alarmed shake of her head.

"Appearances to the contrary." He was acting like a jealous fool, but hell, he had been away half their brief married life. There was no guessing whom she knew.

"I fell. I came to. And there he was."

"Yes, there he was." A jealous fool. No question about it, a jealous fool. He'd spent too many years distrusting everyone. It was a hard habit to break.

"I've been gone almost a month, I'm home two days, and look what happens. What is going on around here?"

"I'd never seen the man before in my life." Her chin tilted. "I thought you were concerned about my health. Not my acquaintances. If you're so worried about them, maybe you need to stay home and watch me."

The strength of her response surprised him.

"Gentle Angel, is that anger I hear in your voice? Do you actually want me around?"

"I want . . . oh, what difference does it make?" Her eyes glistened. "I don't want to do foolish things."

With those few trembling words, she destroyed any anger he felt toward her. He was concerned about everything and everyone connected to his wife. Because, he told himself, she was his responsibility, his worry, as long as she lived under his roof.

That had to be the reason his heart had been beating erratically since Lorcan returned with the empty trap.

"You've done nothing foolish. That's my task, like berating you just now. And I am concerned about your health. I haven't forgotten."

Kneeling before her, he unfastened the top button of her gown. "Very concerned. Let me know if I'm hurting you."

She drew away, then stopped, holding herself motionless. "You're not hurting me."

"You ought to realize," he said, studying the curve of her parted lips, "I've just begun."

She caught her breath as he worked his way past her waist, laying open the front of her gown. The light from the fire and the rich green of the fabric made her appear golden all over. As much of her as he could see, that is, restricted as he was by dress and camisole and what seemed to him at the moment a hundred garments hiding her from his eyes.

Her hands raised to touch his, as if she would stop him and do the work herself.

"You're not to exert yourself, remember. Mrs. MacCabe's orders."

Her half smile tore through him. "We must do as she says." Her voice was barely a whisper. Everything about her was gentle and soft and delicate, and savaging. He was the one with the trembling hands, not his fragile wife.

"Up to a point, Angel. Only up to a point."

He eased the gown from her shoulders and slipped it down her arms. "No bruises yet."

"I guess you'll have to keep looking."

"Most definitely," he said, as always surprised and heated by her boldness.

She lifted her buttocks, and he eased the gown off her. "So many clothes, Angel, so many clothes."

"It's early yet. We've got the night. Unless you need to leave."

When he looked at her, he forgot Scully, forgot the world, forgot everything outside his door. What he needed, what he wanted, rested on the bed inside his room. He didn't question why or wonder that he had never felt this way before.

Pulling back the covers, he laid her on the sheets, then freed her breasts from the confines of the camisole. With a restraint he did not know he possessed, he simply looked. The nipples hardened into dark pink pebbles, unmistakable evidence that she liked his looking.

Reminding himself he needed to go slow . . . that she really had been in a dangerous fall . . . he turned her to her stomach and removed the rest of her clothes, his fingers trailing down each satin inch of her. Her back was smooth, the color of polished ivory, her waist narrow and flaring to full buttocks that almost sent him out of control.

"Are you up to this, Angel?" he asked, trying to be fair, trying to be good. It was certain that he was up to everything.

She turned her head to look up at him. "I'm just a little stiff, that's all."

He could say the same.

"I fear you'll be worse tomorrow," he said, pulling at the tail of his shirt, working at the buttons until it hung open and loose. He liked the way she watched him, liked it so much he had to fight the urge to take her then and there, coming into her from the rear, like the wild animal he was becoming when she was close by.

"We need to work out the stiffness," she said. Her gaze

fell to his trousers and to the evidence that he, too, liked looking.

"Oh, we will. Just let me know if I should stop."

She would also have to let him know how he was to manage that particular feat. Pulling off his boots and socks, he sat beside her, careful not to block the light from the fire. He liked the way flickering shadows shifted across the contours of her body . . . her undamaged body, he was glad to note.

"What's this?" he asked. He gave great contemplation to her right buttock. "You've got a bruise," he said. He kissed a spot gently. "Does that hurt?"

Her fingers clutched the pillow and she burrowed her head in its depths. "No." The word was muffled but distinct enough to convey encouragement.

"Remember how you bruised my neck?" He stroked the rounded fullness of her left buttock. "I ought to return the favor. So that both sides will match."

Her head lifted. "You wouldn't."

"Ah, sweet Angel, you don't know me very well."

He touched her with his tongue, at the approximate place the bruise ought to be. Down went her head into the pillow, and he felt her tremble beneath his lips.

He sucked at her sweetness, his hands stroking her hips, her thighs, then trailing back to the tantalizing curve of her waist. Everything about her taunted him. He needed to be gentle, he wanted to be wild. Like the savage youth he had once been, only this time his savagery would not be directed into fights but into something requiring far more finesse, a different kind of force.

He eased one hand between her legs. She was hot and wet, and beneath the pads of his fingers he could feel her muscles tensing, as if she would draw him into her.

Stretching out beside her and using his fingers, he did not disappoint.

Angel's body set up a rhythmic thrust against his hand,

harder, tighter, faster. And then she held herself still. He could not believe it when she pulled away from him and shifted to her side where she could look at him. Everything about her was untamed, her hair, her eyes, the breath that came in tight, shallow gasps.

"Did I hurt you? Are you telling me to stop?"

In answer, she bent her head and licked his chest, then looked up at him with such heat in her eyes she seared his skin.

"I want you the . . . right way." She spoke softly, for all her fervency somehow shy, touching something deep inside him. He could not swallow, could not breathe.

"There is no wrong way," he said, stroking the dampened strands of hair from her face, outlining her lips with his thumb.

She caught the tip of his thumb between her teeth. Eyes closed, she held on a second, then let go. "You know what I mean," she said, her gaze concentrated on his chest.

He did indeed know what she meant. Undressing quickly, he returned to her side, holding her as someone might caress a precious piece of porcelain. Worldly goods had no meaning for him. And neither did people other than Chad. Never a woman. Never.

But he wanted this one. He wanted her now. Running his hands down her arms, her breasts, her abdomen, tickling the pale pubic hair, then easing his fingers lower to the pulsing bud she lifted to him, he told himself to go slowly, swearing he would stop if she asked him, but she did nothing except offer encouragement, her breasts rubbing against his chest, her tongue seeking his in a deep and forever kind of kiss.

When she parted her legs, he lay as carefully as he could on top of her and, in the manner she had requested, he did it the right way.

* * *

Angel fell asleep in his arms, awakening to find him watching her. In the dimness she could not make out his expression, but she felt no anger in him, she sensed no rejection. She dared to cuddle close, then pulled away, fearing he would think her possessive.

A sentence from one of Raven's favorite plays came to her:

> *O! how this spring of love resembleth*
> *The uncertain glory of an April day!*

She had never understood Shakespeare's lines until now. Love both uncertain and glorious? She understood them now.

"How are you feeling?" he asked.

"Fine," she said, avoiding his eye.

He lifted her chin until she was forced to meet his gaze.

"Fine," she repeated, and meant it.

"Good. Then move back."

"Do you want me to leave?" Firmly said, not the least tremulous, or maybe just a little. She was very proud.

"No. Just shift backwards."

Relief rushed through her. She did what he asked.

He eased from the bed. She watched the play of muscles in his naked body as he fetched the tray of food and returned to set it on the mattress between them. Angel fluffed their pillows against the massive carved headboard, and they both sat upright to eat the soup and bread Mrs. MacCabe had brought what must have been hours ago.

Self-consciously, under her husband's watchful eye, Angel pulled the sheet up to her throat. He left the cover at his waist, and while she honestly tried not to look, she couldn't help glancing from time to time at the pattern of dark hairs across his chest and the way his muscles formed interesting contours across his shoulders and down his arms.

For a man so darkly ferocious, he had small little nipples, almost as pink as hers. Maybe they ought to compare—

She choked on a piece of bread, while Quent just kept on watching.

When they were done, he set the tray aside and returned to the bed.

Here was a new experience for her—dealing with her husband after sex when he did not seem inclined to berate her for anything. She liked it, but she didn't know what to do.

"We left crumbs on the sheets," she said.

"Ah, I forgot your penchant for cleanliness. Shall we call Mrs. MacCabe to clean up?"

He sounded teasing . . . not in the least distressed. But Quent *never* teased.

"No. If they don't bother you, they don't bother me."

"They don't bother me. But I've got a tougher hide than you."

She blushed. He certainly was an expert on just about every square inch of her.

Except her heart. Why, oh why, did such lowering thoughts occur to spoil her happiness? He must have sensed the change in her mood, for she sensed the same change in him.

"What happened in town today?" he asked.

Conscience struck her. How could she tell him about visiting the dock, about arranging transportation to the island for clandestine meetings with Chad?

"I posted Papa's letter, that's all."

That stopped him for a moment, too clearly taking him to other paths of thought . . . like who she was and why she was there. She almost wished she had told him about the boat.

"You're sure?" he asked.

"I went by one of the stores, and then I visited Nellie Ahearne for a while. We had tea."

She played with a small crust of bread, flicking it about the sheet over her lap while she talked.

"What did you do with the trap all this time?"

"I left it in the alley by the store. There was no room on the street. Honestly, Quent, I took care of it. I don't know what happened on the way home."

He covered her hand, stopping her play. "Don't worry. It can be repaired."

Sighing in relief, she said, "Good."

She had to get his mind off her foolishness, and certainly off of town. There was only one way. Somehow the sheet found its way to her waist.

"If you're not too tired, I thought we could compare our nipples."

It was her husband's turn to choke.

She turned to face him, touching her breasts against his chest. "I know what we're doing is meaningless, but it does pass the time, doesn't it?"

He pulled her into his embrace, and he kissed her. She liked the taste of soda bread on his lips.

"Aye, wife," he whispered huskily, "it passes the time."

He'd never called her *wife* before. She almost cried. Rubbing herself against him, she proceeded to do all she could to make them both forget the temporary nature of the word.

Nineteen

Sometime around midnight Quent jerked awake. Angel lay beside him in deep slumber. In the dying light from the fire, he could barely make her out, but still he looked, imagining what he could not see.

She rested on her stomach, her hair splayed across the pillow, her right arm curved above her head, the other reaching out as if to touch him. The left hand was in darkness, but he could imagine the graceful fingers limply curled, one bearing the gold ring he had given her back in Savannah.

Why he had bought it, he didn't know, but it had seemed like the thing to do at the time, making her his for as long as—

He stopped that line of thought. Buying the ring had meant no more than buying the trap. He hadn't even bothered to tell her the horse and rig were for her use, they were of such little importance. So why think of them now?

Never in his thirty years had he fallen asleep with a woman beside him. After sex, one or the other departed. And that included Angel. The novelty of having her still in his bed—for a novelty was all it could be—had him in a strange mood.

The cover came to her waist. He resisted the urge to trace the ridge of her spine with his hand, or better, with his tongue, to lower the sheet and learn if he had really bruised her as he had teased. Given his ready state and her easy-to-rouse passions, to touch her would lead to other things. After all she had been through . . . the fall, the sex, including twice in a short span of time after supper . . . she needed her rest.

Quent admitted to confusion. Usually his stays in Dublin included visits to several female acquaintances. But not this time. Too much business to tend to, he had told himself. In truth, not once in the three-week stay had he been much interested.

Interest returned the instant he arrived at the castle. No matter how much his wife infuriated him, and she could do it better and quicker than anyone he had ever met, she always interested him.

He put the real name to it. She made him horny as hell. Like right now.

Let her sleep, he warned himself. He ought to join her in rest, but he was a creature of habit, used to prowling in the night. On this particular occasion he had a purpose. Easing from the bed, he dressed quickly and quietly, then after making sure she was resting comfortably, hurried from the room.

Vengeance, as much a creature of habit as his master, made little sound as Quent saddled him and took to the road. If Old Tully, sleeping in his quarters above the stalls, heard him leave, he would think it one of his master's regular midnight prowlings.

But this time he did not head for the open country, nor for the deep forests of Kavanagh land. This time he headed for town.

The proprietor of Bantry Bay Tavern, closing for the night, took only a little persuasion to admit that Padraic Scully occupied one of the upstairs rooms.

" 'Tain't alone," he growled as Quent headed for the stairs.

Quent stopped at the room where the proprietor had directed him, gave brief thought to knocking, then with one swift movement kicked open the door.

Scully's naked sticklike figure jumped from the bed, a pale specter in the blend of moonglow and flickering light from a low-turned lamp. The woman who had been beneath him came to her elbows, pendulous breasts resting close to her rounded belly. She must have outweighed her lover by a hundred pounds.

Without looking toward the door, Scully bolted toward the chair by the window, his hands grappling for his trousers. Quent suspected he carried a gun.

"Don't do it," he ordered.

Scully stood still, then slowly shifted to face him.

"You," he whispered, eyes pale and sunken in his haggard face.

Everything about the man was gaunt, including the pencil-like penis that rose between his legs. As he stared at Quent, his erection wilted like the broken stalk of a weed.

The woman lay motionless, exposed, her lips twitching as though she enjoyed the scene. Quent could see striations of red across her white breasts and belly, leading all the way down to her thighs. She looked as if she had been whipped, lightly so as not to break the skin, but hard enough to mark and to hurt.

He looked in disgust at Scully, who took a shaky backwards step toward the closed window. He fought the temptation to shove the bastard through the glass.

"If you come near my wife again, I'll kill you."

Scully shook a long, damp strand of hair from his forehead. "I meant the woman no harm."

"You meant to kill her."

Scully glanced toward his trousers. "I saved—"

"The axle on the trap had been broken halfway through. Purposefully. While she was in town."

"Surely you don't think—"

"Surely I do."

"I never went near that trap."

"Probably not. Who did the dirty work for you? Owney Malone and his dutiful son?"

"They—" Scully stopped and cleared his throat. "I don't know who you're talking about."

"Be careful how you build your lies." Quent spoke slowly, softly, menacingly. "Were you just passing by when Angel went off the road? How many times do you ride up to the castle, Padraic? I've never known you to visit before."

The knot in Scully's throat bobbed. "I was considering putting a business proposition to you."

"The only thing you can put to me is your backside as you ride out of the county."

The woman laughed.

Quent gave consideration to another order, then decided he had said what he came to say.

But he hadn't done what he had come to do. He smashed Scully in the jaw, drew back his fist for another blow, but the man crumpled to the floor without a sound.

Quent stared down at him in disgust while the woman applauded. He heard nothing but clapping as he stepped past the door, which hung precariously on broken hinges, and headed out to finish the business of the night.

The next part was a trickier challenge. Earlier in the day Old Tully had talked to him about the increasing frequency of the night riders, tearing up turf that was already poorly suited for the crops growing on them, frightening the sheep and cattle, terrorizing the countryside, supposedly for the purpose of intimidating those who refused to fight for Home Rule.

"But what are we supposed to do?" Old Tully had asked with a shake of his head. "We're all for it, t' be sure. Methinks they want to stir up enough trouble so that the English will decide we're not worth the effort of keeping us. I'm thinking they'll come to a different conclusion. That we're not capable of ruling ourselves."

Quent agreed. He also suspected the Malones, encouraged by Scully, were deeply involved. He had no proof, just a gut instinct and an understanding of their character. A worse bunch of lowlifes he had not encountered anywhere in the world.

Oh, he had a great number of reasons to scorn the people around Cordangan, reasons that went back for years. Why he remained, he did not know.

Maybe once the matter with Thomas Chadwick was settled, he would leave. Thoughts of the man brought thoughts of Angel and what had happened to her today. He hadn't carried her across the ocean to harm her, just to use her. And any stirring of conscience in that regard would have to be ruthlessly suppressed.

Getting his information from the young gardener Angel had hired, Old Tully told him the usual routes of the night riders.

"Rumor is they'll be riding north o' the town this very night. The lad nay would reveal how he knew, but I suspect he hangs around the tavern in the evenings and hears more than he's meant to."

Finding the marauders meant finding the Malones. Quent made for the dark, rolling foothills of the Caha Mountains toward the north. Here was the most rugged land around the bay, good only for raising sheep and goats and providing cottages for the salmon fishermen who sailed out of Cordangan across the bay and into the Atlantic.

A mist was rising from the water far behind him and moving onto land, as though it would chase him into the hills. Moonlight lit the way. When he was well out of town he pulled off the road into the trees and the cover of darkness, slowing his pace, letting Vengeance pick his way, listening for sounds of other horses, other men.

For a long while, all was quiet. The stallion halted, bobbed his head, and neighed. Quent eased from the saddle. Fallen leaves crackled under his boots, and when he took a step forward, the crack of a twig sounded as loud as the shot of a gun.

Cursing his carelessness, he proceeded more cautiously. A light flickering through the forest beckoned. He moved closer until he could hear the sound of men's voices, pick out the flickers from a fire. He would swear that was Fergus Malone's voice whining about the lack of ale.

Another dozen yards carefully crossed, and he lowered himself to his haunches, his concentration directed to the dozen men gathered in the clearing. Fergus was among them, and Seamus O'Callaghan. Stranger as he was to the countryside around his home, he could not put names to the rest.

Owney was not in sight, but he was around somewhere. Quent could smell his stench.

He started to rise, heard a step behind him, whirled but it was too late. Something hard landed against the back of his head. He slumped to the ground, knowing nothing but the night.

In the dimness of predawn, Angel jerked awake, her heart pounding, her breath coming in gasps. Something was wrong. What, she did not know.

The sheets on which she lay smelled of Quent, and she realized in an instant where she was. Reaching out for him, she touched only an empty bed.

She cried out. Oh, something was terribly wrong, something involving her husband. Her heart told her so more clearly than her mind. She sat up and with the covers clutched to her bosom stared around the room, but all she saw was darkness. She stumbled from the bed and felt for the clothes Quent had hastily thrown aside the evening before. She found her gown, but no trousers, no shirt, no boots.

He was gone.

She tried to still her breath, telling herself it was his absence that alarmed her. He was used to riding in the night. Did she really think her presence in his bed would keep him here?

The argument did little to reassure her. Dressing quickly, not bothering to bind her hair, she went into the hall. The castle was quiet as death.

She shivered. Death . . . what a terrible thought. Making her way to the back stairs, she heard voices from below. They drifted muted but unmistakable in the stillness of the night. She hurried down to find Old Tully and Mrs. MacCabe huddled in their nightclothes by the cold hearth.

They started at her appearance.

"What's wrong?"

Old Tully glanced at the housekeeper, then looked at her. " 'Tis Vengeance. He's come back alone."

Cold terror knifed through Angel. "Where's Quent?"

"We don't know," said Mrs. MacCabe.

Angel turned to Old Tully, so shaky on her feet she could barely stand. "Has this ever happened before?" She knew the answer before she saw the shake of his head.

"Has the stallion been back long?"

"No more'n half an hour."

She looked past Old Tully to the partially opened door, to the darkness, to the void of night. "We've got to do something."

"The sun will be up soon," said Mrs. MacCabe.

"Not soon enough. Quent needs me now. Don't ask how I know it. I just do."

Glancing at Old Tully, she made her decision. "Saddle Solas. I'm going to find him."

She turned toward the stairs.

"It's too dangerous, lass," said Old Tully behind her.

"Aye," echoed Mrs. MacCabe, "far too dangerous. There's a fog this morning. You'll not make your way off the hill."

"Then I'll let Vengeance guide me. Solas will follow." She spoke as the mistress of the castle, one who must be obeyed. "Saddle the mare while I change my clothes."

She hurried up the stairs before they could give her further argument. In a quarter hour she was dressed in riding habit and cloak, her bonnet fastened over her unbound hair, a riding crop beating an impatient tattoo against her leg while Old Tully finished his tasks. He was saddling both Solas and Brenda, swearing he would cripple the horses before he let her ride out alone.

"You'll be left with nothing to ride but Mary O'Callaghan's donkey, lass. You won't get far."

"I'm glad of the company," she said, and meant it.

Vengeance stirred restlessly to one side, his dark stallion's eyes on Solas. Angel stood before him stroking his forehead. "We've got important business tonight, old boy. I promise not to keep her from you tomorrow or whenever you want, but now we have to find Quent." Her voice broke on her husband's name.

Nickering, Vengeance lifted his proud head. Angel knew he understood.

Old Tully helped her into the saddle, then pulled himself onto Brenda's swayed back.

"Let's go find your master," Angel said to the stallion, and with Mrs. MacCabe standing in silence beside the stable door, they rode toward the steeply winding road leading from the castle.

The housekeeper had spoken the truth. A fog rose from the bay, stopping short of the hilltop, spreading its thickness across the valley like a carpet. They rode into its dampness, letting the animals find the path. Always Vengeance stayed in the fore, his hooves sure and steady against the hard ground.

They traveled in silence, past the snarling stone dogs and down the hill, along the road into the village, passing thatched-roof cottages with their dark windows, through the sleeping streets, and past the harbor, where sailors were already preparing for the day, some casting off, some heaving to after a night on the water.

On they rode, until Angel began to question the stallion's purpose. She halted once, and Old Tully did the same, sharing with her a questioning, fearful look, but Vengeance continued and they hurried to catch up.

When they turned from the road and went into the forest, Angel knew they were close to Quent. She could feel him calling her. At that moment, if the fog miraculously heated into fire, she would have ridden through the blaze.

They found him lying on his back at the base of an oak tree. There was no mistaking his dark form, even in the mist-muted light of dawn. Angel cried out, terrified by the sight of her powerful husband now fallen. He was always so strong, so sure of himself. He looked helpless, he looked . . .

She leapt from the horse before Old Tully could help her. Kneeling beside his still body, she touched his face with a trembling hand. He felt cold, too cold. Remembering the lessons she had learned from watching Jeremiah, she felt at his throat for a pulse. When she found it, she burst into tears.

Old Tully crouched beside her. "Is he—"

"He's alive," she reported with a sob.

"So why the tears?"

"I don't know."

Foolishly she leaned against him and let her cries come. When Quent moaned, she got control of herself, sniffling, feeling like a child.

"We have to be careful about moving him," she said, touching his hair, wanting to touch him all over. Removing her cloak, she threw it over him, concentrating on tucking the edges around his prone body. "He'll need to be kept still until we find out exactly what's wrong."

"I've been hit on the head, that's what."

Angel started. Even in the dimness, she could see Quent

looking up at her. She saw, too, the strength in his eyes. She wanted to hug him as hard as she could. Quentin Kavanagh was not a man to stay down for long.

"It's about time you woke up," she said, failing miserably to sound harsh.

"Hard to rest with all the noise around here."

Oh yes, he was definitely the Quent of old. She brushed the tears from her cheeks, so filled with relief she could do nothing but lean close and kiss him right on the mouth. And then she felt a sudden embarrassment because it was such a wifely thing to do.

"This is what you get for riding about in the night. What happened, did a branch get you?"

"Aye, wielded by some bastard who got me from the rear."

She caught her breath. "Someone did this to you?"

Quent nodded, then winced. When he tried to sit up, she helped him, putting her arm around his shoulder, not caring how wifely she appeared.

"You could have been killed," she said, the reality of what had happened coming to her in waves.

"And why wasn't I, when I've been lying here helpless for hours? It's a question I'll be asking myself until I get the answer."

He tried to rise. "Don't move," she said, "anymore than you have to." Then added, because she couldn't hold back any longer, "Who? Who could have wanted to hurt you?"

"The night riders," Old Tully growled, then muttered a curse in Irish.

"Aye," was all Quent said, but there was such a hardness to the single word, Angel trembled in fear at the troubles this night would bring.

Quent slept restlessly most of the day, issuing orders when he wasn't asleep, sending Neill to the library for papers he swore must be read, then ignoring them when they were brought, barely sampling the food Mrs. MacCabe brought him, allowing only Angel to remain in the room.

He was most cooperative while permitting her to undress him. Concentrating her efforts on his shirt, telling him he would have to take care of the other clothes himself, she helped him into a nightshirt that had obviously never been worn.

Late in the day Old Tully visited briefly to report the trap had been mended.

"What we suspected proved to be true," he said without further explanation.

"I thought it would." Quent sounded angry. She must have done something terrible to the thing to rouse him when he was so weak.

"Are ye thinking the night riders are involved?" Old Tully asked.

"Some of them."

The stableman seemed about to say more, but a quick shake of Quent's head and he excused himself for the night.

Alarmed by Quent's sudden agitation, she threatened to give him a bitter tonic if he didn't rest.

"It's a potion Jeremiah taught me to make. I've seen grown men run screaming into the night to avoid its taste."

He came close to managing a grin, then, eyeing her from head to foot, he suggested an alternate cure.

"Later," she said, her voice so filled with fervent promise that he winked before settling back on the bed. While he slept, she sat by the fire, making sure it kept the entire room warm, staring into the flames as she listened to the music of his snores.

When the shadows darkened into night outside the window and she saw him lying quiet and watchful, his eyes on her as she sat by the fire, anticipation flowed like liquid pleasure to all her parts. The *later* she had promised Quent was come.

Twenty

Angel stared at her husband, certain that before long she would be in his bed, uncertain as to precisely how she would get there.

Such matters were far easier when Quent was the one in charge.

Pulling herself from her fireside chair, smoothing the folds of the wrapper and gown she had put on not an hour before, fluffing her hair where it lay against her shoulders, she began to walk toward him.

Quent watched every move. Injured or not, he never missed anything. Nervous, she started to run her tongue around her lips, but that seemed a little obvious, as if she were saying she wanted them wet and ready for whatever he had in mind.

Which she did, but he probably knew it already.

"Remember what you said after my accident?" she asked as she came close to the bed.

He propped his arms on the pillow beneath his head and kept on watching. "I said a number of things."

"I meant the comment about how we needed to work out my stiffness, to keep me from being sore. I thought you might want to know it worked."

"Good."

"I feel like a new woman."

"I rather liked the old one."

"It's just a figure of speech." Angel laughed at herself. "But you knew that. You're teasing me."

"And you aren't teasing me?"

"Maybe just a little."

She sat at the side of the bed, nudging him with her hip to get some room. Unable to look into his eyes, she studied the curve of his arms against the pillow, the way his ebony hair seemed to catch the light from the fire, the line of whiskers accenting his cheeks, the strong nose and mouth, the squared chin. His skin looked more coppery than ever against the whiteness of his nightshirt, and the hairs at his throat looked darkly inviting.

She had never seen him in anything other than black. She very much liked the white.

"It seems strange to see you in bed with your clothes on."

His eyebrows lifted. "Does it now? That can be changed."

Hearing his strong, sardonic voice, feeling the power that emanated from him, she thought of how he had appeared when she first saw him lying unconscious on the ground. Unbidden tears sprang to her eyes. She blinked them away, staring at her clinched hands in her lap.

"You frightened me so. Don't do that again."

"Were you really concerned?"

She wanted to tell him exactly how much, but *I love you* might alter everything between them . . . make everything worse.

"Mrs. MacCabe and Old Tully said Vengeance had never come back alone before."

"Ah yes, Mrs. MacCabe and Old Tully." He sounded disappointed she had mentioned them.

"We didn't know what to think."

"So you came after me. Whose idea was that? No, don't tell me. It was yours."

"Someone had to do something."

"Someone better do something now, Angel, or I'm liable to have a relapse from the pain."

She looked at him in alarm. "You're hurting?"

"Aye, in the worst kind of way." His eyes glittered.

"Oh." Angel understood. She felt a devilish urge to investigate exactly where his pain lay. Her hand crept beneath the cover, exploring his chest and abdomen, pressing gently, lower and lower, stopping at the bulge between his legs.

"I think I've found your trouble."

For a change, Quent's eyes were closed.

"Not quite," he said, not loud, but very, very deep.

Easing up his nightshirt, she wrapped her fingers around his slick, hard shaft.

"Now I have for sure. You've a monstrous swelling between your legs that must be seen to."

He didn't speak for a moment, then finally growled, "Get in the bed."

"I was hoping you'd ask." She stood to slip out of her wrapper.

"The gown, too."

"So many orders."

"I've just begun."

"Not tonight. You're the patient, remember, and I'm the one in charge. The first one to be naked will be you."

Cover down, nightshirt off, both quickly accomplished, his cooperation was all she could have asked. The firelight flickered over his body. She saw no bruises, and she was looking carefully indeed. Just hard muscle and sinews and tight warm skin, with the right touch of body hairs to make him all the more interesting.

And his sex, of course, which did not seemed harmed in the least. She studied it longer than she should, but when she felt his eyes on her, hot as the stones on the hearth, she flushed with embarrassment.

"Turn over," she ordered, more shakily than she would have preferred. He complied. The back of him was as interesting as the front . . . or at least almost as interesting. Especially the tight buttocks that extended into powerful thighs. As good as he looked in fitted trousers and shirt, he looked better with them off.

"No bruises," she said.

"You didn't have any either," he said.

"But you said—"

"I lied."

Angel sighed. "Oh, well. It was in a good cause." She thought back to all he had done . . . could it only be a day ago? Around Cordangan Castle, the hours were either empty or filled with more life, more vigor than an ordinary mortal could stand.

Everything depended on the presence of Quent. He was very much present now, and for the night he was hers.

Smiling in anticipation, very much the way a kitten smiled over cream, she stroked his bottom, then leaned down to kiss each mound. He was as tight and hard as a pair of fists. He muttered something unintelligible, but she didn't think it was a complaint.

She put her hands to work, rubbing the backs of his thighs and knees, then shifting to the inside of his legs, her fingers busily inspecting him from the crook of his knees all the way to the juncture of his thighs. She wedged a hand between them until she could cup his genitals. Again, he gave her all the cooperation she could have wanted.

And then he held still. "Stop." She could hardly believe what she heard. Insecurity assailed her. Until now she could have sworn she was pleasing him. Maybe women didn't do to men the things men did to them.

He looked at her over her shoulder. "I want it the right way."

Whether or not he was a devil, there was devilment in his eyes. Angel's heart did funny little twists as she smiled down at him. "You always throw what I say back at me. As I recall, you claimed there was no wrong way."

Without waiting for a reply, she helped him turn to his back. Whether or not men and women did the same things to each other, she knew exactly what she wanted to do. Slipping out of her gown, she lay on top of him, her breasts full and hungry as they met the solid expanse of his chest. The air was alternately cool and hot against her exposed backside as the heat from the fire came to her in waves.

Wherever she and Quent touched, she knew only warmth. Tickling a strand of her hair across the contours of his face, she drowned in the depths of his hot midnight eyes. If she were making a mistake in anything she did, she told herself, he would let her know. But he just kept on looking, pulling her into his power with nothing but a stare.

Contentment warred with impatience. Wanting this moment to go on forever, she hungered for more. His sex was hard against her belly. She rotated her hips, rubbed her own throbbing sex along his thigh.

And she kissed him, again and again, touching her lips to his eyelids, to his whiskered cheeks, to the corners of his mouth, against the side of his neck, running her tongue in his ear, then moving back to his mouth to kiss him so thoroughly he must surely know what was in her heart.

If she couldn't find words to tell him, she would let her body do so. Spreading her thighs, she lowered herself until the full length of him became encased in her warm, wet sheath. The woman on top . . . she had never heard of such a thing, but he did not complain. Instead, he covered her bottom with his hands and once again made her feel complete.

Sometime in the middle of the night she awoke to find Quent at the window, staring into the night.

"You're going out," she said in panic, not knowing what she would do if he left her again. Follow him, to keep him from harm? If necessary.

He returned to the bed and as he eased beneath the covers he took her into his arms. "The fog is rolling in again, that's all. In the moonlight I like to watch it eat the trees."

"Why Quentin Kavanagh, you're a poet." She nestled against him, relief flooding through her. "And you really love this land, don't you?"

He didn't answer, but she felt his hesitation, felt his withdrawal. What had made her ask such an intimate question? Just because they were lying in a naked embrace didn't mean she could get personal with him. She cursed herself for prying into his heart.

No matter the foolhardiness, however, she could not be completely quiet.

"When Old Tully came in here earlier, he said something about what you suspected being true. And then he wondered if the night riders were involved. What did he mean?"

"Nothing you should be worried about."

Angel knew he lied. Something in the tenor of his voice told her. He didn't realize it, but she was beginning to know him very well. He was keeping something from her, and she could not let the matter drop.

"I've heard Old Tully and the gardener talk about the night riders. Why would they want to hurt you? Are you against Home Rule?"

"I'm not a political man, Angel. Let it go."

She tried to do as he ordered. She really tried. But she hadn't been raised to look the other way when members of her family were in trouble. Whether or not he admitted it, whether he wanted it or not, Quent was her family now.

"If you're not a political man, then what happened to you was an accident. The way my fall was an accident. And we have nothing to fear, do we?"

He kept silent.

"Do we?" she asked again.

"I keep forgetting how stubborn you are. Why, I don't

know, since you are constantly giving me examples of that most unfortunate trait."

Angel let the insult go by without argument, although, if she had wanted to respond, she could have told him that he could out-stubborn her every day of the week.

"You didn't have an accident on the road," he said. "Someone purposefully damaged the axle on the trap."

"What?" Angel shoved herself away and stared down at him. "Who? When? Why?"

"Padraic Scully, or at least his minions. While you were in town. As to why, that's something I'm working on."

The truth of his words shivered through her. Never in her entire life had anyone wished evil upon her—with the possible exception of her husband—and she didn't know how to feel.

Oh yes she did. She felt dirtied in some way, and afraid, not for herself but for everyone around her.

She embraced him once again, holding him tight, as if she could draw his strength into her. "I've made enemies somehow. I'm sorry. I promise I never saw Padraic Scully until I came to and he was staring down at me. He looked so frightening, I almost passed out again."

He stroked her arm. "Scully's not after you, Angel. He's after me. I'm the one who should be apologizing."

"The Micks told me people were afraid of you. Please don't take offense, but it's the truth. And people are, although they really shouldn't be, should they? Not if they know you the way I do."

He held himself very still. "You don't know me, Angel."

There she went again, getting personal. Would she never learn?

Tears of frustration burned her eyes, and tears of heartbreak as well. This was all going wrong. He was supposed to be making love to her because he was falling in love with her, not because he was keeping her safe.

He thought she didn't know him, but she knew him far too well.

"You're right, of course," she said through her heartbreak, giving him the gift of her dignity. He would not want a cloying wife; indeed, he wanted no wife at all.

"I know this is all temporary," she went on, "and pleasant enough for the while, but it's not what either of us wants really, is it?"

This time when she pulled away from him, she had no intention of returning to his arms. What she meant to do was present herself as uncaring, and if that was the most difficult thing she had ever set out for herself, so be it.

Papa and Chad and Morna O'Brien and all the peoples of the past lay between them in that bed, and there was nothing she could do to change matters, not if giving herself to him whenever he wanted, in whatever manner he wished, didn't alter his purpose.

She had been a fool to allow herself to hope.

She sat up.

"What are you doing?" he asked.

"I'm going back to my bed." *Where you think I belong.*

"I prefer you here."

In the dimness she could barely make out his expression, but there was no mistaking the resolution in his voice.

Knowing she ought to leave, she lay back down beside him, but they did not touch.

"Think of this as another sacrifice for Papa."

"That's a terrible thing to say," she cried.

"I'm just more honest than you. We share a hunger for sex, Angel, and there's no denying it. But there should be truth as well. Our marriage is an arrangement from which we've both found an added benefit."

She could have told him no woman called desolation a *benefit,* but he would have another hurtful response, all in the name of truth. She closed her eyes, wishing she could vanish like the morning mist and not have to respond. But this moment was all too real, too hurtful coming as it did after the sweetness they had shared.

"I told you, didn't I, that the letter was posted yesterday?" Her voice was small and soft, but she could manage nothing else. "Papa should be here by the end of the summer." At the beginning of autumn, when the earth began to die.

Quent was a long time in replying. "I promise you this. Thomas Chadwick will find his precious daughter alive and well. Make no mistake, rogue though I am, I keep my word."

She felt leaden, beyond all tears. His assurance came too late, she wanted to tell him. Papa would find a daughter shattered by unrequited love. But that was not Quent's fault. Not once had he pretended to care.

"You'll stay close to home," he said. "It's the only way I know you'll be safe. I have no idea what is in Scully's mind. He was a small-time merchant in Dublin who lost his business through mismanagement. That's all I know of the man, except that when he started showing up in this part of the county, trouble came with him."

"I'll watch out for him."

"I'll do the watching. Coward that he is, I doubt he'll ride close to the castle again."

"But that makes me a prisoner. I can't see Chad."

"If you have a mind to meet him again, I'll make sure the two of you are together before you leave."

She knew it was a concession since he prized his brother above all others. She covered her mouth to stifle a cry. When she could trust herself to speak, she whispered, "Goodnight," and turned her back to him, listening to him breathe.

She felt alone and cold, so cold that all the fires in the world could not warm her. How strange it seemed that two people could lie in the same bed and somehow not share it. But it was no stranger than the way a man and woman could share intimacies in the marriage bed, yet not be truly wed.

Quent listened to the uneven breathing of his wife gradually turn to a regular rhythm indicating sleep. For him, no rest came, and not just because it was his nature to prowl during the midnight hour.

On this night he felt no inclination to leave his bed. Because Angel was here? He admitted it was so. A novelty, that's how he must continue to think of her, although something inside him said she could be a great deal more.

Sometimes it seemed she was beginning to care for him in a way that had nothing to do with her cursed family. Whatever she told herself along those lines, it was to assuage her conscience. Good women did not give themselves to men they did not care for, even husbands. They *submitted*. It was what his mother had done with his father, she had told him often enough.

Angel, good woman that she was, did not love him, no matter how much she believed she should. He was not a man to be loved. She was simply a passionate woman and he was a passionate man, two people thrown together in such a way that their natures took command of their senses. Around each other, they were not quite sane.

Like talking during sex. With his wife, the words, the teasing, the encouragements came naturally. He liked the talk, more than he would ever tell her, although never had he engaged in such a practice before, and no woman had ever talked to him except to call him false names of endearment. It was a blessing that Angel was too honest for such lies.

Somehow in the night she ended up in his arms, curling her warmth against him. Trusting him when he didn't want to be trusted, giving herself to him because that is what she had agreed to do. He had never met anyone like her. She had a purity, an innocence about her that could not be faked. Too, she was an inventive lover who made one of the oldest acts in the world seem new as the coming day.

Knowing he should push her away, he ended up stroking her hair. She purred like a kitten. The comparison twisted harsh memories inside him. Kittens died; women went away.

In a just world she would be back home giving her heart and longings to Jeremiah Godwin. Doctor God, one of the Micks had called him. He was the man Angel needed; he was the husband she deserved.

It was not, however, a just world and Quent was not a just man. A burning anger took hold of him as he thought of her in the doctor's arms.

But that was a world away in another lifetime. While she was under his roof, he would protect her and he would take her to bed again—he wasn't fool enough to deny it.

And when the time came, he would satisfy the vow that had haunted him for half his life, then he would leave the black-hearted knave she called father to her expert care.

Too, he would wonder, always wonder, about his struggle with the past, asking himself after the final retribution just who had won.

Twenty-one

During the next two weeks, no matter how hard she tried, Angel found sneaking away to see Chad an impossibility. Frustrated and anxious as she was, she could not really complain. The reason for her dilemma? One word—Quent.

At least once every day his path crossed hers, and every night he kept her in his room. She had thought such conditions would make her feel like a prisoner, but she had been wrong. If this was all she could have of her husband, these brief daytime meetings and the long intimate nights, she would take them into her heart and into her mind so that she might recall them after she was gone.

With June warming into July, their lovemaking lost its teasing moments, banter turning to low moans and soft cries, and a holding on that spoke more of fervency than it did of joy.

The mating did not always occur in bed. He showed her other places, other "right" ways . . . in the chair with her astride him, riding him as he rode Vengeance (or, so he described it); the rug before the hearth, where they heated up the room in place of the unlit fire; and once, when he returned home late from a trip to the island to find her naked and waiting, he took her against the wall.

All the while, as she grew to love him more, she buried that love more deeply in her heart. The conclusion of their marriage was inevitable. Papa would be getting her letter soon. Papa would be setting sail. Knowing little about the past except what she had already been told, she conceived of no way to soften the meeting with his unknown son . . . and with her husband.

What a poor detective she had turned out to be. Optimism deserted her, as did hope. Disaster lay ahead. All she could think about was making love to her husband, and losing him in the end.

How could she feel any different? Everywhere she turned she was reminded of sex. When the mare Solas's time came, she was mated to Vengeance—under Old Tully's supervision and Quent's disapproving stare. And once she found Neill and Mary O'Callaghan locked in an intimate embrace behind the library door.

"Neill loves you," she had said later when the young woman attempted to apologize. "No matter what else happens, you should always remember that."

"You don't understand," Mary had responded. "You've got your husband, and it's plain he's the man you want. Who have I got waiting for me? Fergus Malone!"

Angel had been unable to think of a single encouraging reply.

When the women began returning to the castle to help in its restoration, Angel threw herself into the work as though the place were really her home.

"Me man says there's evil on this hill," one of the women said early one morning while they were outside beating one of the carpets Angel had rescued from the tower. "I say he has only to meet you, Mrs. Kavanagh, t' see the foolishness of such talk."

The others echoed her sentiment.

"There's trouble at home over your coming here each day?" Angel asked.

"Arrah, lass, there's always trouble when folk don't know for sure if they can keep a roof over their head. Humble though it may be, me cottage is me castle, and I'm grateful for the generous wages you're providing."

Again, the other women agreed.

"There's talk of better times," she went on, "of higher prices for the sheep, of a mill starting up, even the fine handwork of the womenfolk bein' sold in faraway lands. Maybe it will come about. Or maybe it's ale talking, and dreams. We've been through too many hard times to count on pots of gold from the little people." She whacked at the carpet. "Give me wages for work any day."

Raised to labor for her living, Angel felt a kinship with the women. "What do you know about Padraic Scully?" she asked, venturing to ask them questions she could ask no one else.

"A Dubliner. Never cared much for cityfolk meself."

"Stays about the taverns too much t' suit me, buying drinks, encouraging the menfolk to laziness."

"A skeleton, that's what he is, overdue for his own burial."

All the responses came fast.

"How does he make his money?"

" 'Tis a question we've asked ourselves. The menfolk are not so inclined to question, but they listen to that fool Owney Malone."

The talk turned to a discussion of Malone and his son and what a worthless pair they were, and then on to the night rides, which had eased over the past few weeks, and at last turned to whether they shouldn't cease beating the poor rug, else they would be taking it down in pieces.

They did not speak of Mary O'Callaghan, or of her father Seamus. Having demonstrated a talent for handling the antique tapestries, Mary remained mostly in the tower. Good at both penmanship and ciphering, she had volunteered to inventory the contents of the observatory before they were placed in the refurbished rooms, and Angel had readily agreed.

Thinking of Mary, worrying about the lost look that never left her eyes, Angel went to find her. When she stopped by

her room, she glanced through the window in time to see
Quent riding Vengeance away from the castle. Heart quick-
ening, she hurried back downstairs to the stable, where Old
Tully reluctantly revealed her husband had ridden out to
inspect sites for the proposed mill.

"That should take some time," she said.

"Aye." Old Tully's eyes narrowed suspiciously.

"How is Solas getting along?"

More suspicion. "She'll be foaling by next summer,
never you fear."

Angel did not want to think where she would be when
the colt or filly was born.

"Is it all right to ride her?"

"For the next five to six months. After that, she should
be put to pasture 'til the business is done."

Put to pasture . . . like Angel. Permanent pasture, although as far as she knew she carried no new life within
her to ease the fated departure.

Her heart turned to lead. So many things were left for
her to do, and so little time. She stared at the open stable
door. "I'd like to ride her now."

"Nay, lass—"

"Don't worry. I'm not going into town." She covered his
weathered hand with hers. "Please. I'll be all right."

They looked at one another for a long while. "It's important t' ye, is it not?"

"More important than you can know."

"He'll have me head on a platter, but run along and get
into your togs. The mare will be ready when you've returned."

He was as good as his word, and within the half hour
Angel, dressed in one of Nellie Ahearne's riding habits, was
reining Solas down the road and into the trees leading to
the bay. Not just any point by the water, but one in particular, the potential meeting place for the boatman Hogan
who, weeks ago, had agreed to take her to Calluragh Island.

She went without hope. Surely he had forgotten the arrangement. Long ago he must have stopped watching for the red signal flag she was supposed to raise. Still, she had brought the thing, and after tying Solas in a stand of grass, she tied it to the highest limb she could reach.

Waiting was the hardest part, pacing the narrow, rocky stretch of beach, then sitting on a wide flat rock, chin resting on bent knees while she watched for a boat on the bay. She waited an hour, and then another. He wasn't coming. She stood to leave, asking herself why everything seemed to be turning out wrong lately, feeling as though she would never be hopeful again.

And then she saw the small craft cutting through the choppy water, making straight for her. She stood and waved. On came the boat. She glanced toward the island, a nervous smile on her lips. Soon she would see her brother again.

What would Quent say if he knew? He would be more than furious. He would probably hate her, so much he might never touch her again.

Pressing her fingers to her lips, she stifled a cry.

"My darling," she whispered to her absent husband, "I'm doing this for you."

The saddest part of all this was that even if he believed her, he wouldn't care.

With its white walls, green shutters, and colorful flower bed across the front, the cottage was exactly the way she remembered it. So, too, was her nervousness as she walked toward the door, her stomach turning a hundred somersaults and her mouth dry as dust.

Calling herself a coward, she was about to knock when the door opened.

"I've been expecting ye," said Agnes O'Toole.

Angel stared into the kindly eyes of her brother's caretaker. The woman was so short she made Angel feel as big as Owney Malone.

"How did you know?" was all she could manage.

"Chad's been skittering about the place for the past hour, hardly able to sit still, remembering the day he had the visit from an angel. He has a sense sometimes for things that are about to happen."

Smoothing a strand of gray hair from her forehead, Agnes stepped aside. "Come in. I've baked biscuits for the two of you. The tea will be coming directly. Yer brother's outside watching the birds."

Your brother. Angel tingled with anticipation.

"Does he know who I am?"

"Nay, 'tis too complicated for him to sort out such relationships on his own, and there's been none t' tell him. If I hadn't been listening when I shouldn't, the day you were last here, I'd not be understanding meself. Meaning no offense, but Master Quent is not by nature a talkative man." She patted Angel's hand. "But few of them are, lass. Ye shouldn't be dismayed."

Despite her stoop, the old woman had a spring in her step as she led her visitor to the back door. "Chad," she called, "someone's here t' see ye."

He stood in the patch of shady ground where he had been working, his smile crooked, his features just like Papa's. Angel couldn't control herself. Running across the yard, she hugged him hard, then backed away, blinking at the tears.

Chad's smile faded. "Did I do something wrong?"

"Sometimes people cry from happiness." Angel brushed at the dampness on her cheek. "I'm happy to see you again, that's all."

"Me, too. I remember your name. It's Angel, like in heaven."

Angel hugged him again. Quent would say she was showing pity for her brother, when in truth she was showing love.

"I'll fetch the biscuits," Agnes chirped. "On this fine summer's day, I'll serve them out of doors."

She did just that, along with tea and sandwiches, while Angel asked Chad about his carvings, inspecting each one in genuine admiration, asking him how he filled his days, what he liked to do and to eat. With his caretaker back in the cottage, he answered her in turn, sometimes putting a question to her about what she liked and what she did.

Not once did he wonder why she asked or why she was there or whether she had an ulterior motive for showing interest in him. He accepted her the way she presented herself. And in the same manner she accepted him.

In some ways Chadwick O'Brien was more like her than he was like Quent. A traitorous thought, it would not go away.

More than once she wished that Flame and Raven could be here to meet him. They would love him with the same instant enthusiasm she had felt. And so would Mama because she was a good and loving woman with a nature as generous as any of her daughters.

As for Papa . . . she wasn't so sure.

Right away she rebuked herself for so little faith, yet her worries would not go away. Quent had based all his schemes on the belief Papa would be devastated. In the beginning he had felt that she, too, would feel the same, especially when he wrenched her from her home and carried her off to sea.

Things hadn't worked out quite the way he planned . . . for either of them.

"You're going away," said Chad. "The way Quentin does sometimes."

It took her a minute to realize what he meant.

"You mean I went away in my mind. But I didn't, not really. You're in my thoughts a great deal."

"I was thinking something, too. About you and the birds. You're prettier than the gulls."

She clapped her hands together. "What a wonderful compliment. Do you walk around the island much to watch them?"

Chad nodded. "There's different birds with different nests from one side to the other."

She was vaguely aware that Agnes had returned, a silent reminder that it was almost time to leave. But she couldn't, not right away. There was no telling when she would return, once Quent found out about today.

And he would find out, if for no other reason than she didn't want him to.

"Do you ever sail on the water?" she asked, dragging out the afternoon.

"I fish sometimes," he said, "but Quentin doesn't like me to go in a boat."

"How long have you been here?" she asked.

"A long, long time," he said, not looking in the least happy.

"Nine years," Agnes said with a shake of her head.

"Nine years!" Angel stared at her in dismay. "That couldn't be." And yet it could. Mrs. MacCabe had told her Quent moved him here after the death of Dermot Kavanagh. And that had been . . . nine years ago. She just hadn't put all the facts together.

"He lived on the far side of the island at first, then Master Quent built this cottage, mostly with his own hands, but ye can believe Chad did no little part, clever craftsman that he is. Made the shutters himself, under his brother's eye, and he's a wizard with a paintbrush, I can tell ye. Keeps everything looking like new."

Angel studied her proudly smiling brother. "Do you remember the castle?" she asked.

"Oh, yes," said Chad. "I can see it from where I go to fish."

"What about the room where you stayed? It was high in the tower."

Chad nodded, and she could detect no sign the memory was an unhappy one, even though she had been told he was seldom allowed to leave. Life for him had been little more than a series of prisons; it was a tribute to his good, strong nature that he could so readily smile.

"I looked out over everything. Quentin didn't like it there very much. I didn't like it all the time. But it wasn't so bad." He hesitated, smiling shyly at her. "Could I see it again?"

"Now, now," Agnes said, "ye know Master Quent would not be liking yer asking such as that."

Chad sighed. "I know."

There were so many things Quent didn't like, thought Angel. And he always got his way.

She toyed with the idea of insurrection.

Don't do it, her inner voice warned.

Nine years, she answered in return.

She looked around her. As charming as the cottage was, would she or Quent or anyone want to spend a lifetime here without ever leaving? You might put someone in such a place if you pitied him, but if you truly cared for his happiness, you would listen to his wants.

Quent was the one who pitied Chad, not her.

She could hear his steely denial and see the cold scorn in his eyes. How dare she question him? She who was nothing but a temporary wife.

She who loved him more than life itself dared a great deal. What did she have to lose? Papa would be here in little more than a month, and all would end for her.

What about Chad? Would she be doing him a terrible disservice in tearing him from his nest? What would Raven do? Or Flame? In that instant, thinking of her sisters, looking into her brother's wide brown hopeful eyes, she made up her mind.

"Excuse us a moment, will you?" she said to Chad, then hustled Agnes O'Toole into the cottage, where she gave instructions to pack a change of clothes for the two of them, enough to last at least a couple of days.

"We're all going to Cordangan Castle," she explained when the woman looked too dumbfounded to ask why.

Fear replaced puzzlement in the woman's pale gray eyes.

"My orders," said Angel. "It's not anything my husband won't expect of me." And nothing he would like. Still, she had made up her mind.

"Hurry now. The boatman I hired to get me here and back is waiting at the shore. There's room for us all."

It took another quarter hour of wrangling, but at last Agnes understood that Angel had made up her mind.

"Yer a match for the devil himself," the woman muttered as she went about her tasks.

After months of marriage, Angel knew that she wasn't, but pointing out the fact seemed a fruitless pursuit.

Hogan did not appear much pleased at the extra passengers, but he was willing enough when Angel doubled his fee. By the time the sun was halfway toward the horizon, the unexpected party was on the mainland, Agnes sitting precariously atop Solas, brother and sister walking on either side of the horse's high white head. The way up to the road from the water was slow-going, but they made it without incident. They were almost to the castle gate when disaster struck.

As always, disaster took the form of a stormy-eyed, black-clad man who was furious with his wife. He stood at the castle steps. Despite the distance, even Chad sensed his brother's anger, dropping his waving hand, swallowing his smile.

Agnes let go of the saddle long enough to make the sign of the cross.

Angel stood her ground and waited for Quent to walk to

them, more because of weak knees than of a carefully thought out strategy.

They met by the snarling dogs.

No one spoke. Quent looked at Chad, at Agnes, then settled his gaze on his wife.

She cleared her throat. "This was my idea."

"I didn't doubt it."

"Are you mad at me?" Chad asked.

Quent took a deep breath. "You're supposed to stay on the island."

Chad turned. "I'll go back."

"No," Quent and Angel said together.

Quent cocked an eyebrow at her. The rest of her words died in her throat. In that moment the entire Atlantic Ocean flowed between them. It was a distance she knew not how to cross.

"I'll take care of them," he said to her. "Please let Mrs. MacCabe know we have guests."

She stepped around him, determined not to cry, swearing she would not question what she had done. After all, what could he do to her? Send her away?

"Angel." His voice stopped her like a shot. "Wait for me in the library. Alone. I have some things to say that you would not want anyone else to hear."

Twenty-two

Quent stopped in the library doorway to stare at his wife. She stood by the window, gazing into the dying of the day, bathed in the final glows of the sun. In the hour since he last saw her, she had changed from her riding habit into a gown, and had arranged her hair loose. He didn't want to notice such details about her, but he did.

He closed the door, and she shifted her gaze to him. How brave she looked, and how worried. He wanted to . . .

Hell, he wanted to do too many things.

"Are they settling in?" she asked.

"You might say that."

"I was thinking maybe we could all eat together in the dining room." She twisted her hands at her waist. "It's not decorated yet, but—"

"This isn't a social gathering, Angel."

"We still have to eat."

He walked toward her. The closer he got, the clearer he could see the tightness in her lips and the fine lines of worry in her brow.

"Being brave, are you?" he asked.

She looked away from him. "If you must know, I'm trying very, very hard to keep from collapsing."

"I appreciate your honesty."

"Thank—"

"Don't thank me too soon. There's little else I appreciate about you right now."

She rubbed her hands on the skirt of her blue gown . . . the one that brought out the color in her eyes. He had told her once he liked it. She had doubtless remembered. She was a smart woman, too smart for her own good.

"What am I going to tell you?" he asked.

She stared at him in surprise. "Isn't that up to you?"

"Humor me, Angel, as openly as you do in bed."

Her chin tilted. "That's not a very nice thing to say."

"I'm not feeling very nice. I seldom do, but then surely you know that by now."

"All right." She took a deep breath. "You're going to tell me I interfered in matters that are none of my concern. I'm stirring up troubles that I cannot begin to understand. Chad was content, but I have made him discontent and have thus undone all that you have accomplished over the past nine years."

He applauded. "Very good. Not complete, but not wrong."

"It's not good at all because it *is* wrong."

Staying an arm's length away, he kept his voice low, his anger controlled as much as he could manage. "You plan, of course, to point out the error of my thinking."

She returned her attention to the day. "Chad is my brother, too, as you so carefully pointed out when you took me to the island. I wasn't supposed to love him, was I? You expected me to be horrified, and when I wasn't, you decided I pitied him. That wasn't how I felt at all."

"Careful, Angel."

"It's much too late for caution. As for my not understanding, the reverse is true. I see and I know how you feel. He's all you've got—" She paused a moment, as if she would gather courage. "He's all you think you've got in the world, and you want to protect him because you love him."

Her eyes found his, and the depth of her expression shook him more than he could have expected.

"But love isn't always enough. Chad wasn't content. You

can't lock him away, no matter how much you want to protect him. The island was no better for him than the tower. Worse in a way. He told me he didn't really mind staying up there. That's where you put him, isn't it? That's where he asked to sleep. I can see by your eyes I'm right."

"Enough."

"You asked me—"

"I changed my mind." He moved in on her, until she stood with her back to the wall beside the window, so close he felt her breath on his cheek. "You have no idea what you've stirred up. You weren't here when he was younger. You didn't hear the taunts, you didn't watch the village children throw the stones."

"They stoned him?"

"Aye, but the words were worse. He's evil, did you not know? Marked by his tainted evil mother. And I'm the same."

"Oh, no." She touched his cheek. "You're not evil."

Her fingers burned. He crushed them in his hand. "Don't make me out better than I am because you want a happy ending to your stay. Nothing about our marriage should bring you peace. I've used you, for my revenge and for my pleasure. Until today, I've not known a moment's regret."

The blue of her eyes blurred with tears. "Please give me a chance to prove I'm right."

"Stubborn wench, aren't you? You've come a long way from the timid woman who approached me in a Savannah hotel. Wondering what she had to do to make me go away."

He pressed his hips against hers. Curse him for a fool, but he was aroused. He had been the instant he stepped into the room. "The only thing I'll give you is this." He held her waist, spanning it in his hands, and then her hips, her buttocks, squeezing, massaging, letting her feel his hardness against her belly. She did not try to pull away.

"We did it once before against the wall. Would you like it that way again? Here? Now?"

She closed her eyes, tears staining her cheeks. Lips parted, she caught her breath, and he could see the tip of her pink, enticing tongue.

By God, he ought to—

Movement at the window caught his eye. He looked out to see the smiling face of the brother that they shared. He let her go, forcing a nod to Chad, fighting for control.

Her eyes flew open, she followed his gaze, and whispered a shaky, "Oh."

Chad waved and moved on, leaving Quent and Angel to stare at one another. What a lovely creature she was, as foreign from him in every aspect as she could possibly be. Desire was slow in dying, but when it was gone he knew that it could never return. He felt empty inside, as if someone had hollowed him out with a knife.

"He makes a convenient chaperon, does he not? Is that why you brought him? Tired of my attentions?"

Her lips trembled. "Why question me? You will believe what you want to."

There was a finality in her voice, a flatness he had not heard before. He welcomed it. No more would he be subjected to her optimism, her treacherous good will.

He left her standing by the window, moving stiffly, more like one of Chad's carvings than a man. At the library door, he paused.

"You won't be needing protection from me. And you can go back to sleeping in your room. I'll not bother you again. Chad can remain here until your father arrives. As long as there is no trouble, of course. I advise you to see that all goes well."

Over the next weeks Angel threw herself into her work with such abandon she took even herself by surprise. She seldom saw Quent, except for the evening meal when they gathered together in the dining room, an awkward occasion at best with Chad doing most of the talking. She didn't want to see him. Thinking about him was bad enough.

She didn't eat much, and she slept fitfully, she looked terrible with her skin sallow and dark circles under her eyes, but what difference did her appearance make? Chad accepted her as she was, and Quent didn't accept her at all.

Mrs. MacCabe gave her a lecture or two, Old Tully clucked in disapproval around her, and even Agnes O'Toole advised her to rest, but she couldn't. If Quent had his demons, so did she.

Chad took to the restoration work with a joy that was the single redeeming element in her life. The fancy stucco scrollwork in the ceilings and over the windows, damaged by the passing of the decades, caught his attention, just as the gulls had once done. Supplies were brought from town, and he got to work rebuilding the beautiful decorations, his hands as skillful as they had ever been carving stone.

Determined to leave the castle a place of beauty, depending on the advice of the visiting Nellie Ahearne, she ordered crystal chandeliers from the factory in Waterford. With any luck, they could be installed over each end of the dining table before she was gone.

Fighting the centuries-old mustiness that clung to the castle walls, she threw the windows open to let in the summer breeze. There were times she could smell the salt air from the Atlantic at the end of the bay.

Working side by side with the women from town, she scrubbed and waxed and polished and she kept herself very, very busy so that she would not have time to think. Quent, too, was busy with the expansion of his business. As he had promised, he did not bother her again.

Except that with every waking breath she took and with every thought, he bothered her. Nothing removed him from her mind.

The day came when she needed to select a paint for the dining room, the one room she wanted to be perfect. Chad

had completed the stucco work, in particular the circular designs in the ceiling where the chandeliers were to be placed. The portrait of Quent's grandfather in his red cloak was ready to be hung, as was one of the medieval tapestries Mary O'Callaghan had been repairing, a work of art whose crimson and gold threads showed a fair-haired angel of goodness offering solace to a dark-haired man in despair.

It was supposed to be allegorical, a story from another time, but Angel knew different. She wondered how long Quent would allow it to taunt him from the wall.

The paint had to be the perfect shade of cream. Nellie had ordered two different kinds from Cork City, premixed, the "latest thing," she claimed. Word came from town the paint was here. Angel had been isolated for a long while on the hill, but with Padraic Scully seldom seen and the night rides slacking off, she could see no possible danger if she left her cocoon.

As usual, Quent was busy somewhere away from the castle, and Old Tully offered little objection when she asked that he ready the trap for her journey. She made her excuses to Chad, who begged to go with her.

"I won't be any trouble," he promised. They were in the kitchen, talking under the warning eye of Mrs. Maccabe.

But Angel needed no warning. "No," she said firmly, leaving to fetch her bonnet and purse. When she returned, he was nowhere to be seen.

She found him as the trap reached the bottom of the hill. He jumped into the middle of the road, grinning broadly, sweaty from having run to catch up with her, waving his arms enthusiastically in the air.

She reined Lorcan to a halt. "Go on back," she said in her sternest voice.

"I'll run after you. I'm fast."

He spoke the truth. She couldn't believe he had made it down the craggy hill so quickly, yet here he was. Weighing her options, she decided it was better to have him with her than trailing somewhere behind. "Climb in," she said.

When Chad had settled himself beside her on the narrow leather seat, he pulled a handkerchief from his pocket and wiped his face. "Got to clean myself up for town," he said, showing her his initials on the cloth before tucking it away. "Agnes made it for me. She said I should always look my best."

Angel squeezed his hand. "You're a handsome man, Chadwick O'Brien. I'm proud to have you by my side."

Proud, yes, and fearful she was making a terrible mistake. Fervently praying for whatever help she could get, she continued the journey.

All went well at Nellie's. With Chad close by her side and offering good advice, she selected one of the paint shades, purchased what had already arrived and placed an order for more. The paint would do well for the drawing room as well as the dining room, although she wanted something brighter for the Great Hall.

Busy planning, as though the grand old place were hers.

"I'll carry this outside," Chad said, taking the heavy purchases and hurrying on ahead. She paused a moment to thank her dear friend for all her help. The moment stretched out when Nellie tried to discover what brought the worry to her eyes, but there was nothing she could or would reveal. Everything was far too complicated.

Loud voices drew her to the door. She hurried outside to see Fergus Malone weaving drunkenly in the street, behind him his father and a dozen more men she did not know.

"You've come from the grave, you dead bastard," Fergus yelled. "You've taken me Mary, that's what you've done."

"Get him," Owney shouted. "Make him pay," and the other men joined in. Up and down the street, people stopped to stare at the commotion.

Angel could tell at a glance the men around Chad had

been in the tavern too long. Nellie put a hand on her arm to restrain her, but nothing could keep her from rescuing her brother.

Fergus bent to pick up a weapon, a heavy, jagged rock that dwarfed his massive hand. She flew at him with orders to leave Chad alone. Baring his yellow teeth, he brushed her aside. She tripped on the skirt of her gown and sat hard on the ground.

"Serves her right," Owney growled in his coarse thick voice.

"Aye, she's the devil's wife t' be sure," another said.

Chad dropped the paint and went for Fergus, showing no care that the burly farmer was twice his weight.

"No," Angel cried. Chad was not to be deterred. Before Fergus could let loose with his stone, the slighter man rammed his head into his stomach, sending him sprawling in the road not far from Angel.

She scrambled to her feet and grabbed for Chad, but he was a ball of fury, shaking her off, jumping onto Fergus and pummeling him with his fists, the blows doing more harm from their unexpectedness than from their force.

Fergus covered his face and head. "Get him off," he bellowed.

From the crowd fast gathering in front of the stores came the laughter of a woman. "Can't handle the brute, can ye, Fergus?"

More scornful laughter, mostly from the women. Lost to anger, the men yelled all the louder. Owney shook his head in disgust.

It was left to Angel to drag Chad off his enemy. Somehow his shirt had gotten torn at the sleeve and his sweaty face was streaked with dirt, but there was triumph in his eye.

"I never did anything like that before," he said to Angel, turning his back on Fergus.

The farmer lumbered to his feet, looking over his shoulder for support. "He put a spell on me, that he did," he whined, rubbing at his reddened jaw. "He's evil, by God." He made the sign of the cross. "We've allus heard it said, and 'tis true."

The cry of *evil* was taken up by the men, and Angel felt the cold horror Quent must have felt years before when he heard the same mindless taunts.

From the corner of her eye she saw Fergus pick up another rock. She shoved Chad toward the trap; when he leaned down to grab the packages of paint, the missile whizzed close to his head.

Somehow they managed to get aboard, and Angel cracked the whip over Lorcan's flanks. The agitated blood bay proved only too eager to take off at a rapid clip. She kept her eyes straight ahead, vaguely aware of the onlookers they passed . . . Mrs. Dunne, Mrs. Plunkett, others she could not name. She could have sworn she saw Padraic Scully in front of the tavern door, watching like some malevolent bug. No telling who else was viewing and enjoying the ugly scene. Enjoying because it *was* ugly. What kind of people were these?

But one of the women had laughed, and several had jeered the men. She must not forget that. If the mob had turned on Chad in greater violence, perhaps they would have come to Chad's rescue. Perhaps. Willing her thundering heart to slow, she tried to view the scene with more objectivity. As they passed the edge of the village, and the row of cottages that led to the castle road, she glanced at Chad. He grinned in return.

She reined the horse to a halt and shifted to face him.

"Now just what is so funny?"

"I won, didn't I? I never had a real fight before. Quentin takes care of me. But I can do it myself."

Dirty face, torn shirt, disheveled hair and all, he seemed as happy as she had ever seen him. Things might have gone far worse—he might have been truly hurt—but on this bright summer's day that's not the way it had all turned out.

"You were wonderful." She brushed at the smudge on his cheek. He fumbled through his pockets for the handkerchief, shrugging when he couldn't find it.

"Don't worry about looking good. You look better than good. You look wonderful. Fergus Malone is a big bully and a coward. You handled him just fine."

"He tried to hurt you. I couldn't let him. I love you, Angel."

She kissed him on the cheek. "And I love you."

All right, she told herself when she took up the reins once again, it had been dangerous and he might have been hurt, but he couldn't always be protected against the troubles of the world. She wouldn't take him into town again. Once Quent learned of the incident—and he probably already knew—Chad would be watched more carefully than ever. And she would be even more condemned.

But on this one day, in this one confrontation, Chadwick O'Brien had been allowed to fight like a man.

Twenty-three

As things turned out, Quent did not explode. After he had summoned her to the library, using Mrs. MacCabe as his messenger, he just looked at her from behind his wide, neat desk and said the horse and trap were no longer available to her. Neither was Solas. And, if he could help it, he might as well have added, neither were any of the residents at Cordangan Castle.

He spoke as if she were a child. She seethed, as much over the insult as the gulf he kept between them. And her heart broke a little more.

"Have you talked to Chad?"

"Oh, yes. He was very happy. Proud of himself for having defended you. He would take no criticism of the woman who almost got him killed."

"That wasn't the way of it."

"Oh, no? Correct me where I'm wrong."

He spoke so calmly, so coldly, but she could see the twitch of his lips and she knew the anger that burned inside him. She wasn't worth an explosion or an argument, or even a sexual threat as he had been wont to offer. She was worthy of no more than scorn.

She went all cold inside, the way she had done when she learned of Papa's debts. Only this was worse, far worse. She was an ice woman, who could crack and break and shatter at any time.

"If the Malones hadn't been in town, nothing would have

happened to him." Wooden words, spoken stiffly, a rote defense that for all its truth held no hint of hope.

"People like the Malones will always be in town."

It was his final judgment. She stood for a long time just staring at him, trying to gather together all the pieces that he had destroyed inside her, but it was a futile pursuit. She would never be whole again.

"I haven't made a difference here, have I? Not really."

"Oh, you've made a difference, all right." But he didn't say how, and he didn't say that the difference had been wanted, or had been good.

She left him to walk through the Great Hall with its clean walls and floor and the repaired stucco and the fresh scents of outdoors that wafted through the air.

What a wonderful room, she thought, viewing it as a stranger might. It would be even better once the portraits and tapestries were hung and the rugs spread over the cold floor. If such final touches were ever seen to. It seemed unlikely. After her departure she wondered how much time would pass before the mustiness returned.

She ought to care, but somehow she couldn't. A commotion from the direction of the kitchen stilled her musings, and she hurried toward the sound.

A tall, spare man of middle age clutched at the handle of the open back door, breathing heavily, staring at the two people who would deny him entrance, Mrs. MacCabe and Old Tully. Work clothes torn and stained, his face cut, blood dried on one cheek, he appeared to have been in a fight. He looked familiar to her. One of the men who had stood beside Owney Malone, she would swear.

"Where is me daughter?" he bellowed, his narrow eyes cutting around the room. "I've the right t' know where yer keeping the lass."

Seamus O'Callaghan. Of course. Mary's father.

"She's not here, Seamus," said Old Tully. "I've been trying to tell you, but you're too stubborn t' listen."

Angel tried to remember when she had last seen Mary. It must have been late yesterday afternoon.

She caught Mrs. MacCabe's eye. The housekeeper shook her head, as if to say Mary was not available to the father. But that was wrong. Whatever trouble lay between the O'Callaghans was not for others to settle. People needed to talk things out, not keep themselves apart.

She stepped into the fray. "Mister O'Callaghan, I'm Angel Kavanagh. You need a little doctoring, don't you?" She glanced at Mrs. MacCabe. "Could we get a damp rag and some ointment?"

Then back to the farmer. "Sit down, sir, and we'll talk."

"I've no time for talk."

"Oh, yes you have. Old Tully says she's not here, and I've never known him to lie."

" 'Tis the God's truth," Old Tully said. "I've tried to tell the old fool, but he wouldn't listen."

She led Seamus by the hand to the table and fairly pushed him into a chair. Whether it came from surprise at her boldness or from a willingness to cooperate, she didn't question the reason behind his sudden meekness. With the supplies brought by Mrs. MacCabe, she doctored his face.

He sat still as stone until she was done, then lifted sorrowful eyes to her, the animosity in him gone.

"Who did this to you?" she asked.

"Owney Malone."

"I thought you were friends."

"No more. Not after today." The lines on his face deepened to furrows. "I'll not be a part of throwing stones at any man. Especially Chadwick O'Brien. In my youth I did such foolish and shameful things, but surely I'm past the cruelty of it now."

Angel pulled up a chair beside, him and took his hand. "I knew everyone couldn't be against us. I just knew it." She looked up at Old Tully, then Mrs. MacCabe. "Where is Mary?"

Clearing her throat, the housekeeper said, "I'll get some tea."

"Mistress Angel," Old Tully said, "ye'd best hear the truth elsewheres."

"No need t' keep her from me," the father said. "I've come t' tell her she can marry whoever she wants. As long as it's not Fergus Malone."

Old Tully cackled. "Then the two o' ye are of one mind, O'Callaghan, for sometime during the night she took off with Neill Connolly, and there's not been a sign o' them around here since."

The next morning, denied the use of a horse to ride, Angel took off on foot to roam the Kavanagh land, to begin her final goodbyes. Everything seemed settled. Mary and Neill gone to a freer life, Chad off the island in what just might be a permanent new home, the castle as refurbished as she could get it, and even Vengeance and Solas expecting their first foal within the year.

As for her situation, Papa was on his way. She expected him at any time, and it was just as well. Get the meeting between father and son over with, give Quent his revenge— and, she fervently hoped, the peace he sought—then return to Savannah and pick up the fragments of her life.

Which would not include Jeremiah Godwin. In her last letter Mama had written that every eligible female in town was pursuing him; he was sure to be caught before long. Not that Angel could ever look at another man, no matter how good he was, or how lonely the passing years.

For now, she had to have faith in Papa. How could he not love Chad? His torment would come in knowing the hardships his son had suffered in his early years because of his illegitimacy. But those years could not be erased, no matter how much Quent thought they could.

She found herself high on the promontory that held the

dozen headstones marking the Kavanagh family cemetery. Wind off the bay whipped her hair and the skirt of her gown, and in the distance, beyond Calluragh Island and the end of Bantry Bay, she could see storm clouds gathering over the ocean.

Thunder and lightning would be a suitable background for her departure, and rain, most definitely rain. It had been raining the night she arrived. The wind turned chill. She hugged herself, and she wept, for how long she did not know.

"I didn't expect to find you here."

Quent's voice stopped her heart and brought her back from despair. For a moment she couldn't think, couldn't breathe. He was here, alone with her and the sky and the wind and the approaching storm. Hurriedly she wiped her cheeks, but she did not turn to face him.

"I've been to the graves before," she said.

"I didn't know. You never mentioned it."

"It was soon after I learned about Chad."

She felt her husband standing close behind her. She pictured how he looked, the wind in his hair, black shirt and trousers sculpted against his body, his face hard and sharply hewn, his eyes watchful, everything about him darker than the distant clouds.

He stepped to her side. She saw him from the corner of her eye, looking just as she had imagined him, only darker and more brooding as he glanced from her to the bay.

"Do you come here often?" she asked, her hands gripped at her waist to keep from touching him.

"There's little need. This place is restful only for the dead."

"You see that it's cared for. But no flowers. Why not?"

"I'm not a man for flowers. Surely you know that about me by now."

She turned her wedding ring round and round. Since Savannah, she had lost weight and the ring fitted loosely. The better for slipping from her finger when it was time to give it back.

"How is Chad today? I haven't seen him."

"Still proud of yesterday. He wanted to start right in painting the dining room. I told him he ought to wait for you."

"I'm not needed, Quent."

She dared a look at him, but with his eyes on her she could not look for long. She wanted to crawl inside his skin, to dwell with him forever, to love him and care for him, to protect him from himself and from the world he could not accept. He consumed her until all that she was depended upon him. But she could not say so, not because she didn't want to, but because it would do no good.

She returned to a scrutiny of the sky. "Mrs. MacCabe can help Chad, and the other women. Besides, he doesn't need much help. He's very good with his hands."

"Apparently in more ways than I knew. He didn't use to be a scrapper."

And he wasn't now, not really. Quent knew it as well as she.

"We'll have rain soon," she said. "If not today, then tomorrow. I always liked—"

"Angel, there's something I need to tell you."

His voice was different, softer, more personal. Her heart stilled and she could not draw a breath. "Oh?" was all she could say. Stupid, stupid hope warmed her. She couldn't help it; it was the way she was.

"This isn't easy for me."

She didn't think it would be. *I love you* as a flat-out declaration did not come effortlessly for a man.

"I'm not ordinarily given to gratitude."

Gratitude. She felt a knife twist in her heart.

"Before you leave, I want to thank you for all your work, and your care. Until you came, Cordangan was never much of a home. You opened the windows, in more ways than one. For that, I thank you. The castle will never again be the same."

She closed her eyes for a minute, letting his kindly meant words penetrate. Everything seemed to drain from her . . . strength and joy and even the memories of their shared pleasure. Perverse creature that she was, she would have welcomed more willingly his anger, for at least it was an aroused passion.

But he gave her gratitude instead, the way he would to Old Tully and Agnes and Doreen MacCabe.

She turned to him, the tears dried on her cheeks, and swore she would not weep again on Irish soil. Scorn, arrogance, rejection could not sever her ties to him, but gratitude was something else . . . the best he had to give, and the worst. Gratitude had no power in it. She would rather have his hate.

"You think I did it for you?" *I did it for us.* He would not understand the difference.

"I had to pass the time, didn't I?" she said, her voice brittle, as different from the Angel of old as she could be. "Chadwicks are workers, hopelessly middle class, of course. We earn our keep." The longer she spoke, the angrier she became. Quentin Kavanagh was so filled with his own problems, he could not see into the heart of another soul.

"I've earned everything I ever got from you, the clothes, the food, the roof over my head. But I didn't earn your constant anger, and I didn't earn your scorn. Those came from the past and your own warped view of it."

Eyes narrowed, he clinched his fists at his side. "I warn you, Angel, do not go on."

"What will you do? Pitch me off the cliff?" She moved to the edge where the land dropped off in a jagged fall to the trees that grew beside the bay. A clump of dirt broke off under one of her slippers, crumbling to bits as it tumbled down the incline.

He jerked her towards him, his fingers tight on her arm. "Don't be a fool," he growled.

Too late, she could have said. Anger almost brought the words to her lips, and such words she must never say.

She wanted to slap him, she who had never struck another human being in all her life. "If I fell, it would save you a great deal of trouble. Papa would be truly devastated, in case an unknown son isn't enough to ruin him. And you wouldn't be bothered with a messy divorce, or whatever you plan."

He tightened his hold, his eyes as deep as the sky and dark as night. Whatever emotions raged through him had taken control and she would be wise to be quiet.

But the time of caution between them was long past.

"What if I'm like Solas? What if I am carrying a new life within me? You don't want a child. You don't want a family. You've told me that often enough. One simple push—"

"Are you?" He held her so hard she thought he would crush her against his strength. "Are you carrying our child?"

She let the heat of his fury seep into her, wanting every part of him she could get. Even his anger would be something to remember, and the knowledge of how she drove him wild.

But she could not lie. "I'm not pregnant, Quent. It's one worry you do not have." The admission brought another layer of despair. "Please let me go."

"I can't. God help me, I can't." His voice was ragged, and she sensed the pounding of his pulse. "You don't really want me to. You like my touch."

So sure of himself, so sure. With her last ounce of strength, she defied him with the stiffness of her body and the proud tilt of her head.

"All you have to do is kiss me, is that right? Make love to me and I'll not give you any more trouble. At least for a day or two, which is all the peace you can buy at a time and so you'll have to make love to me again. I'm easy to subdue."

He held her hard against him. "You said it, Angel, not I."

"It won't work this time."

He kissed her long and hard, grinding his lips against hers, but she did not grant admittance of his tongue.

"I'll take you here on the grass," he whispered. "With the wind blowing over us and the thunder in the distance. You would like that, wouldn't you? Admit the truth."

His words embraced her as tightly as his arms. "Did you notice the rock ledge a few yards down the hill? There's a cave there. Shallow but deep enough to provide privacy. Does that sound better, just the two of us in the dark with the storm moving in? I'll lie on the bottom, to soften the ground. You like being on top anyway, don't you? You like it a great deal."

Angel had never wanted anything as much as she wanted Quent. Here was the anger she had preferred to gratitude, and the passion that they shared. Everything that she was and ever would be forced her to fight desire.

She held still. "I've never once denied you," she said, her gaze on his lips. "This time I must." She looked into his eyes and saw the hunger that she, too, was feeling. She would leave him unsatisfied, a small, temporary retribution for all he had done to her, and a punishment to herself.

"Let me go," she said.

This time he did as she asked. "If not now, then later," he said.

"No, Quent, our time is done. As you keep reminding me, I'm leaving soon. Sometimes I think you say it often to remind yourself."

"Don't be absurd."

A gust of wind struck her, and, she stepped far from the cliff's edge, looking around her at the cold, unadorned graves, then back at her husband. Overhead a gull cawed, barely audible over the roar of the wind. Her hair blew wildly, stinging her cheeks, but she stood strong against the assault.

"If I'm absurd, I might as well go all the way to impossible. It's taken me a long time to understand completely what took the heart out of you. Morna began it when you were born, abandoning you while she drew within herself. Abandoning her husband, too, and in the doing she caused the greatest rift of all. The one between you and Dermot Kavanagh."

"Enough." He took a step toward her, but she did not back away.

"You've told me that before. Am I to quake and do exactly what you say? If you expect that, you don't know me as well as I know you."

"You know nothing, Angel."

"Not so. I know your mother taught you how to hate when she should have taught you how to love. Chad showed you more than she ever could have about caring for another human being. But you locked him away and he could not teach you enough. You're like your father, you know. A strong man not knowing how to care for someone else."

"Dermot Kavanagh was a brute."

"He was a man rebuffed by his wife and child. What was he supposed to do? He drank, and the drinking made him mean. That's why you shun alcohol. In your heart, you fear you might become like him."

The tears she had sworn not to shed came to her eyes. "Except that you wouldn't because you have Chad. You'll always have him, though you'll have no one else. It took me a long while to figure out why all the treasures of the Kavanaghs were locked away. Self pity drove Morna to strip her husband's house of adornment, as punishment to him because he was not someone she could love. He continued what she had begun.

"And you? Whatever Morna said, whatever Morna did had to be right. And she demanded my own father's ruin. You could do nothing else but make your deathbed vows."

She fell silent, her passions and her anger spent. "The saddest thing of all is that you don't know what you've been seeking all these years. You didn't want vengeance, Quent. You wanted acceptance. You wanted love. It is your mother's final legacy that except for Chad you will never know either one."

Turning, she hurried past the tombstones and down the rocky path that led to the castle, the wind at her back hurrying her on her way. He would have a response for her soon enough, but she knew in her heart that everything of importance between them had already been said.

She heard his footsteps close behind her, but she did not turn and he made no effort to overtake her. Somehow she made the long trek to the stable, to the back door, to the kitchen, Quent always close at her heel.

The moment she stepped inside, she knew something was different. Mrs. MacCabe caught her eye, but she could not read the meaning behind the stark expression on her face. Looking past her, she stared at the figure standing in the far doorway. Exhausted though she was, she felt a rush of exhilaration and relief. The moment she had long dreaded was here, and she could be nothing but glad.

"Papa!" she cried as she flew into the comfort of his arms.

Twenty-four

Quent watched from the doorway as his wife embraced the man he had hated all his life.

His eyes were on Angel. Thomas Chadwick did not matter . . . he had not mattered for a long while, although Quent just now came to the realization. Only Angel mattered. And he had lost her.

Whatever he felt for her, she had become as much a part of his life as Chad, as the castle, as the land that was his legacy.

A sickness settled within him. What a weakling he was. If she had fallen up there by the graveyard, he would have thrown himself after her. He should have told her so, instead of berating her, instead of acting like the irresistible lover who could stroke her into submission.

He should have said she frightened years off his life just standing close to the edge. He should have said . . . a hundred things besides that drivel about gratitude, although it had not been a lie, just a pale representation of how he felt.

And then she could have said she cared for him the way she cared for Chad. Because he needed care. Wasn't that what she told him? That Morna had left him in a condition worse than his simple-minded brother?

He needed only her, but she was pouring out her love to Thomas Chadwick. The ultimate irony. Neither he nor Morna could ever be avenged.

"Angel, lass, where are your manners?" Thomas said, his

arm draped around her shoulders. "Introduce your papa to the rascal who stole you from me. I've long wanted a word with him."

Father and daughter faced him. Papa, beloved Papa for whom the loving Angel was prepared to sacrifice everything. He was short of stature, age thickening his middle and thinning his hair. Brown eyes held an intelligent caution and his ruddy face was lined about the mouth, but otherwise he bore a striking resemblance to Chad, so much that regarding him became painful, and Quent looked at his wife.

The very appearance of her stirred him. Her hair was a mass of untamed curls, her cheeks flushed, her eyes lit with blue sparks. For all her quiet strength, she pulsed with life. She was, in truth, the most beautiful woman he had ever seen.

"Papa, this is Quent. Quentin Kavanagh. My husband." She spoke faintly, barely above a whisper. "Quent, this is my father Thomas Chadwick."

The men regarded one another, neither extending a hand. Wariness deepened in Thomas's eyes. Whatever Angel had written home in her final letter, she must have hinted at the truth.

The moment Quent had long plotted was at hand, but he felt no triumph. This day, already dark with unhappiness, would only worsen before it was done.

"I, too, have been waiting for this meeting," he said.

"I'm glad to hear it. You took my daughter, but you paid my debts as well. I've cogitated over whether I owe you thanks or not." He glanced at his daughter, the wariness in his eyes softening. "I do, indeed, if you've made her happy."

Quent remembered his wife's solemn words on the hill, her accusations, her withdrawal from his arms. He had brought her many things, but happiness was not among them. Best get the business done, and let her go.

"I'm not after your thanks," he said, then to Mrs. Mac-Cabe, "Where is my brother?"

Angel's sharp intake of breath brought him back to her, to the expression of alarm on her face. She ought to see that the inevitable must be confronted right away. She ought to . . . what, trust him? Not in a thousand years.

"He and Agnes are in the henhouse gathering eggs," the housekeeper said. "Old Tully is looking out for him. He's not seen Miss Angel's father."

Quent nodded. "Please get him, Angel, while I take our guest into the library. Give us a few minutes alone, will you?"

"I want to come with you."

"And listen to my tawdry story once again? I'd rather explain our hasty marriage to your father in private. Rest assured I will omit none of my sins."

The struggle of decision was evident in her eyes, but at last she nodded and hurried past him, closing the door sharply behind her. Quent directed her father toward the library and followed, stopping when he felt a hand on his arm.

"Be careful, Quentin Kavanagh," said Mrs. Maccabe. "I've raised you from a babe and I know you better than you know yourself. Do not lose your chance at happiness because of what has gone before."

Never before had she spoken to him in such a way. Never had he seen her stern, strong face so tight with worry, not even in those wild days of his youth when he roamed the county in search of a fight. He saw how much she cared and felt a shame because he had not seen it before. His blindness was another of his sins.

He covered her hand with his. "Aren't you Irish enough to know the fates decree what will happen to us all? There's a destiny been awaiting all my life, dear woman. I'd play the part of fool if I tried to escape it now."

"There's more," she said, not letting him go. "Trouble

in the village. You've much on your mind, but you need to hear it."

The urgency in her voice held him in place, and a deep sense of foreboding took hold of his heart. "Go on."

"The gardener says a young woman has been raped and killed. She was known as the goat girl because of the flock she tended in the hills above town. They found her body last evening in the woods on the far side of the harbor."

"Why are you telling me this?" said Quent, knowing the answer before she spoke.

"She had been beaten. They claim the villain is known. An evil simpleton they'd long thought dead."

Quent's heart and soul cried out against the news. If he believed in God, he would have railed at His cruelty. Instead, he did what he had done as a child, whenever calamity struck: he blamed himself. He should have been more diligent in caring for his brother; he should have kept him from harm.

"Let me know if you learn more," he said, squeezing her hand, then turning toward the library. At least, with Thomas Chadwick waiting in the library, he could see to his revenge. Strange how hollow his driving purpose now seemed, but it was all he had.

He joined his enemy before the unlit fire, listened to the thunder rattling the panes of the mullioned window, and, with their chairs close together, at last began to speak.

He told the tale as he had heard it, omitting only the names of his mother and her betrayer and of their son, ending with the deathbed vow.

"It's a sad tale, to be true," Thomas said when he was done. He stirred uneasily. "But what has it to do with Angel?"

"Only that she had the misfortune to be your daughter, to be in Savannah unprotected when I finally tracked you down. I must assume you did not get the letter I gave to one of the Irishmen you had left to watch over your precious store."

"They were there to watch over my precious child," Thomas responded sharply. "And no, I got no such letter. Just correspondence from Angel assuring us all was well. Her mother and I have been out of our minds trying to believe her, suspecting the truth was otherwise."

"A shame the Micks withheld my message. It reported in brief that with our marriage Morna O'Brien was avenged."

Quent watched for the reaction, for all the implications of what he said to become clear to his father-in-law. He appeared to be genuinely perplexed. "Was she your mother?"

"She was. I'm the legitimate son. Don't tell me you can't remember her. I won't believe it."

Perplexity turned to astonishment, and then to anger. Quent felt glad. Here was fire to match his own.

Thomas rose from the chair, his hands shaking. "This other child—"

"He's thirty-five."

"You think he's mine, don't you? What kind of cruel game do you play?"

Quent stood to face him. "Never in my life have I played games. Except for the games of childhood with Chad, of course. Chadwick O'Brien, my brother and your son."

"Impossible," Thomas hissed, the color drained from his face.

"No, not impossible at all."

They stared at one another, neither backing down as the thunder rumbled in the distance.

A soft knock sounded at the door. Angel stepped inside the library. "He's here," she said, her eyes shifting from father to husband and back again. Lines creased her brow; Quent saw she felt the tension in the air, as stark and lethal as a lightning strike.

Suddenly he did not want her here. She could only be hurt. Angel, the innocent one who was everything good. Surely her father would agree.

But Thomas was not looking at his daughter. All his attention became focused on the slight, casually dressed man who accompanied her.

Chad eased into the room, smiling in greeting at Quent, his expression as guileless as ever.

"Angel said you wanted to see me. There's someone I'm supposed to meet. I like meeting new people, Quentin. Can he be my friend?"

His smile died as he looked at Thomas Chadwick. Father and son stared at one another in silence.

"My God," said the father at last and he sank back weakly in the chair, all the shock that Quent could ever have wanted etched upon his face.

Angel read her Papa's look, an expression she remembered from her childhood when Tecumseh Sherman's soldiers walked Savannah streets.

Dear precious Chad repulsed her father . . . his father. She had long prayed that such a reaction would not occur. She had believed in Papa's charity, his goodness, and the strength of his love. But he stared at his only son in disbelief, the only softening an edge of pity. She knew just how Quent must have felt when he thought she reacted the same way.

And she did what he would have done. Without another word to her husband or her father, she guided Chad from the room, saying the men had business to take care of and didn't he need to help Old Tully brush down the horses?

"They're fighting, aren't they?" said Chad as they hurried along toward the rear of the castle.

"Yes, they are. I suppose. I don't know what they're doing, and to tell you the truth, right now I don't really care."

Her immediate goal was to protect her brother from the men who should be closest to him. Old Tully helped her out, meeting them at the door of the stable and asking Chad to help him with the horses.

"They've taken a liking t' you, Master Chad, that's for sure," he said, nodding encouragement to Angel as he spoke.

She watched Old Tully lead him toward the stalls, then studied the sky, desperately needing to separate herself from the castle and all who dwelled within. The storm clouds had moved in rapidly, but they seemed more filled with rumbling threats than actual harm, and for the moment the wind had died.

Time was what she needed, time to sort things through and let the men come to their hurtful decisions. She couldn't protect one from the other, not anymore, but she also realized a stunning truth. If she had to choose one over the other . . . if she were allowed that choice . . . she would have sided with Quent.

Her steps took her past the flourishing garden, across the rolling fields and through the woods, ending once again at the graveyard overlooking Bantry Bay. She knelt before Morna O'Brien's grave. "He's done what you asked," she whispered. "I pray you rest in peace."

She heard no answering assurance; instead the wind returned to howl over the solemn scene. And with the wind came a darkness as deep as night and the first fat splats of rain. She looked around for shelter, but saw only a scattering of trees. A bolt of lightning brightened the gloom, striking the ground so close she felt a tremor beneath her feet. The accompanying thunder hurt her ears.

Trees would not do for shelter. She remembered Quent's mention of a cave. Lifting her skirts, she hurried to the cliff's edge. Another lightning strike lit the air, and she saw the rocky ledge he had described. It extended from the incline a dozen yards away . . . straight down.

The rain stung, and she felt the first pelts of driving hail. The elements drove her over the edge. Face turned toward the rocky incline, she crept cautiously downward toward the ledge, searching for footholds, grabbing at roots for support. For once, good luck was with her; she arrived suffering no more damage than a soaking and a pair of reddened palms.

The rounded ceiling was too low for her to stand, but the cave offered enough space for her to sit away from the storm. She hugged her knees to her chest and watched the rain. The time must be no later than midafternoon, yet it seemed like midnight.

She watched the storm, trying not to think of the scene in the library, trying not to consider what a disaster her life had become, trying and failing. At last her head nodded over her knees and she gave in to sleep. Minutes . . . hours later she jerked awake to the terrifying knowledge that she was not alone.

She stared at the figure crouching beside her. "Quent," she said, sighing in relief.

He touched her cheek. "You're alive."‘

She managed a smile. "Of course I am. Chadwicks—"

"You can say the name."

"Chadwicks are too stubborn to die."

His face was shadowed, but she felt his dark eyes on her. He filled the narrow confines of the cave, just as he filled her heart. The air was thick and rich with possibility, smelling of rain and green forests and desire. She knew only one thing. Her husband had come to her through the storm, and all her strong words and resolve of the morning faded into nothingness.

He was here, and for that she rejoiced.

"You're shivering," he said. "I brought blankets and dry clothes."

"Oh, Quent," she said with a sob. "I don't need them. You alone can make me warm."

She threw herself into his arms. He caught her, holding

her the way she wanted him to, hard and tight. Pulling her into his lap, he kissed her. She parted her lips and stroked her tongue against his. To the rhythms of thunder and lightning and the pelt of hail only a few feet away, she felt the pulse and the power of the storm, felt them in her heart and in the blood coursing through her veins.

The day descended into wildness, and so did she.

He broke the kiss and whispered, "Angel."

"Don't talk," she whispered. "Make love to me."

He eased her off his lap, spread his cloak over the floor of the cave, and added the blankets. He undressed them both, then lay down and pulled her on top of him.

To protect her from the hard, cold ground.

"You're a gentleman for sure, Quentin Kavanagh," she said, but she said nothing more and neither did he. Lips and hands did the talking for them. She told him as best she could without words that she loved him, and whether he knew it or not, he was telling her he felt the same.

She was insatiable, but she was not alone. He took her once, quickly, and then again more slowly, and later, with the storm abating, they explored each other with infinite care, the returning light of a rescued sun playing over their sweat-slick skin. Each time they came together seemed sweeter than the last, and sadder, too, for their mating marked the time when they must leave their lover's den.

At last came the time when neither could postpone the departure. Each time he started to speak, she kissed him, and after awhile she saw he was teasing her to kiss him again. She dressed in the dry clothes, twisting her wet hair into a knot at the base of her neck, then watched as he dressed, noticing each detail of his legs and his thighs and his sex, of his chest and shoulders and corded neck. She particularly liked the musculature of his arms.

He carried her up the face of the cliff, taking a path she had not seen, then went down for the blankets and her damp clothes. When he returned, she was standing by his mother's grave.

"I don't want to know what happened in the library," she said, as he approached through the wet grass and fallen leaves. "Not yet. But I understand about my father and your mother in that cave so many years ago. A storm was raging, I believe you said. They were young and destitute and lonely. How could they not have made love?"

"Angel—"

"I'm not excusing anyone, or asking that you understand. You will believe whatever you wish, and you have that right. I'm just saying that I see how it must have been."

"Stay with me, Angel."

If Quent had sprouted wings and flown around her head, she would not have been more surprised. Her heart caught in her throat. "What do you mean?"

"Don't go back to Savannah. Live at Cordangan Castle. Be a sister to Chad and a wife to me."

She shook her head. This was too much, far too much to understand. "But you don't want a family," she said, trying to think things through.

"A man can change his mind."

"And you have changed yours? Why?"

He took an eternity to answer. The dark and probing eyes that always seemed so watchful of her for once turned inward, as if he would see into his own heart.

"I've grown used to you here. Chad needs you."

She bit her lip to keep from crying out. *Accept what he says,* the small voice said, but she could not. "And what about the devil of County Cork? Does he need me as well?"

He ran a hand through his hair. The thick black locks, still damp from the storm, separated. She longed to smooth them in place.

"I want you," he said. "My God, haven't I proved it over and over again?"

I want you. Why not *I love you?* He simply wanted her,

and she wanted to weep. For all that had gone before them, she had not reached his heart . . . not enough to set it free. He hungered for her, in very elemental ways. She satisfied him, but she did not know if satisfaction was enough.

"Give me time to answer. Your touch is too much on me for thoughts of much else. And you could say something similar, could you not?" She looked down at the tombstone bearing Morna O'Brien's name. "Why don't you stay here awhile? Before you deal with the living, you need to make your peace with the dead."

"If I've learned nothing else since we met, it is that the past is past."

"That's quite an admission, Quent. I know how difficult it must have been for you. And yet in ways that we can't ignore, the past is always with us, is it not? Please, for your mother's sake, stay here awhile. I can get back by myself. There are a few things I want to tell my father that are best said in private. Surely you of all people understand."

He nodded once, his eyes hot with unrevealed emotion, and she saw traces of the wildness that had been in the puma's eyes on a long-ago sailing ship deck. She saw, too, what she must do.

"There's one thing more I have to say to you. Quickly, before I change my mind about disclosing what is in my heart. Regardless of what happens between us, whether I stay or go, I love you. With all my heart and all my soul and every ounce of life that is within me. I love you, Quentin Kavanagh, and I always will."

Twenty-five

Angel took a long time returning to the castle. Walking, thinking, flushed with mortification and pride over her unasked-for declaration, she postponed confronting her husband as long as she could.

Stay with me, Angel. Quent's words haunted her. She had delayed responding, but she knew now what she must say.

She knew, too, what must be said to Papa. But her husband came first.

Stopping at the edge of a pasture, she watched Vengeance and Solas grazing close together in the high wet grass. The gelding Lorcan and Josephine the donkey were not far away. It was a tranquil scene following the violent storm. If only she could feel that same tranquility in her heart.

She moved on to the stable, expecting to see Quent at any moment for no other reason than she wasn't ready to face him yet. The same went for Papa, but the stable and back rooms of the castle were deserted, as though everyone had been spirited away. A feeling of loneliness shivered through her. She was a person who needed people, and she marveled that her husband had kept himself apart for so many years.

She was relieved to find Mrs. MacCabe descending the stairs into the Great Hall.

"Where's Quent?" she asked.

"He's in the library with your father."

"How long has he been back?"

"Not long. He asked for you, but when you were nowhere to be found, he settled for Mister Chadwick."

"I see." She fell silent, wondering what they said, questioning whether she ought to join them.

"Mistress Angel," the housekeeper said, then again, "Mistress Angel."

"I'm sorry," said Angel, drawn from her thoughts. "I have a great deal on my mind."

"We're all in a bit of a state. You frightened us being out in the storm like that."

"It came on so suddenly."

"An Irish tempest, to be sure. The master was out of his mind. He wanted to rush out after you, and your father as well, but we convinced Mister Chadwick he would only get lost and add to our burdens."

"Oh," she said, dismayed. Not once had she considered Papa's concern for her. Which showed just how much Quent turned her inside out.

Mrs. MacCabe cleared her throat. "I've this to say, Mistress Angel, and then I'll be done. Whatever comes of this day, you have not a single moment at Cordangan Castle to regret. We were not a happy lot before you arrived. I'm hoping that's in the past. If so, 'tis a credit to you."

"Oh," Angel said, warmed. On impulse she hugged her, then backed away in embarrassment.

"I guess a simple 'thank you' would have been better."

The very somber and dignified Mrs. MacCabe grinned. "Not in the least. There's never been much affection shown within these proud old walls. It's long overdue. Now if you'll give me your pardon, I'll see to the evening meal. Vegetables from your very own garden, fresh washed by the rain, and fried chicken, done the way you taught me. I'll serve a meal to your da' that will make you proud."

After she was gone, Angel pondered once again whether to intrude upon Quent and Papa in the library. Decisions . . .

demands . . . declarations . . . she had much to discuss with them both.

She sighed. They were reaching decisions, too, the way men thought they had to do, protecting the womenfolk as though the women were too frail, too emotional to deal with life's hardest tasks. Papa ought to know better, even if Quent didn't. Sire to three headstrong daughters, he had been given example after example of female grit.

Humph, she thought. She'd like to see a man giving birth. She stopped herself. What she would like to see above all else was herself giving birth. To a little Quent or a little Angel . . . no, their children deserved names of their own.

What children? her inner voice asked. Perhaps, she answered, she had conceived that afternoon.

She walked as she thought, going up the stairs instead of toward the library. When she came upon Chad studying the paint in the dining room, she talked him into a late-day walk. In the dying sunlight, raindrops glistened like diamonds on the grass and leaves. The castle grounds had never looked more beautiful, and on this late August day the air was brisk with the hint of autumn.

They walked the winding road that led to the front of the castle, and she told him how she had named the carved dogs Pat and Finn.

"They looked so fierce that first evening I arrived here. Once I gave them names, I found I could talk to them like a couple of friends."

"You talk to them?" asked Chad, his brown eyes wide with surprise. And then he grinned. "I do it, too."

She squeezed his hand. "It's a perfectly sensible habit. People talk to grass and sky and trees all the time." And even tombstones. "They don't really answer back, but sometimes it seems as if they do."

They continued down the tree-lined road away from the castle. "Did you talk to . . . our visitor from America?"

The light in Chad's eyes died. "Mrs. MacCabe said I

should call him Thomas. He didn't want to talk. Least not to me."

"Oh, that's not true, Chad. He was worried about my being out in the storm."

She wanted very much to tell him who this Thomas was, but that was up to Papa. It didn't really matter whether Chad sorted out all the relationships, so long as he felt the love of family that was the most important thing of all.

With a lift of spirits, she felt more charitable toward her Papa. Learning he had fathered a son must have come as a shock. He would sort things through. She would give him little choice, and neither would Raven and Flame, once they heard the news.

Mama would feel the same. She had too much love in her to give room to resentment.

The sound of voices raised in anger came from down the road. Rounding a bend, they saw a horde of men coming toward them, some fifty yards away. Men with sticks, men who had been ready to throw stones two days ago in town.

With a yelp, she dragged Chad back out of sight. Fear froze her for only an instant. "Go get Quentin. He'll handle this."

Chad shook his head stubbornly. "They're the bad men, Angel. You need me to protect you."

"They won't hurt me, I promise. But Quent should be here, too. He was very angry because he missed the village fight." The voices grew louder. "Go get him. Now."

She shoved him up the road. He stumbled, then righted himself. Troubled, he stood staring back at her. And then he turned and ran.

Angel squeezed her eyes closed. What was she doing? What was this all about? Quent could be hurt as much as anyone. Why did she have such faith that he could handle anything?

Because she did, that was all. He would let no one in his charge come to harm. Her duty was to stall the throng.

Once more she rounded the bend. They were closer now, close enough for her to see the swagger and the hate in their eyes. From the scruffy look of them, they must have been at the tavern for hours gathering their courage from tankards of ale.

"There's the devil's wife!" someone shouted. Owney Malone, standing in the fore beside his son.

"Where's the bastard?"

"Kill the idiot!"

"Murderer!"

The shouts came at her in waves, blending until they became one long roar of hate. She halted in the middle of the road to count a dozen, two dozen men striding toward her. At the side of the road, with and yet not quite with the mob, walked Padraic Scully.

Angel fought a rising panic. *Murderer!* What could they possibly mean? Chad? Did they think he had taken a life?

Trembling inside, she kept walking down to meet them. A dozen yards from the Malones she stopped.

"Get off my husband's land," she ordered, hating her too-soft voice.

One of the men laughed, and the others joined in, but they slowed their step.

"Send us the bastard fool and we'll be gone," Owney Malone said.

"What are the accusations against him?"

"Rape and murder."

"No," she cried. "You're wrong."

She looked at Scully, in his suit and high-collared shirt as different from the mob as night from day. "Tell them," she pleaded. "You seem sober enough. This is insane."

But he just kept staring at her. She shivered with revulsion. What a fool she was. He had a part in this, a major part, else why was he here?

By now all the men had halted, close enough for her to

smell their unwashed bodies and the stench of sour ale that fouled the once-fresh air.

Fergus Malone pulled a soiled white cloth from his trousers pocket. "He killed the goat girl. Beat her t' death when he was done with her. And here's the proof."

Angel forgot to breathe. She didn't need to see the handkerchief to know it bore her brother's initials. It was the handkerchief he had shown her on the journey into town . . . the handkerchief he couldn't find on the return ride. He must have lost it in the scuffle with Fergus.

And someone picked it up.

She looked at Padraic Scully. The evil in his eyes terrified her, but it was a fear for her husband, not herself. Scully knew the bond between the brothers, knew Quent would fight to the death for Chad. He had come to watch.

"Out o' the way," Owney Malone growled.

"I'll get her, Da'," said Fergus. "Teach her to respect us men." He staggered forward.

"Touch her and you're dead."

Quent's strong, deep voice stilled even the breeze. She glanced over her shoulder to see him standing at the bend of the road. Relief and joy and fear for him rushed through her all at once. Fergus blinked and crept backward toward the protection of the mob. No one spoke. Angel heard nothing but the raindrops dripping from the trees, and her husband's solid steps as he walked down the road.

"Isn't one bastard as good as another?" Scully shouted into the silence. "Take this one and we'll get the other next."

But the men did not move.

Stopping beside his wife, touching her briefly with his eyes, Quent turned to Scully, and his mouth twisted into arrogant scorn. "I thought I ran you from the county. I see you have returned with your friends."

Scully lost the little color in his face. "Fools!" he yelled to the crowd. "Take him. Use your weapons. Remember the body of that poor beaten girl."

The men stirred restlessly, but no club was raised.

" 'Tis no good, Padraic," said Quent. "My brother has been here since he whipped Fergus Malone in town."

"And who's to say you speak the truth? Your lackeys, one and all. We have proof he's guilty."

Angel could be silent no longer. "They say his handkerchief was found beside the body, but he lost it on the street. Later in the carriage he couldn't find it."

She scanned the faces of the mob, then turned to Quent. "Anyone who calls me your lackey doesn't know me very well."

Their eyes locked for a moment. "Nay, lass," he said, "I'd call you a thousand things before I'd call you that."

Angel was vaguely aware of a muttering in the background, but she could not turn from her husband. An understanding passed between them that was stronger than words, an understanding that swelled in her heart.

Quent looked past her to Scully.

"You like to hurt women, don't you? And the girl was beaten to death. Did she not like your methods? Or maybe, having found my brother's handkerchief, you sought her out to cause trouble for him. Poor lass, to pay the price because of your hate for me."

"You ruined me," Scully snarled. "You have to suffer, too."

"You ruined yourself. Your business was failing when I started the Pride of Ireland, run to ruin by the taking of quick profits. What a miserable bastard you are."

With a guttural cry, Scully pulled a gun from his coat. Quent moved fast to kick it from his hand. The weapon skittered off the road. Scully lunged for it, but Quent caught him by the coattails. One punch sent him to the ground.

It all happened quickly. Angel's heart pounded in fear,

but the sight of Quent, standing straight and unharmed, kept her strong.

He looked across the subdued mob. "Here's your killer. I suspect you'll find he's guilty of other deeds, a few you've blamed on me."

"You own the Pride of Ireland?" said one of the men. He strode to the front, taking the place of the Malones.

"Aye, Joseph Dunne, I confess that I do."

"The same Pride of Ireland that's buying our goods and building the mill?"

"The same. It's where the Kavanagh money comes from. I take no payment from a rascally Member of Parliament who wants to stir up trouble against Home Rule."

"You heard the rumors?"

Quent nodded. "The rumors came from Padraic Scully, did they not? And how would he know such a deed were possible?"

"Because he is the guilty one. The night rides," said Dunne. "He started them, too."

"He had help."

All eyes turned on Owney and Fergus Malone.

"I'm ashamed I went along," one of the men confessed. "Owney himself talked me into it."

"Aye," said another. "Owney and Fergus both."

The crowd stirred. For a moment Angel thought the anger against Chad would be turned on the farmer and his son until she spied a second band of villagers making their way up the hill.

"Look," she said. "The women."

"Your wives and daughters and sisters, are they not?" said Quent. "Have they come to join you?"

Angel took him by the arm. "No, that's not why they're here. They sided with Chad in town, and they're doing the same now. Look at them, Quent. They are our friends."

"Holy Mother of God," said Joseph Dunne. "It's the missus."

Sure enough, Angel's critic from the general store, the formidable Mrs. Dunne, walked at the front of the phalanx. Close behind were the sisters-in-law, Mrs. Plunkett and Mrs. O'Dowd.

The men turned sheepish, and on the ground Padraic Scully groaned.

Quent smiled. Angel's heart soared. Quent smiled, in genuine humor, in what for him was gentle relief. She stared at him with tears in her eyes.

"I've one thing more to say." His voice stilled the crowd. Even the women kept silent as they joined their menfolk on the road.

The watchful eyes that had first stirred Angel outside the family store turned to her in all their power. "In this life I've made the mistakes of a hundred men. But one thing I did was right. I married Angel Chadwick of Savannah, Georgia, and I fell in love with her. She is the kindest, the gentlest, the wisest the person ever to be born."

And then his words were for her. "I love you, Angel. I want the world to know."

From the corner of her eye she saw Chad and her Papa round the bend. They walked arm in arm, but she had eyes only for Quent.

He swept her into his arms and before that selfsame world he had always shunned, the very private Quentin Kavanagh gave her a long and public kiss.

When dark had long descended, Quent nestled in his bed, his beloved wife in his arms. He had no inclination for midnight rides. Unless she accompanied him, he never would again.

After the tumultuous day, quiet had at last come. Padraic Scully was ensconced in the jail at Glengarriff, along with the Malones, the former charged with rape and murder, the latter with disturbing the peace. The men and women of the village had scattered to their separate homes, and underneath the vast roof of Cordangan Castle, only the master and mistress remained awake.

Until this moment their time in bed had been very busy. Angel claimed to marvel at his stamina; he marveled at everything about her.

"I had a long talk with Morna," he said, as she snuggled her head beneath his chin.

"Did she answer?"

"I sensed that she was pleased." In truth, as he knelt beside the grassy mound that was his mother's final resting place, he had felt a peace that he had never known.

That peace had freed the feelings locked in his heart.

Her finger traced the contours of his chest. "Papa and Chad seem happy with one another."

"Thomas and I had a long talk, but it was Chad himself who won him over. When he came hurrying back to get me, it was your father who met him. There's good in the man, lass, because he saw the good in Chad."

He stroked her arm. "He says he never knew my mother's name. That they met on the road and took refuge from the storm. Both young, both half-starved and frightened. The next morning she had disappeared. She told me he refused to follow her; he told me he didn't know where she had gone."

"And you believed him?"

"I suspect the truth lies between the two stories. Perhaps he had no knowledge of her whereabouts, but neither did he try to find her. And when she learned she was with child, she took the defense of having been forced. After a while, she came to believe her own story. Doreen MacCabe has told me she was always fanciful."

"Oh, Quent, so much needless suffering."

"But not all in vain. It brought me you."

"Say it again," she whispered, her breath tickling the hairs on his chest.

"I love you."

"And I love you." She paused a moment. "I have a confession to make. After you asked me to stay, I decided to do just that, whether you ever told me how you felt."

"You frightened the life out of me. Lightning flashing all about, and you without protection. I considered dragging you here and locking you in my room." He tightened his hold. "And then you said you loved me. A breeze would have knocked me off my feet."

"Me, too. I hadn't planned to tell you. It just slipped out." She laughed. "You never can tell what we Chadwick girls are going to do. Sometimes neither can we." And then she sighed. "Besides, I'm not just a Chadwick anymore. I'm also a Kavanagh. It's a volatile combination, wouldn't you say?"'

Quent certainly would.

"You won't be lonely so far from everyone in this old castle?"

"Of course not. You're here. Besides, it's a wonderful castle. There's so much I want to do with it. I've been thinking about the color of the walls in the Great Hall."

"And here I am thinking of the color of your skin."

She thought a moment. "Maybe we could match it, although I rather prefer your darker shade to mine."

Quent thought about the satin ivory of her body, and felt a return of desire. When she started in about the different qualities of paint, he lifted her chin and he hushed her with a kiss.

Epilogue

On a cold, crisp Christmas Day in the year 1883, a year and eight months after Quent took Angel away from Savannah, a crowd gathered in the grand dining room at Cordangan Castle.

Quent surveyed the scene with a sense of satisfaction. It wasn't the crystal chandeliers that made it grand, nor the portraits and tapestries on the wall . . . not even the Chinese rug covering the highly polished floor.

The people made it grand, although he would never disparage his wife's hard work.

At his insistence, Thomas Chadwick sat at the head of the table, and at the opposite end, his wife Anne. Down each side, chattering and laughing, were the members of their large and growing family, lingering over the remains of the holiday meal.

Matt and Flame Jackson had traveled all the way from Texas with their red-headed son Charlie, four-and-a-half years old and guardian of his sister Sarah, not quite two but with her chocolate brown hair and eyes and air of taking control already a ringer for her father.

Sarah sat on a pile of pillows between her brother and Flame and was very much the lady until she flicked a pea at Charlie, who threw one right back.

A warning glance from Matt stopped the imminent, all-out war. Across the table, Thomas Edward Bannerman, Viscount Bradford, who was older than Sarah by three months, grinned at his cousins.

Flame and her sister Raven smiled knowingly at one another.

"The peas may have been a mistake," said Flame.

"We'll get the children outside as soon as we can," Raven said with a nod. "They need to work off some energy before we take them to church."

A third party spoke up. "I'll watch over them." Keet Jackson, the halfbreed Flame and Matt had taken as their own, winked at Charlie. "You'd like that, wouldn't you?"

"That would be great," Charlie said. "We can play with the dogs."

"The stone ones or the real ones?" asked Marcus Bannerman, Earl of Stafford and proud father of the viscount. He looked at Quent, separated from him by an empty chair. "I've never seen so many animals on one place in my life. Since my Aunt Cordelia started breeding bloodhounds, I thought we had the record at our Sussex farm, but you've outdone us."

"Angel's idea," Quent said, missing his wife for the few minutes she had been absent from the room. "She's determined to make up for my lack of pets as a child."

He didn't go on to enumerate all the other things she had done, like restoring the castle to a splendor it had not known in centuries, and getting her husband back in church, and, most important of all, bringing him peace.

As proof, he had extended an invitation for Thomas and Anne to stay at Cordangan whenever they wished. Since two of the Micks, Brendan and Ian, were buying into their store, they had the time. Michael had chosen to return to Texas and help Flame with her mercantile ventures. She reported he and his bride were expecting their first child.

"Our wives are nothing if not determined," Matt Jackson said. "How would we have turned out without them?"

"You would have been miserable and lonely," Flame said.

"And bored," added Raven.

Marcus grinned down the table at his wife. "I'm hardly bored now. What with the theater group you've started and the farm and Tom, not to mention the baby—"

"What baby?" Anne Chadwick said.

Raven smiled at her mother. "I was waiting for Angel to return before I said anything. Marcus and I are going to be parents again next summer."

"That's wonderful," said Angel from the doorway.

Quent stood and felt the same small tremor of surprise and pleasure he always felt when his wife walked into the room. She was still here. His life was still complete.

Even more complete, if such a thing were possible, considering the bundle in her arms.

He walked to his wife's side and lifted the blanket to reveal the face of their child, seven-month-old William Dermot Kavanagh, head on his mother's shoulder, thumb in his mouth. William's dark eyes popped open and he smiled up at his father.

"He looks more like you every day," said Angel.

"Poor lad," Quent said.

The babe squirmed in Angel's arms and practically threw himself at his father.

"He's got a mind of his own, too, just like someone we both know," she added.

Quent shrugged. She was right. What could he say?

He had teased her about naming their son Stormy since he was convinced conception occurred that day in the cave. "The middle name, at least." Angel had laughed, but somehow they ended up using Dermot instead, and Quent saw that it was right.

He looked at his brother, who walked behind her. "What's that you have in the box?"

"Gifts," Chad said with a smile.

"Wonderful," said Anne. "Sit right here beside me and we'll all have a look."

Quent nodded in gratitude to the woman. She had accepted Chad as a member of the family, as much as had her husband and everyone else.

Chad set the box at the end of the table and smiled apologetically. "They're not wrapped."

"Good," said Charlie. "Do I have one?"

Flame shushed him with a roll of her eyes.

"Everyone does," said Chad. "I made them myself."

He proceeded to pull out small wooden replicas of all the animals residing on the grounds of Cordangan Castle: sheep and rabbits and cows, chickens and cats and dogs, and there were some birds, as well.

The single horse he handed to Quent. "It's supposed to be Vengeance."

"Looks just like him," said Quent, and meant it. William lunged for it, but his father thrust it in his pocket, knowing that otherwise it would end up in his son's mouth.

William's eyes sought out the other figures on the table. Just like his mother, always looking for something to get into. Returning to his chair, Quent balanced William on his knee, but his son grabbed for everything within reach.

Mrs. MacCabe appeared from out of nowhere. "I'll take the lad. He's teething and needs something to gnaw on."

Quent swallowed a protest, knowing she wanted to show him off to Old Tully and the rest of the staff dining below. Just as she had served as a nanny to him, Doreen MacCabe was the same to Will. She took to the task with a heart full of love, and he could not deny her.

His wife was of the same sentiment. She must have hired half the female populace of Cordangan to relieve Doreen of her housekeeping chores.

Angel walked closer to study the figures. "Chad used to carve in stone, can you believe it? Lately he's been working in wood."

"They're beautiful," said Raven, joining Angel and Flame beside their brother.

What a trio the women made in the velvet gowns Angel had ordered from Nellie Ahearne—Raven, the dark-haired one, dressed in red; titian-haired Flame in green; Angel in a rich blue. Three jewels: a ruby, an emerald, a sapphire. A star sapphire. It was Quent's favorite stone.

Dressed alike in black and white, the men seemed different as well. Even in his formal wear, Matt Jackson carried the look of an outdoorsman about him, the lines of his copper skin evidence he often looked into the sun. Equal in his physique, Marcus Bannerman would have looked like an aristocrat in baggy workclothes and suspenders.

And Quent? He was dark Irish through and through.

Talk around him centered on Chad's very special gifts. "The man's got real talent," Thomas Chadwick announced.

The sons of Raven and Flame sidled up to the carvings. At Chad's insistence, they made their selections. Not to be outdone, Sarah chose two, but Flame insisted she put one back.

When the others had been distributed, Keet led the boys outside, Sarah toddling along beside him, holding his hand.

"That's quite a young man," Marcus said.

"We're about to lose him as a foreman, I'm afraid," Matt said. "Determined to become a lawyer and defend the Indians. His father was an Apache warrior, but he never knew him."

Quent glanced at Matt and Marcus. "I don't suppose any of us here had the benefit of a father's guiding hand."

"Or a mother's," said Angel. "That's where your children will be different."

Quent winked across the room at her. "Aye, lass."

Angel winked back, then looked at the three brothers-in-law, seated close to one another around her Papa. "Did you men ever settle your argument about which country grows the best sheep?"

"Ireland, of course," said Quent, "and I have proof. Neill

Connolly says he gets orders for Irish wool more than any other."

"Neill and his wife Mary live in Boston," Angel explained. "They used to live here."

"And this Connolly represents the interests of Pride of Ireland, right?" Marcus said. "I'd say his opinion is prejudiced. Everyone knows England has the sturdiest stock."

"Not for long," Matt put in. "Texas is getting into sheep raising on a major scale. It won't be long before we're showing the world how it should be done."

The three men spoke at once, until Thomas Chadwick broke in.

"Argue about sheep all you want, but I know who grows the best babies in all the world. Chadwick women."

The men raised their glasses in agreement.

"Only because," said Angel, smiling at Quent, "we picked as their fathers the best men."

Her sisters readily agreed.

AUTHOR'S NOTE

With this Christmas family gathering in a medieval Irish castle, the tale of the Chadwick sisters of Savannah comes to an end. The fictitious village of Cordangan is based on the Irish town of Glengarriff, and Calluragh Island on Garinish Island, both places of such charm as only Ireland can provide. All other geographic locations mentioned in the book are real.

Trilogies like this one are insidious beasts. Once the stories are done, they are difficult for the writer to let go. Thanks for your support of FLAME (March '94) and RAVEN (February '95). I hope that ANGEL has brought you similar pleasures. While the personalities of the three women differ, their strengths are the same—love of family, loyalty, generosity of spirit, and courage against difficult odds. The strongest of these is love.

Readers, please send me the name and address of your favorite bookseller, along with a self-addressed, stamped envelope (legal size); in return, I will send you a gift.

Evelyn Rogers
8039 Callaghan Road, #102
San Antonio, Texas 78230

SURRENDER TO THE SPLENDOR
OF THE ROMANCES
OF ROSANNE BITTNER!

UNFORGETTABLE   (4423, $5.50/$6.50)

FULL CIRCLE   (4711, $5.99/$6.99)

CARESS   (3791, $5.99/$6.99)

COMANCHE SUNSET   (3568, $4.99/$5.99)

SHAMELESS   (4056, $5.99/$6.99)

Available wherever paperbacks are sold, or order direct from the Publisher. Send cover price plus 50¢ per copy for mailing and handling to Penguin USA, P.O. Box 999, c/o Dept. 17109, Bergenfield, NJ 07621. Residents of New York and Tennessee must include sales tax. DO NOT SEND CASH.